A Tale of Extinction

Heroes of the Remnants

R.C. Peters

PublishNation
www.publishnation.co.uk

About the author

Ryan is an aspiring writer, duh. He could ramble on in the third person about how he also loves his day job and that he wishes he could stay at this point in his life forever like some sort of nerdy Peter Pan. However, he'd rather get on with writing books so that you can enjoy the sequel one day.

If you want to harangue, harass, sass, troll, flame, or otherwise contact Ryan, your best bet is to follow him on twatter (yes, he swore he'd never get it, but he'll just have to learn to live with himself for selling out) or facebook, both of which use the handle @TheRealRCPeters

Alternatively, you can scrawl 'gullible' in black ink over every mirror in your house to summon him.

Special thanks

Edna - your hard work on the cover art has really put the icing on the cake. I really like icing sugar, so may there be many more cakes to come, each with a different yet equally delicious type of icing. Perhaps even a gingerbread man. Alright, this metaphor is getting away from me a bit now. For anyone who'd like to support a fantastic artist, check out:
http://3dn47h.wixsite.com/greenbrush

Ann-Louise - of all the feedback I got during my drafts, yours was by far the most negative. Thank you for realising that criticism is just as vital to improvement as compliments, and for having the guts to be honest.

Prologue

The sound of the colossi demolishing buildings nearby didn't distract Maximilian as he kicked in the door. Once upon a time he would've received a lecture from his father for such an action, but nobody in Lyonis would give half a rat's arse about their front door by the end of the day. "Abby!" he screamed through the hallways.

He moved through the house frantically, sword drawn and chainmail rattling with every step. He only got as far as the kitchen before seeing the truth of the matter, however; everything worth taking was gone - they must've already packed and taken off into the street.

He dashed back outside, pausing to check that none of the elementals were approaching him. "Abby!" he screamed again.

There was a response this time. "Max!" Not from Abby, but from Maximilian's father, Alexander. The call and response continued as Max moved, relief washing over him like rain just from knowing that they were still alive. They were nearby, but it was hard to figure out exactly where over the many sounds of the dying city. Flames roared, melting the winter snow; buildings crumbled, chunks of masonry cracking the street; the air was littered with screams.

"Abby!" he yelled one last time.

"Max!" It was from Abby herself now. She was nearby, he was sure of it, just through a plume of thick smoke drifting around the next corner. He pushed through it and saw the five of them up ahead; his family.

"Is it true? Are they evacuating?" asked his mother, quickly wrapping her arms around him.

He returned the hug, but it was a half-hearted afterthought as he rushed through an explanation. "It's true, all of it. You need to head east. The king left a week ago, and everyone sensible is following. Do you have everything you need?" he questioned.

They nodded, holding up a variety of bags for him to see. "Get to the wagon then," Maximilian instructed. "You've got time to get out with everything, but it's going to get crowded quickly."

He didn't think twice about what he had to do - he'd made peace with this course of action when he'd received his orders ten minutes ago. He gestured for them to follow and took off through the fine districts, trying not to look at the burning and mutilated corpses all around them.

The sounds of carnage faded behind them. It was almost peaceful, until an elderly man hit the cobblestones just in front of Max, splashing brains and gouts of blood everywhere. Max heard his mother scream behind him, but he was too busy looking for the source of the body to try and calm her down. There were a few of them up there on the rooftops, just waiting to jump, trying to work up the courage. It took Max a few moments to figure out what was going on; they were the disconsolate, unable to stomach the thought of taking their chances on the road, unable to look after themselves as the world collapsed around them. He felt sorry for them, and not just because they'd all be dead before the day was done.

There were more bodies ahead, and Max fell back alongside Abby, putting his free hand over her eyes. "Don't look. You don't need to see this," he insisted.

She didn't resist, clasping his hand with her own. She was as scared as he'd ever seen her, and who could blame her? He was scared, too, and not twenty minutes ago he'd seen grown men piss themselves in the face of death, trained warriors begging for their mothers with their final breaths. He kept moving, guiding her around the numerous corpses. His mother followed his lead and covered Carmina's eyes, too. She was the youngest, only fifteen. His father was guiding Max's shocked younger brother by the shoulder, but he was making no effort to shelter him from the horrors all around them.

A cascade of rock resounded across a street to the left, and Max steered them all down an alleyway in the opposite direction. "We're almost there!" he encouraged them, hoping the incoming elemental hadn't seen them. The encouragement was a cheap comfort of course, as the distance had never been the issue; it was what was between them and their destination that was problematic.

He rounded the corner into a narrow street, proceeding towards the nearby stable. A horrible wail choked out into a gurgle somewhere up ahead, and a moment later a detached torso skittered across the street in front of them, organs trailing behind it in a grotesque rope. Max almost lost what was left of his calm, but just about managed to swallow his panic and hide himself against the side of the nearest building. "Hold on a second," he muttered into Abby's ear, planting a kiss on her cheek. She nodded, noticeably calmer now that she couldn't see the chaos around her.

Maximilian's heart skipped a beat as the elemental jogged past. It was one of many monstrosities in the city presently, a seven foot man of animated stone; this one was a mixture of pale marble and cobbles from the street. It didn't look towards them or waver in its course, but it did idly toss a pair of legs their way, no doubt the other half of the torso up ahead. They bounced, rolled, and came to a stop in front of Max, and he fought down the urge to spew up his breakfast as he got a nice look at every little detail; intestines and the shattered edge of a spinal column protruding from the torn trousers. He tried to lift Abby over the limbs, wishing for the first time in his life that she didn't eat so much.

"I can walk!" she insisted.

Max pushed her forwards gently. "Watch your footing," he advised her. She almost stumbled on the partial corpse, but managed to get over it with Max's hand still blinding her. She obviously didn't understand what she'd just stepped over, for which he was grateful.

He hurried them all around the next corner, quietly following the elemental. Thankfully, it was already further away, jogging after some unseen prey.

"We're not going to have much time once we get there. Don't stop for anyone, alright? Get out the east gate and don't slow down until you're clear of the city," insisted Max. He took his parents' lack of argument as obedience and hoped for the best.

He finally removed his hand from Abby's eyes as they reached the stables. "Don't look around. Just get the gear in the wagon," he ordered. There were still corpses nearby, but they were distant enough that the family could make an effort to avoid seeing every grisly detail. The bags were chucked carelessly into the wagon - speed was more important than delicacy right now, and each of the five of them had been loaded with as much as they could carry.

Max ran straight to the horses. A couple of them were riled up from the carnage, but Abby's charger was as stoic as ever. They could be glad that the fires hadn't yet reached this end of the city, at least. He led the horse out and started hitching it to the wagon. Abby was soon helping him, though neither of them really knew what they were doing. "Should I ride?" she asked.

"Let Aurelius do it," ordered Alexander.

"But I'm the best rider here!" she rebuked.

Alexander took Abby's hand in his and guided her around to the back of the wagon. "Yes you are, but let Aurelius do it," he insisted. Abby didn't protest further, fear seemed to have mollified her ability to contest the point.

Max exchanged a hug with his brother and helped him up onto the horse, no time to fit a saddle. "Good luck," he offered.

"And you," Aurelius returned, looking back at him with concern.

Max wished that he could say his goodbyes properly, but he only had enough time to say one the way he wanted. He walked back around to the others and wrapped Abby in a tight hug. "I love you, sis," he said, simply enough. It was the best he could manage without crying, but Abby didn't fare so well. She began to weep as she returned the gesture.

"Please, come with us?" she begged.

It was a little cruel to pick favourites, but Abby was his, more than Carmina, Aurelius, or even his parents. He knew that she'd miss him the most, too. "You know I can't," he responded. He felt the tears beating against his eyes, forcing themselves out of him. "It's my job. I can save others, get them out of here. Duty before self, remember that."

Abby nodded glumly and let her arms fall by her side. "I will," she promised.

Max moved over to embrace Carmina next, but spared no time for words. His parents were last, both at the same time. "Promise me you'll take care of her," he demanded of them.

"I swear I will," agreed his mother.

"We won't need to. She'll be taking care of us a month from now, just you see," insisted his father, little more than whispering in the embrace. "Should I tell her?"

"Never," Max insisted. He took a step back and swallowed hard. "I'll catch up with you down the road. Go! Now!"

He knew it was a lie. He knew that they knew it, too, but it was a beautiful lie - the kind you have to tell just because the words make everything alright for a little longer. Max turned away so that his family didn't see him break down into tears as they left. He heard Aurelius bring the horse into a gallop, and then they were gone, no trace left of them but tracks in the snow.

Maximilian prayed twice; once that Corsein would spare those he loved, and once that Rendick would put steel in his veins until the very moment of his death. He took a deep breath and took in the sounds of the dying city, then readied his sword and charged towards the last enemy he'd ever know.

1
The Survivors

The surrounding area could safely be considered a wasteland. There was the occasional tent, jagged outcrop of rock, and even sparse flora, but the only thing that Abby thought to be worth looking at out here was the evening sun disappearing in beautiful layers of orange and pink.

Little grew here. The sky was barren of clouds, and the earth too dry and infertile for reliable crops, at least by the standards of those from the kingdom. Of course, this land *was* part of the kingdom now. Just about all that was left of it, in fact. Everything else had been ravaged.

She eventually managed to tear her eyes from the sunset in order to finish her stroll down to the water. She paused at the very edge of it, listening cautiously for people nearby. All was quiet, and as quickly as she could manage, she began to unburden herself of equipment.

The majority of what Abby had, she'd kept from her training. A simple combined back and breastplate adorned her torso, and four simple metal plates covered the fronts of her legs. An iron-rimmed roundshield completed the protection of her front.

The shortsword she'd had, had been lost to the elements - the element of fire, in particular. Presented with a choice between burning her hand to a crisp or losing the weapon, she'd chosen the latter and retreated as fast as she could. In its place, she'd taken up a simple claw hammer. It wasn't made for killing so much as carpentry - it was poorly balanced, and she would've preferred something more military, but the threat of being struck by it had kept some of the more common threats at bay, at least.

Her skin was stifled by a layer of dirt that had built up over time. Her sweat was sticky beneath her arms, and she could feel that unpleasant accumulation of it around her breasts and thighs, too. With a grimace, she pulled her barbute off and guided the tangled, ginger hair back over her shoulders.

Entirely unencumbered of her armour and weaponry, Abby paused once more to listen. Hearing nothing but a gentle wind scraping along the barrens, she stripped naked, making sure her shield and hammer were at the very edge of the water. People had grown wary of thievery whilst washing, and even Abby was no different in that regard. Although she liked to believe the best of people, she'd seen too much in her journey to leave her weapons out of reach when she was in public areas.

Striding into the murky liquid, Abby gritted her teeth. Having not been fully graced by the sun for hours now, it was a little chilly, but once the temperature had settled on her skin the refreshment was instant. It caressed her body so very softly, and she couldn't help but moan happily as she relaxed. Resisting the urge to just float there in contentment, she pushed herself deeper into the water and began to scour her skin with only her hands as a tool, leaving no crevice as dirty as it had been when she'd entered. Faint patterns of grime formed around her in the water, a perfect circle of filth ruined by the rippling disruptions her movements caused. She dipped below the surface briefly and repeated the process for as long as she could hold her breath, scrubbing her face and neck. Resurfacing with a gasp, she set to work combing her hair with splayed fingers. The hair was always the hard part, especially as she'd opted to keep hers long despite the heat. The grease was removed easily, but disentangling it from itself took a while.

Refugee, she thought to herself as she cleaned. *I never thought the word would apply to me.* She'd had conversations like these with herself frequently in order to kill time; conversations regarding the use of words that seemed to be more common than they were a year ago. 'Apocalypse' was one of the main ones. She was, of course, guilty of perpetuating the problem herself; she used the word when conversing with strangers or acquaintances, more for the sake of ease than anything else. However, despite the destitute nature of their living conditions, she disliked the A-word. It seemed incorrect - an apocalypse, to Abby, implied finality for the planet itself. *No*, she thought, *what this is, is an extinction. The destruction of a species. Or rather, three species.*

If it was an extinction, though, she knew that she was doing quite well for herself. Although she had lost a significant amount of weight over the year or so they'd been fleeing from and fighting the elementals, she was not yet scrawny. She may have lost her plump figure by her twentieth birthday, but she'd gained a significant amount of muscle in its place. Most importantly, she was still alive - a fact of which the value could not be overstated.

She cleaned herself more quickly as she began to feel the onset of chill from the water. She wasn't quick enough, though; just as she began to finish, she heard unfamiliar voices from over a nearby hill. "How should I know?" one of them responded to a question Abby sorely wished she'd heard.

"Well it's worth a try, even at this time of night," claimed another. Deciding that now would be a good time to conclude her bathing, Abby quickly splashed out of the water, grabbing her hammer and shield. Three men came over the hill, two of them holding battered old firearms.

Abby couldn't name the sort for the life of her, as she'd never educated herself in the matter of guns.

The three blanched at the sight of her, as bare as the day she was born and shivering a little from the residual cold. The best she could manage for decency's sake was to decide which of her more intimate areas to hide behind the shield. She settled for covering her bosom, since the lower had its own natural covering. Despite that fact, she scrambled to pull on her trousers without relinquishing a firm grip on her weaponry.

The man without a firearm approached her. His skin was dirtier even than Abby's had been prior to the bath, and he had an odour to match. His weapon of choice was a shortsword not unlike the one she'd owned until recently, simple steel. "It's warmer if you bathe while the sun's out, you know," he joked, eyeing her up.

Abby was far from ashamed of her body, but the way the trio looked at her and moved predatorily closer made her wish she'd had time to pull on a shirt, too. "I find there aren't so many people around late at night," she replied, trying to stay calm.

"Well, we're around," he stated the obvious, stepping closer. "Not scared of us, are you?"

The same part of her that always saw the best in people wanted to say no, but everything about him set her on edge. She settled for the political answer, her teeth chattering momentarily as her body adjusted to the temperature change. "Should I be?"

The three chuckled amongst themselves. One of the gunmen spoke up next. "Just give us your gear, love. We won't hurt you."

She shook her head firmly, the cold beginning to dissipate from her skin. "If I give you my gear, I'm as good as dead anyway."

"Well, what are you going to do, love? Fight us for it?" questioned the foremost man, running his fingers warningly over the blade of his sword. A horribly smug look crossed his face, and she didn't bother to respond, instead settling in with the grim expression of someone resigned to a fight - which is exactly what she was.

She adopted her fighting stance, even though she felt exposed as she raised her shield to shoulder height. The man stepped closer, reaching out to pick her helmet off the floor. Abby kicked his hand away angrily. "Back off!" she snapped.

The man took a step back, paused outside of striking distance, and shared a malicious grin with his comrades. In that moment, Abby was certain that he had no intention of passing up on what he believed to be a weak young lady. She was right; all of a sudden, he darted forwards and swung his sword at her, slicing through the air in a downward arc.

It was a poor choice of opening attacks, and she'd been prepared for it, but neither of those facts made it less frightening. The adrenaline that had been pumping through her veins erupted properly as she let the blow slide off of her shield. With a fierce yell, she rammed the iron rim of it into the man's ribs. He had no shield of his own to protect him, and had as little skill in his defence as he had in his attack. Abby didn't really stop to think, but if she had, she'd have known right then and there that a few of his ribs were broken. She left no room for retaliation, raising her shield again just in case, and slamming her hammer into the side of his knee. His breathless lungs tried to yell in agony as he collapsed under his own weight, his brain only just catching up with the damage his body had sustained.

She saw the guns rise to point at her, but had no intention of stopping there; a floored opponent is just an opponent that will strike at your legs, after all. Before the man could recover from the pain, Abby swung the hammer one last time to shatter his wrist, the bones spilling out into an arrangement they weren't designed for. Still struggling for breath, the man dropped his sword and screamed at the damage she'd done.

"Stop or we'll shoot!" yelled one of the others, but Abby was already yanking her victim up to kneel in front of her as a human shield.

"Bad idea. Leave and you can take him with you," she offered. The two men exchanged a few glances, no doubt silently debating whether to shoot or not. That delay would cost them significantly, as it gave her time to formulate a plan of attack and carefully slide the shield between herself and her writhing hostage.

It seemed that the man was worthless injured, as two gunshots rang out. Abby dipped her head instinctively, and the man she was holding shuddered as the bullets bored through him. One struck him in the skull - the other must've torn through his gut and out the other side, as Abby felt something batter her shield.

She wasted no time; what little she did know about guns told her that they had to reload now, and would take a significant amount of time to do so. She burst forwards, knocking the fresh corpse over in the process and charging the pair down. They didn't flinch, simply turning their guns in hand so that the wooden stocks were ready to use like clubs. She picked the left, dashed towards him until she was almost close enough to take a swing, then changed direction suddenly and closed the gap to the other. The bandits were far enough apart that the left one fell well short of her when he tried to strike. The other tried to retreat in panic as she approached, swinging the weapon heavily at her as he did so. It battered against her shield, striking the face head-on rather than glancing off. It wasn't an ideal situation, but it allowed her to open his guard up and quickly render him unconscious with the hammer.

Abby ducked as she heard movement behind her, trying to spin and face her final opponent. Her back erupted in a line of brutish pain, forcing an angry gasp from her. Crouching may have saved her from a blow to the head, but he'd still managed to strike along the right-hand side of her exposed ribs. It set her off-balance, forcing her down onto her rump as she faced the irate man.

He swung at her again, another overhead strike. She blocked this one poorly as well, taking the full force of the blow directly to the face of the shield again. She could feel the wood splinter, adding to her troubles as the energy behind the attack rippled through her body, bruising her arm and exacerbating the problem of her aching back. She swiftly corrected herself, angling the shield in preparation for the next attack.

The man resembled a labourer setting up a marquee, hammering pegs into the ground with inelegant strikes. The sheer amount of force he was trying to put into each blow was foolish, and each time he raised his arms it gave Abby time to angle the shield, deflecting the weapon and letting the ground feel the impact rather than herself. Twice more he struck the earth, and when he next lifted his weapon, Abby lunged forwards and brought the hammer up into his crotch with all the strength she had. The man dropped the rifle and collapsed, literally crying from the pain. She scrambled to her feet, then performed the somewhat debatable mercy of bludgeoning him into unconsciousness with his own rifle.

She stood there for a moment, taking time just to gather her breath and her wits. The adrenaline began to wear off, and pains started to shoot through her back periodically, sharp and sudden. She was fairly certain she'd cracked at least one rib, but that would take care of itself with time. Abby set about dressing herself, taking care to avoid any motion that further aggravated her injury. Next she gathered everything of worth on the three, right down to their boots, and placed it all in a pile. Her family wouldn't survive on good intentions alone, after all.

Deciding that waiting was preferable to having to do any heavy lifting right now, Abby sat on the pile of liberated equipment and waited for the others. They must've heard those gunshots.

It wasn't long before the first of her victims stirred; he groaned and clutched his head where Abby had battered his skull, the realisation that he was dressed in nothing but breeches slowly dawning on his face as he looked down at himself. "Fuck," he muttered, sitting up slowly.

"Mind your language," warned Abby, a frown creasing her brow. The man froze, mouth hanging open slightly as he saw that she was still present. He stood swiftly, probably thinking it best to flee from her now that she was armoured. "Sit down," she ordered, holding up the shield threateningly. She liked to think that she'd done her best to abate any doubts he might've had about her lethality.

The man seemed to consider the option of running, briefly, but came to his senses and carefully lowered himself to the floor again. "You're not gonna kill me?" he asked, his tone level. He seemed surprisingly accepting of the possibility. Abby supposed that banditry wasn't an occupation one got into without being aware of the risks. Regardless of his feelings on the matter, she shook her head.

"What are you gonna do to me, then?" he pressed.

Abby sighed. "I'm not certain yet," she admitted. "It seems to me I may as well just let you go, now that you've got nothing to hurt anyone with." Unsurprisingly, the man seemed agreeable to that proposal, nodding swiftly. "Go. Take your friend with you before the others get here," she allowed after a moment's deliberation.

"Thank you!" he replied, relief in his voice as he scrambled to grab his unconscious friend. He carried him off as quickly as he could - which wasn't all that quickly.

Soon enough, Abby heard panicked voices coming from down the path. She recognised the smooth tones of her little sister, though she couldn't make out exactly what was being said. Heavy footsteps jogged closer, and Abby forced herself to stand again.

"Abby!" called her mother, dashing ahead of the others. She slowed as she came closer, skidding to a halt and eyeing the corpse, ventilated skull and all. "We heard gunshots! Are you alright?"

Abby nodded and stepped up to give her mother a firm hug, instantly regretting doing so as it mounted pressure upon her injury, even with the breastplate in the way. "Be careful," she groaned. "I think I cracked a rib." Her mother stepped back abruptly, raising her hands apologetically.

Before anyone else could try to hug her or ask what had happened, Abby gestured to the pile of equipment. "A few of them attacked me for my gear. I think if we trade this it might solve our food problem."

Aurelius chuckled and stepped over to admire the equipment. "Nice catch, sis," he commented gleefully.

"So, shall we head back?" her father queried after a few moments of quiet awe.

Abby nodded. "No use hanging around here," she grunted, and took as much of the gear as she felt comfortable carrying. Everyone else followed suit, and together they strode off along the dusty path. Not too long ago there hadn't been a path out here at all; It had been beaten out by all the thousands of people that had passed through, each of them looking for a light at the end of their metaphorical tunnel.

Aurelius sidled up beside her as they walked, lowering his voice. "Three pairs of boots, but only one body?"

"I let the others go," Abby explained. "It's not like they're going to do any more harm without their gear. They'll be lucky to even live." She didn't feel too good about that fact, and Aurelius didn't push the subject further. He knew exactly how she felt about killing.

The short journey passed them by quickly. The Koning family hadn't moved their camp along the road for about four days now, which was the longest they'd stayed in one place for quite some time. All of the vast, sprawling caravans that they'd become used to had vanished into the distance or dispersed evenly around them, many of them setting up camp just as Abby had with her parents and siblings. Some of the larger tents had become landmarks; the closest thing this shattered community of scared refugees had to a town hall or tavern. The word going about was that they'd already begun to rebuild up north. It seemed logical that they would've, given how long they'd had to do so. Abby had been counting the days since they first left Lyonis; three hundred and eighty-three, now.

She left the gear she'd carried to the others when they got back to the camp, letting them decide what to keep and what to trade for food. Sleep was the only thing on her mind after the sudden violence, and so she went straight to her own tent. The rib stung even as she sat down on her sleeping mat. Finding a comfortable position to rest in that night would be an arduous task.

***

She awoke the next day with a groan, not so much from the throbbing pain in her back as the poor quality of sleep that it had caused her. The injury seemed to have improved overnight, the initial shooting pains subsiding into a constant and predictable, dull ache, but that didn't stop her from wishing that she hadn't defaulted to sleeping on her back as she normally did.

As Abby sat up she heard voices outside, her family chatting merrily. The sun was already high in the sky, washing a faint orange light through the fabric walls around her. With a sigh, Abby eased herself to her feet, trying to flex her back as little as possible. She'd never cracked ribs before, but she'd heard enough stories to know that it'd be at least a couple of weeks before the pain subsided properly. Until then, she'd have to think very carefully about every other motion she made.

Whilst inching her clothes on, she noticed one unfamiliar voice amongst those of her family. It belonged to a man, his words dry and tired as he spoke, though friendly enough. "Reckon I might settle here for a while. More wildlife about than back west," he claimed.

11

Abby eased her shirt on, the movement of her arms tugging at the damaged bones. She slipped her feet into the only shoes she owned - a pair of battered, dark brown leather boots. Hunching to tie the laces turned out to be a mistake, the bending of her back causing a wicked jolt of pain to lash through her. She gritted her teeth and got on with it. *Blasted bandits.*

Stepping out of her tent, she was immediately greeted by the smell of cooking meat, and the sound of her mother's voice. "Good morning, sweetie. Are you feeling alright? You slept in."

Abby nodded. "There's definitely at least one cracked rib. I'll be fine, though," she insisted, stifling a yawn and moving around her family to shake the stranger's hand. She noted his wedding ring in the process. "Hi, I'm Abby," she greeted cheerily.

"Eric," he returned. He must've been in his thirties, she reckoned. He was sporting a rugged beard and moustache that matched the black of his hair, and he had a build that lent itself to physical work. "Your family told me about last night. Heard you got 'em good."

"Something like that," Abby chuckled. She took a glance at the food that Carmina was tending, her stomach complaining at being empty when the smell of food was so evident. It looked a little like venison. "Is that yours, Eric?"

He shook his head slightly, scratching his beard. "Not anymore. Had most of somethin' that looked like a deer, traded it on for the guns."

Abby nodded slowly, glancing thoughtfully at Eric as she connected the dots. She noticed the sadness in his eyes as she examined him, a kind of resigned look that a lot of people got out here. "You're a hunter?" she asked with a sweet smile.

"I am. Or was, maybe," he responded, scrutinising her right back as they talked. If she'd been wearing anything flattering it might've been enough to make her blush.

"Did you ever live in a log cabin out in the woods?" she questioned enthusiastically, easing herself down to sit beside the huntsman. Her family chuckled at her excitement, though Eric barely cracked a smile.

"Not exactly. Used to have a little supply hut out in the area I'd hunt, but that was barely the size of a small room," he claimed. Abby grinned.

"Abby, we were telling Eric that it's about time Aurelius learned a thing or two about hunting, or anything other than accountancy for that matter," interrupted her father. The main disadvantage of having been raised in a well-to-do family just years before the extinction, was that a large amount of what they had learned in their lives was now useless. This was especially true of Aurelius and Alexander, given that money was now only worth the metal it was made from. Abby was very glad indeed that she'd taken to training as a paladin; even the small amount of experience she had smithing was useless out here, without a smithy in which to do it.

"Perhaps you could all go with Eric some time and learn a thing or two?" suggested Abby's mother.

"I'd like that," agreed Carmina. Aurelius nodded, as did Abby.

"So, we're staying here then?" Abby asked her father, peering around at the landscape.

"For a little while, at least. We'll see how it goes. It's been months since the last attack, after all," he replied. There was no argument on the matter. It might've been some sort of desperation that drove them all to believe that they could be safe out here, but they were all so very sick of travelling. Even Abby found that her almost endless supply of cheer was dwindling.

She watched hungrily as Carmina scraped the venison out of the pan, serving it up into wooden bowls. "Are you hungry, sweetheart?" asked their mother.

"Starving," Abby admitted, trading a timid smile with her little sister as she took her portion. Breakfast passed slowly; it was the best anyone in the Koning family had eaten for weeks now, and nobody rushed their unusually reasonable portions.

"Well," Eric spoke up once they were done savouring the meal. "I should clean up those rifles, see what I can do with 'em."

Abby got to her feet to see him off, smiling pleasantly. "It was nice to meet you, Eric. Perhaps once my rib's a bit better I'll join you hunting," she offered.

"You'd all be welcome to. Take care," he returned, nodding politely before he left. His hushed voice and apparent inability to smile gave Abby the impression that he'd lost a lot lately, but she was far too polite to ask strangers personal questions. Besides, he would be far from the first out here to have a sob story. *No parents, kids, or wife, with him. Go figure.*

Abby watched Eric disappear into his tent, about ten metres across the path. "So, what's the plan then?" she asked her parents.

"Well, since we've still got those carrot seeds, your mother and I were thinking we could trade some of the equipment you uh..." her father trailed off, a look of slight embarrassment touching his face as he searched for a more graceful way of putting it than 'looted from all those men you beat up.' "Acquired," he settled for after a few moments.

"We'll trade some of it for spades and try to grow the carrots," his wife finished for him.

Abby nodded and stacked her empty bowl with the others. "Perhaps when my ribs are better I'll give you a hand with that. For now, I think I might just go and sleep some more," she excused herself. "I'll clean those bowls when I wake up."

"Sleep well," chorused Abby's family as she returned to her tent.

"Have a nice day," Abby chirped back before disappearing inside. She stripped naked and settled down on the sleeping mat again, trying her hardest not to extract more pain from her ribs than was necessary. Sleep found her far more easily that time, laying on her side rather than her back.

Two weeks passed rather slowly as she began to recover from the injury. She stuck to the dullest of chores at first, though even washing pots kept sending painful aches through her ribs.

More tents settled in around them over time. There was something about the place and the people in it that seemed to attract others, though Abby wasn't quite sure what it was. She'd found plenty of time to greet newcomers, putting on a cheery face even when she was growing rather bored of her self-imposed lack of entertainment. Of those Abby had met, five had settled in for the long term - three of whom were another family, just the mother and two young children left. She hadn't had the heart to pry into what had happened to the father.

A dark-skinned old woman from the southern lands of the Redanin Empire had introduced herself as Mrs. Elani, but didn't seem to have brought anyone with her. From what Abby had gathered whilst helping her settle, she'd once been something of a traditional medicine woman.

The most recent of the settlers Abby had met was a young man named Carl. 'Young man' was perhaps enduring its most literal usage ever in the context of Carl; despite being only eleven, he was by himself, and seemed to have adjusted to that way of life already. Abby had tried to talk to him once or twice since he'd moved in, but he mostly kept to himself. He was also always busy, constantly in the process of making or repairing something with whatever materials he had available.

Of course, settlers were not the only ones about at any given moment. Many people still passed through, not all of them nice. Sometimes there were complaints about small thefts just after strangers left, and Carmina swore she'd seen Eric setting up a bear-trap in his tent for any would-be intruders whenever he left to hunt.

A sudden yell roused Abby from the middle of an afternoon nap. She jerked upright, and pain shot through her immediately. Wincing, she began to pull her trousers on as fast as she could, ignoring her body's complaints at the rapid motions. Another yell rang out - she was more alert for this one, it was definitely Eric's voice. She pulled on her shirt as she heard more voices join in nearby.

Abby left the tent in a rush, leaving her shirt only half buttoned. She didn't bother with boots, the source of the disturbance had been close enough that she probably wouldn't need them. She broke into a jog as she stepped outside, her ribs protesting the vibrations with every step.

It took all of a few seconds to see what was going on; Eric and a few others were clustered around an injured man, carrying him towards some uncertain destination. She could see another stranger directing them. "What happened?" Abby questioned, moving alongside the group. She didn't recognise the man they were carrying, though she could tell from the blood that his wound was bad. He was already unconscious.

"Bandits," grunted Eric. "Took him out hunting with me, got shot at. Shot one of them back, but he got it in the gut," he explained, pointing at the injured man's stomach.

"Where was this? Perhaps we should go and deal with them?" Abby suggested. She noted a little blood trickling out of a small rip in Eric's trousers, but the lack of any noticeable limp told her that it wasn't as bad as it looked.

"No use, they'll have scattered by now. Probably took the gear off their dead, too," Eric insisted.

Abby nodded glumly. He was right. As much as she hated to admit it, there was little to be done against wandering bandits until they struck. All she could do now was pray for the man. The man whose name she didn't even know. "What's his name?"

"Uh… Henry," Eric recalled. Abby nodded and took note of it for when she had a moment to pray. Perhaps it was unwise to judge a book by its cover, but Henry looked like a decent sort.

"Set him down here," ordered the man who'd been directing them, gesturing to a sleeping mat on the floor of a rather spacious tent. Those who'd actually been doing the carrying followed the instruction, and it immediately became clear that the man giving orders was a doctor, as he fetched a leather bag and pulled from it the tools of his trade. "Out, all of you," he commanded. "I need to focus if he's to stand a chance of living through this." Nobody questioned the doctor's orders.

Eric gently took Abby by the shoulder as they left. "Mind if I borrow you a moment?" he asked.

Abby nodded and led him out of the way of the others for a little privacy. "What is it?" she asked.

"I need to clean my injuries, but I reckon they might come back with more men. Mind coming with me?" he asked.

Abby forced a smile and shook her head, her eyes scanning him for injuries now that they were both stationary. It was clear he'd received a handful of cuts in the fight, but none of them serious. "Sure," she agreed. "I'll fetch my weapons and catch up with you."

Eric nodded appreciatively and set off towards the bathing pool, Abby catching up only a minute later. "Do you reckon they were anything to do with the ones who attacked me?" she enquired, finally buttoning her shirt up fully.

Eric let out a short, bitter laugh and shrugged. "I dunno, didn't get much chance to talk to them," he commented. "Seems likely, though. Can't say I know much about being a bandit but I imagine they'd fight if there was more than one gang in an area."

"I guess," agreed Abby. "You managed to fight the rest off, then? How many were there?"

"Think it was six to begin with," Eric claimed. "Killed at least two of them. Maybe three."

"I thought you said you only shot one?" Abby queried.

"Shot one, stabbed one, and caved in another one's head with the butt of my rifle," he clarified.

"Sounds pretty rough. Shame Henry didn't get away so lightly," Abby commented. With that, the conversation grew still once again until they reached the water. Eric probably hadn't known Henry particularly well, but the hunter still seemed on edge from it all. It was a reminder of their vulnerability out here, after all. *As if we need another reminder of that.*

Eric hesitated at the edge of the water, turning to hand his weapons to Abby. "Uh... you don't mind if I undress, do you?" he mumbled.

Abby shook her head. "Go ahead," she allowed. Even if she hadn't been of the opinion that Eric was handsome in a rough sort of way, it wasn't anything she hadn't seen before. The huntsman stripped, being careful not to worsen the tears in his garments. That was wise; they were small enough that Carl could easily repair them.

Abby couldn't help but admire Eric's body as he turned to descend into the water. He rippled with muscle from a life of hardship. She did eventually manage to tear her eyes from him in order to keep watch, though, listening for any sounds aside from those of Eric cleaning the blood from himself and his clothes. "So, where were you when it happened?" she asked as she scanned the horizon. The question was a staple of post-apocalyptic small talk. Everyone remembered the moment that Borsenine had been wiped off the map - either the event itself, or receiving the news.

"I was almost across the border to Borsenine," Eric claimed.

"Guess you really dodged a bullet there. How come you were headed that way?" Abby enquired, perceiving a tenuous pause.

"Me and this other fella, John, we travelled together for a time. We were both headed down there to take care of some personal stuff," he elaborated.

"Can I ask what happened to him?" she asked, a little hesitant.

Eric's response was not so laboured that Abby imagined the subject of John upset him. "He died."

"Too bad. We were all in Lyonis at the time, waiting out the siege," Abby recalled. "We didn't hear until after the city had been taken. Strange to think that such a big area can be destroyed like that, without everyone just knowing right away."

"If you'd been where I was, you'd have known," Eric continued. "Was like watchin' the gates of avared open. And the noise... I'd have thought it could be heard all the way to Lyonis." The sounds of water splashing gave way to those of feet on soft earth, and she turned to hand Eric his equipment back. Once again she found her eyes straying, but if he cared or even noticed, it didn't show. The huntsman dressed and gestured to the path ahead of them. "Thanks for keeping an eye out," he grunted, and set off again.

"Glad to help. If you ever want company out and about, feel free to ask," she offered. "I know the area as well as anyone now, I guess."

"Just as well you do," he commented, glancing down at her bare feet.

"There's not much to hurt your feet on. Just dust and water out here."

"And bad neighbours, apparently," he added, tapping a small cut on his shoulder. It had already clotted, just a couple of dried, bloody flecks at the edges.

Abby smiled. "But plenty of good ones, too."

2
The Most Dangerous Game

Abby watched Aurelius' technique as he nocked an arrow. "That's it. Remember what I taught you," muttered Eric, his voice soft.

Another two days had passed in relative peace and quiet, thankfully, and Abby's ribs were just shy of painless during normal movement. She was at the point where she could be a little bit more active again, and so she'd finally got around to joining Eric and her siblings on one of their little excursions. They'd travelled a few miles north-east, keeping well clear of the other tent settlements that were springing up here and there, and they'd eventually arrived at a large area of sparse grass and trees where Eric claimed to have done most of his recent hunting. He'd skipped the formality of trying to sneak up on prey, and led the siblings straight to a watering hole that attracted the local wildlife. Sure enough, their target had soon wandered up within range of an ambush.

"Alright, go ahead," insisted Eric, gesturing at the unfortunate beast. Tinarus was a scarcely documented continent, and some of the refugees had expected the animals here to be naked of fur due to the sweltering heat. Although a few of the creatures had lived up to these expectations, the majority weren't vastly different from back on the mainland. This one was something like a deer, though with strangely shaped horns rather than antlers. If the creature had a proper name, Abby was clueless as to what it was.

The understated swish of the arrow cut through the silence at last. It fell short. The deer - for lack of any other name - glanced over in panic as the arrow embedded itself in the nearby earth. Immediately, the creature turned to run - and run it could; it was incredibly fast, bounding with remarkable ease and grace. It was beautiful to watch, but for all its elegance, it wasn't as swift as Eric's bullet. Abby winced at the gunshot, clasping her ears.

"Don't worry, lad. You'll get there," Eric promised. The four of them stood, watching the creature succumb to its injury; it struggled on for a few more steps, then toppled onto its side.

"Can we make sure it dies quickly?" requested Abby.

Eric nodded and turned the rifle, beginning to load it from the muzzle. "Think maybe I hit it in the gut. You run on over and finish it off," he agreed.

Abby nodded and strolled over. She didn't waste energy jogging, knowing that they were going to have to carry the deer back. It probably weighed about as much as she did.

"Do you want me to deal with it?" asked Aurelius, shouldering the bow and pulling out one of his knives. Abby nodded, uncertain if she had the stomach to take the creature's life in such a way, even as a mercy. Carmina also seemed quite content to let him do it.

The deer was evidently in a lot of pain, struggling for breath and weakly flailing its head. Blood was running copiously from the small hole in its side; if Abby's assumptions about its anatomy were correct, the bullet must've ruptured at least one lung. She crouched to place a gentle hand on the creature's head, stroking its soft fur. "Shhh. Rest now. I'm sorry," she muttered to it. It seemed to relax a great deal at her touch, its head slumping peacefully to the ground and its breathing coming more slowly, though still laboured.

"How'd you do that?" asked Aurelius, circling around the deer and silently moving his knife into position at the base of its skull.

"I don't know. Remember my rabbit?" she recalled. Sadness crossed her features as she watched the sharp motion of her brother's weapon. The creature let out one last little spasm before it fell still.

"I guess you're just good with animals," Aurelius shrugged. "So, who's carrying it first?"

"Carmina is, once we gut it," Eric ordered as he approached them, handing Aurelius' errant arrow back to him. "Weakest first, then she won't be as tired by the time we get back."

Carmina rolled her eyes but waited patiently for Eric's lesson on how to properly gut the animal. He rolled the creature onto its back and lifted the rear end, readying his knife. "Trick here is to cut around the anus in a circle, real careful. Not too deep, if you give it a wide berth you can get the colon and such out without making a mess," the hunter explained. The siblings watched in silence as he continued to educate them all, expertly cutting around and removing its entrails.

It took them until sundown to get the freshly gutted creature back to camp, the chill of the night kept at bay by the effort of hauling the beast. Abby was taking her turn carrying the creature when they arrived, and so she was the one that drew her mother's attention first. "Abby! We were beginning to worry!"

Abby grunted and adjusted her burden. "You worry too much," she replied, which was perhaps unfair given that two out of four of their hunting party had been attacked by bandits just recently.

"Oh! An impala!" Alexander exclaimed delightedly, turning from his tending of the carrot patch to admire their catch.

19

Abby lowered the creature to the ground with a grunt and looked at her father curiously. "How do you know what to call it?"

"I read, of course!" he claimed, chuckling and running a hand through his thinning, grey-brown hair. Abby remembered when he hadn't looked quite so world-weary - perhaps her memory was playing tricks on her, but she could've sworn he'd had a full head of hair when they'd left Lyonis. All brown, too, like Aurelius'.

"Anyone who wants to see how to skin and butcher this, I'll be doing that in a few minutes. Just need a quick break," announced Eric, picking the carcass up by a leg and hauling it away. He'd set up a wooden frame in front of his tent a few days ago with Carl's help, and as he took some rope and hung the creature from its rear legs, Abby understood the purpose of it.

"Will it take long to prepare?" asked Carmina, evidently hungry. They all were, of course; none of them had eaten a thing today.

Eric shook his head. "No. It'll get cold out here overnight, we'll do part of it tonight and the rest tomorrow. Should be in even better shape for working with by morning," he informed them. "Normally I wouldn't get the meat out of them this early, or it tastes too gamey, but we can't cure it, so if we wait any longer it's gonna start rotting before we finish it."

Abby willed time to pass faster. Gods of the Maralor, she was hungry. She settled in the entrance of her tent in order to deposit her gear inside, and was soon joined by her mother, sitting beside her with a smile. "Is everything alright, pumpkin?" she asked.

Abby nodded, even though it wasn't entirely true. "Aside from the hunger," she corrected herself, casting her eyes down at her complaining gut.

"I know. We'll have a big supper. Breakfast, too. Don't worry, we'll be eating like kings for a few days," her mother assured her. "Oh! Have you met the doctor yet? We met him while you were all out," she quizzed in a tone that Abby knew all too well.

"Is this your way of saying I need to get myself a boyfriend?" Abby asked, grinning.

"You know me too well," she admitted. "But you should talk to him some time. He's nice."

"I sort of met him, but he was busy with a patient at the time," Abby admitted. She made a mental note to ask if Henry had survived, when she next crossed paths with the doctor.

"Elizabeth dear, don't hassle the poor girl about boys. She's far too young to be dating," Abby's father called out from the carrot patch, his tone jocular.

"Oh nonsense, Alex! You had me pregnant before her age," Elizabeth countered. "Besides, it wouldn't be her first boyfriend." Abby chuckled and shook her head, cheeks reddening slightly at the topic. She had no intention of getting pregnant when she could barely eat for one.

"Well, she's still our little girl. There'll be plenty of time to date when I'm dead," Alexander grinned, stepping over to join them. Abby couldn't help but laugh despite her efforts to try and look disapproving. "But the doctor *is* very nice, in an entirely un-courtable way. Besides, he's... well, a doctor. It's good to have one about, isn't it."

Abby smiled to herself. "I'm going to get a drink. Try not to argue too much over who I can and cannot make love to," she said, getting to her feet and leaving hurriedly before her father saw the broad grin spreading across her face.

Alexander feigned fury behind her. "Making love?! That's out of the question until long after I'm dead! I'll haunt you!"

She found herself wandering across the camp with a smile, observing people's nightly attempts to keep themselves entertained. Some of the luckier ones had books, and others had each other to fill the nights with laughter. Often, she and her family would do the same, but tonight her siblings seemed too exhausted. Carmina and Aurelius probably would've gone straight to bed if it wasn't for the prospect of food.

Carl and Mrs. Elani were the ones she felt most sorry for. They never seemed to have anyone to share time with, and whenever Abby had offered Carl some company he'd barely said a word, just working away on whatever project he'd had at the time. Abby had done her best to take good care of the old lady, though, helping her with any tasks she could, and sharing food when there was enough to spare.

She meandered over to the drinking pools and fetched herself some water. It was best after dark, cold and refreshing. She splashed a little on her face, too, scraping sweat from her skin. A full bath seemed like too much effort tonight.

A slight chill ran down her exposed arms as the night truly began. She headed back over to Eric's, staring at the dead impala. It hung still, like a thirty-five kilo, fleshy windchime. "Bless you Ersei, mother of love and life, for sacrificing one of your children so that others may live," she offered in quiet prayer. She considered waiting for Eric, but soon felt the call of nature. Rubbing her arms to stave off the cold, she made her way over towards the unpleasant smell of the latrine.

The beauty of twilight on the horizon made for a pleasant view, and any distraction from the stench of human waste was a welcome one. Abby knew that they'd soon have to bury this latrine and dig another one further out to accommodate the expanding group of tents.

21

She'd just finished her business when she heard it - a muffled cry from the midst of the nearby tents. Frowning, she pulled up her trousers and tightened the length of rope that she'd taken to using as a belt. Stalking closer, trying to fathom the source and cause of the sound, she heard it again - a woman sobbing a weak cry of protest. Abby continued towards it, suddenly wishing she'd brought her hammer and shield with her.

There was a faint clinking of glass and metal as a man burst from Mrs. Elani's tent. His hands were laden with a heavy-looking sack, and he wasted no time in running for open ground as people began to look outside, searching for the source of the commotion just as Abby had done. Mrs. Elani limped out of her tent in pursuit of the fleeing criminal. "Thief!" she whimpered, her voice weakened by age and pain.

Abby broke into a sprint, glad she'd kept her boots on. The thief had a head start, but Abby reckoned he also had more weight to carry than her with that sack. The man disappeared over the top of a hill and she followed suit, stumbling a little as a stone slipped underfoot. The dark wasn't doing her any favours there, but she was slowly gaining on the man despite her exhaustion. "Stop!" she yelled after him, feeling rather stupid for expecting the kind of man who'd rob an old woman to stop just because she told him to. Typically, he instead glanced over his shoulder and panicked at the sight of her rapidly bearing down on him. All it did was make him run faster.

She forced herself to more than match his pace, though her stomach protested the recent lack of food, informing her that she didn't deserve to be able to maintain this speed. Still, she saw the man tiring and carried on after him, her determination redoubling at the sight. The thief reached the top of another hill and stopped, dropping the sack to the ground.

The wind whipped across Abby's face as she closed in on him, her ginger locks blinding her. Pain exploded in her left arm. She cried out as she felt it tear through her, and swung her other arm wildly, hitting nothing. Her hair settled long enough for her to see what had happened; the knife was deep in her bicep, blood already coursing like a crimson river down to her fingertips.

Something in her flipped like a switch. The pain was forced to the back of her mind, and she stepped backwards, gasping as the knife was yanked from her flesh. A golden shimmer ran over her hand as she clouted the man with a closed fist. There was a sickening crack, the bare knuckles causing damage that they simply shouldn't have been capable of, shattering his jaw like glass. He fell down like he'd been kicked by a horse.

Abby stared at her hand for a few moments, then at the thief. His jaw was visibly deformed even where the skin was still intact over it. She knelt over him, clutching her ruined bicep and inspecting the damage done. There was a lot of blood from both of their injuries. "Help!" she cried out, terrified both by what she'd done, and by what had happened to her. For reasons she didn't quite comprehend at the time, she began to pluck the dislodged teeth from the thief's mouth. They joined the blood pooling in her palm, forming a grim scene.

A gnarled hand on her shoulder steadied her. "You did him good. Let's get you to the doctor," said Eric.

She couldn't help but feel as if she was going mad; like some princess from a story, she swooned in his arms as he lifted her. His black beard brushed against her cheek, his ruggedly handsome face looked down at her with a hint of concern; those strong arms holding her tightly as he carried her off towards safety. *Stop it. This isn't romantic, you're just going loopy from shock*, said some small part of her that was still thinking rationally.

She was losing blood rapidly, massive gouts of it spurting from the wound and streaming through her fingers. The trials of the day soon caught up with her, and she had to close her eyes, gritting her teeth through the pain. She heard everything that happened around her, but understood nothing. Confusion and blood loss eventually exhausted her, and she fell asleep despite the throbbing pain in her arm.

3
Adocalypse Now

She awoke the next morning, almost as confused as she had been when she'd passed out. She barely remembered what had happened to her after being carried off by Eric. *Has Mrs. Elani been returned her belongings? Did I hallucinate that golden light? What happened to the thief?* These questions and more swam in her head, the most important amongst them being where she was right now. Eric's tent, possibly. *How sweet.*

Abby frowned and scolded herself for having the most inappropriate timing for flights of fancy. She glanced at the bandage on her arm; it was thoroughly crimson. As if her mind had only just remembered that she was injured, pain surged through her and forced her to focus. She hissed and attempted to gather her wits, examining the rest of herself. The blood had been cleaned off and her boots removed, but her clothes remained. She brushed some hair off of her face, a pang of annoyance striking her as she recalled the blindness it had caused at just the wrong moment. She should've tied it back - it was not a mistake she intended to repeat.

The entrance flap rustled, and the doctor who'd tended to Henry stepped inside. He and Abby stared at each other for a few awkward moments, reciprocating each other's uncertainty on how to begin the conversation. Eventually, Abby settled for an inappropriately chirpy "Good morning."

He smiled, looking somewhat relieved at the mildness of her greeting. "Hello," he returned. His face was gaunt and tired, his stature slender and tall. His clothes were surprisingly smart, although they looked like they'd seen better days - she recognised the orange-brown wash of blood that just wouldn't quite come out of an otherwise white shirt.

"I'm Abby," she offered clumsily, easing herself up to sit.

The man smiled. "I know. I'm Doctor Ellis, but just call me Johann," he introduced himself. He looked a little young to be a doctor, Abby thought, but considering the lack of any other physician here, she wasn't about to complain. "How does the arm feel?" he enquired, gesturing to the bandage.

"It feels like it got stabbed by a great big knife. Will I be alright?" she asked in turn. A pained smile briefly crossed her face as she recalled that her mother had wanted her to meet the doctor. This probably wasn't quite what she'd had in mind.

"In time, probably. Fortunately for you I was able to get straight to it. With a little luck, any infection will be minimal," he claimed.

Abby crossed her legs under her, waves of pain still slicing through her arm. "What happened to the thief?" she asked, recalling that she'd made an effort to stop him choking on his own teeth.

"Dead. I heard that some of the less forgiving folks finished the job," he informed her, his feelings on the matter hard to gauge.

Abby didn't much like it herself, but vigilante justice was the only type to be had here. Besides, after what she'd done to him she would've been surprised if the thief had survived anyway. "Did they at least return her things? Mrs. Elani, that is," she questioned.

"They did," Johann nodded dispassionately.

She smiled through the pain, glad that it hadn't all been for nothing. "I should check my family are alright," she blurted out, trying to stand. She was a tiny bit dizzy from the blood loss, but she still just about managed to walk.

"Take it easy!" ordered Johann, sounding impatient.

She paid little attention, but paused to kiss him on the cheek. "Thank you, Johann," she offered "What happened to Henry, by the way?"

The doctor stood in silence for a few moments before he answered. Whether that was because of the kiss or the question, Abby wasn't sure. "He didn't make it, I'm afraid. Gut wounds are bad news."

Abby nodded glumly and staggered off barefoot between the tents. It was still early, and everyone seemed to be going through their morning rituals, which may include eating if they were lucky. She forced herself to discard the thoughts of whether or not Henry had left anyone behind, and pointed herself in the direction of her family's little cluster of tents. She approached her own to see Aurelius and Carmina being instructed by Eric on how to butcher the remains of the impala, and - not wishing to interfere or distract others from the lesson - she watched quietly from a distance.

Eric was about halfway done when Elizabeth rounded the tent corner, almost ploughing straight into Abby. "Arboneth Koning, get in bed this instant!" her mother ordered furiously. The anger was clearly just a veil for her motherly concern.

"But-" protested Abby, flushing with childlike embarrassment. All thoughts of food and impala butchery instantly left her mind.

"No buts!" her mother snapped back, grabbing Abby by the good arm and marching her around to the front of her tent. "In! Rest. Now!"

Abby gave an exasperated, apologetic look to everyone who'd begun staring, including Eric and her siblings. Feeling slightly guilty for having worried her mother, she clambered into her tent and sat down. She heard heated discussion from outside, the exact words of which were indistinct through the walls of the tent, though it was clearly her parents arguing. Relief struck Abby when her father eventually stooped into the tent, appearing far more reasonable than his wife. "Hey sweetie," he greeted, shuffling over and carefully embracing her.

"Hey dad," she murmured, returning the hug, grateful for the comfort despite the pain it caused her.

"Please don't hold it against your mother, she was worried sick," he continued, planting a kiss on her cheek. "But I'm proud of you for doing the right thing."

Abby smiled and gave him a little squeeze about the waist, wincing as the motion pulled on her ruined bicep. "I'm afraid it might be quite some time before I'm able to do so again, though," she lamented.

"Johann said you'll recover. By his reckoning you'll have lost a lot of strength by three months, but by half a year it'll probably be like it never happened," said Alexander, leaning back out of the embrace to smile at her.

"Six months is a lot of time," she responded, knowing that this would confine her in much the same way that her damaged ribs had. She also knew that her father was taking a very optimistic view on her potential recovery.

"I know, sweetie, but it'll all be fine. Don't worry."

She did worry, though. Only a madwoman wouldn't, in her position. "What if they catch up with us out here?" she asked.

Her father shook his head firmly. "Don't think about that. We've still got Eric, Aurelius, Carmina, and even Carl. They're not incapable," he reminded her. "Besides, if it gets too bad we'll move north. There are supposed to be more forests and animals that way. It's cooler, too."

Abby gave him a curious look. "Father, where did you hear all this stuff? You've never been here before have you?" she quizzed him.

Alexander chuckled and shook his head. "No, I've not. But you know, your old man had dreams back in his youth. Wild and silly ones."

She'd never thought of her father as a dull automaton, but she'd never enquired as to his childhood aspirations, either. She'd been too busy trying to live up to her own. "What sort of dreams?" she asked.

He grinned, placing a hand on her shoulder. "Well, when I was a bit younger than Carmina is now, I thought I was going to be an explorer. I read reams and reams of books on the matter," he explained, scratching his stubble.

Abby laughed, shaking her head in faint disbelief. "Why didn't you mention this before, when we first arrived here? We could've gone exploring!"

Alexander shrugged. "Well, we *did* go exploring. Yesterday I saw an impala, and before that, more than a few other creatures that I've always been curious about. Truth be told, I never thought I'd come to Tinarus after your mother became pregnant with Maximilian. I wish it had been under better circumstances, but in a strange way, I *am* fulfilling some of my childhood dreams now," he admitted. "Silly as they are."

Abby briefly struggled back against memories of her older brother. "They're not silly," she insisted. "Everyone deserves a little happiness."

"I've got all the happiness I need right here," he claimed, gently tapping her nose. "But I wouldn't say no to seeing an elephant or a zebra, or-" he shook his head, refocusing on the matter at hand "I promised your mother I'd let you rest. Are you tired?"

She shook her head firmly. "Not even a little. I just woke up."

"I'll let the others know that they can see you soon, then. Could you at least pretend to rest for a bit, though? Just for your mother's sake," begged her father.

"If I must," she agreed.

"Thanks," he offered, backing out of the tent. "I love you."

"I love you too," she returned. Silence filled the tent again, and Abby lay down and closed her eyes, doing her best to actually get to sleep.

She must've drifted off at some point after all, because she woke up to the sound of Eric easing himself inside her tent. "Hey," he greeted, his voice low and level as always.

Abby smiled and sat up, rubbing the sleep from her eyes. "Hey," she returned. "Mother let you in, then? I thought she would've been standing guard with a spade or something."

Eric grunted a chuckle. "Yeah. She's just worried about you. Mothers are always like that. Still, that was a brave thing you did."

Abby shrugged. "I guess. A petty thief with a knife isn't exactly a foe of heroes, though," she commented, adjusting herself under the covers.

Eric remained silent a few moments longer before pressing the issue further. "In the war, we used to say the difference between a hero and a warrior isn't about who they fight, but when and why."

"You fought in the war?" Abby quizzed, leaning in closer as intrigue got the better of her. "I thought you said you were a hunter?"

"I signed up when the war got too close to home," he elucidated. "Before that I was just a hunter."

"Thomas or Mathew?" she enquired.

"Lord Hariton, for Thomas. Everyone knows Mathew had the gods against him," Eric claimed.

Admittedly, Abby would've been surprised if Eric had told her he'd fought for Mathew, regardless of whether or not it was the truth. Though he had been the legitimate king, it was a common belief that Mathew's tinkering with magical technology was the reason for the extinction. "Ah. Anyway, you were saying? When and why warriors fight, or something," she enquired, gesturing for Eric to continue.

"Warriors fight when they have to, because they have no choice."

Abby nodded slightly. The description seemed fitting enough for her. She didn't like violence; even when she knew she was fully justified in its application, she preferred to find an alternative where possible. She'd always been like that, though, with everything - her mother said she had a strong conscience. "And what about a hero?" she continued to pry.

"Only when they have to."

"But-"

"Because it's for the greater good."

That seemed to make sense, though perhaps it wasn't very specific. "What about people who fight when they don't need to?" she asked.

Eric let out a tiny little chuckle. "I guess they're just brutes."

Abby grinned. "So does that make me a brute, a warrior, or a hero?"

"I guess it's hard to say. Question is, would you have done the right thing even if you'd have lost?"

"Well, probably. You think that's what heroes really are, then? People who'd throw themselves into the fire for the right cause?"

"If you fight for good, knowing you might not win? Maybe," Eric contemplated.

Abby considered the point, old memories of Maximilian burning in her mind and behind her eyes again. "My older brother. He was a hero," she claimed.

Eric's hesitation made it clear that he was more sensitive to people's feelings than he looked. "Was?" he eventually quizzed.

"He died when they first started evacuating. We were meant to leave together, but he was a city guard in Lyonis. He stayed to hold them off as people fled," Abby elaborated. It had been over a year, but she still struggled to hold back tears as she explained it. Maximilian had always been the light for her, whenever there had been darkness. He could see the good in anyone, the other side of any situation; the silver lining to any misfortune. He'd been just like her.

"Sorry," Eric grumbled. "Shouldn't have asked."

Abby shrugged, feeling marginally better for having got it out of her system. "Did you ever have a brother, or any family?"

Eric nodded and moved to leave the tent. "Aurelius wanted to talk to you. I'll tell him you're awake," he muttered as he left.

Abby let out a drawn out sigh and lay back down, silently cursing herself for broaching the subject of Eric's family in such a stupid way.

She couldn't get back to sleep this time, though that wasn't a concern, as Aurelius was scrambling inside the tent only minutes after Eric left. "Abby!" he grinned, shuffling over beside her. She smiled up at him, not bothering to sit up this time. "Does it hurt?" he asked, gawking slightly at the thoroughly red bandage.

"Yes, it hurts! I got stabbed!" she exclaimed, unable to stop herself from chuckling incredulously.

"Didn't the doctor give you laudanum or anything?" Aurelius asked.

Abby shook her head, her hair dragging softly against her sleeping mat. "He may be a doctor, but I doubt he's got stashes of medicine to spare. We're not exactly doing well for supplies," she reminded him.

Aurelius nodded sheepishly. "Can I see it? The doctor said he'd need to replace the bandage today anyway."

Abby rolled her eyes and began to unravel the bandage, the sticky residue of dried blood adhering it to her skin. "Alright, if you must," she agreed.

"It looks really deep," he commented as she revealed it, grimacing at the thick red line running lengthways down her bicep.

"Yeah, it feels really deep, too. It'll definitely scar," Abby noted. She wasn't sure how she felt about that. She'd never had a scar before.

Aurelius grinned and manoeuvred an eyebrow suggestively. "Well, you know what they say; women like scars."

Abby sighed and put the bandage back on, not bothering to tie it properly. "Honestly, you'd think I was yesterday's loaf or something. Mother's trying to set me up with the doctor, and you're trying to set me up with a woman."

Aurelius chuckled and shook his head. "Seriously, though, it's a good story to tell. Makes you look tough," he claimed.

Abby smirked. "Alright, alright. Give me a hug and get your vicarious thrills elsewhere," she insisted, sitting up and reaching out to wrap her good arm around him for a quick cuddle.

"I'm glad you're alright," he said, giving her a pat on the back that caused her mending ribs to jolt with pain.

"Well, I'm not exactly *alright*, but I'll live. Could you get Carmina to go to the doctor with me later?" she requested. "And... some food would be good. I never did get to eat after yesterday's hunting trip."

Aurelius nodded agreeably. "I'll get on it," he assured her.

"Thanks. Oh, by the way - did you see the thief's body? Was there anything wrong with his jaw?" she enquired before he could leave.

"Something wrong with it? Yeah, that'd be one way of putting it - he didn't have much of a jaw left. It was a total mess, chunks of bone everywhere. Why, was that your doing?"

Abby grimaced. "Hard to say. Everything got kind of hazy after he stabbed me. I know I hit him at least once."

"More than once, I'd guess. Anyway, I'll go see about that food," Aurelius excused himself.

"Thanks," Abby called after him, smiling. She'd rather be out talking to people, or perhaps checking that Mrs. Elani was alright, but she knew that she wouldn't be able to keep herself entertained for long anyway. She settled back down, and slowly but surely, sleep took her once again.

***

Johann grimaced at the unsightly wound. "Yes, that's definitely an infection," he confirmed. It'd been an incredibly dull week for Abby, and it seemed that things would get worse before they got better. She'd mostly occupied herself chatting with Carmina or watching Eric and Carl work on whatever projects they had. This morning she'd woken up to a different kind of pain in her arm, and gone straight to the doctor. "I don't actually have anything to treat this properly," he admitted, giving her an apologetic look. "The best I can do is clean it and hope it doesn't get any worse."

Abby sighed and nodded. "Sugar."

Johann peered owlishly at her, no doubt mistaking her meaning. "I beg your pardon?"

"Sugar?" she repeated tentatively.

"Yes, but what about it?" he asked.

Abby chuckled, though her throat felt dry from worry at the bad news. "Just... exclaiming," she explained.

"Oh. Like, shit?" asked Johann.

Abby nodded. "Like that, just not."

The doctor shrugged and began to soak a cloth in a bucket of water. "You know, I'm impressed with how well you handled the pain. What exactly are you?" he asked.

"Well I'm not really anything, to be honest. Job prospects aren't all that great lately, in case you hadn't noticed." Abby wasn't usually so pedantic, but right now her nerves were eating away at her.

Johann smiled to himself and strolled over. "Well then, what *were* you, before all of this?"

Abby considered for a moment which of her previous hobbies and occupations she should mention, opting to skirt around some of the less successful ventures. "Well, I was in training as a paladin of the Maralor for about six years. Before that, I volunteered at an orphanage. What about you? I suppose you were being trained as a doctor until recently?"

30

Johann nodded and gently grabbed her wrist, extending the arm so that he could start cleaning the wound. It stung a little, but not enough to bother her greatly. "I graduated only a month before the apocalypse. I was on my way east at the time, and I sort of latched onto the people already moving as they passed by. Just my luck to finally get a decent job as Panora comes to an end," he joked, smiling faintly to himself.

"Well, look on the bright side," she told him. "You can still help people who really need it, out here." *People like myself.*

"That's true. I don't get paid well for it, but I do get kissed by pretty women, sometimes," he commented flirtatiously.

"And even some slightly less pretty ones," she said, turning her head slightly to hide a cheeky grin from him. In truth, she loved that sort of attention when it came for the right reasons. She just wasn't sure that it *was* for the right reasons, yet.

"Oh, that's hardly fair. You've lured me into a conversational trap!" Johann insisted, continuing to smile to himself as he worked. "Now I either have to assume that you were calling yourself unattractive and reassure you that you're pretty, or outright agree that you're not."

"Well, fortunately for you I have absolutely no illusions as to exactly how pretty I am," she replied. She'd never been the most attractive girl, even in her own family, and she'd frequently been called things like 'butch' in her youth. Still, she never let it bother her greatly. She refused to succumb to the shallow expectations of men and women.

"Is that supposed to help me *out* of the trap, Abby? Because it seems like you're digging a hole to bury me in right now," replied Johann.

She laughed and shook her head. "I wouldn't intentionally be so mean, even if you are starting to come across as a flirt."

"Is it a bad thing to flirt, then?" he asked, unperturbed.

"Not necessarily, but I can tell that you're rusty with the ladies."

Johann sighed. "You're not wrong. The apocalypse hasn't exactly been kind to anyone's sex life, I'd imagine."

Abby smiled mischievously. "I don't know, it's been about the same for me," she jested, leaving deliberate ambiguity.

"Well, now I'm not sure if I should be jealous or feel sorry for you," muttered the doctor, moving off to fetch a fresh bandage. "You're going to have to take care of this dressing until the wound heals over entirely. It could take weeks," he warned her, unravelling the thing and beginning to wrap it around the injured arm.

She could understand the need to ration supplies. He only had finite bandages, and although only the most serious of injuries necessitated their use, once they were gone it was unlikely he'd get hold of any more. "Thanks for all of this, Johann. You know, you should come by some time when Eric and the others have gone hunting," Abby offered. "We tend to share fresh meat so that it's all eaten before it starts to rot."

"Maybe I'll do that," agreed Johann. "But I'd rather like another kiss, if that's an option for payment instead."

Abby smirked and got to her feet. "Well, not now that I know you're lusting after it," she said. "I'll see you around, Johann."

The doctor sighed as he watched her leave.

Her arm continued to show signs of infection over the next few days. It worsened steadily, causing Abby and those who cared for her to fear for her continued use of the limb. She peeked at the wound under the bandage every morning when she awoke, but four days later that was no longer necessary; the putrid red and purple of the affliction had begun to peek out from beneath the dressing, an expanding spot of concentrated disease. She staggered to her feet and dressed as quickly as she could, so sick with worry that she didn't even think to pull on boots before leaving.

Johann startled as she burst through the flap of his tent. "Abby?" he questioned. She gave him a concerned look and showed him the arm. "Oh bugger it. I don't think that's going to get any better naturally," he commented.

Abby grimaced and struggled to keep her voice level as she spoke. "What are my options? Be honest."

"Amputation probably won't do much good in all honesty, as the infection is just as likely to reappear on the stump if we can't clean it," he admitted. "I can't believe I'm suggesting it, but Mrs. Elani may be able to help more than I can, at this point. When it comes to an infection of this scale, there's nothing I can do without proper supplies."

Abby nodded and took a calming breath, trying to cling onto the hope that he was right about Mrs. Elani. "Thanks, Johann. Wish me luck," she said meekly.

"Of course," agreed the doctor, giving her a sympathetic smile and stepping over to hold the tent flap open for her. It was an unnecessary gesture, but appreciated. "Good luck."

Her mind struggled to suppress silent fits of panic as she left to see the medicine woman. Pausing to take some more calming breaths outside of the old woman's tent, she called out. "Mrs. Elani, are you busy?"

"Not too busy for you, young lady," came the response from within. Abby stepped inside and tried to force herself to smile at the old lady, but the best she could manage was keeping the tears back.

"I knew you would come," Mrs. Elani claimed.

"How?" asked Abby, initially sceptical.

"Rumour spreads, as does infection. Both, if left untreated, can be a deadly thing."

"Ah," said Abby. "Well, that saves me some explaining."

Without a word, Mrs. Elani stooped and took a glass jar from an entropic pile of objects. She handed it to Abby with a faint smile. "I've been working on this for you since I heard of your infection. It's aqueous ammonia, to clean the wound. It may leave it stinging and sore for some time, but better that than festering."

Abby considered the jar for a few moments, turning it slowly in her hand. It appeared as if simply water - but then again, so did many things that weren't. "What do I do? Just rub it into the wound?"

"Leave it in the wound for as long as it takes to boil water," Mrs. Elani clarified. "When the water has boiled and then cooled enough not to burn you, rinse it out. Do this every two days until the wound is clear, but ration it carefully - it takes some time to make more."

Abby nodded and finally managed to force something like a smile onto her face. "Thanks, Mrs. Elani."

"It's the least I could do, after what you did for me. Go. Use it now, while you still can," the medicine woman insisted.

If she hadn't been so concerned about her arm, Abby might've paused long enough to be happy that she'd made a good impression. As it was, she simply scampered off towards Carmina's tent, trying to ignore any negative thoughts swirling around in her mind. *It's going to work. It's got to work.*

"Carmina!" she hissed softly, gently slapping the side of her little sister's tent. She heard a waking moan from within before any sort of actual response.

"Abby? It's still early," groaned Carmina.

Abby ignored the adolescent complaints and spoke up. "I need your help with something! Bring the axe."

She heard the slow, fumbling motions of her sister dressing within the tent. "I'll be out in a minute," she agreed.

Abby took advantage of the brief pause to leave the jar in her tent. She remembered to pull on her boots this time, and tucked her hammer into the rope about her waist. She may not be able to put up too much of a fight with only one arm, but it was better than nothing.

When at last Carmina did emerge, she was bleary-eyed and clearly disgruntled. "What is it?" she demanded.

Abby lifted her arm slightly to show the spread of the infection from beneath the bandage. "It's getting worse. I've got something that will clean it, but we need to boil some water."

Carmina nodded and hefted the axe, resting it over her shoulder. "So we need wood? Alright. Just the two of us, then?"

Abby nodded faintly. "We'll be fine."

"Famous last words," her sister muttered before turning to lead the way towards their regular source of wood. "Does it hurt?"

"It stings. Kind of like bad sunburn, you know?" Abby described. They all knew what bad sunburn was like, of course. Everyone in the family had had it at least once since they'd come to this staggeringly hot island-continent.

Carmina rubbed her eyes tiredly, squinting at the painfully bright sun. "Hopefully this cure of yours works. Johann's doing, I suppose?"

Abby shook her head. "Not exactly. Aqueous ammonia, from Mrs. Elani," she explained, trying her best to convey her hope through a numb voice.

"Her way of thanking you," commented Carmina.

They were usually comfortable in each other's company, but Abby felt that the following pause was not as normal. Her little sister's hesitant glances gave away that there was something bothering her. "Something on your mind, Car?" Abby enquired.

Carmina nodded and dived on the opportunity. "Do you like Johann?"

"You don't just mean as a friend, do you?"

"No, I mean as a lover."

Abby shrugged, so very glad of a distraction. The change of subject calmed her panicking mind, taking her thoughts off of the permeating negative. "He's a nice guy. I don't know - there are lots of nice people about, but I don't really think too much about relationships these days, to be honest. Not that I ever did anyway."

Carmina laughed softly. "Don't you miss the sex?"

Abby shook her head. "Sex isn't worth missing unless you're missing the person it's with, Car. There are better things, despite what some of the men might be telling you by now."

Carmina looked away in an attempt to hide her blush. "So, is this about a boy you like?" Abby pried. "I know Johann's not your type."

"It's not really a boy…"

Abby looked quizzically at Carmina. It was the first she'd heard of this from her. "A girl?"

"A man!" corrected Carmina, blushing furiously. "Eric!"

Abby couldn't help but chuckle at her own mistake. "Oh, right. I probably should've guessed you'd take an interest in him."

Carmina smiled. "Yes, I know I'm a walking cliché - but what do you think about him?"

Abby slowly moved around and put her good arm across Carmina's shoulders. "Listen - I like Eric, and normally I might encourage you, but it seems like he's not over whoever he lost. I honestly don't think you'll get far with him."

Carmina nodded in awkward agreement. "I guess you're right."

"He is handsome though," admitted Abby, grinning playfully.

"Well, so far your advice about men is better than father's."

Abby laughed. "Father's just joking around. I bet he would've walked you down the aisle a long time ago if it wasn't for the whole of Panora falling apart. You're almost seventeen, after all."

Carmina fidgeted slightly. "Yeah, I guess so," she agreed. After a few more moments of silence, she had further personal matters to discuss. "Mother always said the only reason you weren't wed was because you were busy with all the other things."

"Mother was being polite. It's partly that, but also because you stole all the male attention," Abby admitted, craning her neck to plant a kiss on Carmina's cheek. Her little sister was reluctant to be boastful about her looks, as young women had a tendency to be. Abby knew better, of course; there was no point trying to dress up the truth about attraction, or anything else so inconsequential for that matter. Much like Maximilian, Carmina had inherited their mother's stunning blonde hair. She'd be a paragon of Luthanian beauty, one day.

Abby gently removed her arm from her sister's shoulders and picked a less awkward subject - more for Carmina's sake than her own. "How are the lessons going, anyway? It seems like I'll never learn to use a bow if I don't stop getting injured."

Carmina nodded eagerly. Evidently, Eric had left a good impression in more ways than one. "Good! Aurelius actually hit something when we went out last time. I'm getting there, too. And Eric showed us how to make some traps! But... those were pretty complicated."

Abby smiled across at her. "Why don't you tell me about those? They could be handy." It was a distraction, in truth, another thing that Abby was glad to cling to in order to keep her mind from straying. That didn't make it any less true, though - traps were useful for any number of prey. Carmina began to kill time by explaining in great detail the things that Eric had taught her and Aurelius; deadfalls, snares, pits and more.

They eventually arrived at the woodlands, if they could be called that. The trees were frequent, but still sparse enough that one could see clearly for quite some distance beyond and between them - savannah would perhaps be a more appropriate term. It seemed to stretch on for miles like that, a small line of stumps evidencing the fuel needs of those camped nearby.

Whilst finishing off an explanation of how to properly cover a pit trap, Carmina strode up to a young tree and carefully placed the head of her axe against the wood. Abby sighed softly as her little sister set to work, hacking slowly but surely through the wood. It made her feel so useless in her current state, but at least this meant that she might one day have the full use of both arms again.

"Do you reckon we should chop it up here, or carry the whole thing back?" Carmina asked, panting softly from the exertion.

"It's probably best to carry the whole thing. I wouldn't be able to carry much firewood with only one arm," Abby pointed out.

"Yeah, I thought so," muttered Carmina. Even though she wasn't particularly strong or fit, she soon had the tree at the point of felling. Abby walked over, pressing herself against the trunk and ramming her shoulder into it. With a loud crack, the sisters eased it down into their waiting arms.

The effort of carrying it meant that conversation was more of a strain than it was worth, and so the pair continued silently, the journey back as dull as it was strenuous - and painful, in Abby's case. Their father came out to greet them as they dumped the tree behind his tent. "There you are! I was beginning to think you'd both eloped, with Carl and Johann," he commented. Carmina blushed, and failed to compose herself enough to scowl.

"Why would I do that when I could make love in my tent?" Abby questioned, grinning mischievously.

Alexander clapped his hands over his ears. "Lalalalala," he vocalised, drowning out Abby's voice until his wife slapped him on the back and gave him a disapproving look.

Carmina smirked at her little victory and called out. "Aurelius! Get your arse over here and chop this wood, we did the hard work already."

"You mind your language!" scorned Elizabeth.

Carmina rolled her eyes for only Abby to see and walked off to her tent, muttering quiet indignation to herself. "Hey! Thanks, Car," called Abby before her sister could disappear.

A brief explanation of what was going on led to the assembly of a fire, with Aurelius having split the logs as demanded. Abby fetched the jar from her tent, her face wrinkling involuntarily at the stench as she opened it.

"That smells like someone squatted over a fish," Aurelius grimaced.

"I'm glad I don't have to drink that," she agreed, and removed the bandage entirely from her arm. The motion, gentle though it was, seemed to scrape unpleasantly against the infected skin.

She waited for the wood to catch light before pouring the odorous mixture into the wound. It stung, but not as badly as she'd expected, and definitely not badly enough to stop her using it. She closed the jar again and waited patiently for the water to boil. It was in the hands of the Maralor, now.

4
Prayer

The weeks passed slowly and painfully, the afflicted arm becoming red and sore as a result of the treatment. Still, the unpleasant colours of infection faded as the wound healed, and that was what mattered.

Abby had always considered herself a devout follower of the Maralor. She'd managed to bring a copy of the Faralex with her all the way from Lyonis, though she rarely got it out for fear that the holy book would get damaged or in some way blemished. Still, having time to kill had brought faith back to the forefront of her mind. Although Maximilian's death had left her with so many questions, and the long road here had left her with little time to grow spiritually, she found herself praying more often now that her life had some guise of stability.

"Besigur, tailor of creation, bless our works, and grant us the patience to better ourselves through labour. Corsein, oracle of fates, grant us wisdom, and if so willing stay the treacherous tides of time for one more day. Ersei, mother of love and life, teach us compassion and restraint; remind us that there are two sides to every story, and that to love and respect is the best option wherever possible. And should compassion not prevail, may Rendick lend us strength and honour that we might smite the wicked."

She smiled to herself. It felt good to say the familiar words again, her very own prayer. It was a reminder to her of what was truly important in life. She found bliss in worshipping them.

Resolving to maintain that side of herself, Abby got to her feet and dressed before heading over to see Johann. The doctor had taken a look at the infection the day after her first treatment, and had been confident that it hadn't grown worse. Abby hoped that he'd have even better news for her today.

Johann was not particularly busy when she entered his tent. He rarely was; due to the lack of proper medicine, his treatments largely consisted of advice such as 'keep it away from dirt' and 'don't pick at it.' "Ah, young Miss Koning!" he greeted.

"I'm only a year younger than you, Johann," she smiled at him.

"But infinitely prettier," he countered. "I suppose you're here about the arm?" She shrugged off his flirtations and held it out for him to see, stepping closer.

He reached out, gently gripping her tricep to hold the limb steady for inspection. "Well, the infection's obviously cleared up, and the wound's almost closed. I'd recommend stopping treatment now, before you do yourself more harm than good. Just keep it away from dirt."

Abby beamed and wrapped Johann in a hug with her one good arm. "Thank Corsein for that."

"Corsein, and Mrs. Elani's urine concoction," Johann corrected her, chuckling softly and returning the embrace.

"Don't remind me," she begged. Johann hadn't informed her of the source of the ammonia until halfway through the treatment. If she hadn't seen the infection shrinking for herself, she probably would've thought it was a cruel joke.

"So, how about that kiss?" Johann tried.

Abby rolled her eyes and planted a brief peck on his cheek. "There, you pest. Now, I need to go and thank Mrs. Elani as well. Thanks for your help."

Johann smiled at her, calling out as she left. "It'll probably be at least a couple more months before you can really use it again properly, so go easy on it!"

She walked the short distance to the old woman's tent. "Mrs. Elani?" she called, wrinkling her nose at the smell of the strange and pungent concoctions being brewed within.

"Come in," came the reply.

Abby eased herself inside. She was unable to contain her smile; for the first time since they'd left Maximilian behind, she felt like everything would be fine. "I wanted to thank you. Johann says I'm on the way to recovery, as long as I keep dirt clear of the wound."

Mrs. Elani seemed pleased at her manners. "See that you do. And you're quite welcome, the only thanking I shall require is my jar back," she insisted, her face crinkling along the lines of old age as she smiled.

Abby nodded. "I'll bring it on by in a bit. Really, though - thanks. I don't know how much longer I could've survived if I had lost the arm."

"I'm glad I could help. Take care," Mrs. Elani smiled. She waved Abby off, returning to brewing whatever that foul smelling mixture was.

***

Four hundred and seventy-one days since we left the capital. With a soft groan, she forced herself up and glanced at the progress her bicep had made. A month and a half more had flown by in an endless cycle of gradually toughening menial chores and exercises to return strength to the injured arm. The muscle was still small and pathetic, but the flesh had healed over firmly, leaving only a ghastly, straight scar. Aurelius had commented that it looked 'hard as nails', whatever that was supposed to mean. He always had read too many violent books full of grizzled, tough men, though.

She knelt and clasped her hands in prayer. "Besigur, tailor of creation, bless our works, and grant us the patience to better ourselves through labour," she began, the same prayer she said every morning and most nights. She'd kept the promise she'd made to herself and continued actively practicing her faith.

Repeating the words was a meditation exercise as much as a prayer, forcing her to confront her actions and assess her successes and failures under the scrutiny of the Maralor. She liked to think that there were more successes than failures, but there were still some things that she wasn't proud of. In the time that her arm had been more or less useless the camp had swollen in numbers, and anonymous, petty crime had taken a grip. Limited in her usefulness with just one arm, Abby had sat back and done nothing about it one too many times. She'd only have made things worse for everyone if she had tried to intervene.

Considering a much-needed bath for the first activity of the day, Abby began to dress. She froze halfway through getting her boots on as she heard the scream; at first she wondered if this would be another of those horrible moments of helplessness, but as more screaming and yelling came in waves all around her, Abby realised that this wasn't an everyday problem. She laced up the boots in a hurry and grabbed her hammer. There was little point taking the shield, she still couldn't block a half-decent blow.

Aurelius and Carmina emerged from their tents mere moments after Abby, fully dressed and already stringing their bows. People surged past in a panic, the majority of the campsite fleeing from some imminent threat. "Avared's bells, what's going on out here?!" called Alexander, poking his head through the tent flap. Nobody stopped to answer, but Abby was already certain of the source of the terror.

The crowds thinned out swiftly as they fled, and there it was; one of the earthen sort, all seven feet of it. It had in its hands a man she didn't recognise, but despite this position of detachment, she couldn't help but feel furious as the creature crushed its victim's torso with terrifying strength. It walked slowly; not because it was extremely heavy - which Abby knew from experience to be the case - but because it was confident in its victory. She glanced over to where her father had been, but he seemed to have disappeared back into the tent whilst she was distracted.

Carmina and Aurelius nodded at each other and took aim. The arrows flew through the air, deflecting uselessly off of the elemental's head. It walked on, inexorable, its expressionless face mocking them for thinking that such an attack could ever have worked against stone.

Their father re-emerged, fully dressed and swiftly followed by his wife. "Run!" he barked at the siblings, and they did so. Adrenaline burst through Abby's body.

It was intimidating, the speed at which such a thing could move when it wanted to. It was gaining on her, the details of its form becoming clearer with every worried glance she threw in its direction. It was almost as if the creature had been sculpted with the mockery of mankind intended. Its musculature was chiselled in the most literal sense, and it bore a face with features that were disturbingly flat, yet human in a most unsettling way. Abby was stuck at the back of the group, not because she was slow but because pushing forwards any faster would displace others. Given no other choice, she darted left, sprinting off between the tents.

She didn't need to glance back to tell that the elemental was still in close pursuit; its footsteps pounded out a rhythm behind her. She passed a particularly large dwelling, and a moment later heard the telltale sound of tearing fabric as her pursuer upended and ripped through the entire thing. She darted around corners, hoping and praying that the sheer weight of the elemental meant that it was forced to either slow down to turn, or have its momentum reduced by going straight through the many tents.

Abby saw a young couple emerging from a tent up ahead, confused and in a state of half-dress. "Run!" she urged them, and they did. They lacked her speed, however, and she was ahead of them in mere moments. She winced and forced herself not to look back as she heard the crunch of bone and short-lived screams. Footsteps began to catch up with her again, revealing that the elemental hadn't really stopped to kill them, so much as it had ploughed straight through and over them. Her heart pounded. She cornered sharply and headed for the road again.

Abby groaned at her carelessness as she skidded to a halt on the beaten track. Although everyone else had long since run as far as they could, Mrs. Elani was still hobbling along, unable to even jog. At her age, it wasn't at all surprising that she had fallen behind. Abby turned and ran west, hoping to steer the monster away.

Once again, the sound of footsteps gave away its movements - this time it wasn't coming for her. She stopped and pivoted, her mind racing for a quick solution. "Stop!" she yelled, but it did no such thing. The poor old lady stood no chance as the elemental picked her up like a ragdoll and shattered her spine over its knee.

Abby choked on a wretched sob and raised her hammer. "Why?" she demanded, her eyes straying to the shuddering remains of Mrs. Elani as the stone manifestation dropped them to the earth.

The elemental moved towards Abby once again, and she came to her senses just in time to dart to the right and avoid a grabbing hand. There was no way she could fight this thing alone, its very body was armour. The pursuit took full speed once again, tears blurring Abby's vision with every furious movement of her legs until adrenaline and fear forced her mind away from the murder of Mrs. Elani.

It was only a matter of time before fatigue set in, something that the elemental evidently didn't share. She tried to take a right again, her tired legs unenthusiastically preparing to hop more tent pegs, but she found herself hauled off of the ground by large, stone hands. She didn't even have time to make peace with the gods before a gunshot rang out nearby and it dropped her.

She scrambled away the moment she hit the ground, ignoring the pain in her arms from the impact. The elemental turned moodily, and she could see a large chip in the back of its head where the round had struck. The pebble that had been used as ammunition was still firmly lodged inside, and Abby forced herself upright to yank it out with the claw end of the hammer, leaving a vulnerability in the otherwise smooth stone. She went to strike the new weakness, but the monster rounded on her too quickly, lashing out with an open palm. She ducked back and took a glancing blow to the shoulder that sent her reeling.

It charged at her, but she leapt aside at the last moment, clutching her agonised shoulder. Once again, the sound of tents being shredded came from behind her as the elemental's momentum caused it to overshoot. Abby lurched forwards and regained her balance, breaking into a jog towards the source of the gunshot.

The sight of Eric gave her hope, even though the sorrowful calm that usually graced his face was gone. A terrible fury had taken its place. "Distract it!" he barked, placing powder in his gun's pan.

Abby moved back towards the tents, working in little squares around them as the stony monster tried to catch up with her. She moved almost instinctively, just following Eric's order and hoping he killed her pursuer in time to stop it crushing her. It skidded and nearly lost balance trying to turn sharp corners, far less nimble than Abby. Her legs weren't going to hold out much longer, but thankfully another gunshot soon diverted its attention back to Eric.

Though it made no sounds of distress, it seemed to feel pain, which was reassuring. She capitalised on that fact by ducking around it and reinforcing the damage, finally landing a proper blow of her own on the back of its head. A large chunk crumbled and fell away along with the second pebble, and again as she struck a little lower.

Lingering for the second strike proved to be a mistake, as it kicked backwards at her. The blow went between her legs rather than instantly shattering her shin, for which she would've been grateful if she could think about anything other than the pain flaring up in her crotch. The force of the strike sent her skidding backwards onto her rump.

It turned and raised a foot to finish her off, but Eric charged past her before it could stamp down, slamming the stock of his rifle into its face. Its nose crumbled slightly, giving Abby time to crawl forwards in agony as the elemental switched targets once again. She spun her hammer so that the claw-end of the tool was on the impacting side this time, and dragged herself up the body of the elemental, leaning against it to stay upright as she slammed her weapon into the back of its weakened skull. It staggered, and she wrenched the hammer back out, repeating the action over and over. Eric joined in from the other side, and its head caved inwards into a dusty cloud of crumbling rock. It toppled over backwards as Abby moved out of the way, whatever semblance of life it once had, extinguished.

Eric didn't seem satisfied with just that. The frenzied look on his face turned to bitterness as he crushed what remained of its head, swinging the rifle brutishly. Abby lowered herself to the floor and checked the severity of the blows she'd taken; despite the pain, it seemed she would get away with just heavy bruising today.

The huntsman eventually started pummeling its torso as well, making no progress there other than to dent the wood of his gun. "Eric. Eric! It's dead, Eric. You can stop hitting it now," Abby called out, trying to calm him. Surprise struck her when his bitter anger turned into a flood of tears, the rifle going from weapon to crutch as he supported himself on it, then gave up on standing entirely and used the destroyed elemental as a seat. Abby forced herself to her feet and sat beside him as he wept into his hands. "What's wrong?" she asked, putting an arm around his shoulders.

"It killed them!" he managed between sobs.

"Yeah," she affirmed, struggling to remain composed as the thoughts of Mrs. Elani returned to the forefront of her mind. "I'm afraid so."

Abby chewed awkwardly on her lower lip as it occurred to her that Eric hadn't been close to any of the victims. He probably wasn't talking about them. She decided not to pry whilst he was crying, and simply wrapped her arms around him in sympathy. They sat there a while, Eric just dripping from his cheeks until he'd run dry.

"Do you think we ought to go and fetch the others?" she asked when the moment finally felt right.

Eric glanced around at the sea of demolished tents and shook his head. "They'll come back to get their gear once they realise this thing's not chasing them anymore," he claimed.

Abby nodded and removed herself from him, getting to her feet. "I'm going to bury Mrs. Elani. I'll be around if you want to talk," she offered. Eric just nodded, not budging from where he sat. Abby doubted he would come to her for comfort; he just didn't seem the sort to do so.

With a weary sigh, she strolled over to Carl's tent to borrow a spade. She knew he wouldn't mind - he'd liked Mrs. Elani too, at least a little. Fresh tears stung at the back of her eyes when she returned to find the frail corpse of the old lady. Carefully adjusting the spade in her arms, she struggled, hauling the body past the outskirts of the campsite and to the first suitable location she could find for a grave. Digging proved almost as hard as carrying, her left arm protesting at the abundance of exercise. Others would've volunteered to do it for her, she was certain, but she didn't want them to. Although the two of them had only shared a few sincere moments, she knew now that she'd never repay the debt she owed Mrs. Elani for saving her arm. Doing this felt like the closest thing Abby would receive to absolution.

She was about halfway done digging a shallow grave when she heard her mother's distant voice. "Abby!" it called, the worry evident despite the forceful volume. Abby embedded the head of the spade into the earth and wiped her brow before turning to look.

"Abby!" came another voice, her father's or Aurelius' she imagined.

"I'm over here!" she yelled back, her throat dry from all the exertion.

They came into her line of sight within moments, their faces awash with relief. "Oh thank the Maralor!" cried Elizabeth, darting over.

Carmina was faster, however, wrapping Abby in a hug so tight that it made her ribs tingle with the ache of old injuries. "What happened?" she questioned. "We heard gunshots."

"Eric and I killed it. I'll tell you all about it later," Abby explained glumly, returning the embrace and quickly extending it to her mother despite her arm's protesting aches.

Aurelius and Alexander remained out of reach, preoccupied with staring sadly at Mrs. Elani's body. "I'm sorry," her father condoled once the reunion hugs were over. "Do you want me to help dig?"

Abby shook her head and turned right back around to continue. "No. I want to do this myself," she insisted. Her family nodded respectfully, watching in silence as she shoveled the earth away. Her weakened bicep felt about ready to burst by the time she was done, but she didn't care.

Aurelius piped up as they got Mrs. Elani into the ground. "Should we bury her with her boots on?" he questioned hesitantly.

Abby considered for a moment and shook her head. Resources were important, no matter how small and insignificant they might seem. "No. She would've wanted someone else to make use of them," she decided.

Elizabeth gingerly leaned over to remove the boots, and handed them to Aurelius. There was a moment of ceremonious sadness shared as Abby stood at the head of the grave, covered in Mrs. Elani's blood. She spoke up, offering one last prayer for the dead. "Ersei, mother of love and life, we thank you today for giving us the gift that was Mrs. Elani. Truly, she was a woman worth your blessing, even if she did not worship you herself. Corsein, oracle of fates, we thank you today only for staying your hand as long as you have."

5
Moving On

Abby stuffed the tatty excuse for a sleeping mat into the old bag along with everything else that she wouldn't or couldn't carry in her arms. The tent went in last - Carmina's had been torn in two by the elemental, and Carl hadn't had the materials to repair it, so Abby had been sharing shelter with her sister for the last couple of days whilst they prepared to leave.

Nobody had been the least bit surprised when Alexander had insisted that they move north as a result of the attack. It was far from the first time an elemental offensive had compelled them to keep moving, and it was unlikely to be the last. Unfortunately, despite Abby's attempts to persuade him otherwise, Eric had insisted that he'd be fine here and informed the Koning family that he wouldn't be joining them. No one had said it, but they all knew they'd probably never see him again.

She tossed the tent pegs into the bag and set to adorning herself with her armour. She hadn't worn it since her bicep injury, and it felt heavier than she remembered; she probably should've continued wearing it, if only to help her stay in shape.

Despite Abby's handicap, the sisters were still the first of the family to be ready for the road. Carmina went over to help Aurelius, but three people around one small tent would be a little much, and so Abby sat down beside her bag to rest.

Eric came over and sat beside her. He'd been somewhat withdrawn around Abby since he'd wept in front of her, and although he'd said goodbye to all the others at one point or another, he hadn't extended the same courtesy to her, yet. Still, she was glad of his company. "I'm going to miss you, you know," she told him.

"Yeah, I know," he responded.

She turned to face him and forcefully pulled him into a hug with her good arm. "And you're going to miss us, too," she teased.

He cracked a fraction of a smile at her. "Yeah."

It didn't surprise her that he was being terse, even now. "See, tough guy? Sometimes letting things out helps."

Eric smirked. "You're some kind of special, you know? Stay strong, Abby; folks need people like you now more than ever."

She nodded. "And you," she managed as he stood to leave. It seemed an underwhelming way to say a final goodbye, but she hadn't for a moment imagined that he'd be breaking out the waterworks again.

She got up and strolled through the remains of the campsite, heading for the recently constructed well. All around her was a mass of ruined tents and torn families. Many of them were also moving on, the sense of community shattered along with the illusion of safety.

Johann's voice came from behind her as she drew water. "Abby," he called. She glanced back, her gaze drawn to the enormous, leather travel bag he was holding by his side. It was in far better condition than the one she'd just packed. "I'm ready to go," the doctor stated flatly. Johann and Carl had been adamant that anywhere was better than here, and the pair would be accompanying them on the road.

She let the bucket drop back into the water and turned to face him. "Good. Are you sure you've got everything you need? We'll be leaving soon."

Johann nodded, shrugging the bag indicatively. "I didn't have much to pack," he claimed.

Abby could tell that there was something else on his mind; he looked nervous as he stepped closer - timid, even. She smiled as cheerily as recent events allowed, trying to gently encourage him. "I think that we should be together," he said, carefully pacing his words.

"Why's that?" Abby enquired, trying not to sound disparaging. She had expected Johann to try and make another move at some point, but she hadn't expected it to be this forward, nor this awkward on account of him.

"Well, because I think you're the best thing going for this place. A little slice of civilisation out here," he remarked.

Abby was pleased by the compliment, though she tried not to let it show too much. "That's just an observation," she returned.

Johann sighed. "Well then, because you're exactly the kind of woman I'd always thought I'd marry before this, and I don't see why that's any different now," he tried.

Abby's smile broadened somewhat. "Well, I'll be honest, Johann, I don't normally marry on the first date. But I do like your reasoning." She turned back around to draw the water again.

"Is that a yes?" he dared to hope, his confidence clearly bolstered by her reaction.

"Yup," she said, and drank her fill. She felt him press up against her, his arms wrapping around her from behind. Despite the armour, she had to admit that it felt awfully nice to be held like that again. He pressed a kiss to her cheek before she gently shook him off.

"Come on, my parents will be waiting for us," she insisted, romance far from her biggest concern at that moment. Johann followed her over, the bag swaying heavily in his hand.

Soon enough, the seven were on the move together, the endless road ahead of them. Abby found it pleasant to have more people than just her immediate family to talk to, and by the end of the day's travel she'd even managed to get some half-decent conversation out of Carl, though he never talked about his life before the extinction had begun.

"Life out here isn't at all what I'd expected," Johann claimed as they all went about setting up their tents for the night.

"What did you expect, then? Steak raining from the sky?" chuckled Aurelius.

"Not quite. But when they opened that 'portal' thing in Dratha, I had imagined they'd be evacuating us to green and pleasant lands, so to speak," Johann clarified.

Abby smiled and shook her head. "If there were green and pleasant lands to go to, I expect someone would've colonised them properly before the extinction began. Not this dustbowl," she commented.

Johann nodded thoughtfully. "I suppose so. In retrospect, such hope was a fantasy. Still, everyone needs a little hope."

Abby could agree with that. People who didn't have any hope had an unpleasant and unfortunate tendency to commit suicide, after all. She remembered Maximilian covering her eyes as they exited Lyonis. Her family had felt the need to protect her innocence from such sights back then. Not anymore.

She finished setting herself up for the night before moving to help Johann. His tent was larger and more fiddly than her own, but between the two of them it would get set up quickly. "Can I share a tent with you?" enquired the doctor, lowering his voice as she approached him.

Abby glanced across to her family and called out. "Carmina, are you alright with Johann sharing our tent tonight?"

"Not a bloody chance," snapped Carmina and Alexander in unison. The doctor turned scarlet in the cheeks.

"Language!" barked Elizabeth, giving her husband a harsh glare before turning her gaze to Carmina. "I don't recall raising you in a barn, young lady."

Carmina rolled her eyes and otherwise ignored the comment. She stepped up to Johann, cornering him despite his clear discomfort with the situation. "You've got your own tent, I don't. Three's a crowd," she growled before walking off in an apparent huff.

Abby shrugged and gave Johann an apologetic smile. "Well, I guess that's a no, then."

Dinner was pleasant, once Johann got over his awkward moment of humiliation. There was more than enough meat for all of them, presently,

47

though Abby imagined that would change before long, forcing them to hunt again. With some luck, Eric had taught them enough to survive out here without his assistance. They'd managed more than a year without his guidance, after all, when supplies had still been good and most people were decent.

She said a hasty goodnight to the others once they'd all eaten, and settled in bed with Carmina. "Was that what I think it was?" she asked as Abby lay down beside her.

Abby grinned. "Probably not, he just wanted to share a tent with me. Can you tell it's been a while for him?"

Carmina laughed and nodded. "You know, if you want to get laid I'm fine on my own."

Abby gawked in disbelief. She understood that Carmina was at that age now, but where had the sweet and innocent little sister of her youth gone so suddenly? "Carmina!" she exclaimed.

"Oh come off it. Mother and father might still be trying to dot every i and cross every t, but there's no point to it anymore. We're no better than anyone else, out here, and there's no point being coy to try and prove otherwise."

Abby frowned slightly. "It's not about being better than anyone. It's about being polite!" she insisted. It was true, too - at least for her.

Carmina smirked. "If you say so. But don't let me get between you two. In either sense."

Abby simmered down and shook her head. "You're not. He's just trying to rush into things I won't, that's all."

"If you're sure. Goodnight, sis."

***

Four hundred and seventy-five days since we left the capital. Abby yawned and stretched, disentangling herself from Carmina's limbs. "Whose turn is it to cook breakfast?" she groaned. She'd forgotten who they'd agreed upon yesterday.

"Aurelius'," insisted her little sister, barely awake.

"Five more minutes then?" suggested Abby. *Her laziness must be contagious.*

Carmina nodded. "Mmhmm."

It took a few days to get used to the routine of travel again. Walking all day every day was exhausting, and they spent a significant amount of time looking for water and food. The local wildlife seemed to grow in density as they moved north, and once or twice they were given pause by awe, gawping at the magnificent creatures. Elephants and giraffes were amongst the most fabulous, though Abby wasn't certain if anyone called

48

them that, other than her father.

They passed numerous camps in their travels. They even stopped in some overnight, but Alexander always insisted that they were to continue northwards. The further they went, the more they understood why; the weather became milder, still warm but vastly more tolerable for their pale complexions; trees became more frequent and densely packed; dusty, dry earth turned into something more like the soil they'd known back in Luthania. Even the freezing nights warmed to an uncomfortable cold.

The four hundred and ninety-ninth day dawned just as all the others. They had breakfast, packed up camp, and walked - as usual - for miles. It wasn't until evening that their travels took a turn towards the unfamiliar. "Look at that," instructed their father, pointing at the horizon as they reached the apex of a particularly large hill. They were used to the setting sun displaying silhouettes, but these were unlike anything they'd seen since arriving in Tinarus. The shapes didn't move in the wind, and their edges were too straight to be tents.

"Buildings?" questioned Aurelius, squinting at the skyline.

"I think so! We may have found something resembling civilisation!" exclaimed Alexander.

"That can't be more than ten miles. We could be there tomorrow," Elizabeth said cheerily.

"I hope so. I'm tired," contributed Carl.

Abby smiled to herself. The five hundredth day would be the start of something new for them, it seemed. She dared to hope that it was something good.

***

Five hundred days since we left the capital. The buildings stood fifty metres from them, the wood damp from the downpour of rain that was soaking the travellers through. It didn't particularly bother them, the heat meant that they'd dry out in minutes as soon as it stopped.

"I can't believe this! A whole village! I knew somebody had to have made something worthwhile in this wasteland," exclaimed Aurelius.

"It's more like a large hamlet, really," corrected their mother, less easily impressed.

"Be fair, darling, they're still growing," insisted Alexander, pointing to the wooden frame of a shack under construction. It was surrounded by tents, presumably those of residents to be, or perhaps just passers by. The place seemed oddly quiet at that moment, probably because of the rain.

Abby smiled cheerily to herself as they ventured onwards into the hamlet, more structures and tents revealing themselves the further they

49

went. "What should we do? Do we just knock on a door or something?" asked Carmina.

Abby shrugged. "Maybe. We could set up the tents and wait for the rain to pass, then see who comes out?" she suggested. She didn't know what to expect of the residents, for all she knew they could be hostile to strangers. She certainly hoped they were at least as friendly as the group they'd left behind with Eric.

"That seems like a good plan, there's no need to impose on them immediately," insisted Alexander. "We'll set up behind that barn."

Abby examined her surroundings as they proceeded. It seemed just as pleasant up close as it had from a distance, and the dwellings were arranged in a way that was too neat to be coincidental. The whole place seemed incredibly well equipped, relative to the tent encampments they'd seen thus far. Although the buildings were minimal, there were little things about them that indicated access to proper resources; the metalwork on door hinges and nails either meant that there was smithing going on somewhere, or that these people had carried a lot of unusual supplies with them all this way. Even more important than the village itself was the earth that it was built upon; it had a thin spread of grass all over, indicating its fertility.

Abby hummed cheerfully to herself as Carmina helped her set up their tent. "This place seems nice," commented Johann, assisting the sisters before unpacking his own gear.

"Yup. Hopefully the people are nice, too. Maybe you'll have more patients here, it's certainly bigger if you count all the tents as well as the houses," Abby contemplated, handing Johann her hammer.

"One way to find out," he grunted as he went to work on the pegs. Abby settled for using her feet, stamping them into place.

"Do you think they're growing any cotton or linen?" Carmina asked. "I could do with some new clothes."

"You don't *grow* linen, you grow flax and process it into linen," corrected Johann. "But if there's one place we've been that's likely to grow either, it's here."

Carmina seemed pleased that her hopes of something half-decent to wear weren't immediately crushed. They'd worn the same tired garments for too long now, and having left most of their clothes behind to begin with meant that they were in danger of sprouting holes. They were quite fortunate not to be rudely exposed already.

Carmina got comfortable inside whilst Abby and Johann set up the other tent. They'd become quite good at cooperating to swiftly establish camp during their journey, especially as the condition of Abby's arm had gradually improved. It barely hurt at all when she exercised it now, though the muscle was still quite weak, really.

"Do you think they have any sort of government in place?" Abby wondered. "Anarchy is quite tiring, even in its most passive form."

Johann shrugged. "I don't think it counts as anarchy when you're there to protect people," he commented.

Abby considered the point for a moment as she continued to stomp the pegs into place. "I'm just one woman without any sort of authority, or even anyone holding me accountable. If anything, I think that me imposing my will actually constitutes anarchy to a greater degree."

"Oh, nonsense!" called Johann from the other side of the tent. "I am Arboneth Felicity Koning! I am the law!" he jested, doing his very best impression of her.

Abby laughed and shook her head. "That's nonsense and you know it... I'd never use my full name!"

"Indeed. I'd still think you had a vaguely normal name if it wasn't for Elizabeth," commented Johann.

Abby grinned and ducked inside the tent to get the supporting poles in place, making a mental note to tell her mother never to use her full name again. "Look who's talking. I can't even remember all of your middle names!"

He stepped in behind her, reciting in his most pompous voice. "I am Doctor Johann James Giuseppe Francis Ferdinand Ellis, finest physician in this campsite!"

Abby shook her head, struggling to comprehend why his parents had given him so many names, and how he could remember them all. Then again, she still occasionally found herself wondering why her parents had given her such a vile name when her siblings had such nice ones.

Soon enough, they had everything unpacked and set up. "I suppose I'll see you when the rain stops?" Johann questioned.

"Actually, I think I'll stay in here for a bit if you don't mind," she corrected, beginning to remove her armour.

Johann jumped the gun a little and rushed over to help her out of it, boyish excitement on his face. "Of course! You're welcome to, really."

Abby smiled at him and eased the breastplate onto the ground along with her shield. "Close your eyes," she ordered, a teasing tone to her voice as she began to strip entirely of the wet clothes and armour. He obeyed her, and then promptly turned around to avoid embarrassing himself by opening them again.

She wrapped her arms around him from behind, pressing her bare skin against his back. He moved in her embrace, trying to face her, but she held him more tightly, silently requesting that he stay put. She undid his belt first, helping him out of his clothes. "Calm down," she murmured, noticing his arousal as she assisted him into nudity. She had no intention of going further with him at that moment, content merely to lay in his embrace on their sleeping mat. She could tell he wanted more, but he politely refrained from trying his luck. It was as pleasant a way to wait out the rain as any she knew.

It felt like hours before the repetitive rhythm of rain beating against the tent stopped. Johann had eventually realised he wasn't getting lucky just yet, and settled for gently grasping her backside instead. "We should get dressed and see if anyone comes out," said Abby.

"Do we have to?" Johann complained, eyeing her naked form.

"Yes," she insisted, removing herself from his embrace and standing. He lay there as she dressed, continuing to watch her body for as long as he could. "Come on! Up, dress!" she ordered with a grin as she buttoned her tatty shirt. He forced himself up, seeming less reluctant now that she'd hidden her breasts from view.

She stepped back outside once she was geared up again, enjoying the warmth of the sun soaking through her damp clothes. Carmina sat in the entrance to her tent, watching water evaporating from the rooftops in a faint mist. "Any signs of life?" Abby asked, strolling over.

Carmina nodded and pointed to a particularly large and solid shack across from them, at the end of a row of smaller ones. "I saw a man go into that building there. I don't think he noticed us, though."

Abby sat beside Carmina and nodded. "Well, I guess we'll wait until they do." *And hope they don't form a mob.*

The others soon joined them, their spirits high after the opportunity to rest. It wasn't long before people came outside, going about their lives. "Look Carl! There are some kids your age you could play with," Abby suggested. She blushed as her motherly tones earned her a disparaging glare from the young man, and unslung her shield to fidget with it as a distraction. It still had a nasty, splintering dent in its face.

They spent a short while observing the villagers before some of them approached. An elderly man with a wispy beard and a large bald patch in the middle of his snow-white hair led the ensemble, just behind him a middle-aged man, and two more that looked a little younger than Abby. It seemed that they were a family, or at least similar in appearance - all but the eldest man had the same thick, light brown hair.

"Afternoon, folks," greeted the old man, eyeing the lot of them with what Abby thought might've been suspicion.

She smiled brilliantly at him and raised a hand in greeting. "Hey there!" she returned, hoping that her friendliness would be reciprocated.

"Hello, I'm Alexander," Abby's father introduced himself after a brief hesitation. "And these are... well, most of them, are my family."

The old man smiled and stepped up to shake Alexander's hand, his suspicion seeming to dissipate. "I'm William Marshal. This here's my son Patrick, and my grandsons Daniel and Samson," he introduced them.

Abby beamed. "I'm Abby," she said cheerily, getting to her feet to shake Patrick's hand. The greetings were awkward, but one by one they encouraged everyone to give their name, even Carl. Abby found it a little disheartening that living outside the rule of law had turned simple greetings into such a trust exercise. Still, the two families swiftly grew friendly enough to talk on important matters.

"So, we thought we might settle down here. The land's more fertile than down south," explained Elizabeth.

"I reckon you'd do well here, probably. You survived so far and we welcome anyone who can provide for themselves without thieving," agreed William. Patrick also seemed keen on the idea.

Johann nodded sternly. "You'll find no thieves amongst us, I assure you. Quite the opposite, in fact."

"We've managed to keep track of everyone who moved in so far," claimed William. "Originally it was just us - a load of folks from a village called Cray, back before the elementals ruined it - so we called this place New Cray. We've been keeping a list of skills people have, trying to work together to build a proper community, see. Think you could tell us a little bit about what it is you all do?"

"Well, I'm a doctor," Johann piped up immediately.

Alexander went ahead and explained for all the family before they could offer to. "Aurelius and I were good with accountancy before, but these days I farm with Elizabeth and he hunts with Carmina. Abby's always been a little more on the practical side of things, thank goodness. She was training as a paladin of the Maralor, and learned a little smithing on the side."

The men nodded faintly and glanced at Carl. "What about you, little guy? Did you learn any trades?" queried Patrick.

Carl glowered at the patronising tone, but Abby decided it would probably be best to patronise him further by talking for him before he said something rude. "Oh, Carl's great at making things! Cloth, leather, wood. People used to go to him for repairs with all sorts, back south," she informed them.

Patrick eyed Carl moodily for a moment before nodding at Abby. "Alright, how about you all come with us? We'll give you a tour of the place and write all that down."

They spent the majority of the day getting settled. Once the official records of New Cray had been updated with an almost intrusive level of detail on the lives of the newcomers, they were shown what there was to see. The barn they'd been camped next to was a bit empty at the moment, but William expected that they'd find ways to preserve food soon enough, and begin storing up for harder times. They had vast fields here, crops growing strong under the burning sun.

Crops weren't the only worthwhile resource in New Cray, of course. Between the populace of the village they'd amassed quite a reasonable collection of skills. They had a smithy, but materials were scarce and so only things of utmost necessity were actually made there. They had a tailor and a weaver - a married elven couple who worked straight out of their house and grew flax into linen. Carl had shown rare enthusiasm meeting those two, revealing that the favourite of his many skills was needlework. There were also masons, carpenters and architects, all of whom had worked with a town planner on the development of the village. It turned out that they were attempting to replicate the original Cray as closely as they could from memory at the moment, more for nostalgia's sake than any practical reason. There was also a hamlet neighbouring them to the north, smaller than New Cray but still growing. It went by the name of Lapden.

They eventually settled down to discuss the finer details of housing arrangements and work. When it came to Abby's turn, Patrick took her aside along with his sons. "My boys never had any formal training, but they're real tough. They taught themselves," he explained. "If you're gonna protect this place when things get rough, you're gonna have to meet their standards, you understand?"

Abby smiled brightly. "Sure," she agreed. She'd once had higher military aspirations than guarding a sleepy hamlet, and so she didn't imagine she'd have too much trouble making the cut.

Patrick continued, gesturing to a muddy patch off the side of the unpathed street. "I'd like to see you spar it out with each of them."

Abby nodded agreeably and strolled over to the makeshift arena. "Go easy on my left arm though, will you?" she requested. "It's recovering from injury." Turning to prepare for a fight, she was surprised to see that Samson - the older and larger of the two - had drawn his sword. She raised a brow. "Are you sure you want to get weapons out before we both know where we stand? We might hurt each other."

Samson seemed to find something about that funny, and just nodded. "Elementals won't fight fair, nor will bandits. Unarmed won't do you much good out here," insisted Patrick.

Abby disagreed, personally, but since they insisted on armed combat, it's what she'd give them. Samson didn't have a shield, and so Abby left hers slung for now, sticking to just the hammer. "When you're ready," she chimed. She was hoping for good things; both boys had the toned physiques of warriors.

Samson instantly lashed out with the sword. Whatever he'd 'taught himself' was clearly incredibly wrong, because he put far too much shoulder into the strike. Abby was inside his guard before he could even bring the blow down, the sword swooping uselessly behind her. She smacked the top of her hammer into his gut. Winded, Samson stood no chance as she snaked a leg around one of his own and tripped him over it, forcing him to fall on his backside. She stood on his arm with a little more restraint than she'd show a real opponent and leaned over, twisting his wrist to take the weapon from him.

Patrick and Daniel gawked at Samson's failure. Abby almost felt bad for not giving him a real chance, but she wouldn't be party to fooling these men into thinking that they could handle themselves, when they so clearly couldn't. "Alright. Do you want to try, Daniel?" she asked.

The young man nodded and stowed his sword. "Unarmed's fine," he insisted, stepping up warily. Abby's expectations were significantly lower this time.

The fistfight didn't last much longer than the armed one had. Daniel did exactly the opposite of what Abby had asked, and immediately tried to take advantage of her injury, grasping her left wrist in order to tug at the arm. She deflected a solid punch he threw with the other hand, letting it scrape harmlessly over her shoulder. Circling him rapidly, she forced the arm that held her to twist around his body, and before he realised what she was doing she'd pinned it firmly between his shoulder blades. Avoiding a blind and crude kick directed at her legs, Abby bent Daniel over and lowered him gracelessly onto his stomach. She sat down on his back, causing him to grunt at the pressure. She'd honestly expected more of a challenge from the two, but at least there could be no arguments that she met their standards, and then some. "So, do you have any official resources or anything I should know about?" she asked. *Maybe some people who can actually fight worth a damn?*

Patrick looked particularly sour at seeing his two sons defeated so easily. "No. I'll let you three figure out how you want to go about it. Just keep me and William informed," he insisted before walking off in a strop. It reminded Abby somewhat of Carmina, a few years ago.

"Can I get up now?" Daniel gasped from below her.

She stood and helped him up, smiling at the brothers. Daniel smiled back gingerly, though Samson seemed less than friendly about the whole affair. "Well, it's going to be getting dark soon. Perhaps I'll see you two tomorrow," she said, waving cheerily and strolling off before they could make the situation any more awkward than it already was.

She made her way back to the others, who were busy discussing what they had agreed with William. It had been clear from the get-go that there would be no free meals here, but none of them had expected otherwise. They'd been appointed an area of land to farm in about half a mile to the north-west. At the moment there wasn't much in the way of competition for farmland, so they could simply sort out between themselves who would farm where, without having to worry about any potential conflicts.

Johann had been pleasantly welcomed as the only doctor in New Cray, and would probably be provided with everything he needed as long as he proved effective in his role. Given the lack of genuine medical supplies, it was really quite difficult for him to prove his competence or lack thereof.

Carl had been told he'd need to help farm, as they couldn't guarantee that there would be enough work with the tailor and weaver to make those skills alone worth any food that they could spare. They chattered excitedly about how promising everything looked as they headed back to their tents for the evening.

They were setting up a cooking fire when Daniel approached their campsite. He seemed to be alone, and uncertain of himself. "Hello again, Daniel. Is something the matter?" Alexander greeted him.

Daniel shook his head. "No, nothing's wrong. I was wondering if I could talk to Abby for a moment?"

Abby stood. "Sure. You'd best come inside," she suggested, gesturing to her and Carmina's tent. He nodded eagerly and hurried inside.

Daniel settled down within and turned to smile broadly at Abby as she followed him in. "That was amazing! How did you do that?"

"You mean the fighting? I was training as a paladin of the Maralor, remember," Abby chuckled. "Combat's the most important part of that, you've got to be able to fight in wars." It was nice to receive some praise for her talents, but it didn't tickle her ego too much, given how unskilled Daniel and his brother were.

"Could you show us how to fight like that?" he requested.

"I'm going to have to. No offense to either of you, but if you see a proper fight swinging a sword like your brother did, you're going to get killed before you land a blow." She could've pointed out any number of other horrible fates that might await the inexperienced in battle, but that one seemed bad enough to get her point across.

Daniel seemed slightly taken aback by the honesty. "But we've killed bandits before," he claimed. "When we first set up here they'd steal from us sometimes."

Abby frowned. "Really? How many bandits?"

"Well… we only really killed two, but it's something."

"And did they put up much of a fight?"

"Not really," he admitted. "It was over pretty quick."

Abby nodded. "And I bet they barely knew how to hold a sword, either. Anyone can take a swing at an opponent that doesn't know how to defend themselves, but sooner or later you'll find someone that does, and they'll kill you. I'll teach you how to fight properly, on the condition that you don't kill anyone unless it's absolutely necessary."

"When do we start?" he enquired excitedly.

"Tomorrow, if you like. Just remember, it took me six years to learn that stuff, and I was still considered an initiate," she forewarned. That was no exaggeration; although faith and spirituality were an important part of the training, paladins were still expected to achieve a knightly level of martial prowess. Even Abby's incomplete training had saved her family from numerous horrible fates out here. "It won't be quick, but if you're willing to put in the effort then so am I," she concluded.

"I'm willing, Abby," claimed Daniel.

She smiled. "Well then, I suggest you talk to your brother. We can arrange some sort of training schedule. It'll be good to have regular sparring partners as well, to be honest."

Daniel nodded enthusiastically. "Alright, I'll go do that. Thanks!"

He turned to leave, but not before Abby piped up one last time. "Oh, before you go - is there a chapel hidden away around here that didn't get mentioned?"

"I'm afraid not. It wasn't really high on anyone's priorities," he confessed.

Abby sighed softly and moved to follow him out of the tent. "Well, we'll have to do something about that, won't we? I'll see you tomorrow, Daniel."

She had a good feeling about New Cray. It reminded her of how Johann had described her before they'd left the encampment back south. *A little slice of civilisation out here.*

6
Progress

Abby gazed proudly at the wooden chapel. It was hastily erected, rickety, and small even compared to most buildings in New Cray. The windows were still empty, and as of such there hadn't seemed to be any point in fitting a door yet, either. In reality, the only redeeming feature was the stone shrine, but to Abby and the others that had helped her make it, it meant more than just the materials that had gone into it; it was hope. A little light in the darkness.

New Cray was beginning to feel like home, now. Today was the eight hundred and sixty-fifth day since they'd left the capital, but that was no longer Abby's measurement of the passage of time. *Three hundred and sixty-five days since we arrived in New Cray.*

A lot had happened in a year, including Abby's uncelebrated twenty-second birthday. Construction had been swift, and the family had even learned some useful skills whilst helping to build their own dwellings. Aurelius and Carmina were still living in the family home, though it was hard to predict if or when they would fly the coop. Johann was sharing the largest house of their group with Abby, but it had to double as a medical practice.

Travelers of all kinds had passed through New Cray. The word they propagated was that cities were being built far to the north. They went by various names depending on who was talking; Abby had heard Staghelm, Limeon, and Kerel fairly often. There was one rumour that everyone seemed to know, though - King Thomas Forel was alive and rebuilding his kingdom, starting with New Lyonis. A new start, Abby hoped and prayed.

It wasn't all good news, of course. Without access to the medicines he was practiced with, Johann's efforts at preserving life were limited in their efficacy. The young, old, and weak had died off until only the most useful remained. Despite this, refugees had settled in droves and the population of New Cray had actually grown overall. With growth had come petty crime, though. Criminal matters were mostly resolved with ease, whether by violence or diplomacy.

Footsteps behind her turned Abby's gaze away from the chapel. She recognised the approaching man as Michael - the village smith, befitting his surname. "Here about training?" she asked with a cheery smile.

Michael nodded. "William spoke with me this morning, said you'd suggested I train you up because of your past experience," he explained.

"That's right," confirmed Abby. "I began learning so that I'd be able to repair my armour one day. I'm more than a little rusty, but I thought I could help out a little."

"If you come by tomorrow morning we can get you started," Michael agreed. A man of few words that weren't related to his work, he gave her a pleasant smile and turned back to leave the way he came.

"I'll be there!" she called after him, grinning. The prospect of adding to her creative capabilities as well as her violent ones excited her, even if she would never be more than an apprentice. In the spirit of Besigur, Abby set back to work.

The structure of the chapel itself may have been completed, but there was a distinct lack of pews - or furnishings of any kind, for that matter. It wasn't a priority on the list of things to be done, and so anyone with real experience had politely declined to help her with it. Woodworking was not amongst Abby's skills, beyond what she'd learned in New Cray, but the pew slowly began to take shape anyway. As the sun sank lower in the sky, she packed it in for the day and dragged her work in progress into the building. She'd take it to the real carpenter - or Carl - another time. Hopefully one of them could spare the time and effort to finish what she lacked the skill to do.

She joined the other six around the household table for dinner that night. Despite his moody silences and unsociable countenance, Carl had remained close to the family, and they to him. Abby supposed they were the closest thing he had to a family of his own, though he'd grown close to the tailor and his wife - Samiel and Ephenra - as well. He was staying with them until he had a place of his own.

The evening's food was a healthy portion of the last of the carrots. They'd grown a huge number of them over the summer when they'd arrived, but had moved on to growing green beans in autumn. It was neither filling nor greatly delicious, but it was what they had.

"Have you met any of the latest arrivals yet?" asked Johann. Abby shook her head as she crunched down on a slightly deformed vegetable. "Well, I think you'll like them - the ones we met, at least," he continued.

She nodded faintly and planted a kiss on his cheek, ignoring an enormously exaggerated look of disgust from her father. "I'll meet them tomorrow, I guess. I'm pretty beat." There had been so many arrivals in the last year that getting acquainted with them was rarely something that Abby rushed to do, anymore. The ones that intended to settle in and make a life for themselves always ended up crossing paths with her sooner or later, anyway.

Abby's mother smiled at her amidst mouthfuls of food. "The mason did a great job on that statue, by the way, the chapel's looking wonderful. It's just what the place needed."

"Not as badly as it needed a lot of other things," muttered Johann. He wasn't a man of great faith, truth be told. Of their group of seven, only Abby and her mother still actively practiced their faith in the Maralor.

"It is, isn't it?" Abby responded, jabbing Johann gently in the ribs before proceeding to pretend that he hadn't said anything. "I'm working on the furniture now."

They continued to chat after their rations for the day had been eaten, until the lot of them grew weary and headed to their respective sleeping mats. The lack of any sort of proper bedding had left them all sleeping on the floors, but they'd become so used to it during their travels that it barely even seemed worth the effort to try and change the fact anymore.

She knelt to pray once she was home with Johann. "Besigur, tailor of creation, bless our works, and grant us the patience to better ourselves through labour. Corsein, oracle of fates, grant us wisdom, and if so willing stay the treacherous tides of time for one more day. Ersei, mother of love and life, teach us compassion and restraint; remind us that there are two sides to every story, and that to love and respect is the best option wherever possible."

She was interrupted there by Johann's embrace as he planted a series of kisses on her cheek and neck. Despite his lack of faith, he frequently tried to take advantage of the 'love' part of the prayer, interpreting it in the most carnal way possible. "Not tonight, I'm too worn out," she said, softening her voice to let him down and returning a single kiss on his lips. She quickly finished the prayer before joining him to sleep.

The next morning, Abby rearranged her routine a little so that she could pray in the chapel rather than at home. On her way back from breakfast she spied Carmina out front of the tailor's, chatting with a pair of young men that Abby hadn't met yet. She faltered slightly to get a good look and commit their faces to memory; it didn't surprise her one bit that boys might be taking that certain kind of interest in Carmina, but it still made her somewhat uneasy. She decided she'd get the opportunity to meet them later, and moved on with her day, heading to the chapel.

Abby paused once more as she saw the armoured man knelt at the altar, reading from the Faralex that she had left there for public use. She approached slowly, eyeing the blade of the claymore that lay at his feet. It was well above average size, as was the man himself. He wore his grey hair tied back much like Abby had ever since her bicep injury. She strolled over beside him once her initial surprise had passed and knelt for her own prayers, muttering softly to the gods.

"That's beautiful," commented the man.

Abby was a little surprised that he'd been able to hear her. Clearly his senses were sharper than one might expect at his age. "It reminds me of the important things," she said, smiling at him.

He adjusted himself to face her, his features pleasant despite the hard lines of age. "It's refreshing to see another like myself. Not to mention a chapel - not many of them around, these days."

Abby considered cutting the conversation short for the sake of getting to the smithy bright and early, but one more glance at the man's sword dissuaded her. The circular pommel had an inscription in old Redanin, a language she'd been versed in during her overabundance of education. On one side it read 'In Ersei's name, protect.' Abby knew what the other side said without seeing it; 'In Rendick's name, destroy.' The man was a paladin, or at least equipped as one.

"It's not as high on people's priorities as it should be, if you ask me. I didn't get a lot of help building it," she commented.

The man cracked a smile of his own, curiosity crossing his features. "You built this chapel yourself?"

She shook her head. "Not *all* by myself, I couldn't do the stonework for the altar. The Faralex is mine, though - you're welcome to read it all you like, but I'd appreciate it if you left it here when you're done."

The paladin returned the holy book to the altar and stood, then bowed as if conversing with an equal and offered her a hand. Now that he was standing, his full size was made even more apparent. He must've been a full foot taller than her, a giant of a man at almost six and a half feet. "I'm Sir Tahgri Dunwolf of Erdanst. And who might you be, ma'am?"

Pulling herself upright with his assistance, Abby shook his hand. "I'm Arboneth Koning, though I usually go by Abby," she told him. She was about to inform him that she wasn't fortunate enough to be addressed as madam when realisation struck her. "They called you Tahgri Turncoat!" she exclaimed, excitement at meeting a man of genuine renown causing her to speak without thinking.

Sir Dunwolf frowned. "I'm not fond of that."

Abby nodded apologetically. "I'm sorry, I didn't mean to be rude. I just knew your name from stories. I know you didn't fight in the war, but I wasn't judging you for it," she blurted out.

His expression eased up a little at that. "Do you know why I didn't fight?" he asked her, turning and picking up his sword and close-helm.

"No sir. I've heard it said that you're a coward, but I find it hard to believe that a coward could ever be ordained as a paladin."

"Then you believe correctly," he insisted, his tone level. "I didn't fight because Thomas claimed the Maralor's will falsely."

Abby contemplated the point briefly. Unlike issues such as incest and demonology, there was nothing to forbid magical technology in the Faralex. "It was just an excuse to take the throne?" she questioned.

Sir Dunwolf nodded. "It was," he claimed with a sense of certainty.

It seemed as if he had more questions for her, and she certainly had many for him, but she really needed to get to the smithy. "I'm afraid I have to go. It was nice to meet you, Sir Dunwolf. Are you staying for a while?"

"I expect I am. I don't suppose you'd spare some food for a fellow paladin, would you?" he hoped.

She gave him a sweet smile in return. "I'm only an initiate, sir," she corrected. "But if you come and find me by the smithy around sundown, we'd love to have you for dinner." It was perhaps a half-truth. *She* would love to have him visit for dinner, but she had no idea if anyone else would care to share the food.

Sir Dunwolf nodded agreeably, a look of confusion momentarily crossing his features. "Thank you. I'll see you tonight," he promised.

*****

"Right, first things first, Abby, I'm going to teach you how to use all the tools correctly," Michael began. "We ain't got the resources for any big mistakes, so pay attention." She nodded faintly and glanced around the place, feeling almost at home. They were under-equipped, but at least she had experience using everything they did have.

"Once that's done, we're gonna melt down some of the worthless gear that folks bring round and I'll show you how to recover the metal," the smith continued. Abby stepped over to the forge to get started.

The day went quickly; the encounter with Sir Dunwolf had been an unexpected pleasure, and it left her excited for their next meeting, a constant distraction for her mind. Regardless, Michael seemed pleased with her metalwork by the time the sun began to set. "You've got a passable background for an apprentice," he assured her. "I'll talk to William and see about a schedule for you to help out here." She grinned, glad of his approval. Considering that her other duties consisted mainly of farming, she expected that working out a plan would prove to be quite easy.

The sound of clanking armour drew her attention, and Abby glanced over her shoulder as Sir Dunwolf strolled towards them, his gleaming sword resting over his shoulder. "I'm not too early, am I?" he enquired, glancing between the two of them.

Abby shook her head. "Not at all," she assured him before turning back to the smith. "Michael, this is Sir Dunwolf."

The pair shook hands. "A pleasure. I wouldn't be surprised if I have need of your services one day. If you'll excuse us, though, your assistant has offered me the pleasure of her company for dinner," said the paladin.

"Thanks for today, Michael. Just come and find me whenever you want to talk with William? Tomorrow's fine," Abby excused herself. Michael remained wordless but polite, waving them off, and so Abby began to lead Sir Dunwolf towards Johann's.

"So, you didn't finish your training?" the paladin soon asked.

"Finish? I've a long way to go yet. Today was my first day here," she chuckled. "But I had some practice under a smith back in Lyonis."

"I meant your training as a paladin," he explained.

Abby peered back at him curiously. "You thought I was a paladin, sir? I was in training since my fourteenth birthday, but I never finished. I had to stop shortly before Lyonis was evacuated."

Confusion creased Sir Dunwolf's brow again for a short moment. "Initiate," he said softly, as if pondering upon it. "Training didn't stop, though, Abby. I could sense the Maralor's spirit in you from the moment I saw you. You continue to practice your faith, have you kept up with everything else as well?"

Abby nodded thoughtfully and patted her breastplate. "Well, we had to let my horse go because we couldn't feed it, but I've kept practicing my skill at arms. Still - I was never ordained. Formally, I'm barely more than a do-gooder with a little combat experience."

Sir Dunwolf grunted and shook his head. "Being a paladin should never be about the titles. It's about doing good in ways and places others fear to tread, and enforcing the will of the Maralor." Of course, it was easy to make such claims after having enjoyed the wealth and privilege for so long, but Abby was inclined to agree, even if she would love to have been ordained herself.

"Well, I certainly try to do that to the best of my ability," she told him. "But... you said you could sense their spirit in me, sir? I was under the impression that only happens once ordained."

"It does. Or so I thought," commented the paladin, obviously not sure what to make of it. Understanding that he had no explanation for it, Abby pried no further into the matter. Still, she couldn't help but wonder about the implications of such a thing.

"Is this not the doctor's?" Sir Dunwolf enquired as they approached Johann's house.

"The doctor and I are lovers," Abby informed him, hesitating in the doorway. "You're not celibate, are you?"

The paladin firmly denied any such notion with a shake of his head. "I most certainly am not. The Maralor have never claimed anything wrong with the act, and to deny ourselves the pleasures Ersei gives us in our mortal form would be an affront to the rest of my beliefs," he claimed.

Abby grinned and strolled inside. "That's a rather long-winded way of saying you're in touch with your carnal side."

"In touch might be a slight exaggeration these days," he chuckled, crouching a little to get through the doorway unscathed.

"You ought to be able to empathise with me then," joked Johann, making his way over from the other room.

"Johann, this is Sir Tahgri Dunwolf, paladin of the Maralor," Abby introduced them, ignoring the comment on their sex life.

"We met yesterday," claimed Sir Dunwolf, greeting Johann with a lazy wave of his hand.

The doctor stepped up to greet the pair. He was only four inches or so shorter than the paladin, but the lack of breadth in his lanky physique made him seem delicate in comparison. "I had a feeling you two would get along. So, what can I do for you Sir Dunwolf? Or is this a social visit?" Johann asked.

Tahgri looked to Abby, silently bidding that she answer in his place. "Sir Dunwolf will be joining us for dinner," she clarified.

Johann nodded and glanced around. "Ah, wonderful. It's been a quiet day, so I've got no patients right now. Shall we set off?"

The trio departed - and walked all of seven metres to the little house across the road.

"Small village," commented Sir Dunwolf.

Abby nodded. "This is where the rest of my family live."

The paladin eyed the door as it swung open against Abby's hand. "Not big on locks around here, are you?"

"We probably would be if we had the resources to spare for them. Even the hinges are a stretch," Abby explained.

The paladin stooped once more as he followed her inside. "Ah! Sir Dunwolf!" Alexander welcomed him enthusiastically. "I see you've met my favourite and most virginal daughter."

Carmina came up behind Alexander and promptly gave him a sharp prod in the ribs. Abby rolled her eyes and tried to ignore the stupid, boyish grins on Johann and Alexander's faces. The jokes never seemed to grow old for her father, but she'd been hearing them for years now.

"Virginal? Is that what she tells you?" the paladin enquired.

"It's his idea of a joke," Abby smirked, moving over and hugging her father. "I hope you don't mind, I told Sir Dunwolf he could join us for dinner."

Alexander shook his head and smiled. "The beans are coming along nicely. I expect we'll be fine with one more mouth to feed tonight."

Sir Dunwolf smiled gratefully and moved further into the house, making an effort not to bang his head on anything. "Perhaps we ought to eat outside? We're gonna be a little cramped with eight of us around the table," suggested Abby, glancing thoughtfully at the enormous man struggling to get through doorways. Especially at his age, that couldn't be doing his back any favours.

"I'm sorry, I didn't quite catch that, was that Luthanian?" mocked Alexander. "It sounded an awful lot like you said 'gonna.'"

"Oh you're just hilarious," Abby muttered with as much sarcasm as she could muster, kissing her father on the cheek.

"Actually, I'm Alexander," he quipped in response. "Perhaps you're right, though. Sir Dunwolf, would you take my chaste and pure daughter outside whilst I help my wife prepare the food?"

"Certainly," agreed the paladin, smirking and taking Carmina gently by the arm.

Carmina laughed and went with him even as Alexander called out loudly after them. "Not that one!"

Abby followed, the group circling around the house to the southwest corner. It was the only part of the immediate land that had enough grass to sit down on it without getting dirt all over their clothes.

"I'm sure your father loves you *both* very much," Sir Dunwolf tried to reassure them.

"Yeah, he just like to joke about it to help him deal with his daughters growing up," Abby grinned as she sat down.

"He's such an arse about it sometimes. It makes me want to hook up with someone just so he'll stop," muttered Carmina.

"Well, don't think I haven't seen Daniel and Samson looking at you sweetly. And they're not the only ones, either," responded Abby, pulling her little sister into a one-armed hug.

"Ah, to be young and playful again," Sir Dunwolf chuckled.

"Speaking of which, who were those two I saw you chatting with this morning, Car?" Abby enquired.

"Johnny and Sid. They're mine, though, you've got Johann," Carmina warned in jest.

"Somehow I don't think you have to worry about Abby stealing men from you, she can barely even handle me at the best of times," Johann commented.

They were saved from extended conversation about relationships and sex by Aurelius arriving with a large, wooden bowl of sliced carrots. "This is the last of them. We're going hunting tomorrow to tide us over until the beans are ready, so make sure they go the distance," he insisted.

Abby nodded and eased herself away from Carmina, taking the bowl and setting it down in the middle of the group. She noticed the greedy look on the paladin's face as he eyed the food. "How long's it been?" she asked.

"Just a couple of days, but I wasn't exactly eating well before that either, you understand?" he muttered back.

Abby nodded and passed him the bowl. "Go ahead. I'm sure my parents will forgive you," she allowed. The awkward, apologetic looks from her siblings told her that they wouldn't mind, either.

Sir Dunwolf wolfed down a handful of the carrots without hesitation, obviously not lying about his hunger. No doubt any man of his size would've struggled to keep themselves fed out here. Carl, Alexander, and Elizabeth soon joined them, and the meal began in earnest.

They shared stories of their travels, as they often did when making new friends, and were repaid in kind by Tahgri. His journey here had been every bit as long and bloody as theirs. Inevitably, they ended up on the story of Abby's bicep injury, and after showing off the scar, Abby was asked to recite the tale of the three bandits who'd attacked her at the bathing pool as well.

"...so we get there, and Abby's just waiting for us with all this gear, totally relaxed about it like nothing happened," finished Aurelius, taking over from her as she neared the end of the story. The tale itself didn't make Abby smile, but the enthusiasm on Carl's face did. It was always nice to see him come out of his shell, if only a little bit.

"It's a shame indeed that the apocalypse couldn't have waited for you to complete your training. If I may, I'd love to have a chat with you about that," requested Sir Dunwolf.

"Sure, once I've helped tidy up," Abby allowed. She set to cleaning up after herself and the others as they finished. No doubt everyone had noticed Tahgri's appetite taking its toll on the available food, but she felt that it was better for everyone else to go hungry than him, at his age.

"Thank you all so much for the food," said the paladin as they finished up with the dishes.

"It was lovely to have you, Sir Dunwolf," assured Elizabeth, smiling warmly at him.

"Please, call me Tahgri. I think it's safe to say we're on a first-name basis now," he insisted. "So, Abby - shall we?"

"Sure. Thanks for dinner, everyone. I'll see you at home," she told Johann.

The doctor nodded tiredly and got to his feet, grabbing Abby's arm to pull her into a quick kiss. For once, Alexander didn't have any silly comments to make. Nor did he pretend to vomit. "I'll wait up for you," Johann smiled.

Abby led Tahgri out into the lonely plains, far out of earshot. "What's on your mind?" she asked.

"A great many things, Abby," he admitted. "That was just about the best meal I've had in a month."

She nodded and wrapped her arms around him in a sympathetic hug, made somewhat more awkward by the armour. "I'm sorry. I don't think many people have got it easy out here." She was pretty confident that nobody did, in fact. She imagined even the king was far from feasting, if he truly was still alive.

Tahgri didn't respond much to the embrace, simply letting it happen as a hint of desperation entered his tone. "I'll be honest, Abby. I could tell you some nonsense about how I feel a sense of purpose here, but the truth is I'm afraid if I don't try to settle down soon, Corsein will see the end of me sooner than I'd like. I barely made it this far by luck."

"I'll help you however I can, Tahgri, but you're going to have to help out, too." She empathised with the man; like many of the refugees that the elementals had uprooted, he was clearly at a place in life that he'd never been taught how to deal with. Still, there were no free meals in New Cray.

He nodded and gently removed her from around his armoured waist. "I never expected otherwise, but I've never been a farmer or a hunter - I don't know how to do this. Soldier's curse of work, I'm afraid."

Abby ran her fingers back through her hair thoughtfully. "We can help you. Perhaps we can come to an arrangement; a little help on the farm, and you can help train those of us that need it?" She was pleased to see that Tahgri seemed perfectly agreeable to the idea.

"I can do that. Definitely. But I need help learning how to do this... civilian life."

"You'll figure it out pretty quick. We'll show you," Abby assured him. "But in the meantime, there's something you can do for me starting tomorrow, as a little favour?" Tahgri peered at her questioningly. "Those two men who were with Carmina earlier, Johnny and Sid," she began.

The paladin's look grew suspicious, his brow furrowing as he crossed his arms defensively. "What are you asking?" he demanded.

Abby raised a brow at his posture. "Nothing dramatic. I just want to make sure they don't do any harm," she explained.

The paladin relaxed significantly, letting his arms hang by his sides again. "You want me to make sure they play by the rules, so to speak?"

"Exactly that," Abby nodded. "You don't have to talk to them, or even let them see you - but Carmina's a very pretty girl, and I can't always be there for her, if you follow my meaning."

"Say no more. I can do that," he agreed. "As long as you promise not to overreact to anything they might do."

She smiled at him. "I'm asking you to do the reacting for me, Tahgri. That's the point."

"I will, but I've seen the purest of men and women go awry when things became personal, Abby. Swear you won't do anything more than I do. Swear it on the Maralor, and I'll keep her safe."

Abby sighed. "I swear on the Maralor that I'll react reasonably." She didn't believe herself capable of doing anything as bad as was evidently expected by Tahgri, but in all fairness he had only just met her. She could've had quite the temper for all he knew.

He lightened the mood a little with a smile. "Well, that settles that. What's this about training, though?" he enquired.

Abby nodded eagerly, excitement suddenly flaring in her at the prospect of more instruction by a genuine paladin. Although training had gone a long way in redeveloping her arm to its former strength, none of Abby's trainees were close to her level of skill yet. "Well, I've been training my brother and sister. Daniel and Samson as well - but I think you'd see all of us better trained than I could manage."

Tahgri didn't differ. "I'll do the best I can with anyone you wish me to. I can figure out a regime with the others, but right now I'm more interested in you," he admitted. "Tell me, did you train in the knightly fashion?"

Abby shook her head. "No sir, I took a slightly less traditional route. I was brought up and educated properly, so faith came naturally to me. My older brother suggested the whole thing when I grew up broader than most girls, and I undertook the first part of my formal training in Suna; I went on a mission to help bring the faith there."

"Suna?" interrupted Tahgri. "If there's one place that needs the faith it's that land of sand and bandits."

Abby smiled faintly. As much as her work there had pleased the Maralor, he was correct. It had been dull, hard, and occasionally quite dangerous - though she'd have done it again if the gods had demanded it. "They didn't question my purity of faith after a year there, so I returned home for the rest of my training."

"When you returned home, did you continue to practice your faith along with the knightly ways?" Tahgri queried.

"I didn't squire full-time if that's what you're asking, no, but Sir Krensworth tutored me in combat, horsemanship, and tactics whilst I furthered my education. I learned quickly, but because I'd started later than most they said I couldn't possibly be ordained until I was at least twenty-four," she explained. Those were fond memories; the training had been hard work, but incredibly satisfying for her in many ways.

"How old are you now?" he asked.

"I'm twenty-two, sir."

Tahgri seemed to ponder upon the information for a short while. "Potentially two years from being ordained, and you managed to survive out here for this long. I'd reckon you're more than worth tutoring," he commented.

Abby smiled. "I'll see you for training as soon as there's a good moment for it, then?"

The paladin nodded and waved her away. "Rest well. You can be sure I'll be putting you through your paces soon."

Abby grinned exuberantly. "Goodnight, Tahgri. Sleep well," she excused herself before heading home.

She said her prayers in the bedroom. Johann had waited up for her as promised, though he may as well have not bothered. She dismissed his advances that night, returning a single kiss on his lips. "Not tonight. I'll need all the rest I can get for tomorrow." With a sigh of discontent, he resisted his urges and settled down to rest. Abby struggled to sleep, childlike excitement crackling around her mind at the thought of training with Tahgri.

7

A Balancing Act

"You're welcome to sit down, Abby," offered William.

She did so, forming a little triangle of chairs with him and Michael. "So, what's the plan?" she asked.

"Well, that's what we're here to discuss. Michael's keen to take on decent help, but my grandsons are keen to be trained by you, and I don't want to leave your family entirely without your help on the farm, either," William explained. He seemed a little weak-voiced today, which was disconcerting. Nobody expected him to last much longer, given his frailty, but his work to coordinate the efforts of the village had made him popular. The people of New Cray quietly hoped that another such leader would step forwards after his inevitable demise, since few held his son in the same high regard.

Abby nodded faintly. "Well, I reckon my family will understand for the most part, but I think it'd be best if I still helped a bit. It's coming up on time to re-sow and we've got a lot of work to do. After the seeds are planted it'll be lighter work, I know they can handle that without me."

"In the interest of leaving you some time to keep training Samson and Daniel, I think it best you work mornings with Michael whenever you can, and keep afternoons free," returned William.

The smith nodded eagerly. "That ought to be enough," he agreed.

"Are there any issues?" questioned William, looking between the two of them.

"Well, I did tell my brother and sister I'd join them hunting today," Abby informed him.

William waved a hand dismissively. "Take the day, then. You can start tomorrow morning if you like, or whenever you'd prefer. As soon as it's convenient for you."

Abby smiled and stood to shake his hand. "Thanks, William. One more thing, though - have you met Sir Dunwolf?"

"I have. No doubt you're pleased to have another paladin around," he commented.

"I was just an initiate," she corrected. "But yes, I am. He's agreed to train me and the others. I expect we'll all benefit from it."

William nodded faintly. "I'm glad to hear it. We're going to need to be prepared when the elementals come, after all."

"Great. I'll see you both later then, hopefully," Abby excused herself.

"Good hunting," William dismissed her before turning to resume his business with Michael. Abby liked William - he was the kind of man that never had to give stern orders to sound like he was in charge. All he had to do was make suggestions, because his recommendations were always so helpful that you couldn't really disagree with them.

Abby's siblings met her halfway through New Cray. "How'd it go?" asked Aurelius, handing her a bow. She'd never been able to gain much proficiency with it, thanks to her injury, but she'd been learning a little whenever she'd gone out hunting with the others.

"William was happy with it all. I won't have a whole bunch of free time, but I'd rather keep busy anyway," Abby informed them.

Carmina nodded in agreement. "Me too. It's boring here, if it wasn't for your training I'd go mad," she commented.

"Well, maybe you ought to try and make some friends? Or perhaps more than just friends," Abby suggested.

Carmina shrugged. "I was trying to. Johnny and Sid turned out to be a bit weird, they kept giving each other strange looks when I was trying to be nice," she said, sounding a little downtrodden.

"Oh," said Abby, suddenly glad that she'd asked Tahgri to keep an eye on them. "Well, don't worry about that. Boys are weird sometimes. No offense, Aurelius."

"Well girls are weird all the time, so that might explain it," Aurelius muttered back.

Abby playfully clipped him around the ear. "Don't act like you're not interested in women, it'll put them off."

Aurelius snorted derisively. "Put who off, exactly? There's not one woman around my age in this village. Not unless I'm feeling particularly incestuous, anyway."

Abby grimaced and shook her head. "That's disgusting. And I know you haven't met them yet, but I think you'll be pleasantly surprised when Lapden gets closer and we start to mingle more," she hinted. Lapden had expanded in much the same way as New Cray over the last year; there was still over half a kilometre between New Cray's northmost building and Lapden's southmost, but there had already been numerous meetings between prominent citizens of both villages regarding their coexistance. Abby had occasionally been involved, and had met a number of lovely young ladies amongst Lapden's populace.

"I hope so. It seems like everyone's got their eye on someone except me," Aurelius lamented, turning west to face the hunting grounds.

"Don't worry, someone with incredibly poor taste will fall for you eventually," Carmina jibed as they set off.

"Be nice!" Abby snapped before Aurelius could retort.

"Who put you in charge?" muttered Carmina.

"Our mother, when she gave birth to me first," Abby grinned, though she expected the question was rhetorical. She didn't honestly believe age had much to do with leadership, but she was happy to use it as an easy excuse to stop her siblings bickering too much. It seemed to work.

"So, what did Tahgri want to talk to you about last night, anyway? Paladin stuff?" enquired Carmina, steering away from challenging the authority of her elders.

"In a sense. He's going to be staying for a while and helping. He'll be training all of us in exchange for food whilst we get him set up and farming for himself," Abby explained.

Carmina nodded, brushing her hair out of her face as she walked. "That's good. Is he much better than you?"

Abby chuckled. "Well, he ought to be, he's got about forty years more experience than me. More, perhaps - I imagine he started when he was seven."

The trio walked on, chattering excitedly about how training would proceed under new supervision. Abby was glad that both of her siblings approved of the change of leadership in that regard, because she was aching to improve her own skills under Tahgri's tutelage.

Eventually, they came to the solitary tree that served as a marker for the start of their hunting grounds. Large birds - that their father insisted were called ostriches - frequently roamed the plains beyond it. They made for good eating, but there were none visible on their approach, and so the siblings wandered further into the savannah.

"Do you wanna wait by the watering hole, or go looking?" asked Aurelius.

"I'm hoping to get back earlier. We'll sweep by the watering hole and then keep moving until we see something," Abby instructed. They began to amble towards the water, dry, yellow grass brushing against their well-worn boots and trousers.

In the distance, Abby could see what could only be a giraffe, yanking at the leaves of a tall tree. Truly, nature out here was a wondrous thing, especially compared to further south. If it wasn't a case of starvation otherwise, she doubted she'd be able to kill any of the beautiful creatures herself. The others had seen the giraffe too, but they all knew better; not only were they rather heavy, even for the three of them, but they were boney and slender animals. There was far better prey to be had.

They were in luck, it seemed; when they neared their destination, a herd of water buffalo - or so their father had called them - were gathered at the watering hole. Of course, water buffalo shared a similar problem with giraffes in that they were generally too heavy. They'd need a larger hunting party to bring back a fully grown one, and whilst there were occasionally runts or calves that were light enough for small groups to carry, Eric had once told them that killing the young was bad hunting practice; sustainability was crucial. Of more interest to the siblings than the herd itself, were the predators that it might attract.

"What's the plan?" asked Carmina.

"Stay back at least seventy metres and don't spread out too far. Just watch for movement - and remember, we're prey too, out here," Abby instructed. Aurelius passed each of them a handful of the bone-tipped arrows they'd grown accustomed to using and moved off just a few metres to the right. Carmina took the left side, and the three of them stood calmly, waiting for any sign of motion. Eventually, the buffalo seemed to have wallowed for long enough and began to move south. As silently as the tall grass allowed, the siblings stalked the herd.

It took some time for them to spot more suitable prey. They'd been following the buffalo for a while when they finally noticed the motion. "There! look!" hissed Carmina, gesturing off to the right of the herd. Sure enough, subtle as a breeze, something was disturbing the long grass. Adrenaline began to flood through Abby's veins as she looked about for more of the predators. They were rarely alone. All three siblings nocked arrows, just in case the creatures rounded on them.

The animal's coat was so well camouflaged in the savannah grass that it noticed them well before they got a proper view of it. It was no wonder the beast had managed to get so close to the herd. The lioness stood up as they approached it, staring right at them, and Aurelius briefly had time to exclaim "Shit!" before it bolted towards him with a terrifying roar. The three arrows were loosed simultaneously, and the herd of buffalo began to stampede away from the familiar sounds of predation.

Aurelius collapsed under the weight of the animal, grunting heavily. It was dead before its momentum even stopped carrying it; one of the arrows had pierced its eye, and tackling Aurelius seemed to have pushed it further through, right into the brain. "Get it off me!" he groaned as Abby and Carmina rushed over. It was a sizable creature, undoubtedly heavier than the combined weight of the sisters, but between the two of them they managed to roll it off of their brother. "Check for others!" he insisted as he righted himself, nocking another arrow. His arms had sustained some nasty cuts from the claws, though clearly nothing fatal.

They huddled closer together, peering around cautiously for further movement in the grass. Another lioness approached them from the front, snarling angrily. "Only if it charges," insisted Carmina, taking careful aim. "No point killing more than we can carry." The anxiety was evident in her voice despite her carefully measured advice.

"Go on! Fuck off!" Aurelius yelled at the creature. It remained firmly in place, tail swishing as it eyed them hungrily.

"Language!" insisted Abby, blushing faintly as her brother spared her a look of slight disbelief.

"WOULD YOU KINDLY LEAVE!" Aurelius bellowed, shattering the tension of the situation and prompting a slight laugh from Carmina. Abby might've laughed too, if not for the sudden movement behind her. She span on the spot - too quickly, however, the beast was beside her.

Aurelius and Carmina cried out in alarm and backed up, trying to get a clear shot. Confusion settled on their faces as they saw that rather than attacking, the lioness was rubbing itself against Abby in a manner better befitting a small house cat, the beautiful golden fur soft against her skin. She made an effort to distance herself from it despite its apparent lack of aggression.

"What do we do?!" hissed Carmina.

"Just... don't panic," said Abby, feeling dangerously close to doing exactly that herself. It took more than a few moments for her to calm down, but eventually her instinct towards kindness kicked in and she eased herself down onto her knees, timidly brushing a hand over the big cat's ears. "Hey there," she muttered, forcing a soft tone to her voice despite the shake in it. The second creature approached slowly, probing Abby gently with its nose. The pair seemed to settle, comfortable up against her.

Truly, she had no idea what to do or say, simply shrugging at her siblings. "Wait for them to get bored and leave?" she suggested. Aurelius nodded, observing anxiously as the beasts enjoyed Abby's gentle touch. Neither he nor Carmina dared get close to the animals, but to Abby their presence became surprisingly pleasant once it was clear that neither of them were going to suddenly change their minds and bite her.

It was some time before the animals left. After a while they simply strolled off, their purpose forgotten. "What the fuck just happened?" questioned Aurelius.

Abby would've admonished him for his language again, but the same question was on her mind, even if she would've voiced it in a less crude manner. "I don't know, but it beats being mauled," she responded, getting to her feet. "Let's get this thing out of here before they come back, or something that actually *does* want to eat me finds us," she suggested, eager to be out of the hunting grounds.

"Good idea. Think we'll be able to carry it in one piece between the three of us?" asked Carmina, glancing warily around in case of any more would-be predators approaching them.

Aurelius stepped over and carefully retrieved the three arrows from

74

the lioness, then circled around to its flank and tried to lift it. "Nope! I don't think so," he grunted, unable to lever it more than an inch from the ground. "Let's gut it and see if we can get it back that way?"

Carmina nodded agreeably. "Alright. Someone else is doing the anus, though," she insisted. Abby chuckled.

Aurelius took his knife and set to work, mutilating the lower end of the lioness. They'd had to practice what Eric had shown them on all sorts of animals over the past year. No doubt certain creatures of unusual shapes could've been dealt with using different techniques, but the basic principles always remained the same; create an incision that minimises damage to the hide, and pull the guts out without letting any of them leak. Despite it being their first time actually killing a lioness, it didn't take them long to apply the same old methods, and soon enough there was a large heap of guts piled up, fresh and pungent. "Alright. Let's see if we can get it up," instructed Abby, moving over to the rear end and considering how best to carry it.

Aurelius moved to the front, and Carmina took up position in the middle for all of two seconds, until blood dripped on her from the gory incision. "Abby, swap with me?" she begged.

Abby chuckled and moved over, wrapping one arm around the blood-slicked underside of the creature. "Do either of you want the hide?" she asked, struggling over the words as they hoisted the animal. Aurelius and Abby were both significantly stronger than Carmina, but even with the three of them carrying it, it was damned heavy.

"Not my colour," said Carmina, obviously not putting quite as much effort into the lifting as Abby was.

"Too hot for furs," grunted Aurelius.

He wasn't wrong, but Abby's clothes were starting to wear thin again. If nothing else, she could wear it at night when it got cold. Besides, there was no other purpose for the material, and it would've been a shame to waste anything after such a beautiful creature had given its life for their continued survival. "Alright. I guess I can have that then," she said, frowning as she felt lioness blood begin to soak through her hair and onto her neck.

The strain of carrying the creature quickly reduced their conversation to silence as they walked. Circling cautiously around a group of ostriches that had wandered over to the hunting grounds, the trio soon came to that one distinctive tree again. "Let's set it down here and rest a little," panted Abby. They were more than happy to dump the corpse beside the tree and rest in the shade for a while.

"Next time we're bringing Tahgri, too," insisted Carmina, mopping at her brow with the sleeve of her shirt.

"If I can convince him out of his armour, sure. We'll never sneak up on anything with him rattling about," Abby chuckled.

"If you can't get him out of it, perhaps I can," joked Carmina.

"He's like sixty years old," Aurelius muttered in disgust.

Abby smiled at the pair's inexperience. Although she wasn't exactly an expert, there was much she could teach the two about love. That it didn't need to be shallow, for one thing.

"What's that?" enquired Carmina, peering into the distance. A single figure strode northwards. It was humanoid, but the more Abby looked, the more it became clear that it was not one of them. It must've been around nine feet tall, and it strode closer to the roaming ostriches than it should've been able to without invoking an attack.

"I don't know, and I'm not sure I want to find out," Abby admitted after peering for a short while.

"Elemental?" suggested Aurelius.

"Probably, but it's not like one I've seen before," Abby continued, straining her eyes to try and make out more of the creature.

"It could be an air elemental? There could be one for every element, right?" Aurelius suggested. The siblings had seen plenty of earthen and fire elementals, and they'd heard of water elementals, but never air. Who could say for certain - the only thing that Abby really knew about the elementals for sure was that they would go to great lengths to kill her and everyone she loved.

"It does have wings," Carmina considered. "I'm not sure why an air elemental would be green, though."

Abby nodded, and suddenly ducked to the ground as the creature turned its head towards them. Even though she was fairly sure it couldn't make them out clearly from where it stood, its gaze sent chills running through her. "Once it passes by, we get to New Cray and tell them. We may need to prepare for elementals soon if they made it out this far," she insisted.

"Yeah, but for now let's just stay very still," Aurelius recommended. And so they did, observing the distant anomaly with an understated sense of dread.

It slowly meandered off north, and in the end Abby lost sight of it behind a distant tree. "Alright, let's get this thing back double time," she ordered, glad that they hadn't had to rush off before getting sufficient rest. Despite the distance between themselves and the aberration, Abby kept glancing over her shoulder as they carried the lioness back east. None of them said a word until they were safe. It was strange that such a distant encounter with something could leave such anxiety; the air was thick with it.

The exhausted trio took the lioness straight to their parents'. "Can you two butcher this?" Abby requested. "I need to go and tell William what we saw." She wasn't exactly sure what she expected to come out of an 'unknown something' walking distantly past the village, but she felt an urge to make sure it got heard about as soon as possible.

Carmina nodded, and the three of them deposited the creature outside the front door. "We'll get on it. You want the hide in the best condition we can get it?" asked Aurelius.

"Yeah, please. I'll be back in a bit," Abby excused herself before dashing off to find William. She knocked on the door of the Marshal household.

It was Daniel that answered. "Hey Abby, are you alright?" he asked, gesturing to her neck and shoulders. "You're bleeding."

Abby shook her head and took a moment to catch her breath. "It's lion blood, don't worry. I need to talk to William, we saw something weird while we were out."

"He's at Johann's," Daniel informed her, his expression taking on an air of curiosity.

"Thanks Dan, I'll see you later," she replied. Leaving his unspoken questions unanswered, she turned and ran home. "William!" she called as she pushed through the door.

"We're through here," came Johann's voice.

She darted through to the long room he'd set aside for his medical practice. The pair of wooden benches were occupied - one by a shirtless William Marshal, and the other by an unfamiliar woman perhaps five years Abby's senior. "William, we saw something weird out hunting. We think it might've been an elemental but it wasn't like the ones we've seen so far," Abby blurted out.

"Are you alright? You're bleeding," interrupted Johann.

"I'm fine, it's lion blood," she explained again, smiling reassuringly.

"Just the one elemental?" asked William.

Abby nodded. "So far, but you know how they tend to gather."

William sighed. "Thank you, Abby. I'll get Sam and Dan to keep ready for trouble. Your usual spot for hunting I suppose?"

She rolled her shoulders, stiff from carrying the lioness. "Yeah, out past the fields to the west. I could see the boys for you if Johann needs to keep you here," she suggested. With her mind now unburdened she noticed that William looked terrible. Far worse than he had this morning.

He shook his head and pulled his shirt back on. "No, no. We were done anyway. I'll be heading home now," he insisted.

Politeness kicked back in now that the need for urgency was gone. "Alright. Thanks, William. Take care," Abby saw him off.

"And you," William returned, slowly making his exit.

Abby waited to hear the door close before asking. "How's he doing?"

Johann gave her a saddened look. "He has disease of the lungs, and his heart's struggling," he admitted. "But on the bright side of things - Abby, this is Jaina," he introduced them, turning to face the woman sat on the other bench.

Jaina smiled and offered Abby a firm handshake. "Pleased to meet you," she said, her accent as proper as Abby's own.

"And you!" Abby returned, smiling broadly. Jaina had retained proper pronunciation, too, something that Abby couldn't help but notice had faded in the time that she and her siblings had spent in the company of New Cray's more rustic citizens.

"Johann was just regaling me with second-hand stories of your time as a paladin," Jaina claimed.

"Initiate," Abby corrected instinctively. "I hope you've been settling in alright? They found a job for you yet?"

Jaina shook her head. "I was a lawyer, once upon a time. I think I'll probably have trouble finding a fitting job here - I'll most likely end up farming," she said, obviously not pleased at the notion of manual labour.

"A lawyer, eh? I was wondering when we'd encounter our first parasite out here," Johann joked.

Abby gasped, unused to her lover making such harsh jibes. "Johann!" she scolded him.

Jaina laughed merrily, waving a dismissive hand. "It's quite alright. It's not like I'll ever be a lawyer again, that would require some sort of formal law to exist. Besides, I was only in it for the money. It was far from a noble profession."

Abby didn't quite know how to respond to the situation, and simply settled for being glad that Jaina hadn't taken offense. "Well, maybe I'll see you soon, Jaina. I've got lots to do, so I'll let Johann tend to you," she said, placing a quick kiss on the doctor's cheek.

"Oh, I'm not ill, I'm just being social," Jaina claimed. "Perhaps I'll see you later."

Abby went looking for Tahgri, any thoughts of working at the smithy banished from her mind in light of more pressing concerns. She soon found the paladin in the chapel, sitting cross-legged on the floor and deep in meditation. She joined in, seating herself beside him and ordering her busy thoughts.

Tahgri opened his eyes and glanced across, giving her a weary smile. "Welcome back. How did the hunt go?" he asked.

"Weirdly," she chuckled. "We finally caught a lioness, but these other two came up to us afterwards. We thought they were going to attack, but they just started playing with me. Like pets."

Tahgri scratched his stubbly chin with one huge gauntlet. "It's not unheard of," he claimed. Abby looked to him, desiring more explanation.

"You were taught about the powers of the Maralor bestowed onto us," he stated, more than asked.

"Yeah, they explained that in the first year of my training. I was told they manifest in most paladins in some form after they're ordained," she recalled from those lessons so long ago.

"Correct."

"But I haven't taken my oath. I wasn't ordained."

"Then what does that make you?" he asked thoughtfully.

"Naturally good with animals?"

"Blessed, child. The Maralor care for you especially. I couldn't say why you in particular, but since the day we met I could see their power in you as clearly as any paladin I've ever known," he continued.

"I thought you weren't going to give me any nonsense about a 'sense of purpose' here?" she responded, failing to stop her ego inflating at the notion of being favoured by the gods themselves.

"A sense of purpose for you, perhaps. Not for me," he insisted.

Abby smiled at him. "Fair enough, but I've always been good with animals, are you sure that's anything special?"

"Explain," commanded Tahgri.

"Well, when I was very young I had a rabbit. And there were others, too; stray cats, dogs - animals just seem to like me," she said, feeling a little embarrassed for implying the presence of the divine in such silly matters.

Tahgri nodded faintly."Rabbits and dogs are a little bit different to lions, though," he noted. "Have you ever had anything else like this happen to you?"

"Well, I'm not sure if it's related, but do you remember that story I told you about how I got this scar?" she asked him, gesturing to her arm.

"I do," he nodded.

"When I hit the guy, it wasn't just a regular punch. There was this weird light, then his jaw was just... shattered. It was like I'd hit him with a rock. A big rock," she continued. "At the time I thought maybe I'd hallucinated. I lost a lot of blood, and I know that can do strange things to the mind - not to mention the pain - but none of that explained how I could've broken his jaw like that so easily."

"A golden, shimmering light?" Tahgri enquired.

Abby nodded. "Yeah. I think you can see where this is going."

"What you're describing is Rendick's power manifesting in its most physical form," he informed her.

She contemplated for a moment. "What should I do about them, the powers?"

"Train with me. Through the Maralor, the path of the righteous is made clear," Tahgri insisted.

"Do I train the powers as well? I was never taught anything about how to use them," she admitted.

Tahgri shook his head. "You were never told? The powers are not yours to control, but the Maralor's. They will simply occur when they're meant to."

Abby nodded thoughtfully and stood again. "Alright. Thanks, Tahgri. I think I'll pass on the smithy tonight, how about we get started on the training right away?" she suggested, concerned that they may be facing off with the elementals again sooner rather than later.

"I hate to be a pain, but I don't suppose I could eat first, could I? I'm starving," he admitted.

Abby smiled at him. "Come on, I'll cook for you."

The paladin grinned and eased himself upright. "It's been a long time since a beautiful young lady cooked for me," he commented.

"Well, I'm afraid it might be a while more before one does," she replied in good humour.

Hardly discouraged by her refusal to accept false compliments, Tahgri followed Abby back to her parents' house. Aurelius and Carmina had skinned their quarry, the entire stripped hide now hanging proudly on the rack beside the beast itself. They were butchering it out on the porch, dropping the meat straight into buckets. "Who wants to find out what it tastes like? I'm cooking," Abby called out as she approached.

"Sounds good to me. There's more meat on this thing than we can store," claimed Carmina. By the looks of how much meat was yet to be removed from the carcass, she was probably right.

"Car, go and fetch the others will you? I'll get started," requested Abby, heading inside.

"I'll just stay out here and help with butchering this," Tahgri decided, cunningly avoiding the effort of crouching to go through the door. Abby quickly gathered the necessary materials and set right to it, heading out the back door and setting up a fire outside.

Tahgri soon joined her, sitting down beside her and resting a bucket of meat in his lap. "Thanks for all of this," he said warmly.

Abby grinned. "Well don't thank me just yet - I've not tried cooking lioness before," she joked.

The paladin chuckled. "Seriously though, you're a good lass. It's not always easy being the 'good guy' out here."

"Sure it is," she differed. "You just have to be nice to the good people and firm with the bad ones."

Tahgri smiled to himself. "Sometimes I wish I could still see the world that simply. The more I saw, the less black and white it became," he claimed.

"Yeah? What was it like, being a paladin?" she asked him. During her training she'd always thought that she'd be ordained after the war came to its conclusion. She would've liked that, she reckoned, being a paladin in a time of relative peace.

Tahgri seemed to think on his words as Abby began to cook the meat. "It wasn't like you'd think, I imagine. Nobody ever hears anything but the stories of noble deeds. Everyone wants to hear about Willhelm the Enforcer or Blood Oath Gretchen, but a lot happens around and between the tales you hear that isn't so glamorous," he explained.

Abby eyed him questioningly for a moment, hoping that he was going to expand on that. "Are you familiar with them?" he asked, seeming to settle into the same sort of storytelling routine they'd had last night.

"I think everyone's heard of Sir Willhelm, but I've never heard of a paladin by the name of Gretchen," she admitted.

"Dame Gretchen was a bit of an upstart when the war came about," Tahgri informed her. "I barely knew her, but Willhelm was only about ten years older than me. I was already a paladin when his name became legend, and we were actually fairly well acquainted. What the stories don't tell you is that all those bandits he killed were quite well protected because of their blackmailing and bribery. He actually spent five months trying to unpick their whole scheme beforehand; he tried paperwork, he tried talking to the right people, but nothing he did worked. He knew intervening physically with a large operation like that was madness. One well-placed crossbow bolt or - Maralor forbid - a gun, and he could've died. Going up against them alone was the absolute last resort."

"That doesn't seem so bad. Five months is a lot of time but it's not like it was all for nothing," observed Abby.

"Well, that's not the point," insisted Tahgri. "Sometimes it doesn't pay off at all. Sometimes there's nothing legal you can do, and there's always an honourless cause to fight for. Our positions require that we keep the lords of any region we're in happy, as well, at least if we want to eat. Believe me, Abby, some of the men and women I've fought under weren't worth the carpets in their castles."

Abby nodded. "I guess it can't all be prestige, faith, and honour."

"It certainly isn't. Even aside from all that, there's the battlefield if you're ever unlucky enough to find yourself in a proper fight. There are few things sadder than hordes of good men going to their deaths."

The words resonated with Abby. She had often wished that violence wasn't so necessary. "I've never killed anyone before," she admitted.

"Be glad of it, there's no glory in death. You'd be better off dueling or taking to sports if you want something to gloat over," he commented.

Abby was rarely one to gloat, of course, but she understood him well enough. "So, who's Blood Oath Gretchen?" she asked, poking at the meat whilst it sizzled away in the pan.

"Well, as I said, she was something of an upstart. She acquired the nickname from using blood oaths. Not the sort of magic that's looked kindly upon - are you familiar with those from your time in Suna?" he asked.

Abby nodded. "Sort of. I didn't see any of it myself, but I heard they used them to enslave people, right?" she recalled.

"That's right. Slavers would give people a choice between the oath and death, so that they didn't dare disobey. Gretchen repurposed the magic to give criminals a second chance - to force them to obey the law," he explained.

Abby smiled faintly. "That's smart. I'm surprised nobody tried that earlier," she commented, though she wasn't really, in truth; the magic was unpopular with the nobility, presumably due to fear of having it used against them.

"Many are superstitious of the black magics," contributed Tahgri, shrugging as if he didn't understand why either.

"Black magics. What is it that makes a magic 'black', anyway, other than our perceptions of it?" she asked him.

"How philosophical of you," he smiled.

"I suppose it ought to be, I was quite fond of philosophy in my youth. When I wasn't training I was usually reading. Either that or eating my own weight in cake," she grinned.

Tahgri chuckled. "That's a lot of cake for an initiate."

"I suppose it was. I think it's done me some good, to be honest, all this hard work and rationing food. I feel stronger for it."

Carmina returned with the rest of the family, and Carl. "Lionesses!" exclaimed Alexander, obviously fascinated by the wildlife as was usual for him. "I heard they got friendly with you! How was it?"

"Terrifying. I was close to needing new trousers," Abby muttered, prompting a round of laughter.

"Well, I'm glad you're back in one piece. And with food," Alexander continued. Abby smirked, glad that she was at least as important to her father as the food was.

Abby's mother sat down beside her and peered at the meat in the pan. "It smells nice. We've not had lion yet, have we?" she asked.

Abby shook her head as she tended the food. "Nope. Just about the only thing around here we haven't. By the way, could someone see if Johann wants to join us?" she hoped, noting his absence.

"I already did. He's busy with a patient or something, said he'll join us tonight," responded Carmina.

"Alright. More for us, I guess. I think we may have to trade some before it goes off anyway," said Abby.

"I could go with mum later and see who's interested?" suggested Aurelius. Since more and more people had arrived, produce had gained diversity, and trade had become more frequent. No doubt they'd be able to get some much-needed supplies with the extra meat.

"I think Tahgri's going to give us our first training session tonight, though," Abby informed him, glancing at the paladin for confirmation.

Tahgri shook his head and looked to Aurelius and Carmina. "It would be better if I worked once with each of you individually first. That way I can get a good grasp of where you stand. I'll start with Abby, there should be time for both of you tomorrow, if that's alright," he corrected.

Carmina and Aurelius exchanged glances and shrugs, communicating in the most adolescent way they knew. "I'll take that as a yes," muttered Tahgri.

"Yeah, sure. Why not," Aurelius finally verbalised.

The meat was ready soon enough. Everyone took plentiful helpings. "This tastes amazing!" commented Carmina, digging in hungrily.

"Think it might be the best game we've had so far," added Aurelius.

"I preferred the giraffe. It was sweeter," disagreed Abby. "Have you been working on anything special by the way, Carl?"

He shook his head faintly, a wordless frown on his face as usual. "How would you like to make me something from that lioness hide?" Abby smiled, knowing not to be discouraged by his expression.

"What sort of something?" he enquired.

"Well, like a cloak sort of thing I guess. Just, anything that'll cover me when these old rags are worn out," she answered, sticking a finger through one of the numerous small holes in her current shirt. It was easy to forget the state of her clothing, since she wore her armour over it whenever it was practical to do so.

"Sure, I can manage that," he agreed. "Did you keep the brain?"

"It's still in the skull. You want to eat it?" asked Carmina, sounding rather disgusted.

"It's for tanning with," Carl clarified.

"It's inside. I'll get it for you once we're done," offered Aurelius, talking with his mouth half-full.

Carl, the smallest of the group by far, was also the quickest to eat his fill. He moved around to sit beside Abby once he was done, and the pair spent the rest of the brief lunch break discussing ideas for what to make with the hide. The beast was larger than Abby - enough so that it could be made into just about anything she requested, given time and sufficient skill. They settled on a hide vest and a matching sort of shawl or drape.

With lunch dealt with and business with Carl settled, she turned back to Tahgri. "I'll go get my armour on. Meet me out back?" she suggested.

The paladin nodded and got to his feet. "Thank you all for lunch. I'll let you both know about training tomorrow," he added for Carmina and Aurelius' sake.

"Have a nice afternoon, guys. I'll see you all for dinner," said Abby, gathering up the dirty dishes to take them inside. The family wished her a good afternoon one by one, and she headed back to Johann's to arm and armour herself properly.

"...honestly, I've never seen anyone so obviously guilty get away so entirely free," Abby overheard as she entered. Jaina's thick capital accent was unmistakable.

Abby walked through and smiled at the pair. "Just getting my gear," she informed Johann, who grinned broadly at her sudden appearance.

"Hello again," greeted Jaina.

"Heya. Law stories, is it?" asked Abby, pausing briefly to chat.

"Something like that. We were swapping stories, old and new. You seem to have snapped up the last of the good men," said Jaina.

"Oh, I don't know about that. My brother's still single, and if you're interested in older gentlemen there's a wonderful paladin with no ring on his finger," Abby grinned.

"Since when did you start helping people to pull?" enquired Johann.

"Helping people to what?" she asked, prompting a sigh in return.

"Nevermind. You wouldn't get it," Johann insisted.

Abby shrugged and left them to it, moving through into the bedroom. If it was the sort of filth that she required to be explained, she wasn't sure that she wanted to understand it anyway.

"So, what's with the armour? The elementals aren't here, are they?" asked Jaina, following Abby into the bedroom with little regard for privacy.

"Not yet. I'm just training with Sir Dunwolf," Abby explained. She began fastening her armour in place, piece by piece.

"Ah. Maybe we'll catch up some other time, then. In the meantime, I suppose I may as well loiter," Jaina smiled.

"Oh, darling!" called Johann as he came over to join them, crowding the doorway. "Why don't the three of us have dinner tonight? Things would get a little cramped if Jaina joined our usual crowd, I expect, and I'm sure you'd both appreciate the chance for proper introductions."

Abby smiled at the pair as she grabbed her battered shield. "Sure, I'll cook. Why don't you show Jaina around while I train?"

Johann was clearly surprised at the suggestion, but nodded anyway. "Why not," he agreed. "I'll see you tonight."

Abby picked up her hammer and squeezed past them both. "I hope you like lion meat!" she called over her shoulder, heading off to meet with Tahgri.

He was waiting for her behind the family house, his equipment ready. "Unarmed first?" Abby enquired, keeping her hammer and shield tucked firmly away for the moment.

"Yes," he agreed, gently embedding his sword in the earth. "Let's get stuck in. Try to hit me," he ordered. Abby adopted a fighting stance and lashed out at his face with an open fist. Tahgri was remarkably fast despite his advanced age, and he batted the hand aside with ease.

The pair paused unnaturally at that point, Tahgri nodding his firm approval. "Good. Keep going, don't hold back," he insisted. She took a step back before setting right into it, sending a flurry of vicious punches at his torso. He deflected all but a single glancing blow, making it look easy.

The paladin gently held her wrists to give her pause when he was satisfied with her demonstration. "Not bad. Help me out of this armour and let's do this properly," he ordered, beginning to remove the dulled plate. She moved around to help, taking pieces of the armour from him and stacking them against the wall of the house. It was impressive stuff, she had to admit, much more protective than hers. She'd very much have liked a set of her own, but she doubted such a thing would be possible. Iron was hard enough to get hold of out here, let alone decent steel.

"Do you know if any other paladins survived?" she asked as she assisted him.

"I wasn't the best of us, and I certainly won't be the only one to have survived," he said confidently. "But I don't know where they've gone, what they're doing or even if they've kept their oaths."

"You think some of them would break their oaths, then?" she asked, curiosity getting the best of her. She couldn't recall ever hearing of an oath breaker, though it had undoubtedly happened at some point.

"Some, possibly. We're still only mortal, and people tend to behave unpredictably when they're backed into a corner," he contemplated, handing her the last piece of his gear. "Leave yours on. You'll need it."

He put his guard up, ushering her in for another bout. Abby didn't hesitate - she knew that he could beat her senseless before she ever did any real harm to him, and so she adopted a fighting pose and waited for him to make a move. His strong arms lashed out towards her shoulders, and she reacted swiftly, wrapping one arm around his right wrist and moving around him in a circle, trying to bend his arm behind him like she had once done with Daniel. Tahgri's strength proved a little much for her, however, and she found herself rooted to the spot, straining against him. They began to trade leg blows, blocking and pummeling each other, but before she could get any further he snaked his other arm around and yanked one of her legs out from beneath her, dropping her to the ground. She landed on her back and rolled sideways, making a quick recovery and returning to her feet. He didn't attack her again just yet.

"You're fast, but you're trying to fight like you're much larger and stronger than you actually are. Don't let your size discourage you, but that's not going to work against an opponent like me," he commented. "You need to focus on redirecting or avoiding blows entirely, not trading them."

Abby nodded. It was smart advice, and she didn't honestly know why she'd thought such a thing would work against Tahgri. Perhaps she was rusty, too used to untrained opponents; neither the lawbreakers nor the elementals out here fought with anything close to the skill of a paladin.

"We'll get back to that later. Are you any good with a sword?" Tahgri asked, retrieving his blade from the earth once more.

"I am. Sir Krensworth tutored me, and was very pleased with my progress. I was showing promise with a flail as well - but to be honest I've grown rather fond of the hammer," she explained. Although the carpentry hammer had never exactly been a weapon of war, it seemed somehow fitting to her. Rendick was often called 'the hammer of war', after all.

"Show me what you've learned," Tahgri insisted, handing her his sword. She tested the weapon carefully - it was rather unwieldy for her, since it was almost as tall as she was, but she had no doubt that Tahgri would take that into account as he assessed her skills. She demonstrated everything she'd learned, effectively utilising point, edge, and pommel of the sword in fluid motion against a non-existent opponent.

Tahgri seemed suitably impressed by the time she was done. "Sir Krensworth taught you well. To be honest I'm not sure how much more I can teach you with that, but we'll keep you practicing to improve your speed and stamina, and we'll try out other styles and weapons."

Abby smiled brightly and returned his weapon to him. "Thanks. It's a nice sword, but it's a bit big for me."

"That it is. Now, show me what you've learned with that shield and hammer. I imagine I'll be able to teach you a thing or two there, still," Tahgri instructed.

She grinned and drew her weapons of choice, raising the shield high.

8
Mortality

Abby groaned, noting the single, narrow line of light breaking through the shutters. *Four hundred and eighty-nine days since we arrived in New Cray.* She sat up.

She ached all over. The bruises and physical strain of recent weeks had left barely a limb completely absent of the dull pain, and to add to that, after more than a month without sex, Johann had taken to it perhaps a little too vigorously last night.

She dressed and went to shake her lover awake, but he looked so very peaceful in his sleep. He'd started taking house calls recently, tending to ailments in the comforts of citizens' own homes where feasible. Last night's patient - whoever they'd been - had kept him until after dinner, and he'd come back almost too exhausted for sex. Almost.

Deciding to let him have his rest, Abby withdrew from the bedroom and headed over to her parents' to get some things for breakfast. She and Johann had begun to eat alone more often these days, or occasionally have a single guest over. Jaina and Tahgri were often their visitors of choice - they'd settled down well in New Cray, with Abby and others teaching them how to manage their own farming. They would be able to provide entirely for themselves, soon, but until then they'd have to rely on the good will of others.

Abby set to cooking a healthy portion of zebra along with some beans fried in the fat of the creature. Their diet did consist of more than just meat and beans these days, thanks to staggered trade agreements with other farmers for their produce, but this would do just fine for breakfast in bed. She brought the two plates through to the bedroom and sat beside Johann, leaning in to wake him with a firm kiss.

He woke, wrestling lips with her for a few moments before sitting up with a grin. "You're fantastic you know," he commented, reaching for his breakfast.

She brushed a hand through his hair and sat beside him to eat. "You need a haircut again. Want me to sort that out for you today?" she asked.

"Yes please," he nodded, pushing a stray strand away from his face. Johann's hair was naturally curly, and if it was left to its own devices it became excessively puffy, growing sideways rather than downwards and giving him an appearance that Abby found hard to take seriously. "So, what's on the agenda today? More training?"

Abby shook her head, chewing down a mouthful of beans before she answered. "Nah, that's tomorrow. I heard one of our newcomers was a glassworker, though. Thought I'd go talk to him after I get out of the smithy, maybe he'll be able to make some windows for the chapel."

Johann nodded. "Well, I only have one patient so far. I think I'll go help your parents work on the farm after that, so if anyone's looking for me, sen-"

They were interrupted by the sound of the front door bursting open. "Johann!" called the familiar voice of Daniel, the urgency clear in his tone.

Abby gave Johann a reassuring glance and quickly got up to see what was happening, leaving her plate behind. She stepped through to see the young man, panicked tears dotting his face as he carried William's limp form across his arms. Abby inhaled sharply and directed him towards the medical benches. "Set him down, quickly," she ordered.

She turned back towards the bedroom, borrowing the urgency that Daniel had conveyed. "Johann!" she snapped. The doctor staggered out of the bedroom a moment later, shirtless and still tying his trousers in place. Seeing William, he immediately dashed over and checked the old man's breathing.

"Save him!" Daniel begged through his tears. Patrick and Samson bustled through the door to join him, the three of them looking on with concern.

Johann pressed his ear to William's chest, checked his pulse at the neck and wrist, and then simply straightened up and fixed Daniel with an apologetic stare. "He's gone, Daniel, I'm sorry. His heart's stopped."

"You're meant to be a doctor! Help him!" cried Daniel.

Abby stepped over and wrapped her arms around him. They'd all known William would be for Corsein soon, but it hardly made the blow any easier - especially for Daniel, it seemed. "I'm sorry, Dan, he's gone. It's just his time," she tried to comfort him.

The tears spread until William's entire family wept for him. Even Johann seemed close to crying, despite being by far the most acquainted with the bitter truth of mortality. Abby held Daniel tight and thought about how this would affect life in New Cray. It would be bad news all round, but the extent of it was hard to predict.

Daniel waited for some time before removing himself from Abby's embrace, his tears coming to a halt as he just stood there, stunned. She wasn't sure what she should say, or even what she wanted to. After an awkward pause, she settled on an offer of help. "Would you like me to do anything for you?"

Patrick shook his head and stepped over beside his dead father. His voice cracked as he spoke, the emotion proving too much to keep it level. "No, we'll take him out to bury. Think we could all do with a day or two. Just, if anyone asks after him, let them know. Not gonna make a big announcement or anything."

"Sure thing,"Abby agreed, watching glumly as Patrick took William in his arms and led his sons from the building.

"Well... shit," commented Johann, once the door closed behind them. Abby didn't have the strength to remind him to watch his language.

They finished breakfast in sombre silence, their plans for the day feeling more like chores than they had before. "I'll see you for dinner?" she asked as she pulled on her armour.

Johann nodded and perched on the edge of the bed. "Yeah."

Sadness weighing on her, Abby headed over to the smithy, deciding to postpone the acquisition of glass for the chapel. Michael was busy making nails when she arrived. As important as weapons and armour might've seemed, such civilian things as door hinges, nails, and basic tools actually took up the majority of their time and resources. Michael had already taught her how to make most of the essentials. "Hey," Abby greeted, moving to help him without instruction.

They worked in uncomfortable silence for a few minutes before Michael finally spoke up. "Something wrong?" he asked. The smith's absolute refusal to say anything he didn't think to be of importance made him impressively terse - even more so than Carl - so there was no doubt he'd picked up on her lack of cheer.

"William's dead," she responded, trying not to dwell on the matter too long before continuing with her work. As with all grief, distraction was key to recovery.

Michael paused, looking down at his feet. As Abby understood it, he'd been one of the bunch from the original village of Cray, and given that he was a good thirty years William's junior, he would've known him all his life. "May the Maralor rest his soul," said Michael, standing there in silence for a moment. Without further comment, he simply continued working.

In truth, Abby wished she could afford to just curl up in bed and take the day off like Patrick. The hours trudged on miserably, barely a word passing between the two as they worked right up until the warm, orange sun of evening hovered on the horizon.

"It's late," Michael commented morosely.

Abby nodded and began to tidy up after herself. "Are you gonna be alright?" she asked.

"Yeah," he said, though it wasn't entirely convincing. Still, Michael was a grown man. Abby supposed it wasn't her responsibility to fuss over him, even if he had been close to William.

"I'll see you in the morning?" Abby queried. "We'd planned to train in the afternoon, but I'm not so sure Daniel or Samson will be in the mood for it anymore." Michael nodded and dismissed her with a wave of his hand.

She almost walked into Tahgri as she exited the smithy. "Oh!" she exclaimed, jumping slightly at the sudden presence. He was out of his armour for once, which explained how he'd snuck up on her. That could only mean he'd finally obtained somewhere safe enough to leave it.

"My house is finished!" he informed her cheerfully, putting a hand on her shoulder to help steady her.

"Good."

"Is something wrong?" he asked, and Abby suddenly found herself wondering if she was wearing her heart upon her sleeve.

"William's dead," she informed him as she began to walk home.

Tahgri strode after her, and Abby was more than a little surprised when his arms wrapped around her and lifted her into an embrace. It was far more pleasant without his armour on, although being lifted a good five inches from the ground was a little strange. "I'm sorry to hear it, he was a good man. When did it happen?" asked the paladin, setting her back down after the initial squeeze.

"This morning. Patrick and his sons brought him in for Johann, but he was already dead," she explained, turning to face him.

"Will you be alright?" he asked.

Abby nodded faintly. "I liked him, but I wasn't *that* close to him. I'm mostly just worried what it'll be like without him. He did a lot for us, really."

"You and yours will be just fine, don't you worry," Tahgri promised.

Abby smiled weakly at him and nodded. "I hope so. Now, do I get a look at your place before I go for dinner?"

Tahgri rocked his head from side to side as he considered. "I'm not sure it's such a good idea anymore, given the news, but I'd intended to invite you over for dinner, actually. My tomatoes mostly died, but the melons have worked out."

"It's still a good idea," she assured him. "I could do with the company to be honest. Is anyone else coming?"

"So far it's just you. Why don't you invite Johann along? I'd invite your whole family, but frankly the place would be too cramped."

Abby nodded. "Alright. What's for dinner, then?"

"Well, uh… Melon, I guess," he replied, taken off-guard.

Abby smiled, her mood improving due to Tahgri's somewhat amusing incompatibility with cooking. She'd been teaching him bits and pieces about how to look after himself now that he had no initiate or servants to attend his needs, but in some ways he was like Carmina had been when everything had gone south; incapable and somewhat spoiled. "That won't do, will it. I'll cook, but you've got to go and ask my parents for as many different types of fruits and vegetables as they can spare. Oh, and some ostrich - I'll show you how to make a nice, juicy melon-ostrich," Abby insisted.

"Do you mean lemon-ostrich?" he puzzled.

"Have you got lemons?"

"Well, no..."

"Then it's to be melon-ostrich."

Tahgri nodded, looking a little embarrassed. "Alright, I'll go and get the food. We'll meet at my house?" he suggested.

"Sure, I'll be right over," Abby agreed, and headed back home.

Johann was in, sat about doing precisely nothing. His mood seemed like it had been heavy, though he lightened up when she walked through the door. "Hey love," he muttered tiredly, moving over and pressing his lips to hers.

"Rough day? You haven't been beating yourself up over William, have you?" she asked.

"No. There's nothing any of us could've done," he insisted. "But it's never nice when they turn on you. I'll be 'the doctor that let William die' for a little while."

Abby nodded and ran a hand through his messy curls again. "Don't worry, they'll forget all about it next time you patch someone up," she assured him, hoping it was at least partly true.

"I know, but until then it's still going to be somewhat unpleasant," he predicted.

Abby nodded empathetically. "I guess so. They finished up Tahgri's house today, by the way - he invited us over for dinner. How about I cut your hair and we go over?" she suggested. "Lighten the mood a little."

Johann looked momentarily guilty. "Oh. I sort of told Jaina we would go to hers for dinner tonight. I probably should've asked first."

Abby sighed. "Yes, you probably should've. You go ahead, I'll see you tonight."

"You won't come along?" he asked tentatively.

"Nope. Just tell her it turned out I already had plans, she'll be fine with it."

Johann nodded faintly. "Alright. Sorry. Could you still cut my hair, though?"

She wouldn't hold any sort of grudge over such a small matter, and by now Johann knew better than to try and change her mind. Abby retrieved the scissors and sat him down on a chair, removing his shirt and setting about making him look respectable again. The hair fell away lock by lock, and by the time she was done he looked far better for it; gangly, but in no way unattractive or silly. "There we go, all shawn," she joked, placing a kiss on the back of his head.

"Thanks. Want me to tidy this up?" he asked, gesturing to the hair piled on the floor around them.

"No need, I'll tidy it up before I head off. You go ahead now, say hi to Jaina for me."

Johann nodded and got up, giving Abby another kiss as he pulled on his shirt. "Don't have too much fun without me," he called back at her as he left. Given this morning's happenings, Abby doubted anyone would be overdoing the revelry.

She tidied up after them and decided to make herself a little more presentable for the night, removing her armour and letting her hair down out of the bun. It had grown quite long over the last couple of years, and she had to admit that it actually looked quite nice on the rare occasions when she did let it down. Outside, it was getting cool enough to wear the lioness-hide shawl that Carl had made for her, so she wrapped it around her shoulders before leaving. The head of the creature rested atop her own, a proud and fierce hood.

Abby had seen Tahgri's house more than a handful of times during its construction, but this would be the first time that she'd actually set foot inside. Despite William's death still sitting at the back of her mind, Abby found herself smiling at the good news, even if it was something small. She didn't bother knocking, simply pushing through the Tahgri-sized door and brushing her hood back.

The paladin was sat on the floor, two small baskets of food resting beside him. "Why are you sat there?" Abby asked.

"Where else would I sit?"

"Chairs, at a table maybe?" she smirked at him.

"Well, I have neither - so the floor will have to do."

Abby laughed. "You're joking, right? You invited me over for dinner and you don't even have a table?"

Tahgri grinned sheepishly. "Alright, maybe I was a little over-eager to have people over. It's been so long since I had anything to celebrate."

"You've got plenty to celebrate. You just need to be happy about the little things, like still being alive and in good company," she differed. It was an attitude that had prevented a great deal of misery in her early days as a refugee.

Tahgri smiled at her. "You know what I meant."

"You meant that you're sorry for inviting me over for dinner, when I have to do all the work and there's no furniture either?"

The paladin looked unusually embarrassed, even though Abby's tone and expression made it evident that she was joking. She walked past him, into the kitchen. "Come on, let's get stuck in. Bring those through and fetch me some water, will you? I'll make us a salad. Sort of."

He followed her through to the kitchen, depositing the baskets of food on the side for her. Abby borrowed his knife to cut the vegetables, and briefly found herself wondering how many lives had met their end by this weapon that she was now using for food preparation. Although the pair had spent a lot of time together since Tahgri's arrival, they'd talked more about the future than the past. She thought that tonight might be a good chance to change that.

"So, no Johann then?" enquired Tahgri.

"Not tonight - he's having dinner with Jaina. I suppose it was a case of first come, first serve," she explained.

Having had a propensity for gluttony during her youth, Abby liked to think that she was rather experienced with food preparation. Due to the recent increase in variety in their diets, the skills were once again coming in handy, and by the time Tahgri fetched the water, she'd cut all the fruits and vegetables they'd need into perfect little chunks - save for a single melon. "Okay, cut this melon," she ordered.

Tahgri took the knife and made a tentative start, apparently going to cut it into rings rather than slices.

"Stop! Wrong," Abby barked, smiling faintly at his confusion. "Cut it lengthways, down the middle. Yeah, like that."

She proceeded to guide him through the steps, knowing that she was coming across as bossy despite trying to sound encouraging. "Good, now scoop the seeds out and dump them into a bucket. Not that one! It's got water in it already." She pointed to another bucket she'd used, already full of the seeds and soft gunk from the centre of the fruit. "Good, now slice each half into four pieces. Even pieces!" She quickly wrestled the knife from the poor, confused paladin as he threatened to mutilate the precious food into improper shape. She took one half of the melon and demonstrated how to do it correctly, creating four beautiful crescent-wedges. "Now, try it with the other half."

Tahgri, of course, didn't do it quite so expertly. Still, it came out good enough for Abby to use. She didn't expect perfection right away. "Now, cut down through the fruit so that you form little cubes with it. Yep, that's right. Perfect. Now cut the fruit free from the rind and drop it into the pile."

She took the rind from him and set it aside for later. "Do the same with the other slices while I sort through these seeds," she instructed.

With careful deliberation and Abby's supervision, the food came together. It was a mingled salad of fruits, vegetables, and roasted seeds - an odd combination of flavours, but she knew from experience that it would taste just fine. With a smile, she served up two bowls and led Tahgri back through to the bare front room.

"This is good!" he complimented as they began to eat.

Abby grinned impishly. "And you learned something about cooking, too, I hope."

Tahgri smiled faintly and shuffled over beside her, leaning against the wall. "You'll make a cook out of me yet."

"And you'll make warriors of us all," she returned. "Have you ever done anything dramatic, like in stories?"

"Dramatic, certainly. Not worthy of tale, though," he claimed. "I've served alongside knights and men at arms of all kinds, over the years. I helped put down the rebellion in county Monest, too."

"Did you fight in the battle of Peresque?" she asked out of curiosity.

"I did. That's probably the only thing I've ever done that's still talked about, though I believe Dame Ingred was hailed as the truest hero of that battle."

Abby nodded, very much familiar with the battle of Peresque from history books. It was the most recent reminder of the price of dissent; the failed last stand of rebellious nobles. "Was that your favourite thing you did as a paladin, or just the biggest?" she enquired.

Tahgri shook his head swiftly. "The only thing I enjoyed about that battle was knowing it was over. Most who've been unfortunate enough to see war for themselves would understand that," he claimed. "After the rebellion I joined the king's personal guard. Of course, it was only a few years before his brother sprang up and started spewing inflammatory nonsense. Mathew had to let me go when our order sided against him, but I think my time spent guarding him was probably my favourite work as a paladin."

Abby smiled. "You liked him, didn't you?"

"I did," admitted Tahgri. "His experiments were horrible things, truly, but that wasn't who he was as a person. He was a great man, and he could've been a great leader."

"You saw the experiments yourself?" Abby asked, finding herself curious. "They said he turned men into monsters."

Tahgri nodded. "As always, the victor writes history. He did make monsters, but not exactly out of men. He wanted to resurrect the heroes of old as something 'better' than mortal. It seemed like he was getting close by the end of the war, too. Of course, Thomas made that sound like such a bad thing to want. It was also conveniently forgotten that the war only started after he tried to assassinate the king. His own brother."

"Huh," Abby muttered. She hadn't heard that part before, though she supposed it didn't matter anymore. Mathew was dead, and Thomas had taken the crown. Nothing would change that. "What did they look like, the experiments?" she pried, scraping the wooden bowl with her cutlery.

"Ugly, especially at first," he claimed. Many Marathists had viewed Mathew's attempts to create something beyond human, elf, or dwarf as heresy, but Tahgri was probably one of the few still alive that had seen them first-hand. "To begin with they were just big, deformed people. As the war began they were starting to resemble the real thing physically, but in mind they were nought but children. They'd thrash around when they were first brought to life, it became necessary to restrain them to prevent them from injuring people around them. The last I heard, they were dead-eyed and passive things."

Abby grimaced at the thought. "Why did he do it?"

"Why not? What king doesn't want the latest technologies?" Tahgri pointed out. "Or the best soldiers, for that matter."

"I suppose so. So what was he really like? As a person, rather than a king."

"Well, in truth he'd never done all that well with his training; for a king he was remarkably poor with a sword, and he didn't have much of a mind for tactics, either. In other ways he was very smart, though. Almost scholarly, as a matter of fact. He saw no reason that faith in the Maralor and academic progress couldn't live side by side. Between you and me, he was once popular with the ladies as well; well-dressed and witty."

Abby laughed. "But was he nice?"

The paladin nodded. "He could be. Most of the time he was very pleasant, though his mood fell when the war began. I suppose I'm lucky to be able to remember him as he truly was. Fifteen years of war changes men, even the ones who aren't on the front lines."

Abby nodded thoughtfully. She could ask a thousand more questions, but she imagined that more talk of the war might lead to bitter memories for Tahgri, and so she switched subjects tactlessly. "Have you met the newcomer who does glasswork, by the way?"

He seemed confused by the sudden change of topic. "Not yet. Why?"

"Me neither," Abby continued to ramble. "I was going to talk to him this afternoon, but I didn't really feel like it after William. I thought the chapel would look nicer if it had some windows."

Tahgri nodded. "It probably would. Personally, I miss the old stone buildings."

"Are you suggesting we work on that?" she grinned.

He shook his head, smiling faintly. "I most certainly am not. I believe the Maralor would prefer to see real improvements to this place rather than superficial ones. Besides, as I do recall, our masonry coming to life was the downfall of our cities."

"It was," Abby agreed. "I'm not sure we've got the manpower to dedicate to proper masonry yet anyway, even if we did want it."

Tahgri nodded and scraped the last of his food out of the bowl. "Speaking of manpower, do you know if Daniel and Samson will be coming to training tomorrow?" he asked.

"I wouldn't count on it. I'll come by, though."

"People react differently to death. They might even find it a good way of coping, if they're willing to continue," Tahgri suggested.

"We'll see," Abby evaded, getting to her feet once again. "Now, let's get back in the kitchen. I'll teach you how to make that melon-ostrich."

Tahgri grunted softly, his knees betrayed by age as he stood. "Alright, alright. Just a moment," he insisted, stretching a little before following her.

"How did you manage to squire without learning to cook, anyway?" Abby asked. She expected that she would've passed with flying colours, had that ever been part of her time as an initiate.

"Well, I had the good fortune of serving Sir Moriene, who was a fussy eater. He adamantly refused to let me do the cooking after my first attempt. His personal cook stuck with him instead," he explained.

Abby chuckled and began to extract juice from the remaining melons. "Was Sir Moriene a good paladin?" she asked, making sure Tahgri's attention remained on the food preparation.

"He was a knight, actually. An odd fellow, but his heart was in the right place, and he knew how to use a sword."

"Oh right. Who ordained you, then?"

"Sir Eustace Moore," Tahgri claimed. "Now he *was* a good paladin, the Maralor rest his soul."

The rest of the evening went by quickly as they reminisced upon Tahgri's kinder memories and collaborated to prepare a marinade for the ostrich. Eventually they could do no more than let the meat soak, and so Abby hugged Tahgri goodnight and went home to relax as much as she could before she pushed her body to its limits in training again.

Johann was sat up waiting for her in bed. "How'd it go with Jaina?" she asked as she began to undress for the night's rest.

"Oh, it went well enough. Her cooking's improved - I suspect your hand in that," he smiled.

Abby chuckled and knelt for her nightly prayers. It was true; though Jaina had never been as incompetent as Tahgri when it came to culinary matters, she'd still been able to improve.

Johann gently crawled on top of her as she came to lay with him, his hands pawing at her breasts. She pushed him away gently as he tried to part her legs. "I'm not in the mood," she insisted. Still he persisted, pressing passionate kisses to her neck and bosom. It might've been pleasant, had she been at all interested at that moment. Regardless of her desires, he proceeded anyway, trying to gently ease her legs apart once again.

"I said no!" she barked, twisting her body and slamming him into the sleeping mat beside her. "Go to sleep," she ordered. The stunned silence told her that he was done with his advances.

Sleep did not come so easily that night.

***

Four hundred and ninety days. She awoke to find that Johann had returned the favour of breakfast in bed, his hand brushing her cheek to rouse her from slumber. "Hey," he greeted her. "Sorry about last night."

Abby nodded, trying hard to be understanding about it. "Is something bothering you?" she asked, taking the peace-offering of food.

Johann hesitated. "I don't know. It was just a weird day," he claimed.

She could understand that, given the death of William. "Well, don't do it again," she warned him.

Johann nodded guiltily. "I won't."

They ate in uncomfortable near-silence, uninterrupted by death this time, thankfully. "Were you going to check up on the Marshals today?" Johann eventually asked.

"Sort of. We've got training today - if they show up to that I'll see how they're holding up."

"And if they don't?"

"Then I'll check on them tomorrow and see if there's anything we can do for them," she informed him, slowly easing herself out of bed.

Johann seemed satisfied with her answer. "Alright. I'll see you later, I've got plenty of work to get on with," he claimed. Abby doubted that, though she resisted the urge to comment as he pulled on his shoes. The soles were beginning to wear out on them - she imagined that Carl knew how to make some repairs, though they could still do with a proper cordwainer in New Cray. They could do with a lot of things.

Abby dressed once Johann had gone, and made her way over to the sea of tents. They'd all relocated lately, the newcomers staying in the general proximity of the farmland rather than spread out all around the barn. "I'm looking for someone who works with glass!" she called out across the campsite.

There were a few relaying calls, and then a man emerged from his tent and strolled over to her, directed by those nearby. He had a narrow, angular face that didn't suit the big, black facial hair it sported. "Viktor Jacobson," he introduced himself. "What can I do you for?"

"Abby," she returned, shaking his hand. "I was just wondering, can you make windows for the chapel?"

Viktor chuckled. "Not without a glassworks. But yeah, if I had one, I could. I doubt you could get the materials for stained glass, though."

Abby smiled. "That's fine. I'll talk to..." her expression dropped as she remembered that she no longer had William to discuss options with. "Someone... about that. I'll be in touch regarding any requirements, I suppose."

Viktor nodded, clearly confused by her hesitation. "Alright. Catch you around," he dismissed her.

"Have a nice day," she added clumsily before walking over to the smithy. Much to her surprise, she walked in on what sounded like a somewhat heated discussion between Patrick and Michael.

"Ah, good timing," Patrick commented as Abby entered the building.

"Hey, Pat. What's going on?" she asked.

"I want you and my boys in training right now. Michael will be fine by himself," he claimed. She could tell from the look of irritation on Michael's face that he disagreed, and she couldn't say that Patrick's was a logical request, either.

"Tahgri's farming with Carmina this morning. We can't really train until the afternoon," Abby informed him.

"Well, tell Tahgri to drop it for the day," ordered Patrick. "Training's more important."t

"No it's not. Nobody's got anything to spare, and that's not likely to change any time soon. We can't afford to put off farming for the sake of training, or anything else for that matter," Abby insisted.

"Well if Tahgri won't do it then train them yourself. You managed it for a year, didn't you?" Patrick pestered.

"And now Tahgri's taken over. The training going fine as it is, Pat, I'm not going to interfere with it. If Daniel and Samson are up to it we'll train this afternoon, not before," she informed him.

Patrick groaned in frustration. "Abby, how do you expect me to lead if nobody listens to me? You're not helping."

Abby shook her head and gave him a reassuring smile. "Pat - I get it, but it's only been a day. Take some time, make sure you and your boys are alright. Nobody expects you to be a leader right now."

"We're fine, Abby," he insisted. It really sounded like the truth for a moment, though few would believe him. "But people here need someone to look to for guidance. Right now, that's got to be me."

She could see that if Patrick continued like this, nobody would look to him for leadership or guidance - or anything else, for that matter. "If you want to do something leader-like, talk to Viktor Jacobson. He could run a glassworks if we had one, we need to decide where to put it and get some carpenters to work with him," she suggested.

Patrick nodded grumpily and turned to leave. "I'll think about it," he grumbled.

"Prick," Michael muttered as soon as he was out of earshot.

"Be nice," Abby scolded. "It's just his way of coping."

"He's coping fine," Michael claimed. "He wants to be in charge but he hasn't got what it takes. Known that man all my life; born stupid, hasn't learned a thing."

Abby set to work in silence rather than feed the conversation and elicit more unpleasant comments from Michael. They smithed away until noon, Abby's work making nails a welcome distraction from the worries of the world. With that done, she tidied up after herself and said farewell in time for training.

Heading over to their usual training grounds, she was pleased to see that the entire ensemble was there. "How are you holding up?" she asked Patrick's sons, giving the bereaved pair a kindly smile.

"We'll live," insisted Samson, though he couldn't entirely hide that he was still in mourning. Daniel looked even more affected than his older brother, the telltale marks of recent crying on his face.

"Let's get stuck in, shall we?" suggested Tahgri, offering distraction.

They trained until the evening, when they were all exhausted and bruised. The absence of Samson and Daniel's usual enthusiasm was a bit of a dampener on the whole affair, but all things considered they did well for themselves. They'd all improved quickly since Tahgri had taken over training, Abby included. She was glad to be prepared further for when the elementals came. Nobody had seen anything since their hunting trip, but they were always at the back of everyone's mind. It was only a matter of time.

"Right, nice work everyone. I'll see you all again in two days' time?" Tahgri enquired. There were murmurs of agreement, even from Samson and Daniel.

"How would you like to bring that melon-ostrich round to mine and Johann's tonight?" Abby asked. She desired Tahgri's company again more than the food itself.

"That would seem fair," he agreed. "You did make it, after all."

"*We* made it," she corrected him, too used to flattery about her food to not assign credit where it was due. "I'll see you in a bit."

Tahgri strolled off, chatting with Carmina and Aurelius, but Daniel and Samson hesitated beside Abby. "Want to talk about it?" she offered.

"I wanted to say sorry about how I spoke to Johann. I know it wasn't really his fault," Daniel opened up.

"It was nobody's fault. We all have our time, and William lived a good life," Abby insisted. "And believe me, Johann will be fine, he's heard that sort of thing plenty of times."

"I just want grandpa back. After mum died he was always there for us. It was different from just dad, you know?" continued Daniel.

Abby stowed her hammer and embraced him in a stout hug. "I know, sometimes it doesn't seem like it's right. When my older brother died I was the same way. Took me a while to get back to where I am now. Just don't lose sight of what you have because of what you don't have, alright?" It was the best advice she could think of at that moment, though it felt somewhat lacklustre.

"Do you think we could stop talking about the Maralor in training?" Samson requested.

Abby nodded, as much as she disliked the thought. They weren't training as paladins, after all - their faith wasn't greatly important, just as long as their hearts were in the right place. "I understand. I'll talk to Tahgri about it," she agreed, removing herself from Daniel. "Don't be afraid to ask your father for help dealing with this stuff, by the way. I gathered he's not exactly sticking around to talk it over with you."

The brothers exchanged a brief, silent glance. "Thanks, Abby. We'll see you around," said Samson. They headed off, leaving her alone with a melancholic smile and an empty stomach.

Upon returning home, she found Johann chatting with some of his patients, as well as Jaina, who seemed to have nothing afflicting her at present. That much was a relief, as she'd recently suffered a string of small illnesses that had required Johann's attention. "Hey, Jaina. How's the farming coming along?" Abby pried, hoping that her diet was more varied than Tahgri's.

"Quite well, thank you, and I can see that your training is, too. If you get any stronger you'll look like some of the jailbirds I've worked with over the years," returned the lawyer.

Abby raised a brow, sceptical of the 'compliment.' "Uh, thanks? By the way, do you happen to know much about town planning?" she asked.

"A little bit, I suppose. You wouldn't believe how many laws there were regarding property ownership and such in the capital. I've worked with that a couple of times over the years," Jaina said airily, daring Abby to pry into the complexities of her former profession.

"Ah, good. I was thinking you may be in luck; with William gone, the town planner might need more assistance," Abby suggested.

Jaina smiled cheerfully, undoubtedly pleased by the possibility of some less laborious work. Perhaps it was a little cold of her to profit from William's death, but Abby knew that the two of them had barely even talked. Jaina probably hadn't felt much in the way of attachment to him. "I'll look into it," she agreed.

"Give it a few days, though. They only just buried William," Johann insisted. Abby nodded her firm agreement.

"Fine, fine. By the way, do you mind if I join you two for dinner tonight?" Jaina asked, doing her best to smile sweetly at Abby. As an ex-lawyer, it was hard to believe her portrayal of innocence.

"Sure. Tahgri's coming over as well, we should be able to make room for one more," agreed Abby.

Johann soon finished up with his patients. "Why don't you go and get changed, darling?" he suggested. Taking the hint, Abby nodded and strolled over to the bedroom, letting him entertain Jaina in her stead.

She removed her armour and changed into something less drenched with sweat, ready for dinner. The conversation wafted through from the other room; a brief gossip about one of the masons volunteering to make a proper tombstone for William. Most settled for wooden grave markers, if that.

"So, what happens with our northern neighbours now that William's not dealing with them?" Jaina soon asked.

"Good question. I suppose Abby knows more about that than I do," Johann admitted.

"Patrick wants to take over where his father left off, so I guess he'll handle negotiations for now," Abby called through.

"Patrick? Who put him in charge?" questioned Johann.

"Nobody, just like nobody chose William," said Jaina.

Abby strolled through, letting her hair down as she talked. "He's in a bad place right now. Give him time, see if he figures things out."

"I don't think he's got what it takes," admitted Jaina.

"Me neither," agreed Abby. "But if people start doubting him before we know for sure, it's just going to make things worse."

"Have you two considered running for leadership?" asked Johann.

Abby chuckled. "There's no 'running.' People will follow who they choose to," she insisted.

"Yes, but even I know that William was grooming you to take over from him," commented Jaina. "I reckon you'd do well at it."

"Contrary to what you might've heard, William never talked about leadership after his death, nor any plans he might've had for Patrick or myself," Abby corrected. "I learned a lot about how he handled logistics, but that's about as far as it went."

"Well you're still perfectly qualified, and you've certainly got your head screwed on straight," said Jaina, pressing the matter.

"Absolutely. You should do it," agreed Johann.

"I appreciate that you both think I'd make a good leader, but there's nothing to be done about it. I can't tell people what to do, they'll only follow me if they want to," Abby insisted. A knock at the door distracted her, and she turned to answer it, glancing back once more at the table. "How about we change subject? It's still too soon, really."

Abby let Tahgri in and saw him to the table. Once the greetings were over with she took the basket of food he'd brought and headed for the kitchen, tending to the meat as the others chattered away in the front room. She served it up with fried vegetables, the whole thing coming together with welcome ease.

"So you've not found a suitor yet then, Jaina?" asked Tahgri. Abby smiled as she joined them to eat. It was a much easier topic to discuss right now.

"Are you offering, Tahgri?" Jaina asked with a false laugh. "To be honest I'm quite enjoying the single life. I just have to get my thrills elsewhere," she continued before the paladin could respond.

"I can understand that. I never had much luck finding a wife, myself. I might've, if not for the war. These days, romance seems more effort than it's worth," commented Tahgri.

"You and Johann met after everything fell apart, didn't you Abby? Did you have a lover before that?" Jaina enquired.

"We did, yes," Johann answered for her. "But Abby scared off her old lover long before that. He was too intimidated by her training," he claimed.

"He was not!" insisted Abby, a piece of ostrich hanging limply from her fork, highlighting her indignation.

"Well the way you described it made it sound that way," he said defensively.

Abby rolled her eyes and gave Jaina a bemused smile. "A young man called George courted with me for a couple of years, until I was eighteen. My training meant that we didn't see as much of each other as we'd have liked, so it just sort of fell apart naturally because of that. What about yourself?"

Jaina chewed down a mouthful of food and shook her head. "Well, my last steady lover was hanged a fair while ago. A sad case of mixing work with pleasure, but I think I learned a lesson from that. This is really good, by the way," she complimented, jabbing at the food with her cutlery.

Abby blanched at Jaina trivialising her former lover's execution.

"Hanged?! Goodness! Not still licking your wounds from that, are you?" she questioned.

"Oh, not at all. I was over him before they even got him in a cell. He got convicted of murder, you see; I took his defence but there were three witnesses. There wasn't a chance he could have got away with it," Jaina elaborated.

Abby contemplated for a few awkward moments whether or not Jaina would've continued to associate with the man had she been able to worm him out of his punishment, and she had a feeling that everyone else was wondering the same thing. "What about you, Johann?" asked Tahgri, breezing over the matter with welcome grace.

"Well, I was studying up until the apocalypse, more or less. All that reading didn't leave me as much time as I'd have liked for women," responded the doctor.

"You know, I was saying to Aurelius a while back that he might meet someone in Lapden. You might, too, Jaina," Abby suggested.

Jaina grinned and eyed Johann. "Well, we can't all be as lucky in love as you are, but you never know."

They whiled away the rest of the evening discussing partners past and present, courtship, marriage, and even the possibility of parenthood. Although options were severely limited, romance was still a staple of conversation during the extinction. Gossip, it seemed, was as hard to kill as intelligent life.

Eventually, they saw their guests off for the night. The conversation had been just what Abby needed to remind her that life would go on without William. "Do you ever think about children?" Johann asked as they cleaned up after everyone. Nobody had been rude enough to pry about that over dinner, but it had probably been on their collective minds. Their relationship was getting to that point, after all.

"Sometimes, yeah. But we're not exactly in a good position to have any right now," she reminded him, dumping a bucket of filthy water out of the window.

"True, but what if it happens by accident?" he pressed.

"We'll cross that bridge if we come to it. As it stands, Aurelius and Carmina are enough children for me to look after," she grinned at him.

Johann chuckled. "Fair enough. Do you think Aurelius would actually take an interest in Jaina, by the way?"

Abby shrugged. "I'm not sure. I've never asked him, and I doubt he'd talk about it if I did," she admitted.

"You know, we *should* try to find him a suitable partner some time. From Lapden, probably."

Abby peered at him suspiciously. "Why the sudden interest in my brother's courting options?"

Johann shrugged. "I just think it would be good for him to have a partner of some sort," he claimed. "It seems almost cruel for him to be alone when he's coming into his prime."

"Well, we'll see what happens. There are plenty of single women in Lapden for some reason. Probably just as well, since Jaina doesn't seem interested, " Abby commented, considering the possibility that men were actually just a hive-mind dedicated to helping each other get laid.

"I really can't see Jaina together with him, anyway," Johann insisted. He regarded the dishes a moment, then smiled at her. "Why don't you let me finish up with these?" he offered. "You did the cooking, after all."

Abby kissed him goodnight. "Thanks," she agreed, and went straight to bed. There were no attempted advances when Johann joined her that night, of which she was glad. As much as her mood had picked up, she still wasn't interested.

The next day began like any other; prayers, breakfast, and a walk to the smithy. Rather than turning up to find Patrick arguing with Michael, however, the man turned up just before midday to disturb their peace again. "Abby," he called. She could sense the tension between him and Michael from the moment he entered the building. "Did you tell Viktor that I'd help him out with a glassworks?"

Abby shook her head. "I said I'd speak to someone about it and get back to him."

"Well, don't do things like that! You don't speak for everyone here," Patrick insisted crossly.

Abby frowned. "I didn't speak for anyone but myself. I *did* speak to you about it, and if you won't get back to him, then I will. If you're not interested in helping with the glassworks, leave it to me," she countered, managing to resist the urge to give him a lecture on his poor attitude. She didn't want to be that person right now, not whilst he was still grieving.

Patrick reddened with anger, pointing an accusing finger at Abby. "I think you've done enough! It's not your job to decide what industries we invest our time and resources into," he said forcefully.

Before Patrick could continue his rant, Michael rounded on him with competing fury on his face. "Leave us alone you feckless toad! We've important things to be on with, unlike you," he barked, brandishing his smithing hammer.

Patrick clearly wasn't so good at reaping what he sowed. With one last venomous look, he stormed off to do whatever it was he did when he wasn't wasting other people's time. "That's no way to get things done," Abby sighed, putting a calming hand on Michael's shoulder. She wasn't so keen on insults, though admittedly, she might've described Patrick similarly if she was being brutally honest.

Michael shrugged her hand away. "You're too nice. I'm not gonna stand here and let that pasty-faced layabout bully you. Nor me, for that matter."

Abby shook her head. "I can take care of myself, Michael. All we've done now is make an enemy of him."

"Stupidity was already everyone's enemy," Michael muttered, and returned to his work.

Abby set back to creating door hinges in grumpy silence. She liked Michael well enough, but these last couple of days it seemed that all she could think about was finishing up and going home. Time passed by at the pace of a crippled tortoise.

She sat on her sleeping mat that night, thinking over the events of the last few days. She could still barely believe that William was dead, but that wasn't what plagued her mind most, anymore; Patrick's strange mixture of incompetence and confidence was going to make life tricky for them. It was unlikely to be the last time he reacted poorly to people taking his leadership less than seriously, but he clearly wasn't going to be discouraged.

Abby clasped her hands together in prayer. "Corsein, grant us the leader we need."

9
Redchapel

She started awake at the sound of frantic knocking. No light was shining through the cracks in the shutters, and her brain immediately told her that she hadn't had enough sleep yet. *Five hundred and one days since we arrived? Five hundred, if it's still the night before.*

"What the fuck?" muttered Johann from beside her, shifting under the covers.

"Language," scolded Abby, her admonishment half-hearted thanks to exhaustion. She slipped out of bed and held the covers firmly to her front to retain her decency as she answered the door.

Tahgri stared down at her, his face serious. "There's been a murder. You need to come right now."

She stood there in shock for a few moments. Death by natural causes or elementals was one thing, but she'd never imagined that anything like this would happen here. "I'll be right out," she agreed, and dashed back over to get properly dressed, unconcerned that she'd just flashed Tahgri her bare arse.

"What's going on?" demanded Johann, getting to his feet as Abby clattered about the room.

"There's been a murder," she blurted out.

"What?! Should I come too?" he asked.

Abby hesitated a moment. "Yeah," she decided, and waited for him to dress as well.

The three of them met on the porch, still fastening various items of armour and clothing in place. "Where are we going?" Johann asked, looking between the two of them uncertainly.

"Chapel," grunted the paladin. Abby broke into a jog, the others in close pursuit.

The ground was soggy from rainfall earlier in the night. It was the earliest part of dawn, the very faintest glimmers of pink on the eastern horizon. The beauty of it did nothing to distract Abby from the tingling dread crawling through her skin. "When did you find the body?" she asked, slowing to a walk as she approached the chapel.

"Just now. I thought he'd just passed out or something at first, I didn't see the blood until I stepped in it," Tahgri explained.

"Why are you up so early, anyway? It's not even light," she boggled, pausing nervously outside the chapel door.

"Trust me, when you reach my age you'll understand," muttered the paladin.

Abby strode inside ahead of the other two, her nerves eating at her as she saw the body for herself. She eased the victim onto his back to identify him, the blood beneath so profuse that it sloshed around from the movement of the corpse. "Owen James," she informed them.

"I've treated him before. You knew him well?" asked Johann.

"Not well, but he came in here sometimes. He seemed nice enough," she told them. Her gaze was drawn to the Faralex in Owen's hands, soaked through with blood. Sighing, she pried it from his stiff, dead fingers and set it back on the altar. They'd need another copy.

"What do you want to do about it?" Tahgri asked.

"Why are you asking me? I've never dealt with anything like this," Abby pointed out.

"Well that makes two of us," said Tahgri.

"Three," corrected Johann. "But someone has to take charge, and it's not going to be me."

Abby considered for a moment, swiftly deciding that it may as well be her responsibility. "Fine. Uh, what can we tell from the body?"

Johann stepped over beside her. "You want me to do an autopsy?"

"Yeah. Tell me what you find," Abby ordered, stepping back to let him work.

It was still slightly too dark to make out everything in perfect detail, but Johann did his best, Abby and Tahgri listening intently as he worked. "The cause of death is most likely exsanguination. The neck has been cut once - very deeply - by what appears to be a blade of some sort. Not serrated, nothing unusual enough about it to help us narrow down the murder weapon," he explained. "He's cold and in rigor mortis. I'd say this was done last night rather than this morning."

Abby grimaced. "Anything else?"

"The blood splatters up the wall indicate that the murderer didn't get in the way of the blood spray, so we can probably rule out looking for the big, red man," continued Johann. "How about we move him to mine and get some light on him so that I can see properly?" he suggested.

Abby nodded, ignoring Johann's inappropriate humour. She was somewhat used to his detachment by now; he'd always claimed it was just how doctors coped with the constant presence of death in their work. "Alright. Help me with the body will you?" she instructed him. "Tahgri, go and wake some people up, Patrick and his sons at least." The paladin nodded sternly and strode off as they went to lift the body.

Abby took the underarms, trying to get as little blood on herself as possible. That wasn't so difficult, as the body had already bled most of its sanguine contents onto the floorboards of the chapel. With some difficulty, they hauled the corpse over to Johann's. "Should I light a lamp or something?" he asked as they carried Owen inside.

"No. It'll be light enough in minutes," Abby assured him, helping to set the body down on a bench and opening the shutters. The pale grey light of early morning caressed the corpse.

Johann waited a couple of minutes for the sun to better illuminate the room, then inspected the hands again, holding them up to what little light there was and squinting. "It seems like he put up a token fight. We might be able to look for bruises on the murderer," he commented.

Abby glanced down at her own arms and the marks left behind by training. She doubted they'd be able to use that to prove anything, unless Owen had managed to leave any significant injuries on his attacker.

Johann took no notice and turned the corpse over, inspecting the less obvious parts of the body. He frowned as he lifted the shirt, noticing a wound that hadn't been so obvious in the darkness. "Stabbed in the back," he commented, then hesitated. "No. The shirt isn't ripped."

Abby peered curiously as Johann dabbed at the blood, clearing the wound a little. "What's that?" he asked.

"It's the symbol of Corsein," said Abby, recognising it in an instant despite the obscuring blood. "Who would do something like this?"

"No idea. This could either be zeal or blasphemy, depending on how you look at it," Johan commented. "It must've been done after he was dead. The lines are very neat."

"Definitely blasphemy. No good Marathist would think this right, even by Corsein," insisted Abby.

Johann shook his head. "It's about the killer's opinions, not yours."

As much as she hated to admit that it could've been done in the name of the Maralor, she had to consider his point. "I suppose so. We should wait for the others and see what they think. Just so you know, Patrick's been acting weird since his father died. Try not to be too harsh on him if he acts like a-"

"Complete prick?" interrupted Johann. "You're not the only one to have noticed. Some of my patients have commented."

"Well, just be nice. I'm trying not to make things harder for him than they already are, as difficult as that is with the way he's acting."

They waited until Tahgi returned with the others. "Maralor protect us," Patrick growled as he saw the body. His boys stood beside him, observing the scene silently.

"Actually, that's somewhat ironic," commented Johann. He lifted the shirt again to show them all the symbol of Corsein.

"Avared's bells. I hadn't seen that," said Tahgri, looming over the others to observe the wound.

"You've had all that training to protect this place. Fetch Aurelius and Carmina, and start investigating," Patrick ordered.

"Well, this isn't exactly what we were training to defend against, but we've already started investigating. Were any of you out last night? Perhaps you might've seen something," Abby enquired.

Patrick shrugged and looked about at his sons. "I was in all night," he claimed. "So were my boys."

"We all went to sleep about sundown, got an early night. None of us have been near the chapel since grandpa died," Daniel confirmed.

Abby frowned at the mention of the chapel. "I told them on the way here," Tahgri explained before she could question it.

"Alright. We'll try asking around the village once everyone's up. In the meantime, I think we can narrow it down somewhat," she suggested. Stepping closer to Owen, she tapped the symbol of Corsein on his back. "Whoever the killer is, they either really love or really hate the Maralor. Or Corsein, specifically."

"Were I a betting man I'd say it's hate," commented Samson.

Abby paused briefly, wondering if he realised he'd just pointed a finger at his own family. "Well, we won't rule out anything yet. Daniel, Samson - people will start to rise soon. I need a symbol of Corsein just like the one on his back. A wood carving should do just fine. I also need you to gather all the people who are known to have strong feelings about the Maralor."

"You realise that includes - and is, in fact, probably exclusively - you and Tahgri, right?" pointed out Daniel.

"And Samson, unfortunately. But Johann can account for me, and you for Samson," Abby added.

Samson didn't protest the fact, although he was clearly displeased that anyone was considering him as a suspect. "What about you, Tahgri? I don't believe you did it, but you did find the body," he questioned.

"I fell asleep after I ate last night," Tahgri claimed. "But as you know, I live alone, so I suppose I'm the only one here without someone else to prove my whereabouts. I'll have to live with what people make of that."

"Well isn't that just great," Patrick muttered, looking irritated as he took a seat on an unoccupied medical bench. "Hopefully nobody starts pointing fingers at you."

"Alright. Forget about the whole loving or hating the Maralor thing, but I'm still gonna need that symbol. Tahgri, could you watch the body while I fetch Carmina and Aurelius, please? Johann, I want you to stop anybody going into the chapel for the time being." Everyone set about their respective tasks without delay.

She let the door slam a little as she walked into her family's house, hoping the sound would rouse everyone for her. Aurelius stepped out in only his underwear, his eyes bleary. "What's going on?" he demanded.

"There's been a murder. I'm going to need you and Carmina to help me investigate," she explained.

"A murder?" questioned her mother in disbelief, emerging from the master bedroom. "Who's dead?"

"Owen James. You and dad can stay here until everyone else starts waking up, the fewer people involved the better right now," said Abby.

Carmina peeked out of her own bedroom, looking understandably concerned. "Get dressed, and bring your knives just in case," Abby ordered. Her siblings did exactly as they were told, and Abby turned back to her mother, who was clearly upset by the news.

"Does his wife know?" asked Alexander, a strange mixture of shock and exhaustion on his face as he appeared behind his wife.

Abby shook her head. "Not unless she was the one who killed him. I guess I'm going to have to break the news to her. And his mother," she sighed, dreading the thought already. "Get some rest. I'll talk to you two about it later."

Her parents nodded and returned to bed, theorising energetically with each other about the nature of the crime. Carmina and Aurelius soon returned fully dressed, following Abby out towards Johann's house. "You two know the symbol of Corsein, right?" she checked.

"Of course, but I've not really had a lot of time for that sort of thing, lately," said Aurelius.

"Same here. Why?" asked Carmina.

"Owen had it carved into his back. We figure whoever killed him either really loves or really hates Corsein," she explained.

"Well, Samson's not exactly been subtle about blaming the gods for William's death," Aurelius contributed.

Abby nodded. "And anger at Corsein is traditionally associated with personal loss - it occurred to me, but they have an alibi; the whole family was in together last night," she informed him.

"But they're all related! They all lost William, doesn't that mean they could be conspiring or something?" asked Carmina.

Abby nodded. "Of course it does, but it's all we've got to work with. Besides, there's no other evidence to suggest that it might've been one of them. They're hardly the only people out here to have lost someone."

"Alright, fine. So what are we doing about it?" asked Aurelius.

"Well, we're going to need to talk to absolutely everyone we can about this. That'll be a lot quicker with all of us. Also, can you think of anyone other than Samson who's shown a strong like or dislike of the

Maralor?" Abby asked them.

"You and Tahgri. Honestly, you two are the only others that come to mind with any sort of strong feelings towards the gods," said Carmina. "Or maybe mum."

"To be honest, we haven't ruled out Tahgri yet, either. He was by himself, and as much as I don't believe it was him, the evidence sort of fits him, too," admitted Abby. She wasn't concerned about that, though. It was hardly enough evidence to incite a lynch mob against Tahgri - which was just as well, since a mob probably wouldn't stand up too well against him.

"Well that's a kick in the head," Aurelius grumbled as he followed Abby through Johann's door.

Daniel was back already, chattering with Tahgri. "Samson's with Herman. He said he could probably make you a little symbol of Corsein like that out of wood. Shouldn't take too long," he informed Abby.

"Thanks. So, we've got to figure out how to approach this. Everyone in this room is already accounted for at the time of the murder, except for Tahgri. I'm of the opinion that the best route is to talk to everyone it could've been, and try to get them to rule out anyone they were with when it happened," she suggested.

Patrick gestured vaguely to Carmina and Aurelius. "I guess you two didn't see anything last night, either?"

"What's that supposed to mean?" snapped Carmina.

"It's just a question, Carmina. Everyone's going to be asked it," Abby sighed, struggling to remain civil.

"We were both in with mum and dad all night. We couldn't have seen anything," insisted Aurelius, ignoring Patrick's obvious distaste at the moody response.

"Alright. Well, so far we have no witnesses, and only the symbol of Corsein as a lead. Are there any objections to me dealing with the people who were in the chapel yesterday while you all talk to the others?" asked Abby. "After that we can see what we can find by cross-referencing. Perhaps someone was spotted going out late last night, or something."

The assembly glanced around with uncertainty, though they were absent of any objections. "Alright. It seems like you've got this under control, I'll be in my house if you need me," said Patrick.

"But... we do need you. We could use your help," Abby requested.

"This is your job. Let me do mine," Patrick insisted, and left.

Abby sighed, her mood further soured by yet another moment of stupidity from Patrick. "We should probably make an announcement before everyone starts gossiping. Do you think we could gather everyone in front of the chapel?"

111

"Sure. Might take a while, though," said Aurelius.

"So, what exactly are we asking people? I take it you're not going to be questioning the entire village by yourself," Daniel enquired.

Abby nodded. "I was hoping you'd all help me with that, yeah. Just try to ask about who people were with, what they were doing, and if they saw anyone near the chapel yesterday. Anything that narrows down who could've killed Owen."

"Alright. Shall we get this over with?" suggested Carmina, gesturing to the door. Abby nodded, and they all set to it.

She took a few minutes to wander aimlessly and set her mind in order before strolling over to relieve Johann of his position on the chapel steps. The crowd, already gathering, grew further as her assistants fetched more people. "What's the plan?" asked the doctor, putting an arm around her armoured waist.

"I need to appeal for help. Someone might've seen something useful, whether or not they realised it at the time."

The assembly swelled until there were more than four hundred in the crowd. She recognised most of them - others were strangers from the tent encampment. "What are we all here for?" a voice called from amongst them.

Abby looked around briefly, hoping Daniel or Samson would show up to tell her if more were coming, but she couldn't spot the brothers. In favour of not keeping the crowd waiting, she spoke up. "There's been a murder." The reaction was less dramatic than she'd expected; a ripple of whispers spread, and before the noise got out of control she continued. "This morning, Sir Dunwolf found the body of Owen James. He was murdered late last night, in the chapel."

A single cry of sorrow rose above all the others, no doubt Owen's wife or mother. The whispering crescendoed to a scandalised thrum, and Abby raised her voice to be heard over it. "Some of us are attempting to figure out who's behind it, and we'd appreciate it if we could talk to all of you, one at a time, in case any of you saw something that could help us. If anyone's not willing to talk to us, you may as well leave now."

She paused there, but nobody left. There would be certain unpleasant implications to doing so, of course. "Anyone who was in the chapel at any point yesterday, please come and talk to me. Anyone else, please form orderly queues and talk to Daniel, Carmina, Samson, Johann, or Aurelius," she concluded.

The crowd began to mill about, chaotic and confused at first, but soon forming into smaller groups as Abby's assistants led people away into separate areas. A group of chapel-goers approached, including a woman that Abby recognised as Owen's mother. "Are you sure it's him?" she asked, tears threatening to burst forth.

Abby nodded solemnly, struggling to keep her face level. "I'm afraid so, Katherine." The tears began to flow.

Abby would've comforted her, but Owen's wife - Amanda - was also amongst those present, and got to Abby first. The shock was clear on her face, the evidence of her disbelief reinforced by her question. "Can we see the body?"

Abby scanned the crowd. "Tahgri!" she called out. Within moments, the paladin stood before her. "Would you take Katherine and Amanda to see Owen, please?"

Tahgri nodded, giving the bereaved an apologetic look. "Right this way," he instructed, leading them to Johann's house.

Abby turned back to the others that had gathered around her. "Right, let's start with the obvious - did anyone see anything they'd immediately think might be related to this?"

The group seemed uncertain of themselves, glancing at each other to see if anyone would speak up. "Can't say I did," admitted one of them. There was a murmur of agreement that betrayed the fact that she'd find no useful responses to that question.

"Alright. Which of you went to the chapel yesterday morning?" Abby continued. Three of them raised their hands. "And the evening?" The rest all raised theirs.

"But I didn't see any body then," one of them informed her, a young man whose name stuck at the tip of her tongue.

"I gathered as much. Did any of you see each other in the chapel? I'd like to know which of you was the last to leave the building," questioned Abby.

"I saw Margaret as I left. I went in just before dinner," contributed a middle-aged man, pointing out the woman in question.

"Alright. Maggie, did you see anyone come in after you?" enquired Abby, doing her best to seem friendly. If she pushed too hard, she might just lose their assistance entirely.

"Oh yes. Irene and her husband came in after me," Margaret offered.

"And Sophie came in after us," Irene supplied.

"I spoke with Owen outside the chapel after I left," admitted Sophie. She had a measure of worry to her voice, as if she was expecting people to jump to the conclusion that she was the killer because of that fact.

"If you saw Owen before he entered the chapel, that probably makes you the last person to see him alive," said Abby.

"Other than the murderer," corrected Sophie.

"Yeah, other than that," Abby agreed, suffering through the pedantry.

"Steven and I came in after Sophie, but we left before her as well. We glimpsed Owen walking to the chapel," contributed a vaguely familiar woman, gesturing to her husband.

"Alright, thanks everyone. Sophie, was anything amiss in the chapel by the time you left?" asked Abby.

"No. It all looked normal to me," she claimed.

Abby sighed, seeing that this wasn't going to be as simple as she'd initially hoped. "Alright. Did you interact with Owen at all? Did he say or do anything that you took note of?"

Sophie shook her head. "It was nothing unusual. He just smiled at me, and we chatted a little before he went into the chapel. I don't remember what about, it was just the normal sort of thing."

"So you don't remember anything he said? He didn't sound panicked or concerned in any way?" continued Abby.

"No. If anything, it was the opposite. He was... happy. Not really sure why, but he was definitely in a good mood."

Abby nodded. "What time did he leave you to go inside, and where did you go afterwards?"

"Oh, it was late by then. The sun had been down properly for a little while, so I went home. At a guess, I'd say it had been dark around twenty minutes, maybe," recalled Sophie.

"Alright. Thanks, everyone. If you could all go and speak to the others now, I'll grab their attention," Abby dismissed the group. She stood in the chapel doorway and raised her voice as the others ambled off. "Samson, Daniel, Carmina, Aurelius, Johann!"

Soon enough, the five of them stood in front of her, queues of people they'd been talking to gathering behind each of them. "It's confirmed that the murder took place around half an hour after sundown. I'm going to need everyone to tell these five where you all were and who you were with around that time last night. Hopefully, by doing this we can narrow down the list of suspects to people who have no witnesses as to their location, so please try to recall as accurately as possible who was where, and when," she requested. Johann gave her an encouraging thumbs-up and turned straight back to work with the crowd.

Abby left the five of them to it and quickly did another sweep of the chapel. The morning sun had revealed nothing, not a single clue save for Owen's blood, and so she headed back to Johann's, hoping to get some answers from the victim's grieving family.

The sound of heartfelt sobbing filled the air as she entered, and she waited in respectful silence for what she hoped was a good moment to speak. "I'm sorry for your loss. We're doing all we can to find out who's behind it," she assured them.

"You haven't found them yet?" demanded Amanda.

Abby shook her head, mentally preparing herself to stay calm under the pressure to succeed. "We're working on it. We figured out who last saw him alive, and the others are currently narrowing down the suspects to people who weren't with anyone else at the time of the murder."

"Shouldn't you be helping them, then?" Katherine asked, somehow managing to sound bossy even in the aftermath of tears.

Abby nodded. "Actually, that's why I'm here. I was hoping I could ask you two some questions about last night?"

"You don't actually think we had anything to do with it, do you?" snapped Amanda.

"I don't, but that doesn't mean I'm not interested in what you can tell me," Abby returned. "It might help, it might not - but it certainly won't hurt."

The women exchanged an awkward glance, then Amanda stepped up to Abby. "I don't see how I can help, but I'll try."

"Did Owen leave for the chapel after it was dark, or while it was still light? I've seen him there enough times to know that he was out later than he usually is," Abby probed.

"He definitely left after it had gone dark," Amanda claimed after a moment of deliberation. "I don't know exactly how long after."

Abby nodded. "The last person who saw Owen alive commented that he was particularly cheerful. Can you think of any reason for that?"

Amanda began to weep again. It was more graceful this time, though it still caused her to choke on her words a little. "I told him that I'm with child."

Abby lost her words a moment and clasped her arms around Amanda. Evidently this was news to Katherine as well, as the older woman soon pulled her out of Abby's embrace to do the same. "I'm sorry to pry, but knowing all of this helps more than you might think," Abby informed them when she finally swallowed the lump in her throat.

"Did he have any enemies, or even simple disputes with anyone?" questioned Tahgri, finally breaking his silence from the corner.

"No! Nothing like that. I can't even remember the last time I heard him differ with someone," claimed Amanda.

"What did you think when he didn't come home last night?" Abby asked, a question she'd been pondering from the start.

Amanda shook her head. "I didn't. I fell asleep right after he left. This morning... I guess I just thought he was out working the field already."

"Alright. Thanks," concluded Abby, turning to Katherine next. "Were you with Amanda last night at all?"

"No, I was alone all of last night," recalled the older woman. "But I didn't kill my own son!" she added forcefully.

As much as Abby wished that she could rule either of the women out entirely, she knew that she had to consider them to the same degree that she considered Tahgri as a potential suspect. "I don't believe either of you did it or even knew about it," she offered the pair in consolation. "I'd be surprised if there were fewer than fifty people who had no witness to prove their location, and there's still the possibility of a conspiracy to provide witness for false alibis. Nobody's going to be pointing fingers at anyone - especially you - unless we have more solid evidence."

"Good," snapped Katherine.

"Thank you both for your help. I'm going to get back to the others," said Abby, offering them both a coroner's smile before turning to leave.

"Wait," Amanda urged before Abby could get out the door. "What do I do? I'm all alone again, I won't be able to take care of myself *and* the child," she sobbed.

Abby turned back around to face her. "I don't know, Amanda. Appeal to your friends for help, I suppose," she suggested. "I'll give you what I can spare, but frankly I'm not even going to be farming for myself until I've done everything I can regarding this investigation." Amanda simply nodded glumly and sat down beside Owen's body to continue mourning.

Abby strode back out to meet the others, leaving Tahgri to attend the needs of the bereaved. Confronting those two had taken its toll on her, and she paused at the back of the crowds to clear her mind again. It seemed that her helpers had been steadily working their way through the interviews in her absence, though there were still many more to get through. She took up position on the steps of the chapel once she'd gathered herself, and called out over the thrum of people talking. "Okay! I'm now assisting, so please share the load a little and come talk to me if you're near the front of the queues!"

People glanced at her and quietened down as they reorganised, and soon enough she had her own slowly growing queue to deal with. One of her many acquaintances stepped up first, smiling regretfully at her. "Hey, Mark. Thanks for helping," she began.

"Could've been any of us that died," he said solemnly. "It's only right I do my part."

She nodded agreeably and got on with it. "I need to know everything about last night, after sunset - where you were, who you were with, anyone you might've seen about."

"I went over to Ulrich's to break bread. Literally, for once - his family recently had a good harvest of wheat. I was with them all evening, then I headed back to mine for the night," Mark claimed.

"Did you see anyone on the way back?"

"On the way back? I didn't see anyone at all. Not all that surprising, really, it was well after sundown."

"And then you went straight to bed?"

"Not quite, I stopped by the latrine before bed," he appended. "Didn't see anything helpful then, either, I'm afraid."

"Alright. Thanks, Mark. No need to keep you any longer," she said with as much cheer as she could muster. He gave her another smile before wandering off. "Okay, next!"

The day dragged on as they gradually worked their way through the villagers. The impatience on the faces of Abby's trusted helpers slowly grew, matched well with the expressions of those who had waited for far too long to be interviewed. Abby made sure to thank each and every one of them before they left, even though she didn't feel like doing so by the time she neared the end of her queue.

The other interviewers all met her as they finished their work, the load divided evenly enough that none of them kept the others waiting for long. "Well, I was shocked and amazed to find that everybody in the entire village could talk in such detail about how little of interest they did last night," complained Johann.

Abby looked around at the others, immediately gathering from their somewhat vacant expressions that none of them had found anything that seemed to be of particular note. "If we're all on the same page, how about we go back to Johann's and sift through all of this, see what we can find when we put our heads together?" she suggested. Murmuring reluctant agreement, the others all followed her over, quickly settling in around the table in Johann's front room.

Tahgri soon joined them, looking dazed and confused. "The others left with the body," he informed them, glancing back at other room.

"Were you napping?" Abby asked him, squinting suspiciously.

"You *were* gone for quite a while," he said defensively.

"Be fair. Old people need their sleep," muttered Carmina.

"Thanks for that," grumbled the paladin.

"You may as well join us, Tahgri. You're better rested than any of us now," suggested Abby. He came over to the table, the lack of chairs forcing Abby to give up her seat for him. "Alright. I suppose now would be the time to cross-examine what we can remember, and single out anyone whose story was inconsistent with others, or had no witnesses for them."

"That could take forever!" complained Aurelius.

"Nothing takes forever. This is our job for now," Abby scolded, and so they began. The exercise in frustration dragged on for hours; the details of so many stories were somewhat blurry with no written record, and they'd run out of ink before William's death. Nobody knew how to create more from the resources they had available.

It wasn't until late afternoon that Tahgri pointed out the one and only inconsistency they'd found. "That fellow Jonas said he was in his house all night, didn't he? But I'm sure the Wilkinsons' daughter said she saw him near *their* house?"

"I think so?" Abby asked uncertainly, looking around the table. She had a headache from strenuous thought, and got the impression that she wasn't the only one afflicted in that way.

Samson nodded. "That's definitely what Jonas said. Who talked to the Wilkinsons' daughter?" he quizzed.

Johann raised his hand slightly. "That's Michelle, right? I talked to her... and I think you're right." There was a moment of apprehension as everyone silently considered what that meant.

"Alright. Motives?" asked Abby. Nobody had any suggestions, and she certainly couldn't think of any. Jonas was an easily forgettable man that had yet to do anything unusual or unexpected in New Cray.

"I've met him a few times. He occasionally gets ill, but he's no worse off than anyone else here. As far as I know, he barely knew Owen and he didn't have any particularly strong feelings about the Maralor," the doctor contributed.

"Alright. You guys all get some rest - Tahgri, would you come with me to talk to him?" requested Abby.

Normally, Carmina and Aurelius might've been upset at being left behind for something this important, but Abby suspected that they were too bored and tired from the work to be unhappy about being allowed to rest.

"Let us know how it goes," insisted Daniel before getting up to leave. Everyone but Johann followed Abby out the door, dispersing into pairs to go their separate ways.

"Do you know where Jonas lives?" Tahgri asked on the move.

"I helped build his house," Abby told him. "It's near the Wilkinsons', but if he went that way it wasn't just a latrine visit. It's in the wrong direction for that."

"Have you put any thought into what to do if it is him?"

"If we can prove without a doubt that it's him, I suppose we're going to have to find some way to imprison him. I'm not too big on the idea of execution," she responded. Tahgri fell into a foreboding silence as they approached the house. The sun seemed impossibly high in the sky after what felt like such a long day of work.

She knocked heavily on Jonas' door and waited impatiently. There were the sounds of alarmed motion from within, and a short while later the door opened just enough for Jonas to stick his head out. He was clearly at least partially naked, hiding his body behind the door. "Hey Jonas, sorry if this is a bad time. We were hoping you could answer a few more questions regarding what you said earlier," Abby greeted him.

Jonas nodded warily. "What sort of questions?"

"You said you were in all night. You didn't go out after sunset at all? Not even to the latrines?" demanded Tahgri.

"No," insisted Jonas. "That's what I said, and it's the truth."

"But someone claimed they saw you near the Wilkinsons' after dark," continued the paladin. "Care to explain that?"

Jonas glanced over his shoulder nervously. "Shit," he grumbled. Abby raised a brow, unimpressed with his lack of defence but still struggling to believe that it could've been him. "I think you'd better come in. Just give me a moment to get dressed," he insisted.

"Jonas!" exclaimed a female voice from inside, the tone disapproving.

Abby exchanged a glance with Tahgri as the door was shut again. "Any idea who that was?" she asked him. Tahgri shook his head, looking very much ready to burst into action. Fortunately, it wasn't like Jonas could run anywhere, and Abby thoroughly doubted he could fight either of them, let alone both. She waited a few moments more before pushing inside, her patience spent.

Walking into the bedroom, they found Jonas along with the formerly unknown woman, both in a state of half-dress and pulling on the rest of their clothes frantically. "Mrs. Sutton?" Abby gawped. She quickly recovered herself and looked between the two demandingly.

"I'm sorry," Jonas said to his apparent lover. "It was either they know this or they think I'm a murderer," he insisted.

"Explain," demanded Abby, though in truth she didn't need them to.

"Please don't tell my husband!" begged Mrs. Sutton.

Abby raised a hand to quiet the pair. "I can't say I approve, but I'm not here for that; I'm trying to find a killer. Tell me the truth about last night, and I won't tell anyone the truth about *this*."

Jonas sighed and pulled on a shirt, seating himself on the bed to explain. "Last night I paid Francine a visit, and that's the truth of it. Whoever saw me probably did it on my way back home. I left as her husband came back from working the fields."

Abby groaned and glanced back over at Francine Sutton, who was now looking incredibly guilty. "Is that true?"

"Yes, it's true! We didn't kill Owen or anyone else, now leave us to our own business!" she insisted.

The pair seemed genuine enough, and given that they'd caught them with their trousers very literally down, Abby was inclined to believe them. "Come on, Tahgri, we're done here. Thank you both for your

119

help," she muttered, liberally applying sarcasm as they left.

"Unbelievable. Shall we tell anyone about their indiscretions?" Tahgri asked, slamming the door behind them.

"No, I told her I wouldn't. If anyone asks, it was a dead end."

"If you're sure," Tahgri agreed. "What next, then?"

"I guess now I'm going to have to re-interview everyone who had nobody to confirm their alibi," she sighed.

"Well, at least we've narrowed it down a lot."

"That's always a bright side. You should get on with farming, I can handle this part alone. It's going to be dull anyway," Abby offered.

Tahgri nodded and gave her a gentle pat on the shoulder. "Good luck. And keep a weapon on you," he advised. "It could turn ugly if you find out who it is."

The pair went their separate ways, Abby heading over to the nearest well first of all. All the talking today had proven to be thirsty work, and her throat was beginning to feel a little hoarse for it.

"Abby!" called Carl as she hoisted the bucket. She forgot the water momentarily and turned to face him. "They asked me to bring you this," he said, approaching with the symbol of Corsein she'd requested.

She smiled sweetly at him and took the piece of woodwork, eyeing the carefully carved angles. "Thanks, Carl. What are people saying about all of this?"

"Some people reckon it's Tahgri, but I doubt it," he shrugged. "I was wondering if you'd found anything yet, to be honest."

Abby frowned. "Nothing too solid. It wouldn't be right for me to tell you all about it right now, but I can tell you that there's no real evidence for it being Tahgri. Let me know if you hear anything, though, won't you?" she responded.

Carl nodded. "Sure. I'll see you later, Abby."

She tucked the symbol of Corsein into her belt and waved him off. "Take care. Do yourself a favour and stay armed until we figure out who's behind this," she called after him, passing along the advice.

Abby turned back to the well for a refreshing drink before heading off to get down to business once again. She hoped with her new tool she could scare some interesting reactions out of their suspects.

10
Tailor of Creation

She cried in Johann's arms, feeling truly awful. It had been a week since the murder, and for all of her efforts there was not one thing to go on that would lead them to a culprit. Her work with the symbol of Corsein had ruled out a few suspects, but even that couldn't be certain, since the murderer could also be a very good liar.

The rest of the investigation had become a repetitive cycle of cross-referencing stories until everyone had become impatient and unwilling to offer any more help. Amanda had kept asking if there was any progress, and Abby had finally had to confess that they were unlikely to succeed. Owen's loved ones had taken the news poorly, but even if that hadn't been the case, Abby still would've felt awful knowing that they might never see justice for their beloved. She simply sat there being comforted by Johann. At least he wouldn't judge her for her failure; she wasn't so sure about anyone else.

They were eventually pulled from their little bubble of emotion by a knock on the door. "I'll deal with it," offered Johann, planting a kiss on her forehead. She slumped and tried to compose herself as he went to see who it was. She couldn't bear for anyone else to see her like this.

"Good morning," Abby heard an unfamiliar woman greet Johann. "I was told I could find Abby here?" Abby frowned and got to her feet, wiping her eyes and strolling over to see who it was. "Oh, is this a bad time? I could come back later if it's no good for you?"

Abby knew she must look terrible to draw such a reaction. "No, it's fine. How can I help?" she asked, genuinely hoping there was something she could do to take her mind off of her own failure.

"I take it you're Abby, then? I'm here looking for the leader of this place. I understand William died, the Maralor rest his soul, and you seem to have taken over where he left off."

"I am Abby, but we've never really elected a leader. People just try to help wherever they can," she responded, wondering who the woman had been talking to.

"Well, everyone I've asked seems to view you as the leader, so that's good enough for me," the stranger insisted.

Abby took a moment to scrutinise the woman; she was old - maybe as old as Tahgri - but she carried herself with an air of grace and dignity. "Well, how can I help you, Mrs?"

"Vanessa De Burges," she introduced herself, stepping closer and shaking Abby's hand.

"Arboneth Koning, but I tend to go by Abby," she returned. "Have I seen you in Lapden before?"

Vanessa nodded and shook hands with Johann, too. "I'm Doctor Johann Ellis. Abby and I are together," he introduced himself.

Vanessa smiled back, then promptly adopted a businesslike manner. "You've probably seen me talking with William before. I'm here to discuss the merge with Lapden - William knew that it was coming, and we're bordering on interfering with each other now. Our leadership has decided that it would be in everyone's best interest if we had some sort of formal structure, and we'd like to take that up with you, if you're interested," she explained.

"I think it would be best if we all sat down and had a talk, Mrs. De Burges," suggested Abby, leading her inside. Truth be told, even though this opened up a whole bundle of issues regarding Patrick's leadership, Abby was glad that the subject had come up. It kept her mind entirely away from Owen, Amanda, and Katherine.

"Please, just call me Vanessa. The formalities can wait until later."

"I'd offer you something to eat, Vanessa, but I'm afraid there's little to spare right now," Johann apologised.

Vanessa waved the notion away. "It's no bother. So, is there some issue with the idea?" she asked.

Abby nodded faintly and directed them all to the table. "There's an issue, but it's not with the merge. William's son - Patrick - thinks he's in charge around here, but nobody's elected him and I don't think anybody wants him to lead," she elaborated once they were all seated.

"So he has no support? I don't see how that could be a problem, then," Vanessa said confidently.

"Just his sons, and I'm not even sure about where they stand with him at the moment. I don't see why he'd oppose a merge, and I don't see why we shouldn't have some sort of meeting to discuss it," Abby agreed. "I'm just worried he'll try to take charge of something that nobody wants him involved in."

Vanessa smiled. "Well, I'm glad that we see eye to eye on the idea of a meeting, at least. I don't really see the problem with Patrick, though, if I'm entirely honest. He can't take charge of anything if nobody will listen to him."

"I wish it was that simple. I know we could just tell him to leave us alone, but I don't want to alienate anyone," Abby explained.

"I see. Well, Lapden has no such leadership issues, and everyone's eager to begin. Is there any way that we could proceed sooner rather than later?" Vanessa asked.

Abby pondered a moment. "I'm going to talk to Patrick about it. It might seem counterproductive, but I want to keep him in the loop so that he doesn't take it the wrong way. He seems to lack the focus to actually involve himself since William's death anyway."

Vanessa nodded. "Could I come with you, since I'm here already? Perhaps I can be a little less diplomatic with him."

Abby arched a brow. "You want to go right now?"

Vanessa nodded. "What better time than now?"

"Well… alright then." Abby got to her feet, the others soon following her. "But don't be too harsh, will you? He's still mourning his dad, and to make things worse there's been a murder since."

"A murder?" enquired Vanessa, obviously surprised.

"Yes, unfortunately so. I don't suppose you've had any in Lapden, have you?" Johann queried. "We haven't ruled out the possibility that the killer wasn't from New Cray."

"No, thankfully we have not," responded Vanessa.

They made their way over towards the Marshal household. "What do you think Patrick will say about all of this?" Johann enquired as they walked.

"He'll probably insist that he's in charge, then let someone else do all the work anyway," Abby sighed.

"Sounds about right," the doctor concurred.

"By the way, are there any others here that are held in similar regard to you, Abby? We'd much prefer a broader perspective if we were to convene on the matter," Vanessa commented.

"Sir Dunwolf is a paladin of the Maralor. He's a bit newer here than a lot of us, but he's a hard man to disrespect," Abby suggested.

"That hardly broadens the perspective, though, does it? You and him are like two sides of the same coin," pointed out Johann.

"I guess so," Abby considered. As much as she wished to be seen as unique, any faithful member of their order was bound to have a lot in common with her.

"I believe Jaina's suited to this sort of work, and about as trustworthy as a lawyer could be," suggested Johann, grinning cheekily.

Vanessa laughed and nodded. "Well, I do hope you'll give it some thought before the meeting, anyway."

Abby knocked on Patrick's door. "Come in!" called his voice from within. The three pushed inside and walked through to the next room, where Patrick was sat opposite Viktor Jacobson. Samson and Daniel were nowhere to be seen, no doubt working on the farm. "Ah! Your timing's perfect, Abby."

"It is?" she questioned, suspicious after what had happened last time he'd made such a claim.

"I was just telling Viktor that I'd have you take over work on the glassworks. There are more important matters at hand for myself."

Such as walking around delegating all your potential work to other people, and claiming that you're busy. Abby knew full well that if Patrick hadn't dealt with the glassworks by now he'd probably done exactly nothing whilst she'd been trying to investigate Owen's death. "That's not been arranged yet? I assumed you'd dealt with it a week ago," she admitted, hoping to gently illustrate his uselessness. "Still, as you mention important matters - this is Vanessa De Burges. She's come from Lapden to discuss the merge."

Vanessa stepped over and shook Patrick's hand. "Ah yes, I think I recall my father mentioning you. I'll be taking over where he left off," he smiled at her.

"Actually, I've been told that Abby's the woman to talk to if you want to get things done since William passed away - my condolences, by the way. Abby insisted that we keep you abreast of the situation, though," responded Vanessa. Remarkably, she managed to keep any vestiges of intentional disrespect from her voice.

Nobody in the room seemed to know how to take her words; Johann shot Abby an amused glance, whilst Patrick searched for a polite way of replying. Viktor simply hid his smirk behind a hand. "Well," Patrick managed after a drawn out silence. "Abby's right to keep me informed. I'm afraid you've been misled by whoever told you to speak to her about this, though."

"I'm quite certain I wasn't, as it was several different people who were of the same opinion," corrected Vanessa. "Regardless, Abby has expressed a wish for you to join us in meeting, and so I'm here to extend the invitation to you, as well as any others that Abby feels should be there."

Patrick seemed entirely unsure of himself in a manner that Abby hadn't really seen before, even when Michael had practically chased him out of the smithy. She supposed it was easier to know how to react to more direct insults than to Vanessa's brand of polite put-downs. "Yes, yes. I'll be there, then," he spluttered. "Abby, come and fetch me when it's time. Meanwhile, help Viktor here out with this Glassworks. You really should've done that earlier."

Abby gestured for Viktor to follow her and turned to leave before Patrick could bait out her temper. "Well, I can see why you'd think him a potential problem," Vanessa admitted once they were outside. "He's nothing like his father."

"Potential? He *is* a problem. I don't know how you can even tolerate that arsehole, let alone have him involved in something like leadership," commented Viktor.

"Ersei, mother of love and life, teach us compassion and restraint; remind us that there are two sides to every story, and that to love and respect is the best option wherever possible," rebuked Abby.

"Ah, no wonder you get along so well with the paladin," Vanessa smiled.

Abby came to a halt, indecisive on where to begin their efforts for the glassworks. "I was in training to become a paladin myself, up until the elementals first breached Lyonis," she informed them. "What about you two, do you have faith?"

"Perhaps not quite as much as some, but I like to think I'm a good Marathist," claimed Vanessa.

"I guess you'd call me a moderate," contributed Viktor.

"I'm sorry for leaving you to deal with Patrick, by the way. I honestly thought he was going to get that done, and I was so busy with the murder investigation that I didn't think to check up on it," Abby apologised.

"Don't worry about it. I'm just glad to be rid of him," Viktor grunted.

"It sounds like I should leave you two to your work now," Vanessa excused herself. "The meeting's in two days' time at around noon. If you can't find us, just ask someone where the court is."

"Alright. Nice to meet you, Vanessa. I'm sure I'll be there," Abby responded.

"I'd best get back before any patients turn up. May I come along to the meeting, for curiosity's sake?" asked Johann.

"I don't see why not," Vanessa agreed. "Anyway, good luck with the glassworks. Viktor, was it?"

Viktor nodded and shook her hand. "Viktor Jacobson," he introduced himself properly. "Nice to meet you."

Abby kissed Johann goodbye before refocusing on the matter at hand. "I suppose we should pull one of our carpenters off of the housing jobs," she thought out loud as the pair departed. Nobody stayed in New Cray for long without becoming handy with a hammer and nails, and many - Abby included - had volunteered their spare time to help with expanding the village. No mere volunteer would suffice for consultation on the beginnings of a new structure, however.

"How's the smithy around here?" Viktor asked.

"Good, but metal's hard to come by at the moment. Most of what we get is from recycled gear or mined out of rock faces," she explained. They strolled over towards the latest of the village's housing projects, wooden frames and walls on display at various stages of completion.

"Might have some trouble if there's not enough metal to spare for proper equipment," confessed Viktor.

"Well that's alright. You'll probably find that it takes a while to get everything together on something this big. You'll have to farm like the rest of us, at least until you're making glass," Abby told him.

"You still farm? I'd thought you were more of an authority figure, investigations and law and all that."

She shook her head. "There's no real authority here. I do what I can get away with whilst lacking it. I just try to help people, really."

"Well, that woman... Vanessa. She was right. People talk about you as a leader now, since the murder," he claimed.

"Seems like it. I've never led a thing in my life, but I guess everyone starts somewhere," she considered.

Viktor shrugged. "I've never led anything in my life, neither. I make glass, my father made glass, and my grandfather made glass. I wouldn't know about leading, but I know about respect, and I know that until you fuck up good and proper, people here will respect you enough to follow."

Ignoring his language, Abby smiled half-heartedly. "We'll see if that changes when I announce the failure of the investigation, I suppose. You might say I made mistakes there."

Viktor looked right ahead as they walked. "When are you planning to tell them?"

"Tomorrow, when I ask for thoughts on the meeting in Lapden."

"Why don't you wait until after the meeting to tell them you've failed?" Viktor asked.

Abby frowned faintly. "Because pride is a sin, Viktor, and I refuse to withhold the truth to make myself seem better than I am. At least with something this important."

Viktor nodded. "Maybe honesty *is* the best policy."

"Would you ever think it otherwise?" she questioned him, her mind straying all too easily to the suspicion she'd forced upon herself for the duration of the investigation.

"I wouldn't call myself dishonest, but I'm honest enough to admit that I'm not *always* honest," he said with a cheeky grin.

"Well, I suppose that's better than being dishonest enough to claim to always be honest," Abby muttered.

The rest of the day passed by in a blur of activity as she and Viktor accomplished in less than twelve hours what Patrick had somehow failed to do in the last week. At the expense of the very latest housing projects, they convened with the carpenter and the town planner, and chose an appropriate spot for New Cray's latest foray into industry. It could take months to get the woodwork done, and far longer to have a furnace and tools constructed, but it was a start. It also served to take Abby's mind from the murder and the announcement she had to make. By the time she returned home that evening, she no longer felt so helpless.

"So, it seems that I'm sleeping with my boss now. When do I start getting special treatment?" Johann jested as they readied themselves for bed.

"Ooh, you'll have to wait and see about that. Even if everyone still wants me in charge after tomorrow, I wasn't the boss last time we made love," she smiled at him.

He grinned and shuffled over to watch her pray. "Maybe we should change that," he suggested. Abby had been unintentionally abstinent since the investigation began, but he'd have no such luck that night.

***

Abby stared at the ceiling as she awoke the next morning, forming a little speech in her mind that would inevitably go off-plan the moment it began. She sighed softly and sat up to fix her hair. "Morning," greeted Johann, barely awake beside her.

"Morning," she returned, rolling over to press herself tightly against him. "I'm a little nervous about how everyone will take the news," she admitted.

"Let me know if you want my help," Johann mumbled, closing his eyes and wrapping his arms around her sleepily.

"You can help," she said with a smile, letting the silence explain. He opened his eyes and looked at her in confusion for a moment before he understood. He didn't hesitate to crawl on top of her, knowing better than to pass up on sex when he could get it.

***

"Morning! You're looking cheerier - did you find a lead?" Aurelius greeted them as they came over to help prepare breakfast.

Abby chuckled and shook her head, joining her father in extracting the beans from their pods. "I wish. I've got to make an announcement today, would you guys help me gather everyone who's willing to listen, after we've eaten?"

Her father nodded. "We can spare a little time if it's important."

"It's important," she assured him. "Somebody from Lapden came to talk about merging into a township."

"Do you think it'll happen?" asked Alexander.

"It must do! We're so close that I'm not even sure what's to debate, to be honest. A little cooperation and everyone benefits," Abby insisted.

Her father nodded. "So what exactly are you announcing, then?"

"That someone from Lapden asked for a meeting. We need to make sure the majority of people are happy with the representatives, it's only fair. I also need to announce that we've found no more evidence to help with the investigation," she explained.

"I'm glad I didn't join you for the entire week," said Aurelius. "Call me cold, but what a waste of time."

"To be honest, after the first day it was a one-woman job anyway. I guess it was a waste of time, but somebody had to try," Abby shrugged. "Where's Carmina, by the way?"

"Oh, she's talking to Johnny and Sid, I think. I'm not sure why she bothers trying anymore," said Alexander.

Abby peered curiously at her father. "Why wouldn't she? Is there something I don't know, here?"

Alexander didn't get time to respond before Abby's questions were answered rather dramatically; the door burst open, and Carmina stormed into the room, Tahgri ducking to avoid the doorframes as he followed. "What's wrong?" asked Abby, noting her sister's obvious anger.

Carmina stomped over and rather suddenly slapped Alexander across the face. "Stop interfering with me and boys!" she snarled.

"I was only trying to make sure they didn't take advantage of you!" he insisted, rubbing his cheek.

"They're bent you idiot! Both of them - for each other!" Carmina announced.

Abby stifled a laugh with her hand, the situation almost too perfect. "Thank the Maralor," muttered her dad.

"It's not funny!" insisted Carmina, turning to Abby and slapping her, too. "And you sent him to watch me," she continued, pointing at Tahgri "Stick to your own fucking business!"

Abby was too focused on not vocalising her amusement to care about the slap. Even as Carmina grabbed her food and left in a huff, Aurelius descended into laughing fits. "Take note, you two. Being a parent is often a thankless task," muttered their father.

They paid for their humour by way of harsh glares from Carmina over breakfast, and Abby knew better than to ask if she'd help the rest of them gather the villagers. There were enough helping hands as it was, anyway. They set to work as soon as they'd all finished eating, and just as she had when she'd announced the murder, Abby took up position on the chapel steps. People slowly amassed around her, and eventually Tahgri stepped through the midst of the crowd, his armour and height singling him out as they always did. "They're mostly here," he claimed.

She gestured for him to stand beside her. "Come on, I want you with me for this. Jaina and Patrick, too," she instructed. Tahgri nodded and quickly strode back into the crowd to fetch the others.

Patrick deliberately positioned himself to the front of the four, whilst Jaina sidled up beside Abby and Tahgri. "You wanted me?" the lawyer asked, the faintest hint of nervousness in her voice.

"I do," Abby confirmed, pondering upon Jaina's apparent anxiety. Given that she was one of the people who'd been alone at the time of the murder, it was slightly worrying - but since the lawyer had no obvious motive and was - at best - moderately religious, Abby pushed the thought to the back of her mind and faced the crowd.

"Thank you all for coming," she spoke up. "I've got two important announcements that I felt you should all hear. You'll probably be pleased to know that this won't take as long as it did last time we were all here." There was a faint ripple of chuckles; she could only hope they remained so pleasant. "Firstly, I would like to say that despite the best efforts of everyone involved in the investigation, we haven't been able to find any firm evidence as to the identity of the murderer, nor have we been able to rule out the possibility that they don't even live here. Still, if anyone has any further information they can offer I *will* follow up on it. I'd like to suggest that for the good of the community, any of you who can spare resources should assist Amanda James in this difficult time."

She paused briefly to gauge the crowd's reaction. It seemed that they wouldn't tear her apart in a disappointed rage, nor would she be the only one to help Amanda in the absence of Owen. "There is some good news, however," she continued. "As you're all aware, our northern neighbours are still expanding, and we need to start making an effort to cooperate. They've invited the four of us to a discussion on merging the villages, in which we'd represent the interests of New Cray. I'd prefer a democratic approach to select representatives, but there's not enough time to arrange that before the meeting; therefore, I ask that if anyone has any issues with us representing the village, please object now."

Amanda stepped forth from the crowd, scowling. "I have an issue," she said bitterly, just as Abby had expected. "Why should *he* represent us?" the widow asked, pointing at Patrick. "What has he ever done for this place?"

A murmur of agreement rippled through the crowd, and Abby found herself somewhat stunned. Before she could recover from her surprise, Patrick retorted. "I've led as best I could since my father's death!"

"And what is it that you've led?" asked Katherine, stepping up beside Amanda with equal ferocity.

"I got things rolling on the construction of the glassworks!" Patrick claimed, much to Abby's annoyance.

Viktor stepped out of the crowd next, shaking his head. "Bullshit.

That was all Abby's doing and you're a fool to think otherwise."

"And everyone knows you didn't help with the investigation. You don't represent us," continued Amanda. "Nobody even knows what it is you do. Certainly nothing useful."

Abby raised a hand to try and calm everyone down, wondering if the insults were going a little far, even for Patrick. "I can see that there's significant discomfort regarding Patrick as a representative. Perhaps we can settle this with a vote another day, but is there any issue with the rest of us representing the best interests of our village?"

One of the few people she was not acquainted with stepped forwards, his rustic voice carrying. "What will you do about our farmland? Can't expect us to share crops an' such, we're spread thin as it is."

Abby nodded. "There's no need to share, we're out in the middle of nowhere with plenty of room for expansion. If there's anything to discuss I expect it'll be the placement of buildings, coordinating industry, and system of leadership. If there's anything else that people want us to mention specifically, let one of us know before tomorrow and we'll make sure it's addressed," she told them, hoping to assauge any fears.

The concerned man merged back into the crowd, and nobody else immediately stepped forwards. "Thank you all for your input," Abby dismissed them, turning to face the others. Patrick looked like he was still struggling to swallow some bitter medicine.

"Did they really ask for me?" enquired Jaina, grinning and obviously flattered by the attention.

"Sort of. They asked for me, and anyone else I thought might be good for this sort of thing," Abby explained

"Oh. Well, thanks, I suppose," said Jaina, the grin fading a little.

"I'm coming with you tomorrow," grumbled Patrick. He disappeared into the dispersing crowd before any of them could properly object.

"What do we do about him?" Jaina asked once he was firmly out of earshot.

"Nothing," Abby insisted, though she was sorely tempted to advise tying him to a chair. "I'll make no effort to fetch him for the meeting, and even if he's there for it nobody needs to listen to him if they don't want to." Of course, Abby knew full well that if the windbag was there, he would make himself heard whether people liked it or not.

Tahgri nodded. "If you're sure. So, what role do we fulfil in all this?"

"You can help me make decisions, assuming any need to be made tomorrow," she suggested. "I can't be the only one to do it, it needs to be a group thing."

"So what do we do right now?" asked Jaina. "Should we be preparing or something?"

"I don't think that'll be necessary," assured Abby. "I'm gonna get right back to the smithy, so go about your day, I guess. Have a nice one."

"If you're certain," agreed Jaina. "I'll see you tomorrow."

Abby departed and met Michael halfway to the smithy. He seemed to be in a good mood today, probably due to Patrick's public humiliation. They set to work, but even the noisy, metallic rhythm of their hammers didn't distract Abby's mind from thoughts of tomorrow's meeting.

***

Five hundred and ten days since we arrived in New Cray. She awoke feeling excited about the day ahead and the results it might yield. Less so about having to deal with Patrick's childish behaviour.

Johann had snuck back into bed in the middle of the night following another house-call for one of his patients, and he remained fast asleep even as she brought him breakfast in bed. In the end she left for the smithy without waking him and set to work; nails and door hinges, each one unexciting yet satisfying in its simplicity.

Leaving well before noon gave her ample time to fetch the others for the meeting. Before she could locate any of them, however, she was approached by Daniel; "Got a moment?" he asked.

"If you can walk and talk at the same time," Abby smiled at him. *Please don't let this be about Patrick.*

He kept pace beside her as she headed for the farmlands. "I was wondering when we're gonna start training again - that is, if we will. I thought we were, since the investigation's over."

"We will, hopefully soon. I tell you what, I'll speak to Tahgri today and see if I can sort something out for tomorrow afternoon. I'll let you know how that works out, alright?"

"Sounds good to me. Look, about my dad," Daniel continued.

And there it is. Abby shook her head, dismissing it before he could finish. "It's fine, Daniel. I'm being as fair as I can be, but he's not really helping himself."

He nodded glumly. "I know he's being really stupid about this whole thing, but could you at least keep him in the loop? It seems to help him deal with everything."

"I haven't got any reason to keep him out of the loop, yet." Abby assured him, her frustration growing. "I won't play along with any ideas he has about being in charge, but other than that I'm not going to make any deliberate efforts to get in his way."

Daniel nodded. "Thanks, Abby. I'll see you around."

He veered off to go his own way, and Abby kept on walking until she spied Tahgri working his farm. He planted his spade in the earth as he noticed her approaching - it was a far cry from the sight of him with sword and armour. "Time to go already?" he asked

"Yep, just gathering everyone," she explained, gesturing for him to follow. They walked back alongside the farmland together, waving to some of their acquaintances in passing. "I just spoke to Daniel; he was asking when we're going to resume training - I was thinking we could start again tomorrow, continuing as usual?" Abby queried.

"Tomorrow sounds fine to me. I'll see you all after lunch, if you inform everyone for me," agreed Tahgri.

"Will do. By the way, I meant to ask - do you have a copy of the Faralex we could put in the chapel? It seems kind of bare without one."

"I do. Hopefully this one doesn't meet the same demise, I only have one copy," he lamented.

"I'm sure there are a few others kicking about the village, if it comes to it. Still, thanks," she smiled at him, leading the way to Johann's.

Their job was made easier when they arrived to find the doctor having brunch with Jaina. "Ah, good timing. Are we leaving soon?" he asked.

"We may as well leave as soon as you're done," said Abby, gesturing to the food. They nodded and wolfed down the last of their meal. It made Abby hungry, but her excitement outweighed that desire. She led the three of them north to Lapden.

The grass-filled gulf between the two villages made for a pleasant little walk in the morning sun. "Did we manage to sneak away ahead of Patrick?" asked Jaina.

"No sign of him so far. We'll see," said Tahgri.

"Hopefully he stays out of the way," Johann muttered.

"So, where is it?" Jaina enquired as they approached the southern edge of Lapden.

"The court, apparently. Though what that looks like is beyond me," responded Abby. "We'll get directions if we can't see it."

They pressed on until they'd ventured further into Lapden than Abby had ever gone before. It wasn't all that different from New Cray, the distinctions primarily in the layout of the buildings rather than the style. They had the same materials to work with, after all, and probably similar skills.

They acquired directions from the first person they came across. "You can't miss it," the stranger claimed as he helpfully pointed them in the right direction. He was soon proven right; the building stood out from all the others - the foundations of each wall were made of stone, the stairs leading up to the front doors included. It wasn't quite the marble of Lyonis' grander buildings, but it was still beautiful.

"They must have at least one good mason," Jaina commented as they ascended to a pair of double doors.

"Working with whom would be one of many benefits to a closer relationship with Lapden, I'm sure," commented Tahgri, taking to the role of a politican like a duck to water.

Abby pushed through the front doors and into a small lobby, sparing a few glances about. It was less impressive inside, though she didn't get to look about too much before they were accosted by a pair of lightly armoured men. "State your business," insisted one of them.

"We were invited here by Vanessa," Abby tried.

The older of the two nodded and eyed Tahgri's knife. "We're going to need to take your weapons," he insisted.

Tahgri peered at the blade a moment, then offered it to the man. "As long as we get them back," he allowed.

The guard didn't bother to confirm that they would, though Abby was certain that refusing to return them wouldn't go down too well. "Follow me," he ordered once everyone had handed over their weapons. Abby didn't much appreciate his bossy tone - nor did the others by the looks of it - but they all followed, resisting the urge to do or say anything that would make a bad first impression in Lapden.

Either side of an unstaffed desk at the back of the lobby was a set of double doors. They were led through the ones on the right, though they both opened into the same chamber. The size of the structure considered, one might've expected a large council of hundreds of men and women. That was not the case, however; the numerous benches arranged in a semi-circle on the far side of the room were populated by a total of twenty-five men, women, and children. In the very centre of the room, addressing the crowd, was Patrick. "...but if a council is the only way you will all be satisfied with a merge, I believe the people of New Cray will respect that, so long as I have a place on it," he claimed. Abby groaned.

"How the fuck did he get here ahead of us?" Johann muttered.

Their escorting guard cleared his throat loudly, drawing the attention of the room. "Does the council recognise these people?" he asked.

Vanessa stood and waved a hand. "Absolutely, it does. Please, take the floor and introduce yourselves." It didn't take a genius to realise that she was already finding Patrick to be a tiresome man.

Abby shooed Patrick away, more than happy to interrupt his address. She stood on the tips of her toes to get a better view of everyone over the top of the lectern, but spoke confidently despite the intimidating nature of the room. "Good day, everyone. I'm Abby Koning. I'm here today along with my friends Sir Tahgri Dunwolf and Jaina Steward to represent the interests of the people of New Cray," she greeted them all.

"I am too, of course!" Patrick interjected.

Abby ignored him and carried on with the introductions. "My lover, Johann, is here to observe. I can see that won't be a problem," she commented, smiling and gesturing to some of the civilians nearer the front seats. She was certain that not everyone here was old enough to be on the council itself.

A man in the audience stood up, a pleasant enough expression on his face. "Good day to all of you, I'm Montgomery Leyland. I understand that this is perhaps more formal than you are used to in New Cray but we try to maintain strict rules for discourse in this council, for the sake of ease if it is to grow in the future. For today, however, we will suspend these rules to make your welcome more comfortable. You already know Vanessa - she and I, along with Markus Twine and Yasmine Enverson are the elected of Lapden's council. The others present are family or acquaintances, here to observe out of interest - or simply because we can't let them out of sight for too long," he said with a faint smile. Some of the parents in the room chuckled, understanding all too well.

"Perhaps this would be easier if those of us who are on the council would sit on the same bench," suggested Vanessa. There were some nods and a general consensus in the form of the four members of the Lapden council relocating to one of the foremost and lowest benches.

Gingerly, Abby moved to stand in front of them. "So, how do we begin?" she asked, blushing ever so slightly at her own inexperience. She would've felt more at home discussing the philosophy of democracy, rather than organising the practical aspects of it.

"Well," began Vanessa. "I think it's best that we discuss potential leadership going forwards, to begin with."

"Good idea," agreed Patrick, stepping up beside Abby again.

Once more, Abby willfully ignored his cries for attention. "I like this system you've implemented - assuming that is, that I understand it correctly. I can't say for certain that everyone in New Cray would be happy to implement it and expand accordingly, but I don't see any reason why they wouldn't be, either," she said, looking to Tahgri and Jaina for their thoughts on the matter.

Both seemed confident in agreement. "Absolutely. I doubt it would hurt to have a little more legitimacy to our leadership. People respect Abby, and judging by the response we received yesterday, the same can be said of Tahgri and I," contributed Jaina.

"And me," Patrick added swiftly.

The Lapden council exchanged some confused glances with one another after Patrick spoke. Abby found herself wondering how much Vanessa had told them about the situation, and decided to use Patrick's desparation to be seen as a leader to her advantage. "Could you briefly summarise for the three of us how your system works, just to make sure we don't misunderstand anything?" she asked them, taking great care to exclude Patrick by gesturing to herself, Jaina, and Tahgri.

The council swapped further glances and hushed words, swiftly concluding that Montgomery should explain. "Well, it's quite simple really," he claimed. "We have at least one representative on the council per hundred people in the village, and every time we cross the threshold we hold a full set of elections. Anyone is free to run, and everyone old enough to hold a conversation votes for candidates. The most commonly voted for are elected. For example, we currently have a population of just over three hundred and fifty people; our last election saw Vanessa and I stay on; Markus replaced his predecessor - Adam - and Yasmine took the open spot."

"And how do you make decisions, now that you're elected? The majority again? Is there any weighting?" Tahgri asked.

"There's no weighting to it. We're all equals on the council, and the majority rules. So far we haven't had any even splits, but if we ever do we're going to have to defer the decision until we can persuade at least one person to change their mind," Vanessa explained.

"What happens if there's an even split and nobody will move their position?" Jaina asked.

"Then I suppose the decision is postponed indefinitely," said Vanessa.

Jaina smirked and nodded. "That's democracy I suppose. Everything gets done fairly, even when nothing gets done."

Vanessa raised a brow imperiously. "Are you proposing a change to the system?" she demanded.

Jaina shook her head. "Not yet. Although I am interested to hear what Abby and Tahgri think of that particular flaw," she said, turning to look at them.

"I see your point, but I'd rather have a slim chance of that happening, than have to organise a complicated alternative," said Tahgri.

Abby shook her head. "Complications won't be necessary. Jaina's correct - it could cause that problem. However, I'd like to point out that the population of New Cray is currently at around four hundred and seventy, if memory serves. That would mean by these rules we get five representatives, and nine in total can't reach an even split on a binary decision."

"And when the population crosses the threshold and we're forced to make it an even ten representatives?" continued Jaina.

"Simple - we keep it an uneven number at all times," Abby suggested. "Whether that means more, or fewer representatives per one-hundred population than we currently have."

The Lapden council exchanged a series of approving looks. "I could get on board with that. Hypothetically speaking, would anyone present have an issue with that system?" asked Vanessa.

"I have one," said Patrick. "What if I was to adamantly disagree with a decision? Surely I could overturn some things, within reason?" he enquired.

Vanessa shook her head, explaining slowly and carefully, verging on patronising him. "That's the point of democracy, Patrick - a majority are happy. There's no perfect system, but it's certainly better than having one person making all the decisions."

"One person in charge worked fine for us when it was my father," Patrick insisted.

There was a subtle sigh from the collective Lapden council. "It clearly did. But the people of Lapden couldn't possibly agree to have a single person in charge of everything. Especially not before they've had time to integrate and see - as we do - that we're all going to be working to the same ends. That we're on the same team, as it were," Vanessa insisted.

"Well, it seems to me that despite all this talk of democracy, you're uninterested in compromise. I don't believe the people of my village will benefit from any sort of deal with this sort of attitude at its heart," continued Patrick. Abby groaned in disbelief and hoped that someone would control him before she was forced to do something mean.

"Well, it seems that there's a clear disagreement between you and your representatives there, Patrick. Still, you are clearly in the minority," contributed Montgomery.

Patrick laughed derisively and shook his head, waggling a finger at the Lapden council. "You're speaking as if this system has already been implemented; as if my colleagues here have already been elected onto this council. But they haven't been, and they're not in charge yet," he insisted.

"And who elected you to make such a decision then, Patrick?" asked Montgomery. The council seemed to have some understanding of the situation, now.

"Elected me? Nobody. But it is what it is," Patrick continued with surprising confidence. "Nobody elects kings, but they still rule." Credit where it was due, he certainly knew how to polish the fetid dungheap that was his reasoning.

The assembly scowled at him, including the others from New Cray, their expressions universally intolerant. Vanessa stepped forwards from the bench, looking between Patrick and Abby with an expression that seemed like it could set people on fire. "I'm sorry Patrick, but I'm going to have to be blunt; you're not a king, and nobody wants you to lead. It's nothing personal but from what we've seen, people in your Village would trust Johann to lead more than they'd trust you," Vanessa insisted.

Abby winced at the less than delicate approach. "Oh it's fine, I'm just the baseline of trustworthiness," muttered Johann.

Patrick began to bubble with fury. "My father built New Cray! He gave it order!" he spat.

"Your father, not you! William was undoubtedly a great man, but you're not William. I have no reason to believe that anyone will be the least bit upset if we don't treat your words as equal to those of the representatives, and if you don't understand that then you're going to have to leave. Come back when you've proven you're wanted as a leader," ordered Vanessa.

Patrick opened his mouth to speak, but only managed to turn a furious shade of red as he glared at the council. His gaze turned to the children present, and then without further comment he stormed from the room, his fists clenched and trembling.

Vanessa slowly returned to her seat, her expression returning to calm as if nothing of note had happened. She had to wait for a few of the youngest members of the audience to stop murmuring in excited tones, however. "So, I suppose the first issue to address is this obvious problem with the legitimacy of power. I think everyone would benefit if you could make arrangements to settle it once and for all. Could we come to some sort of agreement on that today?" she asked.

"I'll ask if everyone's willing to make this transition, and organise a fair system of voting if they are," Abby responded. "Just give us a week to arrange elections." She didn't know if she'd be voted in as one of the five if it went ahead, but she was certain that Patrick wouldn't be.

"Well, I shall look forwards to hearing from you about that. Do keep us informed on the proceedings, won't you?" requested Vanessa.

Abby nodded. "That shouldn't be a problem. If you don't hear from us straight away, you can probably assume things are going smoothly."

"Before you leave, I'd like to add that we're finally planning a proper mine, since we believe that the hills to the northeast are rich in metals," announced Montgomery. "If anyone from New Cray is interested in sharing in the venture, we'd welcome them to join us."

"I'll mention that whilst we deal with the election, thank you. Is there anything else before we go?" Abby queried, smiling.

"Just one thing," said Johann. They all glanced across to where he was pointing, a young woman hastily scribbling with a quill. "Do you create your own ink and paper?"

Yasmine spoke up, a touch of humour in her voice. "We do. And I'm sure we could arrange to share, were a merge in the works."

Abby nodded her approval. There seemed to be an ever-growing list of reasons for the merge to take place, and very few for it not to. "Well, I'm sure we'll hold you to that, if this goes as well as I expect it to. We'll be in touch soon," she concluded.

"Thank you all for coming. We'll look forwards to having you again, I'm sure," Vanessa excused them.

Abby turned to smile at the others. "Shall we go and get this started?" she suggested. They all said their goodbyes to the Lapden council before making their exit.

They paused to retrieve their weapons from the guards. "It seems change is afoot," Tahgri commented as he sheathed his knife. "Village politics could be interesting."

"Yup! And the smithy will certainly a bit busier if we can get any sort of reliable iron supply from that mine. We'll make Besigur proud," Abby enthused, leading the group back to New Cray.

"Did anyone else notice how much posher Abby sounded when she was addressing the council in there?" Jaina teased, grinning broadly.

Abby's cheeks tinged with embarrassment, though she couldn't help but laugh. "I guess it reminded me of Lyonis, somehow." Suddenly, this place felt even more like home.

11

A New Tomorrow

"So who counts these votes, then? It would be easy for someone to lie about the results," Amanda called out from within the crowd.

"Good point. I suppose nobody related to any candidates, and close friends should probably be excluded as well. Are there any volunteers?" asked Abby. A series of hands went up, much to her approval.

People had taken to the idea of democracy with enthusiasm, though Abby suspected that the possibility of further humiliating Patrick had been somewhat more persuasive than the system itself. "I'd like to suggest that Johnny and Sid count the votes. I don't think they could be considered especially close to any of us," Abby continued as she noticed the withdrawn couple amongst the volunteers. They stepped forwards, and nobody seemed to disagree with the idea - not even Patrick, who'd done his utmost to paint the whole ordeal in a bad light.

Truth be told, Abby didn't know anything about Johnny and Sid beyond what Carmina had revealed about them. The pair kept almost entirely to themselves, and even if they were closer to Patrick than she knew, they'd have to come up with a pretty clever system of cheating to help the most hated man in the village win a glorified popularity contest. "If nobody objects, I suggest we take a week to establish who will put themselves in for the running and allow people to make up their minds. For now, would anyone who wishes to run for a place on the council please step up here with me?" Abby requested.

There was a flurry of movement as people rearranged. A handful of Abby's acquaintances stepped up, whilst Tahgri and Jaina simply sidled closer to her. Johann soon decided to join them in the electoral race, and the entire Marshal family made their presence known as well. Shortly after the latter, Michael took to the chapel steps.

"I suppose anyone else who's considering running has until the time of the vote to make up their mind. If anyone has any further questions for me, I'll be in the smithy," Abby concluded. She waved off the crowds, but hovered beside Daniel a moment before leaving. "Training resumes as normal, starting tomorrow."

Michael soon joined her in the smithy. "I'm only really running so that arse of a man can't get elected by default," he confessed.

"Good thinking. I'm trying to be nice to him, but I would've done the same," Abby admitted. The pair set to work with silent cheer.

Fighting against all odds, Patrick spent the week trying to convince people that he was the man for the job, vilifying the other candidates and spouting rhetoric about protecting New Cray during the merge. Despite his obvious bitterness over recent events, his sons didn't make training awkward for Abby. It seemed that they realised their father was in the wrong, though they were understandably reluctant to confront him about it.

Patrick wasn't the only one actively trying to win the affections of the populace; Johann did a good job of convincing everyone that his role as a caregiver made him an ideal choice to look out for New Cray's best interests, and Katherine and Amanda soon joined the running, following Michael's example to make sure that Patrick stood no chance of placing.

The week flew by as Abby settled back into her routine of farming and smithing. She even finished the pews for the chapel at last. Though she made no conscious effort to convince people to vote for her, she was confident that people would know the right leaders when the time came; anyone but Patrick.

The five hundred and seventeenth day arrived, and rather than begin her day as she usually did, Abby decided to forsake the smithy in order to help with the electoral preparations. They'd borrowed ink and paper from Lapden; Johnny and Sid would simply make a tally of the votes each person received, and compare the totals at the end. It didn't take them long to prepare, and though they had initially planned to begin at midday, to postpone for the sake of an arbitrarily arranged time seemed pointless to Abby. They started early, gathering people to the little stall they'd set up at the base of the chapel steps.

Patrick and his boys hurried forwards to cast their own votes first. Abby imagined each of the three had voted for themselves and each other, though she had no idea of their other choices. When it came to her turn, Abby voted for the most obvious candidates; Amanda, Johann, Jaina, Tahgri, and Katherine. Not content to simply wait for the results to come in, she killed time by going to work in the smithy.

A few hours and large quantities of nails later, Tahgri turned up to fetch her. "They're just finishing up now. Are you coming back?" he queried.

Abby nodded and set down her work in progress. "Just a moment. Good luck, by the way," she offered, quickly tidying up her mess before heading back over to see the results. If the crowd had ever dispersed, it had reassembled just as quickly - she joined it from the back, watching as the very last voters had their choices noted down by Johnny and Sid. She toyed with the idea of organising a way to avoid people being able to vote twice next time; it wasn't a problem right now, but it could become one after the merge, since they would have more faces to recall.

"That seems to be everyone!" Johnny called out.

The crowd eagerly closed in to witness the results as the tallies were counted and compared. That part didn't take so long, and after a swift discussion with his partner, Sid announced in the unceremonious tones of someone who'd spent too long trying to be enthusiastic about something fundamentally boring. "Our five elected are Katherine, Johann, Michael, Abby, and Jaina."

Abby smiled and stepped forwards. She would've rather had Tahgri than Michael, but she supposed some regarded him with suspicion since the murder. She was still happy with the results. The respect that people held for her was confirmed. It was a good feeling. "I'd like to thank everyone who helped to organise this. Especially you two," she called out, smiling at Johnny and Sid. They mostly looked embarrassed by the attention. "I'm going over to Lapden to inform Vanessa, and it would be great if all five of us went."

"I would, but I should probably make myself available as a doctor at least once today," Johann chuckled, stepping out of the crowd.

Abby nodded. "I'll see you later, then. Anyone else?" she asked.

Jaina seemed to consider, but shook her head as she stood beside Johann. "Seeing as they've already met me, I think I'll sit this one out as well. I'll be there for the next one, though."

It made a poor first impression in Abby's opinion. Still, she imagined they'd have plenty of time on the council to make up for it, and the other two stepped out of the crowd looking somewhat keener. "I'll come," agreed Michael.

"And me. I think I'd like to meet the council there," added Katherine.

With a bounce in her step, Abby led the pair north to Lapden. Soon enough they reached the buildings on the southern edge of the village. "Sort of didn't count on actually getting voted in. Just glad that shit-for-brains didn't," Michael admitted.

"Likewise. I'm not even sure what it is he does. His boys seem to do most of the farming, and he certainly never did anything to lead when he had the chance," gossiped Katherine.

"Yeah, well, hopefully this puts an end to his childish behaviour," agreed Abby, observing the construction efforts in progress. They'd already made good headway on the buildings since a week ago, the frames of new houses beginning to take form ahead of the recently completed ones. Much like before, Abby asked the first person she came across for directions - this time to Vanessa's residence. She pointed out the court on the way there.

Michael refrained from unnecessary comment, as usual, which made

Abby wonder - and not for the first time - how he was going to get along in a role that was almost purely about communication. Katherine, on the other hand, was as chatty as ever. "So that's where they work, then? It's awfully fancy with all that stone, isn't it."

Abby smiled at her. "Yeah, I like it. Just a shame it's all the way out on the north side - still, I guess they couldn't have known we'd be using it when they chose the location."

"So the council building will be in Lapden, even after the merge?" asked Katherine, sounding slightly suspicious.

"Well, in a manner of speaking, yes, but there won't really be a Lapden after the merge; no 'them' and 'us'," insisted Abby.

"I guess so," Katherine bumbled. "Maybe we can swap houses with some of the newcomers so that we're closer."

Vanessa's house wasn't far from the court. It was only slightly larger than average, but it was marked out by a handful of carefully carved wooden ornaments littering a small porch. Abby knocked on the door, knocked again, and waited until it became clear that nobody was in. She took the time to admire the decorations. Sometimes she found herself thinking that even the simplest of ornaments were incredibly pretty, these days. There could be little doubt that her standards had slipped since leaving Lyonis.

"Perhaps they're in the court already?" suggested Katherine.

"Yeah, maybe. It's worth a try," Abby agreed, and led them right back the way they'd come. She ascended the stone steps of the court and pushed through the double doors.

The guards immediately approached them. "State your business," ordered the older of the two. They were the same men as last time, surly and overzealous in their duty.

"We're here to see the council. They'll want to hear from us," Abby assured them. They seemed to recognise her, and the eldest gestured back to the doors. The younger exchanged a glance with his superior and quietly led them in, not that such was at all necessary. Abby knew that it was perhaps a little petty of her, but she almost felt insulted, having been elected and then treated like a prisoner being escorted about.

"...the location of the latrines may seem a non-issue at present, but if it rains heavily there's a good chance of contamination of the water supply. The last thing we need when we have no real medicine is an outbreak of disease," Montgomery addressed the rest of the council.

Abby waited politely for a break in the discussion, Katherine and Michael following her example. "Those who are in favour of moving the latrines in such a manner that solves the issue presented, raise a hand," ordered Vanessa. Unsurprisingly, there was no argument on that matter, and all four hands on the Lapden council went up. Abby was sure that if Jaina had been there she would have made a joke about democracy requiring four officials just to legislate human waste.

"If it's alright with all of you, I shall deal with this one tomorrow. It shouldn't take long," assured Montgomery before turning his attention to Abby. "It's good to see you again, Miss Koning. I trust the vote went well?"

Abby smiled and led her friends to the lectern. "Please, call me Abby. And it's great to be back. Good news all around - we have five elected; Johann and Jaina you've already met, plus myself. Today I'd like to introduce you to the rest of us - Michael and Katherine," she said. Given Michael's taciturn nature, she decided it a good idea to introduce him more thoroughly on his behalf. "Michael's the village smith. I've been working as his apprentice for a little while now."

Katherine stepped up to the lectern, peering around Abby to address everyone. "I mostly just farm with my daughter-in-law these days," she informed them. "But it's nice to meet you all."

"Likewise. I'm Vanessa De Burges - Montgomery, Markus, Yasmine, and I comprise the council. I gather the other two will not be joining us today, but would it be possible to make some decisions without their input?" Vanessa enquired.

Abby glanced to Michael and Katherine for their opinions. "I expect so, depending on the nature of the decisions," she concluded from their vacant expressions.

"Excellent. When William was in charge, we joint-reviewed plans for any and all new buildings relating to the southern expansion of Lapden, and the northern expansion of New Cray. We would appreciate it if we could find a way to continue this system with you, until such a time as the merge is complete," proposed Vanessa.

"Well, that makes sense to me," said Abby. "Does anyone disagree?"

"Those against, raise your hands," ordered Vanessa, formality taking over the process.

Only Katherine did so. "I don't really know much about building or design," she pointed out.

"Neither do I, but we have a town planner of our own. At least we can represent issues he brings up," Abby pointed out.

Katherine nodded and lowered her hand. "I suppose so. What happens after the merge? Do we still have to review every single building?" she questioned, sounding somewhat overwhelmed.

Vanessa shook her head. "Once we've bridged the gap between our villages we could probably work out a simpler system. The structures built here have all been reviewed by our town planner and at least one council member before construction could begin."

"Sounds sensible," concurred Abby. "That's pretty much what we've always been doing, though it was with William rather than a council."

"Does anyone object, then?" asked Montgomery. There was silence.

"We should tell Jaina and Johann, but if you don't hear news of their objections you can probably assume there are no issues. I'd also like to recommend Jaina as the go-to for reviewing any building plans," Abby proposed.

"She has experience with it?" asked Yasmine.

"In a sense. She was a lawyer, once upon a time, so she knows the laws from Luthania relating to property . Some of that could translate well to this," explained Abby. There was a murmur of approval from the Lapden council.

"Something to consider in the near future, then," agreed Vanessa.

"I have a question," Markus interjected, breaking his previous silence. "When we go through with this merge, what do we do about the name?"

It occurred to Abby at that moment that Markus and Yasmine were not so involved compared to the other two. There may be no weighting to the votes, but a natural sense of leadership seemed to come from Vanessa in particular. Abby found herself wondering if she'd take the same position amongst the New Cray council members, or indeed if she had done so already.

Awkwardness filled the room when nobody immediately dared to suggest their opinion on the matter of the town's name. It had been inevitable that they disagree on something sooner or later of course - they were fortunate enough that it was something so insignificant. "I suppose we'd all prefer it if our own village's name was adopted for the town," Abby finally offered. "Obviously, there can only be one name. It doesn't matter that much to me, but I'm aware that many of those we represent were from the original village of Cray, and therefore might be attached to the name of New Cray in some way."

There was evident contention from the Lapden council, but after more murmuring, Vanessa spoke up. "The name of Lapden was agreed upon early during the construction of this village, and - beyond these last couple of years - is unimportant to us. I propose, as a sign of good faith, that we adopt the name of New Cray once the merge is complete. All in favour, raise your hands."

Of the Lapden council, only Vanessa was in favour. Unsurprisingly, both Katherine and Michael joined Abby in agreement. "Well, that's democracy," said Montgomery with a stiff chuckle. Even with two of New Cray's council out of the picture, they were outnumbered.

"I appreciate the gesture. Is there anything else you'd like to resolve without Johann and Jaina?" Abby asked.

"Well, possibly," said Vanessa. "We've discussed the suggestion you made last week, and it seems to us that we should vote on whether to over-represent or under-represent in order to prevent an even split in the future."

Abby nodded. "I suppose we should retake the vote on the idea of a permanently uneven number of council members first, since we have new additions."

Katherine cleared her throat. "I'm sorry, I'm not quite following - why would it need to be an uneven number?"

"Because this way we can't possibly reach an even split, which means that decisions are never postponed," Montgomery clarified.

Vanessa eyed Katherine for a thoughtful moment, then instructed the assembly once again. "Those in favour of keeping an uneven number of council members, raise your hands." The outcome was unanimously in favour.

"Those in favour of over-representing rather than under-representing, raise your hands." There was a little more division this time; Markus and Yasmine raised their hands, but they were the only ones. The decision was clear.

"Well, that settles that," said Vanessa. "But we probably shouldn't get too far ahead of ourselves without everyone here. Now that we're all acquainted I'd like it if we could perhaps have dinner tomorrow and go over the formalities of how we normally conduct a discussion here."

Abby glanced around at the others to gauge their reactions. "I finish training in the evening. Around sundown's fine with me," she agreed.

"I guess I could take an evening off," agreed Michael.

"I'm free then," Katherine said cheerily, quite clearly glad to be done playing politics already.

Vanessa smiled. "Well then, I'll see you all there. If you can convince Johann and Jaina to come along as well, that would be wonderful."

Abby chuckled. "I'm sure I can, and I'll bring something nice over if I can find anything to spare." She was just being polite, of course - she knew full well that there was nothing going unused.

Vanessa waved a hand dismissively. "No need. We have more than enough food for all of us. Just bring yourselves."

"If you're sure. Until tomorrow, then," concluded Abby. The two councils said their goodbyes and went their separate ways, the three from New Cray returning home and chattering excitedly amongst themselves until they had to disband.

Tahgri intercepted Abby just before she got back home. "Abby," he greeted her. "How did everything go?"

"Pretty well. It seems like everything's going to work out nicely, and tomorrow we're going over to Vanessa's for dinner," she summarised as she approached Johann's door. "Is something wrong?"

"Wrong? No, I was just curious. Chaperoning was rather uneventful," said Tahgri.

Abby nodded, then paused with the door held open against her hand. "You haven't been stalking Carmina again, have you?"

The awkward expression on his face told her that he had. "You never asked me to stop," he pointed out. "Should I?"

Abby sighed. "*Carmina* told you to stop. Besides, Johnny and Sid aren't exactly going to pounce on her, as you might recall."

"Fair enough," commented the paladin. "I thought perhaps other boys might take an interest, but it's really only Samson at the moment. I'll stop."

Abby heard the sound of Jaina's laughter from the medical room and strolled over to join them. "Welcome back," the lawyer smiled as she entered, dismounting from her perch on one of the medical benches.

Johann stepped up to give Abby a quick peck on the cheek. "You're back earlier than I thought. How'd it go?" he enquired.

"Well enough to get invited over to Vanessa's tomorrow evening. Can you both make it?" Abby asked.

They nodded hurriedly. "Of course. Could you fetch me when it's time?" asked Jaina.

"We certainly can," assured Johann.

"For tonight, though, how about you and I have dinner with my parents?" Abby suggested to the doctor.

"You're going to leave me all alone?" Jaina asked with a perfect hint of a pout.

"I'm afraid so. We'll see you tomorrow, Jaina," Abby smiled. She was certain that Jaina had no shortage of single men who'd love to have dinner with her, anyway.

"If you'd care for some company, Miss Steward, I would too," said Tahgri, confirming Abby's thoughts.

Jaina grinned. "Only if you agree never to call me that again. I think we're on a first-name basis by now, Tahgri."

The paladin chuckled. "Certainly, Jaina."

"You two can let yourselves out when you're ready," offered Abby, taking Johann by the hand and leading him to the front door. Dinner was no unusual affair that night, despite them being congratulated on their positions on the council and answering the accompanying questions. The future looked bright, and it was in a good mood indeed that Abby and Johann later went to bed.

146

The five hundred and eighteenth day came. Both of Patrick's boys showed up to training that afternoon, and thankfully neither seemed to care nearly as much as their father had about the results of the election. According to Carmina, the look of bitterness on Patrick's face had been priceless when they'd left him behind. Naturally, Abby took no joy in his unhappiness - she couldn't deny that there was a certain pleasure in knowing that she was above him now, though. More powerful than him in every way.

Tahgri lunged at her, his fists frantic. Only a single proper strike got through, to Abby's credit, the rest of them glancing relatively harmlessly across the length of her forearms. He began to mix kicks in, but his age started to show and soon enough he was about done with the melee, simply grabbing one of her wrists mid-blow to indicate that she should stop. "Are you alright?" she asked, noting his ragged breathing.

"I'll be fine after a little rest," he insisted. He took a seat on the dry earth to watch the others, gesturing for Abby to do the same. Together, they watched Aurelius and Daniel brawl.

It was a brutish affair, though far less so than it had been when she'd been training them herself. The last year especially had seen them change greatly, and not just in terms of their combat ability. Whilst Daniel had been every inch Samson's younger brother when they'd first come to New Cray, he looked almost like Aurelius' twin now. Not all the men had aged equally.

Daniel won the fight, eventually, a decent manoeuvre of his legs and hips sending Aurelius tumbling to the floor. They nursed their bruises; though they didn't receive quite the same pummeling as Abby usually did from her more advanced conflicts, they had the disadvantage of not having their own armour. Abby hoped that might change, if the mine proved successful.

Her attention strayed to Samson whilst Tahgri instructed the other two on how to improve their technique. Despite being the eldest of the brothers, he was far less capable when it came to violence. It wasn't that he lacked the stomach for it, nor the physique - simply the skill. Still, he'd been slowly improving like everyone else, and Tahgri was convinced that he'd hold up well in a real fight, eventually. He was supposed to be sparring with Carmina, but rather than proper brawls they were trying out singular techniques on each other to practice the motions of grappling - and having a good time about it, despite the bruises. Whilst Samson had inherited Patrick's unpleasant temperament, he seemed to get along well with Carmina. Abby strongly suspected that personality alone wasn't the reason for that; her sister had aged too, but she'd only become more beautiful for it.

"Alright, ready for more?" asked Tahgri, tapping Abby's shoulder. She got to her feet and prepared herself, adopting the fighting stance again. Round and round it went, sparring with weapons or fists until Tahgri was done in and had to take a break. Each time, he would take advantage of the pause to advise the other four.

Eventually, the sun dimmed in the sky, and Abby decided it was late enough to start making a move towards Lapden. "Alright, I've got to get going. Thanks, Tahgri. I'll see you all in a couple of days," she excused herself. They all said their farewells, and Abby strolled back over to Johann's.

Jaina was present at the doctor's house once again, making the task of fetching everyone that much simpler. "I don't suppose you two could fetch Katherine and Michael could you? I need to dress down," Abby requested. "I'll catch up with you all?"

"Why not. I'll see you soon," Johann agreed, giving her a quick kiss.

"We'll meet you in the gulf," Jaina added, before leaving with him. Abby didn't imagine they'd have trouble locating the others.

She stripped off her armour and quickly changed into another set of clothes; thin and plain linen that hung loosely and unromantically from her form. It was far from the sort of finery that her father would have had her wear for dinner parties back in Lyonis, but she didn't mind one bit. Practicality was her preferred style, now.

Her battered boots were something of a contrast to her newer clothes, but they were still holding together. Deciding it too hot for the lioness-hide shawl despite the setting sun, Abby left looking respectably plain and regrouped with the others in the gulf between the villages.

"What do you really think of their system?" enquired Johann.

"I like it, within reason. Else I wouldn't have agreed to be part of it," Abby pointed out, hoping he wasn't getting cold feet about the whole thing now.

"Yes, but having everyone on the council as equals with no distinct roles… it's somewhat different from having ministers for different issues, don't you think?" continued the doctor.

"Yes, but there's no point complicating the system when there's such a small population, is there," contributed Jaina. "The systems in Luthania came into being, presumably, because it became impossible for any one person to fully understand the workings of everything that happened in the kingdom. As it stands, it's quite easy for one person to understand everything that goes on here."

"Exactly my thoughts," agreed Abby. "For the time being, I think this system suits us just fine. If our population keeps on growing, we might have to consider a change one day, though." *One day.* Perhaps she was presuming too much about the lifespan of New Cray, or even the length of her stay in it.

Johann smiled. "I suppose I'm better at medicine than politics."

"Well, I don't like to think of politics as an entity in itself, personally. It's about understanding the various spheres of life and how they interact with one another," claimed Jaina.

"Well, I'm just glad we're getting a proper say now. Ruling, rather than being ruled," said Katherine.

"And not being pestered by Patrick," added Michael. Nobody would disagree there.

They continued to discuss styles of leadership both democratic and otherwise as they walked. The king was, as far as any of them knew, still very much alive and well. Perhaps they'd be ruled again one day, if he ever learned of New Cray.

They reached Vanessa's house without difficulty. It was thankful that they'd known the way already, as the streets were dark and devoid of anyone to give them directions, this time. An elderly man answered the door, his clothing putting all of theirs to shame; fine wool, fancier even than Johann's bloodstained waistcoat. "Good evening!" he greeted. "You must be our newly elected. I'm Arthur De Burges, do come in."

Abby smiled and allowed him to usher them all inside, shaking his hand as she passed. Each of them offered him their name in a most formal fashion as they entered. "We were just setting the table. Do come on through," he insisted.

The house was nicer inside than out, efforts having been made to cover the bare walls. In the absence of paint, simple wood had been embellished with ornaments like those outside. Religious iconography both modern and archaic; carved folklore figurines; even a single piece of three-dimensional art intricately carved from a rectangle of wood. They certainly knew how to decorate - even the placement of furniture was quite effective in distracting from the small inadequacies.

Even more impressive than the decor was the feast that had been prepared for the seven of them. There were fruits and vegetables in vast amounts, sprawled across a table that was obviously well-suited to events like this. There were even large helpings of meat, still steaming on the bone. "It's lovely to see you all again. I trust you're hungry?" greeted Vanessa. Everyone was, of course. Most of them hadn't even had lunch, and those that had would still be happy to eat more than their fair share. Food was still unreliable out here after all, it was best to eat at any given opportunity.

"I definitely am. That's a beautiful dress, by the way," commented Abby. She took a seat as she admired Vanessa's attire, well-fitted to her

149

waist and frilly about the bosom. "I didn't think anything like that would've survived the journey here. My sister and I both lost a lot of our clothes before we even reached Tinarus, let alone New Cray."

"Kind of you to say. We managed to save one set of proper clothes each, as difficult as it was to do. We wear them only for occasions such as this, of course," Vanessa explained.

"If I may ask, what is it that the two of you did before all of this?" enquired Jaina, seating herself beside Johann.

"I was something of a dilettante, and Vanessa is the second daughter of a baroness. As you might imagine, the marriage was one of political convenience to begin with," explained Arthur. "We try not to talk too much about all of that now; it makes us seem so very stuffy."

"Not to mention it greatly reduces our appeal to the voters. These days it's better to appear one of the people than to adopt an air of superiority," added Vanessa.

"That's probably just as well - I'm not sure I'd know how to act superior in any way other than medical knowledge," Johann chuckled.

"Did you grow all this yourself? And catch it?" Katherine interrupted, somewhat in awe of the mass of food.

Vanessa laughed and shook her head. "Goodness, not all of it. Barely any of it, actually, we're too old to take care of anyone but ourselves. Most of this is what you might call a tax. All of us on the council are entitled to it, naturally."

"People are happy to just give you food?" Michael quizzed.

"Some more than others, but it's not so much to ask; one or two extra mouths to feed between a hundred people," Vanessa said dismissively.

"Not during good times, at least," the smith commented.

"Well, do help yourselves. There's plenty for everyone, I believe," insisted Arthur, and so they began, eating more greedily than any of the five had for quite some time. Full introductions were brief affairs over the food, since Arthur had already heard so much about the New Cray council members. Jaina and Abby, in particular.

"So, I hope you don't mind us talking business at the dinner table, but work and gossip have sort of melded together with this whole voting thing," said Johann.

Vanessa chewed down a mouthful of salad and shook her head, gesturing for him to continue. "By all means," she allowed.

"I found myself wondering what sort of professions the people here have, currently. I suppose there are ways to optimise a workforce even with a population of under a thousand," the doctor theorised.

"Well, as it happens we currently have no doctor of our own. From what I've heard, you've already had a few patients from here, and that number will probably grow as the merge progresses," said Vanessa.

"Perhaps you should move closer to the centre of town when that happens, like I was saying yesterday," suggested Katherine. Johann shared a glance with Abby, clearly considering it just as she was.

"We have some tailors who are always busy. A smith as well, whom we'd very much like Michael to meet at some point," continued Vanessa.

"Carl would make a great apprentice to the tailor," suggested Abby, jumping in while she could. She reckoned the young man would be every bit as excited about that as Michael clearly was about meeting another smith.

"I'm sorry, Carl? Have we met him?" asked Vanessa.

"Not yet, no. He's very talented with that sort of thing, though. He makes all sorts," Abby explained.

"Are there any other lawyers?" enquired Jaina, no doubt more out of interest than any particular purpose.

"Misery loves company," jested Johann. As usual, Jaina took the jibe well, appearing genuinely amused. Picking up on that, some of the others laughed tentatively along with her.

"No lawyers that I know of. Of course, one never entirely knows - people don't always talk about their former professions, and there's little use for the formalities of real law without anyone to enforce it," claimed Vanessa.

"You have guards at the court though, don't you?" Abby quizzed. Somewhat rude guards, as she recalled. She decided it would be better to bring that up later.

"We do indeed," Vanessa smiled.

"Friedrich and Harame. They've served me for most of their lives. They got us here safely, and now they protect the council when it's in session," Arthur explained. "They're not so duty-bound to the law out here as they are to their own consciences."

"There were more of them, but they were the only two that made it all the way with us," Vanessa lamented. No doubt the others had died doing their duty.

"So there are no others? No town guard or such?" Abby asked.

"No. We can't all be as fortunate as you and have a paladin around," Vanessa explained. "The people here are used to taking matters into their own hands."

"He's training more of us, you know. Myself, both of my siblings, and both of Patrick's sons," Abby informed her.

"Well, between the eight of you there ought to be ample protection and enforcement, for what little can be enforced or protected," Vanessa anticipated.

"Perhaps. We could invite Friedrich and Harame to train with us some time if they'd be interested?" suggested Abby.

Arthur nodded his approval. "Perhaps Sir Dunwolf could even train some others for us. Lots of people here have weapons, but very few know how to use them properly. I fenced a little in my youth, and even now I can't help but wonder how most survived for this long, with their lack of technique."

"Fencing for sport is quite different from the style of a knight or paladin," Abby pointed out. "Still, you're probably right. Samson and Daniel were awful when I first met them," she reminisced, chuckling to herself.

"Well anyway, we also have several woodworkers," Vanessa steered the conversation back on track. "Most of us dedicate all of our time to farming crops, though some of the dwarves have begun rearing the less dangerous animals; the stripe-horses, especially."

Abby smiled. "Do you mean the zebras? The ones with black and white stripes."

Their hosts exchanged a glance and nodded. "How do you know that?" Vanessa enquired.

"My father. He read a lot about Tinarus, way before we came here," Abby explained, evoking pleasant smiles from Arthur and his wife.

"How do we go about this 'tax', by the way?" Katherine butted in. "My son and his wife used to help support me after my husband passed away. We might struggle now," she admitted glumly.

"Why's that?" asked Vanessa. Awkwardness descended upon the table, and Abby couldn't decide whether or not it would be disrespectful to explain on Katherine's behalf. Thankfully, Vanessa corrected herself before anyone had to do so. "Ah, a sensitive subject. My apologies. Well, we can arrange the tax once the merge goes through. It's not all that difficult," she assured Katherine.

Abby smiled. She didn't intend to abuse the idea of taxation by any means, but she'd certainly appreciate being able to take care of her family if things got tougher. It was also greatly comforting to know that Katherine would be well looked after.

Johann poured himself a mug of water from a crude, clay jug, and proceeded to share it all around the table until everyone had something to drink. "We may not have wine, but regardless - a toast; to New Cray and Lapden, and a brighter future together," the doctor proposed.

Abby smiled and raised her mug with all the others. "To a brighter future. Together."

12
Heat

The construction had proceeded with renewed vigour between the two villages. Most had accepted that the whole place would formally be named New Cray, but the word 'town' didn't quite apply yet, as there were still a few hundred metres of bare ground separating them. People still referred to the northern village as Lapden, of course, and Abby suspected that it would become something like an unofficial district name even after the physical distance was bridged. That didn't matter, though; unity by any name was still unity, and it was good for them all. Unfortunately, there was bad news as well. The heat had continued to intensify throughout spring, and if it continued at the same rate, there would be a drought soon. The crops were doing well out of the intense sun, but everyone knew that wouldn't last if the weather didn't relent.

The farm had proven difficult to work. Abby had forsaken both the smithy and training for the day in order to carry bucket after bucket of water to the field. Many had suggested that proper irrigation be looked into, but the truth was that they were only farmers by necessity, not by trade. All they could really do was hope that someone with the correct knowledge came along sooner or later.

Abby admired her family's hard work one last time before walking away from their farm. She had little care for the beautiful sunset as she returned home; the sun had become a source of annoyance once again, causing her tan to take on the red hue of sunburn. She was so exhausted from the heat that she couldn't even be bothered to make dinner that night.

Johann lifted a tired hand in greeting to her as she passed. He was busy fanning patients in the shade, heatstroke a most common affliction lately. He'd spent some nights in the houses of the afflicted to make sure they didn't overexert themselves and expire as a result. Abby hadn't missed his warmth at night, but she had missed his company.

She flopped limply on top of the bed and strew her clothes about the room before struggling to find sleep in a puddle of her own sweat. In the time since the election, she'd regularly dreamed of herself as a beloved leader, and that night was another such instance. She hadn't told anyone of the dreams in case they thought her egotistical - which was perhaps a fair conclusion - but she kept having them. Whether it was leading the people of New Cray into battle, preaching sermons to a crowded chapel, or being praised as a queen, she always imagined herself in a position of power. Whether the power came with privilege or just responsibility, she liked feeling as if her potential was being fulfilled. She liked feeling as if she was a moral authority.

***

The heat went on and on, a terrible scourge, and more terrible still the idea that summer would only get hotter. The spring harvest was strong, the efforts to manually water the crops paying off in conjunction with the oppressive sunshine, but the reality was that nobody could continue to work the fields as it grew hotter and the water became scarcer.

Most other jobs couldn't be attended either. Every industry of New Cray suffered in one way or another - they were pale men and women of Luthania, far from home and unused to such conditions. Construction ground to a halt early in the summer and only ever saw progress when it rained. The same was true of Michael's smithing, Tahgri's training, and even relations with Lapden; their northern neighbours hadn't fared any better in the heat, and the best that could be done to aid them was to help them ration and divide crops so that nothing was wasted. Though many tried to sow seeds again at the first reprieve of the summer rains, they couldn't frequently tend them. Everything died in the soil almost as soon as it had been planted.

Once again, the harshness of the land began to claim the lives of the weakest; the old, the undernourished, and even the unborn. Fever and starvation had taken more than a tenth of the population of New Cray by the time they reached the mark of the seven hundred and fiftieth day. People kept mainly to themselves, and it could be days at a time without knowing who'd lived and who'd died, sealed away in the shade and solitude of their houses.

***

Abby ran the damp rag over her father's forehead. He was capable of doing it himself, as was Elizabeth, but Abby and her siblings had been taking good care of their parents during an episode of heatstroke. It was day seven hundred and sixty-three, and summer had begun in earnest. She was long since twenty-three now, another year older with nothing done to celebrate it.

Johann was at Jaina's today. She too was suffering from heat stroke, and knowing that Abby was more than happy to tend to her parents herself, the doctor had left the five of them to use his place as they desired.

154

"How long before it cools down again?" begged Carmina, wiping sweat from her own brow.

"I don't even know the date," admitted Aurelius.

"Nineteenth of June, sixteen-forty-nine," Abby muttered after a few moments of calculation. They looked at her as if she'd just told them the meaning of life. "I've been counting," she shrugged.

"So a couple more months, I suppose," concluded Aurelius.

"Afraid so," she agreed. Part of her was terrified of how many would die by the time the heat of summer began to fade. She tried to reassure herself and others with the knowledge that there had once been natives on Tinarus that had lived through worse than this. Perhaps there still were - it seemed unlikely that the Redanin Empire had killed *all* of them when they'd voyaged here so long ago.

"I'm going to lie down for a bit. Mind if I use your bed?" Carmina asked.

"Go ahead," Abby allowed. Aurelius took over from his younger sister and joined in with the gentle rhythm of repeatedly washing their parents' foreheads. It was almost enough to lull them all to sleep.

Rather suddenly, the tranquility of the routine was shattered by a feminine scream from outside. Abby startled, unintentionally slapping her father across the face with the wet rag. "Ugh! What on Panora was that?" he demanded.

Abby darted to the shutters and flung them open, squinting as sunlight burst around the previously shaded room. Her throat tightened at the sight before her, thin ranks of them striding confidently through the streets of New Cray. "Fire elementals."

Her parents immediately sat up, but Abby slammed the shutters and blocked her father's path before he could stand. "Lay down, you can't help this and you can't go out in this heat. Aurelius, Carmina, come with me. We'll get your weapons and fetch the others," she ordered, gently forcing her father back down onto the bench.

"But-" complained her mother.

"No buts!" insisted Abby, darting through to her room. She ignored Carmina's state of semi-nudity and grabbed her hammer and shield. There was no time to take the rest - the simple armour would hinder more than help her beneath the glaring sun, anyway.

She trusted that Carmina would be close behind her and followed Aurelius out the door. Wisely, he chose to retrieve his weapons first, waiting for a gap in the elementals before darting across the path to their parents' home. Abby helped her siblings to fetch their gear - swords, arrows, and bows - before pausing to assess the situation. The elementals seemed to be stalking aimlessly through the streets rather than actively destroying anything, for now, but they were between the siblings and Patrick's house. Abby left by the back door and led the way to the Marshal household, being careful to avoid being seen wherever possible.

She was just about to give further orders when Patrick's door burst open up ahead of them. Samson and Daniel came out with swords at the ready. Of course, this immediately drew the attention of the elementals. There were five in the street nearby, two of which shambled towards the brothers, crackling with heat.

Carmina and Aurelius began to string their bows, but Abby could tell that they weren't going to be done in time. Fighting back against the fear gripping her heart, she charged at the elementals, taking advantage of their turned backs. She slammed her shield heftily across the back of one flaming skull, and her hammer into the other. She felt them crumble beneath her assault, and a second blow with the hammer went clean through, sending flaming fragments spinning through the air and forcing Abby to withdraw before she received serious burns. The one that was still in one piece swung furiously at her with blazing arms. She was faster than she used to be, and deflected them with ease. Then her shield burst into flames.

She shook her arm and flung the shield away. Two arrows thudded into the elemental's chest, instantly igniting along the shafts before falling back out along with a crumbling, black mess. Daniel brought his sword down through the creature, severing it from shoulder to hip, and Abby leapt backwards even further as the elemental fell towards her and scattered all over the ground. She looked over the others for injuries; Samson seemed frozen by his fear, but they were all fine. Their house was catching fire, however.

"Put that out!" she ordered, edging around the coal-like remains to try and pat out the flames with her shirt and bare hands. With some very minor burns and a little singed clothing, they managed to prevent the conflagration from taking a proper hold.

A distant woman's yells for help reached Abby's ears. "All of you stick together. Don't waste arrows on them if you can help it - keep out of reach and use your swords, and definitely don't fight near buildings," she instructed the trainees. Daniel was surprisingly collected, and she hoped he'd keep them from panicking in her absence.

Where are you going?" Demanded Carmina.

"I'm gonna fetch Tahgri," Abby told them. "Good luck!" She broke into a jog, the heat starting to get to her as she took off towards Tahgri's house. The temperature wasn't helped by the proximity of her scorching opponents.

She pulverised another flaming skull with her hammer in passing.

Like the earthen elementals, they were mockeries of the human form; skeletal men made of charcoal. Their bodies crumbled easily under a fierce blow, but even in defeat they could cause serious damage with the burning fragments of coal left behind.

She realised that they were now pursuing her, almost matching her pace as she neared Tahgri's house. "To arms!" she called as loudly as she could. Not willing to risk a blaze, she steered clear of the building itself, circling widely around to glance at the door. It was already open, no sign of Tahgri inside. Perhaps he was already fighting.

Her hesitation there gave one of the elementals time to close the gap and take a swing at her. Abby went to deflect it instinctively, yanking her arm back as she received a narrow, painful burn where she was used to having a shield. She retaliated by dipping out of the way of a second blow and driving her hammer up through her opponent's ashen jaw.

"To arms!" she cried as she took off again, fleeing from her pursuers and heading towards the sounds of yelling. Smoke billowed in the sky ahead of her, the source of it a pair of houses ablaze around the next corner. More of the elementals strode onwards, their fiery gaze seeking anything organic. Thankfully, they didn't seem intelligent enough to deliberately burn people out of their homes.

She destroyed another elemental as she passed, using her momentum to drop it to the floor with a single blow. Her fingers complained when the hammer became lodged momentarily, flames licking at her digits for the briefest of moments. She carried on, and soon came to the well where Tahgri already stood, his claymore in hand and a pile of smouldering remains scattered around him. Amanda was busy drawing water beside him, terror writ on her face in a stark contrast to the calm determination of the paladin. It was a thing of beauty to watch him fight, even in his old age. He brought the sword down and across in perfect arcs, destroying any that dared near him before they could get within reach. Abby helped him clear a crowd of oncoming opponents, their focus so drawn to the paladin that she could disassemble a few of them from behind without receiving further injury.

Tahgri darted forwards, almost barreling Abby over as he struck down one that had, in turn, snuck up behind her. "Thanks," Abby gasped, wiping sweat from her forehead as she moved around him.

Amanda splashed them both with water, steam hissing up around them as the remains of the elementals were doused. "Orders?" Tahgri requested, facing Abby without even pausing in his annihilation of their opponents. She considered telling him that he was in charge, given that he was by far the most experienced combatant in New Cray, but she forced herself to take responsibility. She wanted to be the leader she was

157

in her dreams, and what better time to start than right away. "Ma'am?" Tahgri growled, forcefully pulling her backwards with one arm and decapitating a pair of elementals with the other.

"Uh, drink up! If the heat gets to you, this is over," she instructed. Thankfully he'd had the same insight as her and left the armour at home. "Amanda, keep people hydrated as long as there's still water in the well. Tahgri, can you fight your way back to Johann's? Meet up with Aurelius and the others, and bring them here."

"And you?" he asked.

"My weapon's too short. I'll round up the civilians and get them to safety?"

"Don't ask, Abby. Order!" he insisted.

Quite why he was so obstinate about her taking charge, she didn't know, but she wasn't about to complain. She could just imagine it now; Captain Koning. "Go! Save as many as you can. Don't fight near the buildings if you can help it, they can set them on fire even after they die," Abby reminded him.

Tahgri nodded and yanked the hammer from her hands, giving her his sword in its place. "Use this. I'll be fine with your hammer," he insisted.

Abby set to work, but not before taking a great gulp of water from Amanda's bucket. She darted back the way she'd come, knocking on house doors and cutting down elementals as she moved. People had obviously heard the yelling, as many were already dressed, ready, and sometimes armed when they answered the door. "Get to the eastern well! Bring any weapons you have and keep clear of the buildings!" she insisted to each and every one of them. They all followed her orders without hesitation.

She winced as she saw a dwarf come out from his home, trying to beat down one of the attackers with what appeared to be a table leg. One of the elemental's arms crumbled under the assault, but the other took hold of the makeshift weapon, setting it ablaze. The dwarf could do little as the creature advanced on him, and though Abby ran as fast as she could manage, she sliced though the elemental too late. The civilian was already unconscious and dying, his head entirely ablaze and his eyes melting in his skull. The best she could manage was to shift his limp form away from the wood of the house to prevent it igniting.

She'd already got most of the village to safety by the time Tahgri caught up with her, his trainees in tow. "There are some fires and some dead, but I think we got most of them," he informed her.

She nodded and wiped the sweat from her brow again. "Ignore the fires, there's no time to put them out now. Gather all the civilians and get them into the houses around the eastern well. Tell them not to come out unless we fetch them," she ordered.

"What about mum and dad?" demanded Carmina.

"They'll be safe if they stay put. I'll go and tell them not to move. Meet me in Lapden once everyone's secure," she ordered before dashing off to check on her parents. Tahgri didn't seem to have taken care of as many elementals as he thought he had, and she had to slice her way through another handful of them as they shambled her way. The sword wasn't designed for Abby's height, but the length alone was enough of an advantage that the balance barely seemed to matter against unarmed opponents. She shouldered the weapon and banged on the shutters as she reached Johann's house.

Her dad opened them, looking exhausted from the heat though still pleased to see her. "Abby! What do we do?" he demanded.

"You'll be alright as long as you stay inside and keep the shutters closed. Don't let them see you. Just stay put and keep cool, alright? We're taking care of it," she assured him.

Her mother joined Alexander at the window. Scepticism covered her features, but she leaned down to kiss Abby on the cheek regardless. "Good luck, sweetie," she said before withdrawing inside again. Her father spared her a forced smile and closed the shutters.

Without delay, Abby took off towards Lapden, sweating buckets as she jogged. It was only when she reached the small gulf between the two villages that she realised the full gravity of the situation; the creatures marched as far as the eye could see. Where they were unobstructed, they moved east to west, often setting small blazes in the patchy grass. There must've been thousands of them, though only a relatively small number seemed to take an interest in Lapden. For the first time, Abby found herself properly contemplating the intelligence of the elementals. It had never seemed a concern before, but if she was going to command she should make efforts to understand her enemy.

Had the situation been less dire she might have stood and waited for the flaming army to pass them by, but she could see the pillars of smoke throughout Lapden, and suspected that the situation was worse over there than it was in New Cray. Praying for Rendick to guide her, she took off in a jog, cutting down foe after foe in the perilous crossing.

The density of her opponents was great enough that many came close to her despite the whirling blade, leaving several small and painful burns on her arms and thoroughly ruining her shirt. Still, despite exhaustion and pain, Abby continued to batter her opponents. She noted that the elementals ahead of her didn't pause to look back despite all the noise she made. They simply continued their apparently aimless wandering, oblivious to anything that wasn't in front of them.

A matter of minutes felt like an eternity of battle, but she eventually came to the southernmost buildings of Lapden. Their streets were full of the invaders, and it was little wonder why; everywhere Abby looked and went there were citizens fighting with whatever weapons they could find, proper or improvised. Corpses littered the ground, and not just those of the elementals. She realised now that it had been a mistake to fight when they could've hidden, but a lesson learned from this was something gained for the future.

She helped wherever she could, trying to spare her energy and be as efficient as possible with the borrowed sword. All of Tahgri's training had paid off, and she slowly but surely made her way towards Vanessa's house. "Everyone with a weapon, follow me!" she yelled, her voice tired from exertion. Most followed her, though some ignored her orders even as she saved their lives.

She felt lumps of the coal-like flesh of the elementals beneath her boots as she walked, like hot, jagged stones digging into her soles. It slowed her progress just as much as the still-animated enemies, but she fought on anyway. Eventually, she reached Vanessa's house. It was still perfectly intact and the door was closed, hopefully with both Vanessa and Arthur still inside. As long as they stayed in there, they were safe.

Abby continued on towards the court next, knowing that she could defend from the stone steps without risk of fire. She made swift progress, a growing crowd of people following her. Friedrich and Harame seemed to have had the same idea - by the time Abby arrived they were already taking advantage of the inflammable court steps to battle off a swarm of aggressors with their bastard swords. The youngest of the two warriors was soon pulled down into the midst of the abominations, his screams of agony swiftly fading as he was held in place within the collective blaze of the monstrous crowd.

Abby and her civilian comrades battered into the blazing enemies from behind. The elementals fell quickly to the superior numbers, and the older man - whichever of the two he was - pulled his comrade free from the pile of smouldering bodies. It was too late, though; he was unconscious and hideously burned already.

"Anyone with a proper weapon, stay on these steps. Anyone else, get inside the court," Abby commanded wearily. She took up position beside the other guard as she watched the crowd mill about. "Are you Friedrich or Harame?" she asked, catching her breath.

"Friedrich," the man replied gruffly. Abby nodded and prepared herself for further combat.

Three of the civilians stayed on the steps with them, two with wooden clubs and a third taking up Harame's dropped sword. They formed a line

160

as the elementals swarmed in again. Friedrich was good with a blade, and even the clearly untrained man to Abby's right did enough damage by slashing the elementals mercilessly across their heads. The two with the wooden weapons didn't fare so well, their clubs catching light after just a couple of strikes. They managed to kill a few more, but it wasn't long before both of them were weaponless and massacred just as Harame had been. Their screams and the stench of burning flesh sickened Abby as they cooked alive, writhing on the stone steps.

The defenders that remained were forced to lose ground and back up in order to protect the entire width of the steps. They held there for some time, slaughtering their opponents in waves and recovering as much as they could when they weren't under attack. The swarms became less coordinated as time dragged on, formed of elementals that wandered in one after another rather than assembling in denser packs. Abby was glad of the reprieve, as she was growing dizzy from the heat.

Help arrived by the time they no longer needed it; Tahgri approached with all the others in tow. He demolished his opponents so very casually with Abby's hammer, not even breaking stride as he dodged their flailing arms. It was a good reminder that no matter how much she learned from him, his experience would always be superior. He eased himself up the steps towards them, swaying slightly from all the effort. "I tried to get as many civilians as I could inside. If you've done the same here, we should be alright," he panted.

Abby nodded tiredly. "Good job. I just need to sit down a minute," she responded, then promptly slumped forwards as she passed out.

***

She wiped the sweat from her brow, glancing around in confusion. "Hey, love," Johann murmured, sat in a chair beside her.

She looked over at him as her senses returned to her. She was on an unfamiliar sleeping mat, and completely naked. It also wasn't sweat she'd wiped from her brow, but water that Johann had been cooling her with. "I passed out?" she mumbled, sitting up.

"Take it easy!" Johann ordered, frowning at her. He waited until she'd laid down again before answering her question. "You did indeed. The heat got to you, I suppose. How do you feel now?"

She looked herself over briefly. The burns on her arms had turned sore shades of red and pink. They might scar a little, but she knew they'd be fine given adequate time to heal. "A bit of a headache. Sore, but not awful. Where are we?" she enquired.

"Vanessa's bedroom. You weren't unconscious long, Tahgri brought you here."

Abby looked around again. "Vanessa and Arthur don't share a bed?" she questioned, struggling to imagine two adults of any size fitting comfortably onto this sleeping mat.

"Apparently Arthur snores something awful," Johann smiled.

Abby chuckled under her breath and stared at the ceiling, trying to recall everything that she'd been thinking last time she was conscious. "Is everyone alright?" she asked.

"Well, not *everyone*, unfortunately. They're still counting the dead, but your family are just fine. Daniel got a bad burn on his arm, but he'll be alright if infection doesn't set in."

"Jaina?" she enquired, doing her best to remain calm.

"She's fine."

"What about Michael? And Carl?"

"Still indoors, nothing to worry about," he tried to assure her. "Just relax. Don't think about all that just yet."

Abby exhaled and closed her eyes. She'd have time to get a proper accounting of the casualties and the structural damages later. For now, she'd thank the Maralor that her friends and family were alive. "Are you sure you're alright?" asked Johann, lowering himself to the floor beside her.

"I'll be fine. It's much cooler in here," she assured him.

"I'm not talking about the heat. Apparently it got pretty rough out there," he explained. "I thought you might want to talk about it."

"Nothing I haven't seen before, Johann. I'm just tired," she assured him. It was perhaps a half-truth; the men burning to death so close to her on the steps had been a particularly unpleasant experience, and one she hoped was never to be repeated - but for better or worse, Abby was more numbed to those sorts of horrors than she used to be.

"If you're certain. You know, people reckon you're a hero now," Johann claimed. "There's going to be a meeting at the court tonight. I think everyone would like your input, if you're feeling up to it by then."

Abby smiled, making no effort to protest such a status. "Shouldn't you be insisting I stay right here and get plenty of rest?" she chuckled, enjoying the gentle sponging of water on her forehead once again.

"Would you listen?" he queried.

"Probably not."

"Then I won't waste my breath. It'll be at sundown anyway, so the heat won't be such an issue."

Abby nodded and opened her eyes again, just so that she could grab Johann and pull him into a kiss. "Thanks."

He stayed with her for most of the afternoon, until she'd managed to convince him that she was just fine. Ignoring her stomach's complaints of hunger and a general feeling of exhaustion, she dressed in the singed linens and set out into Lapden once again. Her first port of call was the nearest well - she'd only intended to get a drink, but as it happened she found Tahgri talking with Vanessa, and got a full update on the situation. Ten had died in New Cray, and thirty-three in Lapden. A total of nine buildings had also burned down between the two villages. Ever in search of the bright side, Abby was informed that the coal-like remains of the monsters could, in fact, be used exactly like coal. It probably was coal, despite its unnatural source. The smiths would surely have an abundance of fuel for some time to come.

Abby promised the pair she'd be at the meeting and had her fill of water before going to the court to wait out the last of the sunshine. She opened a single shutter to keep track of the time, watching the shadows lengthen and blend together as she pondered what they'd learned from this attack. She was eventually pulled from her train of thought by Jaina and Johann wandering in, laughing at some unheard joke as the light faded. "Hey," she greeted them.

They turned suddenly, seeing her lurking in the shadows of the back row of benches. "Oh! Abby! Are you feeling any better?" asked Jaina, obviously a little surprised that the room hadn't been empty.

"Much better, thanks. I'm glad to see you made it through without a scratch," Abby responded. She got to her feet and made her way down towards them.

"As am I, though I must confess that I was hiding under a bed for the whole affair," said Jaina. "The others should be here soon, by the way."

The three of them sat down on a bench together, conversation scant. Abby couldn't help but feel that she was bringing the mood down, but given the events of the day she didn't imagine they'd hold it against her. People soon began to file into the chamber - all the council members were easily recognisable despite the gloom, and Abby noted that most of those who'd swept through the streets of Lapden alongside her were present as well.

The room became quiet as everyone took seats. Everyone except Vanessa, who stood at the lectern. "If you'll excuse the lack of our usual formality, this is not formally a council meeting," she greeted. "I'd like to start by thanking those of you who fought today. Many of you are from New Cray, and it's reassuring that even in these dark times we can count on you as our allies. I'd like to ask first of all, does anyone have reason to believe that such an attack won't occur again?"

Tahgri stood up, shaking his head. "It's common knowledge that the elementals come from their favoured environments. In this case, they may have been drawn by the heat. Unless you believe it's going to get cooler rather than hotter, they *will* show up again," he asserted.

"Does anyone disagree?" asked Vanessa. There was silence. "Most of us aren't fighters. Even those of us lucky enough to have weapons aren't necessarily that good with them," she reminded the audience. "If we don't have some sort of plan to deal with these elementals, we're not going to last all that long. I'd like to ask those of you with knowledge of combat for advice."

"Don't," instructed Abby.

Vanessa looked at her questioningly. "Excuse me?"

"Deal with them, I mean. There's no real need to," Abby stated. A few people murmured around her, no doubt questioning her sanity.

"Are you suggesting we flee?" asked Vanessa.

Abby shook her head and slowly rose to her feet, walking over to take the lectern. "We can't fight them. There are too many, and in this heat we're struggling to stay outside, let alone fight - but I don't think they were actually doing all that much harm until we started trying to kill them. The vast majority actually passed us by, as I understand it. Where they were going and to what end, I don't know, but they did pass. That's why I was quick to secure civilians inside."

There was another murmur as people seemed to catch on to what she was getting at. "Katherine, was Amanda the first one to notice them?" Abby asked. "I think it was her screaming that drew my attention in the first place."

Katherine nodded firmly. "It's like you said. They were just passing on through until they saw her."

"They seem to keep clear of the buildings unless lured to them by us, and I think they're deaf - I was running right behind them and none of them turned around - so in reality, they only pose a threat as long as they see us," Abby informed them. "Given that we're keeping the shutters closed at this time of year, that's mostly just an issue when fetching water. Amanda *was* fetching water, wasn't she?"

"She was," confirmed Katherine.

"We should have an announcement for each of our villages," Abby proposed. "Look carefully to make sure there are no elementals outside *before* fetching water. If there are, try to wait as long as you can for them to move on. If the water is needed too desperately to wait, try not to be seen when you fetch it. If you're seen by the elementals they *will* pursue you, *don't* run inside, because it's possible they'll follow you and set the whole building on fire. If you can, lead them into a secluded area and kill them with whatever weapons you have available. Even a good heavy stick could kill one or two of these things before it burns up."

Vanessa looked around, gauging reaction. It seemed to be generally positive, though there was obviously still a little apprehension. "We're not trained fighters, not like you," one of the civilians pointed out. "You say it like killing them is the easiest thing in the world."

"Try using a lengthy weapon," Tahgri contributed. "That'll work well against them - training or not. Anyone could stand a decent chance of fighting them safely, given enough distance."

Vanessa nodded and peered around the room again. "And what if that doesn't work?" she asked nervously.

"Then scream as loud as you can, and hope that someone who knows how to fight comes to you," commented Friedrich.

"It's also possible to outrun them. They're not all that fast," Abby recalled.

"That settles it, then, unless anyone disagrees?" concluded Vanessa, leaving ample time for others to contribute. Nobody did. "Until such a time as there's cause to change tactics, we'll simply hide from them. Thank you all for your advice. I'll be sure that announcements are made as soon as possible."

"Likewise. If anyone would like to help me gather people tonight, that'd be great," said Abby, looking to the other elected of New Cray in particular. She ambled to the door, but was intercepted by Friedrich and Tahgri before she could leave.

"Miss Koning. I wanted to thank you for your assistance earlier. If you hadn't arrived when you had, many more could well have died. Myself included," said Friedrich.

Abby smiled weakly at him. "Please, Friedrich, call me Abby. And you're welcome. I couldn't just leave you to die, we're in this together now, even if we're not merged just yet."

He nodded approvingly. "That sort of attitude is exactly what we need more of if we're to survive. I'm sure we'll return the favour."

Did Harame survive, by the way?" she asked, though she feared that she already knew the answer.

"He survived, but we had to…" the guard swallowed hard, his face tingeing with repressed sorrow. "He was in a lot of pain. It was a mercy, really."

"I'm so sorry about that. You did the right thing, though," she tried to assure him. She would've gone in for a hug, but her arms still stung from the burns, and he probably wasn't the sort to appreciate it anyway.

"Thank you," Friedrich responded before passing her by. It was like being at a funeral, one of any number of relatives offering condolences and saying little else.

Tahgri matched her pace as she left. "You did well today. You may still have things to learn, but you played it smart. Few things are more important to winning a fight than using your brain, just you remember that," he commented.

Abby was glad of his approval, though her mind was still too busy dwelling on Harame to show it. "Thanks. Now, seeing as I'm giving the orders all of a sudden, come and help me gather the civilians."

Tahgri put an arm around her shoulders. "Yes ma'am."

13
Vultures

Aurelius spat the inedible part of his second and final carrot out, his dissatisfaction as clear as the nose on his face. "Alright, that does it. Hunting?" he suggested. Breakfast had been as small and unfulfilling as it had been every day for the previous week, and though they'd rationed and eaten consistently, they'd only become hungrier over time.

"Hunting," chorused Abby and Carmina, getting to their feet.

"Shall I come with you?" asked Johann.

Carmina gave him a judgemental look and shook her head. "Stick to what you're good at, Johann," she grumbled.

"The river runs red," muttered the doctor.

"Cut it out, both of you!" snapped Abby. She chalked it up to hunger, as she'd had to restrain her own undeserved anger once or twice in recent days. Johann sighed and simply walked off home before anyone could trade more barbs with him.

They fetched their gear, not that there was much to fetch, and soon enough they headed out. "Good hunting! Take care!" their mother called after them.

"Something big today," insisted Aurelius. He'd find no arguments there; although carrying prey back was made more difficult by empty stomachs and extreme temperatures, they were all starving. They'd take as much as they could feasibly carry.

The savannah, once so full of beautiful creatures, was empty. Even past the tree that had traditionally marked their hunting grounds, the watering hole had dried up in the heat, forcing most of the animals further north or west. Resultantly, hunting had become more problematic for the citizens of New Cray, exacerbating the food issue.

On and on the siblings walked, the blazing heat causing them to work their way through their water faster than they'd have liked. Aurelius soon stripped off his shirt and tucked it into his belt, his back dripping with sweat. It wasn't long before Abby and Carmina followed his example, the overwhelming heat overriding any concerns they might've had over exposing themselves to their brother.

"Hey," said Carmina, a tired grin spreading across her face. "How much do you think dad would whine if he knew his 'sweet and innocent daughter' was out like this?" Abby just chuckled, her throat too dry to give a proper reply.

They walked for what felt like hours, until they were long past the empty basin that had once been a watering hole. They hadn't been so far west since they'd first arrived in New Cray. "Hey, is that an ostrich?" Aurelius dared to hope, gesturing off into the distance.

"Nope. That's just a big rock," claimed Carmina, inducing groans of disappointment from her siblings.

On and on they walked, until at last nature stood beautifully before them once more. It was just trees at first - not that there had been an absence of these in the savannah - but they came in gradually increasing density until it could be fairly described as woodland, the only break in which was a rocky stream as clear and fresh as could be hoped for. They dashed over to it, their pace matching their thirst, drinking greedily and refilling their water skins.

"How about we creep along the stream bank a while? We might find something that way," Aurelius suggested once they were refreshed. Abby nodded agreeably, her stomach growling at her.

"May as well. I like our chances," said Carmina. They all saturated their shirts with water before covering up again.

Signs of wildlife were all around them as they began to creep steadily north-west. Some birds even showed themselves, and though they were too small to be worth the effort of trying to shoot down, the trio sated their hunger temporarily on the raw eggs they found in nests - shells and all. It wasn't long before they were deep within the woodland, no sign of open ground to be seen, and only the stream to guide them back. "Hold up," insisted Carmina, gesturing off to the left. The trio stopped dead in their tracks, pressing themselves against trees and observing.

It took Abby a few moments to realise that what she was looking at was not a fallen log between trees, but a great reptile basking beneath a gap in the canopy. "Sugar, is that a snake?" she asked rhetorically, the sleek black and brown scales drawing her eye.

"Biggest I've ever seen," gawked Carmina.

Aurelius remained in stunned silence for a few moments. "Do you think it's edible?" he eventually asked.

Abby nodded, still eyeing the magnificent length of the creature. "It must be worth eating. It's like a six-metre-long sausage!"

"Alright. How do we kill it?" asked Carmina.

"I'll try and get close to get a shot at the head. Carmina, come with me. Aurelius, stay here, and if it moves just hit it anywhere you can," Abby ordered. Carmina followed her, moving through the undergrowth as quietly as possible - not that it made any difference; unbeknownst to them, the creature's senses were so keen that it had known of their presence long before they'd seen it.

Abby and Carmina took all of five steps towards the serpent before gunshots rang out; three of them in rapid succession, from beyond their line of sight. They immediately panicked and dashed back over to take cover beside Aurelius.

"Fuck, what now?" he asked, pointing to the snake slithering away rapidly.

A fourth gunshot broke the stillness of the woodlands, and Abby watched the direction it had come from cautiously. "Everything worth eating's going to have run off now. Just wait for them to move on and hope they don't do anything stupid, I guess," she whispered.

They watched and waited in silence. Out here, anyone could be at the mercy of bandits, and Abby didn't want any unnecessary conflict. She'd rather live and let live.

Three men erupted from the tree cover ahead of them, panicking and sprinting straight towards the siblings. Two more gunshots rang out, and two of the men collapsed. One of them landed face-first in the dirt, his foremost leg falling out from beneath him as a bullet tore through it. Another man rolled onto his side, screaming and clutching his gut.

The last of the three men sprinted straight towards the siblings' cover, another two shots ringing out behind him - one spat up fragments of bark right beside its intended target, but the final shot caught him in the arm. He staggered and ground to a halt as he saw them hidden amongst the foliage. "Abby?" he questioned.

She looked to the man's bloodied arm, and then his face. She could hardly believe it; although his hair had greyed a little and his beard had grown wilder, he was unmistakable. "Eric!" she exclaimed, surprise putting her off-balance after witnessing the cold-blooded murders. She grabbed him by the wrist and tugged him into cover. "Who are they? Can you still fight?"

"My arm's fucked. I don't think I can aim this thing properly, but I can load it," he informed them, gritting his teeth from the pain and reloading with slow, laboured actions.

Abby glanced around the tree to see the attackers advancing directly towards them. The live and let live option was officially off the table. "Try and take out their legs," she whispered across to her siblings.

"Or just kill them," responded Aurelius, leaning out and firing off an arrow. Abby frowned, but this was hardly the time for a discussion on the ethics of dealing with criminals. Judging by the lack of any sounds of pain, Aurelius had missed his target anyway.

Abby leaned out from behind the tree and took a shot at one of their unknown opponents, an elf of dingy appearance. It embedded itself into the wood of the tree he was cowering against, and she ducked back into cover as he and his comrades returned fire. She waited a few seconds and then popped out again, rapidly loosing two more arrows at the same elf as he retreated to better cover. One of them struck this time, embedding itself in the back of his left knee and extracting a yell of pain as he fell. Abby hid again, giving them time to waste further rounds.

"What are you waiting for?" grunted Eric, pushing his gun towards her. "They'll take a good twenty seconds to reload."

"Right, yeah," she muttered. She knew that, of course, she'd simply been worried that she hadn't accounted for all of the opponents. Perhaps one of them still had a gun ready, waiting for her.

Abby stayed in cover anyway, for safety's sake, then briefly peeked out to encourage them to waste their next rounds. Gunshots screamed, but hit only trees and earth. Her confidence bolstered by Eric's reminder, Abby slipped out from behind the tree, an arrow ready to loose. One of the villains was knelt over the man that had been shot in the leg, slitting his throat to finish the job. Abby narrowly missed the bandit, but another arrow flew straight past her and plunged into his back, causing him to stumble and crawl away to cover. She took another shot at his shoulder to incapacitate him, but fell short yet again.

Short on arrows, she dipped back to grab Eric's gun, then advanced hurriedly through the woodlands. Dropping the borrowed weapon to the ground, she loosed two arrows in pursuit of a woman on the retreat. Though she'd aimed for the legs, she was fairly sure all she'd done was clip the woman's hip.

A dwarf emerged from cover, taking aim with a gun that seemed a little too large for him. Another arrow from one of her siblings narrowly missed him, but it caused him to flinch and put his shot off, spitting up dirt beside Abby. He tried to retreat, but she took up Eric's gun and aimed low. Truth be told, 'aimed' might've been an exaggeration, as she'd never fired a gun before. The scarcity of gunpowder made them impractical to practice with.

She didn't stay still long enough to see if her shot had hit after the weapon bucked. The elf she'd shot in the knee had reloaded whilst on his back, and raised his rifle. Abby hid behind a tree until the gun went off, then ducked back out and loosed her last arrow at him, a clean hit to the shoulder. She grimaced as her siblings finished the job unnecessarily, one in the chest and one in the neck.

Abby replayed the frantic seconds of combat in her head, trying to remember how many there had been and what had happened to them. Moving cautiously out of cover, she spotted a pair of legs protruding beside the base of a tree. She snuck closer, shouldering her bow and turning the rifle in her hands to wield it like a club.

The man still had the arrow sticking out of his back; Abby gathered from his laboured breathing that it had gone right into the lung. He thumbed back the hammer on his rifle, oblivious to her presence. "Drop it," she warned once she was close enough to take a swing at him. He took one look at her and blew his own brains all over the tree he'd been leaning against, evidently preferring a quick death. Abby turned her head away sharply, trying not to see the messy results.

The woman who had so far got away lucky was already back on her feet and trying to reload. Abby charged at her fearlessly, certain that she had time to get there before the weapon was primed. The stranger raised her rifle, but she wasn't fast enough; Abby knocked the barrel off to the side with her own weapon and grabbed the end of it, forcing it in an arc away from her and aiming it up at the treetops. She winced at the loud roar of the weapon so close to her face and promptly kicked the woman in the gut to wind her. She proved an unimpressive opponent when she wasn't cowering behind a firearm, and a quick bit of footwork brought her to her knees. Abby yanked the rifle free of her hands and opened what little guard she had left with a boot to the crotch.

She pushed the barrels of both guns harshly into the woman's neck. They may not have been loaded, but they could still hurt enough to keep her where she was. "Not an inch," Abby growled, her ears ringing from the gunshot. Confident that the woman was too distracted with the pain in her crotch to do anything incredibly stupid, she glanced back to check on the others. They were gathering up the weapons of the dead, and Eric seemed to be doing alright despite his injury. He was quick to put one of his fallen comrades out of his misery, still squirming and crying from a gut shot. There wasn't a chance that he would've survived all the way out here.

"I think that's all of them," Aurelius called out as he approached. He came up beside Abby, drawing a knife with his free hand.

She realised just in time what he intended to do, and used one of the rifles to bat away the weapon as he attempted to finish off the woman. "Stop!" Abby demanded.

"She's a murderer, Abby. You want to just let her live?" questioned Aurelius, frowning.

Abby glared and tossed away the rifles, putting herself between the two. "Since when did we decide who gets to live or die for what crimes? This isn't right!" she snapped at him, struggling to believe he would take the life of another so lightly.

"Since when? How about just now," he insisted, gesturing across at the dwarf. Abby hadn't even looked before, but now she could hardly take her eyes from what she'd done; there was an unpleasant hole in the back of the dwarf's skull, blood pooling beneath his face. Repressing her guilt, Abby brought herself to stop Aurelius from slitting the captive's throat just in time, twisting his wrist and throwing him to the ground angrily.

"You may be in charge in New Cray, but this isn't New Cray!" he shouted, getting back to his feet.

Abby's reply was weak-voiced despite the conviction she felt on the matter. "I'm in charge in New Cray and everywhere else, as far as you're concerned, and you're not executing anyone."

"Just kill me already. It's better than whatever you'll do to me if I live," insisted the captive woman.

"See?" pressed Aurelius.

Abby turned to glare at the woman. "Nobody's doing anything to you yet, now be quiet."

Carmina stepped up to survey the situation, Eric not far behind her. "I appreciate you saving my arse, but what are you going to do with her if we keep her alive?" the hunter enquired.

"I don't know! You haven't even told me who these people are yet!" Abby complained, looking to Eric for explanation.

"Just bandits," he claimed. The captive didn't argue with that.

"We could make her carry for us," pointed out Carmina.

Aurelius put his knife away, scowling at Abby as he did so. "Carry what? In case you hadn't noticed, our meal slithered away," he reminded them.

"I wouldn't say that," grunted Eric, glancing across at the dwarf.

"What do you mean?" enquired Abby, struggling to keep back the tears of guilt as she looked at the man she'd killed. It was a few moments before realisation struck her.

"You can't be serious," commented Carmina.

"I haven't eaten in days. If you've got any better meals, I'll take you up on that," Eric argued.

Aurelius was the first to cave in to the pressure. "Well, he does have a point," he admitted, then squinted at Abby. "Are you crying?"

She tried to swallow the lump developing in her throat and nodded. "Forget about it. Let's deal with this," she insisted, though she failed to prevent the tears from reaching her voice as she refocused on the matter at hand. Carmina's uncertain expression revealed that they were alike in opinion - they could hardly deny that there were a lot of arguments in favour of cannibalism right now, the main one being not starving. They'd have to spend a significant amount of time to locate any animals after all those gunshots, and none of them wanted to be left out here after dark. It was literally a matter of life or death. None of those facts made it seem less disgusting, however.

The bandit turned to peer at her. "What the fuck are *you* crying for? I'm the prisoner here," she commented.

"You watch your mouth!" Abby ordered tearfully, trying to act like she wasn't crying and that nothing was wrong. "I guess we're eating them. It beats starving to death," she admitted, wiping her eyes.

"So, what's the plan? She helps us carry them back, then we kill her?" asked Eric, generously complying with Abby's pretence that everything was fine.

"Funny way of persuading me to help," muttered the woman.

Abby glared at the prisoner once again. "Shut. Up." she emphasised. "She'll help us carry them back. Are we going to have to gut them before we make a move?" she asked, hoping for a no.

"Yeah, we are - but where are we going?" asked Eric.

"New Cray - our village," Abby explained. "We'll tell you all about it on the way, but right now I'd like to get out of here before we get eaten by the giant snake or something."

"They don't tend to go for people unless you bother them," claimed the huntsman.

"Point taken, but we should still get out of here," Abby insisted. Eric nodded and turned to gather the corpses into a line, former comrades and enemies alike. Aurelius joined him, leaving the women alone.

"What's wrong?" asked Carmina, clearly distressed by the emotional outburst.

"This isn't the time for it, alright?" Abby insisted, drying her eyes again. "Help the others, I'll make sure this one doesn't go for a gun."

Carmina gave Abby a concerned look, but went off to join the men. "You don't mind if we eat your friends?" she asked Eric.

"Not my friends. Just allies, barely know 'em," he claimed. No doubt there was a story behind that, but it could wait for another day.

Abby looked the captive woman over, sat there glumly. "You know how to gut an animal?" Abby asked her.

"I know how to gut a person," she responded.

Abby decided that the woman was genuinely trying to be helpful, rather than threatening her. The outcome was better for everyone that way. "Then get up, take that knife you were thinking about reaching for, and get to work on the dwarf," she ordered.

The woman reconsidered her hands. She'd been trying and failing to be subtle as she reached for the knife tucked into the back of her trousers. "How'd you know?" she asked, getting to her feet.

"You're not cut out for this sort of thing," Abby told her.

The woman gave Abby a wide berth as she approached the dwarf, and set to work, stripping the corpse of clothes and cutting an incision in its stomach. "So what's the plan then?" she asked. "Let me slave away until I drop dead?"

"We'll see," Abby returned, tears slipping freely down her cheeks now that her family wasn't around to see them.

"What's with the crying?" asked the captive. "Family troubles a bit much for you?"

"Not that. I just didn't mean to kill the dwarf," Abby vented.

"He had it coming, if it helps at all," the woman claimed. It didn't, nor would Abby dignify it with an answer, and so the bandit continued in order to fill a void in the conversaton. "Look, you're obviously the law and order type, so just do me one kindness, will you? If you're gonna see me punished, give me a quick death."

Abby resisted the urge to look away as the woman castrated the dwarf and slit him from sternum to anus. The smell as she began to remove the organs was fouler than it tended to be with their usual game, even from further away. "I promise that if you're to die it'll be quick," she agreed. Hanging was a worst case scenario - if it came down to it, she'd see if Tahgri was willing to behead the woman.

"Good enough. So, Abby huh?" asked the prisoner.

"Yeah."

"Jenna," returned the woman, gagging slightly at the stench of the removed bowels. "Want me to remove the head?" she asked.

Abby glanced over at Eric a moment. He was busy patching up his arm with torn strips of cloth. "Is the head worth eating?" she called out, trying to forget that she was talking about a person.

"Not really. Cut it off - too much weight. Blood drains quick from the neck, too," responded the hunter. Abby tried not to dwell on the question of how many people he'd eaten so far.

Jenna shrugged and cut around the base of the skull before standing up and stamping down repeatedly on the neck. The entire head snapped off with an unpleasant cracking sound. Abby supposed it was better than blunting her knife by sawing through bone, even if it was nauseating to watch.

"There's two more bodies back the way I came," Eric called over.

"Get moving," Abby ordered, steadying her voice at last. The bandit obeyed calmly, leaning the dead dwarf up against a tree to drain before heading further into the woodland.

It didn't take them long to find the other bodies, laying close together and bleeding out slowly into the dirt. Jenna set to work without orders, understanding her role for the moment. "I suppose you'd not be too

174

happy with me if I tried to make a run for it?" she asked, eyeing the equipment left behind by the dead.

"I suppose not," agreed Abby.

"Don't seem very cautious about stopping me," Jenna commented.

"Like I said, you're not cut out for this sort of thing. I doubt you'd get far before Eric caught you, even if you did manage to shoot me. The way I see it, even someone stupid enough to take up banditry has to realise that their chances are better playing nice with me," explained Abby.

"Got this all figured out, don't you," Jenna muttered. "Don't make me regret not running, won't you?"

"You'd regret trying to run more, believe me."

The bandit continued her work in grumpy silence as Abby gathered all the gear. There were plenty of weapons they could use, and water skins to keep everyone hydrated on the way back. "How bad's your wound?" Abby enquired as Jenna finished her grisly task.

"Just more than a scratch. Can I deal with it now?" the bandit asked.

"Come on, get by the stream so you can wash it," Abby agreed. They grabbed one body each, dragging them along with blood still seeping from their neck stumps. Aurelius and Eric were still busy with the rest of the corpses, whilst Carmina seemed to be struggling not to vomit at the smell of the mutilations. Abby watched with disinterest as Jenna cleaned the wound and made a makeshift bandage from torn clothes.

Making sure to first confiscate any weapons on Jenna's person, Abby led her back to the others, where they gathered everything of worth and optimised the load between them. There had been seven corpses, far too many to carry between the five of them, but some additional deboning and amputation allowed them to leave only one body behind as they headed home.

The siblings were excited to see Eric again. Carmina and Aurelius told him about everything that had transpired since they'd parted ways. The hunter didn't say a word more than he had to, leaving his presence up here unexplained. Nobody pestered him about it, though - the carrying was tiring enough without wasting breath, and Abby's mind was still occupied with her own guilt.

The return journey took far longer, requiring occasional breaks when the load grew too heavy. Abby refused to let Jenna speak, often silencing her with a firm slap when she tried to do so. She hoped it would reduce arguments over what they should do with the bandit.

Amidst concerns that they'd lose their way home at sundown, the solitary tree at the edge of their old hunting grounds proved to be their saving grace, guiding them with its twilight sillhouette. They couldn't see the village yet, but at least they now had a good point of reference.

175

"So, what do we tell mum and dad about all this? And everyone else, for that matter," asked Carmina.

"The truth, I guess. We were attacked by bandits, these people were dead anyway, and the alternative is starving to death," suggested Abby. She'd read about cannibalism before, often associated with savages and barbarians. The people of New Cray were neither of these things, and Abby had no idea how to approach suggesting the act to them. She was really just improvising and hoping for the best at this point.

"It's about the best we're gonna manage to stop them freaking out," agreed Aurelius. "I have no idea how the rest of the village will react, but I doubt it can be much worse than carrying on eating four carrots a day."

"Do you think dad will find this better or worse than bringing home a boyfriend?" jested Carmina.

"That depends on the boyfriend," Aurelius grunted. Despite the whole morbid situation, Abby couldn't help but smile.

"I think I see it," commented Carmina, using the arm of the body she was carrying to point at the distant shapes of buildings in the dark. They pressed on, silent determination interrupted only by Jenna's question as they finally reached New Cray.

"I'm starved, don't suppose I could have any of this, could I?"

"No," Aurelius muttered indignantly.

"If you behave yourself, yes," Abby corrected. She couldn't see the expressions of the others in the dark of the night, but she imagined they all disagreed with her decision. "If she's to die, it may as well be on a full stomach. We can eat her, too, if you're that concerned about wasting it," she continued, making sure nobody had good cause to argue.

They made their way home, relieved at finally being able to set down their loads "We're back!" called Aurelius as he walked through the door.

Pausing to take Jenna aside, Abby lowered her voice. "Go on in. Be polite, and if you don't cause any trouble I'll let you eat."

Jenna seemed to have made up her mind by now; it was better for her to chance Abby's mercy than risk the wrath of the others. "Not one bit of trouble, I swear," she agreed.

"Eric?" Abby heard her father's surprise inside.

"Alex," returned Eric. "You're still in one piece... it's good to see you all again."

Abby stepped through the door, setting her grisly burden down. "It's wonderful to see you too, Eric," agreed Elizabeth. "But what in avared's bloody gates is all *this*?"

14

The Other, Other White Meat

Johann looked at the corpses with great indifference. "Well, at least you removed the organs. It's not well documented, but I believe some of them could cause terrible disease if consumed. I'm not entirely sure which ones, either," he commented. It had taken a little explaining, but hunger had got the better of Abby's parents. Johann, on the other hand, hadn't been at all put off by the suggestion of cannibalism, which was equal parts disturbing and relieving.

"So what do we do? Just invite people over to eat them?" asked Alexander, still a little queasy over the sight of the mutilations. "I mean... not to eat *them*, but-"

"I know what you meant," Abby interrupted. "But no. You wouldn't invite people over for raw meat - we'll butcher it and cook it, then I suppose we offer it to people, just as long as they know what it is."

Johann nodded and grabbed a knife. Being a doctor, he was the most qualified when it came to butchering a human carcass. "You're gonna want to shave them all first, it's just like preparing a hog," Jenna advised from her corner, no doubt keen to appear helpful and therefore worth feeding.

"Well, I've never butchered a pig," Abby chuckled.

Jenna grinned sheepishly. "Want some help? I slaughtered a few hogs back home."

She considered the offer a moment. Jenna's assistance might've been appreciated, but the idea of the bandit holding a knife anywhere near her parents made Abby uneasy. "Were you raised on a farm, Jenna?" she enquired.

"Raised? More than just raised I suppose, worked it all my life. Or until it got attacked by elementals, anyway."

Abby joined Johann in shaving the bodies, working the knife harshly against the grain. "You stay right there, Jenna. I don't suppose you know anything about irrigation, though, do you?"

"What's that mean?" asked the bandit.

"Like, getting water to the crops without carrying it all across the farm yourself," Abby explained.

"Oh, yeah... guess I know a bit about that. Weren't a big farm, but big enough," Jenna considered.

Abby grinned. "Well, I guess we've got some use for you, then."

"If you don't kill me," Jenna sighed theatrically, shamelessly taking advantage of any purpose she was perceived to have.

"I'm going to see if I can have some of that elemental coal from Michael. I'll fetch some water, too," Elizabeth interrupted the exchange, turning to fetch her shoes.

"Good thinking," agreed Johann. Abby suspected that it was an excuse to get away from the bodies, but it was at least a useful excuse.

Some of the knives required sharpening, either before or during the process, blunted by the sheer quantity of hair. "By the Maralor, this is what you guys do to your faces?" asked Carmina as she made a raw mess of some of the hairier skin. Eric raised a brow at her, his beard answering the question for him. Carmina rolled her eyes and glanced to the doctor instead.

"I wouldn't be so rough with myself, since I'm... you know, alive," said Johann. "Don't be afraid to really dig the knife in with these, it's fine to damage the skin."

It took quite some time to shave all the bodies. Each of the six had been a fully grown man, hairy to the last crevice. Elizabeth joined in when she returned, somewhat reluctant at first to handle the cadavers. Still, as the process continued and the butchery began, the flesh became dehumanised, more and more resembling any other meat. None of them slacked, exhausted though they were. They worked well into the night, deboning and cutting. It wasn't a perfect job, even with Johann's precise anatomical knowledge, but at that moment in time, even imperfect cuts were beginning to look like dreams come true.

It was past midnight by the time they'd created something resembling more traditional cuts of meat. Residual blood covered the floor, bones strewn around the room in loose piles. "I can make something with the skin and bones. Why don't you get started with the meat?" suggested Elizabeth.

Abby nodded and began to gather masses of flesh into clean buckets. "Jenna, help me carry some of this. Aurelius, grab something to cook it on will you?" she requested before leading the way to the middle of the village.

Jenna spoke up again when they were finally alone. "So how does this work, then? Me and you, that is," she asked.

"Well, I guess for now you just keep on behaving yourself. Gonna have to tie you up while I sleep so you don't do anything stupid, though," responded Abby.

"I won't do anything stupid," Jenna insisted. "The way I see it, I try anything with you the others will kill me. Biting the hand that feeds and all that."

"I'm not so gullible as to trust a murderer to make good on her word," Abby retorted.

"Attempted murderer," muttered Jenna, as if that made everything alright. "I never actually *succeeded* in killing anyone."

Aurelius and Carmina soon joined them, and they set up a makeshift grill over a simple coal fire. Without hesitation, Abby began to preside over cooking the meat to perfection. "Your mother's cleaning up with Johann," Alexander informed her as he joined them. "You're sure you want to do this?"

"Yep," Abby responded simply, hunger welling up inside her as she watched the human steaks dribble fat. "Would you go and start waking people up? I'm sure they'll forgive us, as there's food involved." Her father set down the pile of wooden plates he'd been carrying and left to do as requested.

Jenna drew close as the first of the steaks finished cooking, like a dog begging for scraps. Of course, like the runt of the litter, she was to be served last. Abby offered food to Carmina and Aurelius first, instantly filling the empty spaces left on the grill with more steaks. Her siblings tucked in ravenously - they were so hungry that they didn't even spare time to thank Abby or comment on the qualities of the meat as they tore into it. She saved another three for when the others returned to them, setting out food for Eric, Johann, and her mother next.

A small crowd of citizens began to form a little further back, peering inquisitively at the strange sight of the midnight feast. Abby waited until her father had returned, and served him, herself, and finally Jenna. Only then did she address the crowd. "Don't be shy. Gather round," she called.

Enticed by the sight and smell of the meat, they were quick to come closer, desperation on their faces. Abby almost felt bad that she had to add a caveat to the offer. She silently prayed that they'd understand the necessity of her actions. "Carmina, Aurelius and I went out hunting today, and we almost came back empty-handed, thanks to bandits. We were forced to make a tough decision," she began. "We're faced with starvation here. If we can hold out just a little longer we'll be able to grow crops again, but we won't last any longer without a little extra food. All the meat you see here is from the bandits. Actually... it *is* the bandits."

She observed the shock that spread through the crowd, but continued before anyone could voice a knee-jerk reaction. "I know this may seem disgusting. I thought so too, but at the end of the day we've got a choice to make between keeping our old values, and eating. In this case, I'll choose the latter. Besides," she said, taking a bite out of her own steak and chewing thoughtfully. "It tastes a bit like pork."

"Is that what we are now? Savages? Are we going to start eating our own? Our loved ones?" asked one of the older men, stepping through the crowd.

"Absolutely not!" reassured Abby. "This is a desperate measure, and if I can help it I'll never eat this again. We're not murderers or villains; as it happens, we killed these men in self-defence. If you want some of this, you're welcome to join us. If you don't, then I wish you the best of luck with finding other food, and I sincerely hope you're still with us by next harvest."

Amanda stepped forwards, her face gaunt. She'd lost a lot of weight, and not just from the miscarriage. "I'll take what you can spare," she begged.

It was just what Abby was hoping for. One desperate person showing their acceptance would be like a gate opening for the others. She took Aurelius' empty plate, placed one of the juicier steaks on it, and handed it to Amanda. Tahgri stepped forwards next. "The Maralor would not have you starve. It is the lesser of two evils to eat of the dead," he told the crowd as Abby served him, too, and before anyone could pass further judgement, the more open-minded people crowded the fire.

"This could take a while, ladies and gentlemen. You may as well form a queue," said Abby, filling the empty spaces on the grill.

A small number of people declined the offer, whether aggressively or passively, and as much as she worried for their continued survival, Abby didn't blame them. Still, far more had gratefully accepted the offer than had refused it, and Abby continued to cook through the night. Everyone got a reasonable portion in the end, probably the best any of them had eaten in weeks. There was even a little spare for the next day.

The sun eventually peeked over the horizon, and Abby glanced at the dispersing crowd. "Jaina, Katherine, Michael. There's something we ought to discuss before it gets too hot again," she called out. Johann joined them as they gathered around, no doubt aware of what she was referring to.

They all looked weary from lack of sleep, as was Abby. Eager to get it done quickly, she grabbed Jenna by the wrist and pulled her over. As promised, the bandit was unresisting in the matter. "This is Jenna. She was one of the bandits that attacked us - we didn't kill her in the fight, obviously," Abby explained.

The others exchanged some quizzical glances. "You're keeping her alive?" asked Katherine.

"Well, I wanted to get your opinions. You're my peers, after all," Abby reminded her. She might've been tempted to keep the decision to herself, but that wasn't what democracy was about. Besides, if she'd done so it would only have been a matter of time before people learned of the deceit and grew angry.

"Well, by law, if she killed anyone then she should be hanged by the neck until dead," Jaina claimed, fixing the bandit with a cold stare.

"Far be it from me to question the law," agreed Katherine.

Abby didn't feel a need to remind her that *they* were the law, out here. "Jenna, did you kill anyone?" she asked, recalling the bandit's earlier claim.

A glimmer of hope appeared on the woman's face as she shook her head. "No. I hit your mate... Eric. But only in the arm. That's the worst I did," she claimed.

"Attempted murder then. Is that still hanging?" Abby asked Jaina.

The lawyer considered for a few moments. "She should be sentenced to restitution for a period of no less than five years to make up for her misdeeds. Probably some other things, too, but generally it would be a sentence like that. Of course, we don't really have the capacity to stop her running off," Jaina emphasised.

"I'm sure I can think of a way," differed Abby. "Or Eric could, since he's the one that Jenna should pay restitution to."

"I think we should just kill her before she tries to stab one of us and escape, to be honest," said Jaina.

Abby had been afraid that such an argument would come up. It was certainly no light decision. "Well then, all in favour of putting her to work?" she asked. With some hesitation, Katherine and Michael raised their hands. "And those for execution?"

Johann seemed slightly unsure of himself as he raised his hand, but Jaina didn't hesitate to pass a death sentence. "And what about you?" she asked Abby.

"I suppose I'm for the former," she responded.

"That's three to two, then," said Katherine, smiling timidly.

"Well then, all in favour of her being Abby's responsibility?" asked Jaina.

Abby chuckled and raised her hand. "Alright, I'll deal with her," she agreed. Everyone except Johann was in agreement on that. "Thanks, guys," Abby dismissed them all. They saw each other off, ending the day with the strange sight of the rising sun.

"We may as well get started right away. Help me clean up this mess," Abby commanded Jenna. The bandit seemed to consider rebellion for a brief moment, but logic prevailed and she soon set to it, carrying as much as she could.

Johann joined them, helping to get it all back home. "How do you think we're going to look after her?" he demanded. Abby's problem was now his due to proximity, and he clearly wasn't happy about it.

"We'll figure it out. For now we'll just tie her up overnight," Abby replied calmly.

"I'm not comfortable having her in my house," Johann grumbled, completely unconcerned by the fact that Jenna was within earshot. Of course, all she did was scowl to herself.

"Then I'll stay with my parents for a while and keep her there," Abby responded diplomatically.

Johann sighed. "Please don't do this."

Abby shook her head and carefully adjusted the stack of plates in her arms. "Well someone has to watch her tonight, and it should be someone who can deal with her if needs be," she insisted.

"It's not just going to be tonight, though, is it? Who wants to keep one eye open every night for as long as she's here?" Johann pointed out.

"I'll speak with Tahgri when we wake up," Abby tried.

"What makes you think he'll be interested in watching her?"

Abby smiled. "He probably won't be, but that's not what I need him for. Have you ever heard of Blood Oath Gretchen?"

***

She sat on a rock with Eric, waiting for Tahgri to return. Jenna was out of earshot, but not out of range of Eric's gun. Not by a long way. "So, what brought you up here then? Was it the heat?" Abby asked. It had taken him a week to decide, most of which he'd spent hunting far north of the village anyway, but eventually he'd settled in New Cray, if only for the company at present.

"Heat was part of it," he admitted, fidgeting with the bandage on his arm. "But mostly I just kept catching myself wondering what the fuck I was doing with my life."

"How do you mean?" quizzed Abby, briefly tearing her gaze from Jenna to look Eric in the eye.

His instinct to clam up kicked in for a few moments, and Abby put a reassuring hand on his shoulder. "You don't have to tell me, if it makes you sad."

Eric sighed and looked back over to Jenna, his eyes not wavering thereafter. "You remember that elemental we killed?"

"How could I forget," she commented, briefly recalling the death of Mrs. Elani.

"One like that killed my family."

Abby nodded. "I figured it was something like that. You were pretty angry."

"I guess I thought I'd feel better about it if I stayed down there killing more of those things," he elaborated.

"Did it work?"

Eric shook his head. "It wasn't what she would've wanted."

Abby fell silent a moment, but she couldn't help but pry. "She died on the way here?"

"No, it was at the end of the war. I sent her to Borsenine, see - I got her pregnant while she was following camp. Told her she'd be safer down there."

Abby grimaced. She couldn't imagine living with the consequences of that decision. At least he was finally getting it off his chest. "About eight months later I got a letter from her, telling me I was a dad now," he continued. "Year after that we won the siege at Rothlin. War was about over, so there was no more work for soldiers in the south. We all got discharged. Best day of my life when I left to see her."

She clung to him in an attempt to provide comfort. He didn't resist. "I'm sorry, Eric. I didn't mean to pry."

His face was haunted by the next part of his story. Still, he continued despite his composure threatening to fail him. "I was so close when it all happened. So bright I couldn't even look at it straight. Didn't have a clue what was going on, of course. Thought it was the Maralor's wrath at the time; may as well have been. She was nowhere near the blast itself, but there was one elemental just like that earthen. Got there before I did."

The huntsman tried to dry his eyes, his voice threatening to give out under the weight of emotion. "I couldn't even get their bodies back. Gods above, I would've given anything just to see my son's face." He leaned against her, taking a moment to pull himself back together. "Took me a while to realise it, but I think she would've wanted me to move on and do something with my life. So here I am."

"Well, I'm glad you're back," she commented, one arm still around his waist. "It was never your fault. Nobody knew it was coming."

"You know, I never thanked you properly for saving me back there in the woods," Eric responded, returning to his old habit of avoiding the subject.

"Any time. Just a shame so many had to die," Abby lamented.

"Is that why you're trying to keep her alive?" Eric probed, gesturing towards Jenna. "Guilt?"

Abby shook her head insistently. "No. I'm just doing the right thing, even Jaina had to agree that the law was in favour of her living. I just hate it that everything out here seems to turn to violence."

"You never had a problem with violence before, with the thieves and such," Eric commented.

"That was different. I never killed anyone then, the only one that died was shot by his own friends. This time... I killed that dwarf, and helped with the others. Even though I didn't want to, they're still dead."

Eric peered across at her, his brow creasing. "That was the first time you ever killed anyone?" he asked. He sounded surprised.

"Yeah," Abby admitted. She'd bottled the whole thing up somewhat, but the truth was that she'd had to wrestle with her conscience every time she'd thought about it. Those who hadn't been present for Abby's initial outburst weren't aware, and of those who had been, only Carmina had so much as pretended to understand the way she felt.

"Don't worry, it gets easier," Eric claimed.

"I don't *want* it to get easier. I don't *want* to have to kill people, but it seems like I'm constantly getting backed into this position where I have to fight," Abby vented.

"Life has a way of putting good people in bad situations. Especially lately," claimed Eric. "But you know what, better you than the others. You can fight, and you're trying to do the right thing. You did the best anyone could expect back there."

Abby wasn't entirely convinced that Eric believed she had done the right thing, given his protests about Jenna living, but his words were comforting anyway. "Thanks," she returned softly.

"Any time. Now, I'd best leave you two to your black magic," he teased, gesturing back as Tahgri approached.

Abby smiled faintly and wiped a thin line of perspiration from her brow. "Take care, Eric. I'll see you around."

"Alright, shall we get this done?" asked Tahgri, adjusting the bundle under his arm. It had taken some persuasion to assemble the resources for the ritual. Still, with any luck it would be worth the effort.

"Jenna!" snapped Abby, waving her over. The woman came to them, apprehension clear on her face though she didn't voice it.

Tahgri began to lay everything out in a small circle; wooden runes, roughly carved figurines, even a straw doll of some sort. With only a bone knife and a tattooed piece of hide left in his hands, he forced Jenna into the circle. "Hold out your hand," he ordered.

Jenna grunted as the sharpened bone sliced a neat line across her palm, but despite - or perhaps because of - her ineptitude at banditry, she was tough. She barely even winced when Tahgri began to prod roughly at the wound with one finger, using the sanguine ink to trace the runes tattooed into the hide.

"We make this oath by blood, and only by death can it be broken - be it yours or mine," began Tahgri. "Do you promise to uphold the law without compromise, on pain of death and the eternal torment of your soul?"

"Yes?" mumbled Jenna, the dramatics clearly making her nervous.

"Say it like you mean it!" barked Tahgri, his face serious. Abby slowly circled around and stood behind Jenna so that the bandit couldn't see the amusement on her features.

"Yes," repeated Jenna, taking a deep breath thereafter.

"And do you promise to obey and be loyal to both myself and Abby, without question or compromise?" the paladin demanded of her.

"Yes!" Jenna squeaked again, her shoulders slumping as she signed her life away. Tahgri finished painting the blood runes and held the hide aloft for them both to see - it was actually quite beautiful in a primitive sort of way. It was a shame what was going to happen to it.

Tahgri gripped Jenna's bloodied hand in his own. Abby could see from the pain on the bandit's face that he was perhaps being a little more rough than was necessary. Still, it all added to the drama of the moment.

The paladin began to chant in a language that neither Abby nor Jenna were familiar with. In fact, Abby knew with certainty that there wasn't a person alive that understood it, not even Tahgri - because this whole thing was one elaborate hoax. Tahgri didn't know how to do a blood oath. Like all magic, it was no small matter and required at least a little proper training, not to mention the natural affinity for magic that nobody in New Cray seemed to have. That was why Abby was currently stood behind Jenna, struggling not to laugh at the nonsense that was coming out of Tahgri's mouth. Credit where it was due, he managed to make the nonsense sound appropriately sinister, and very magical indeed.

The chanting continued. Taking a pot of oil from the ground, Tahgri poured some over the blood-painted runes and set the piece of leather down. He then pulled out a fire-lighting glass and angled it, magnifying the sun's intense light onto the hide. It burst aflame, shriveling into a wicked-looking and blackened thing. "We make this oath by blood, and only by death can it be broken - be it yours or mine," concluded the paladin.

Abby gave him a thumbs-up as she did her best to compose herself. She'd considered doing the fake ritual herself, but the truth was that she couldn't lie worth a damn. She probably would've given the game away instantly with her attempts not to laugh, looking like she'd just sucked on a particularly sour lemon. "It's done," Tahgri informed them.

Jenna sagged and clutched her hand. It would heal up soon enough of course, Carl had carved the bone knife especially for this faux ritual, and they'd taken great pains to clean it in hopes of avoiding disease. "Go and sort your hand out," Abby advised her. "You've got a lot of manual labour ahead of you." All they had to do now was hope that the idea of eternal torment was enough to stop her from ever testing the oath.

15
Serial Serious

She writhed under Johann's touch, panting softly as he took her with hasty, eager motions. Though the harsh temperatures had begun to relent a little, it was still too hot for her liking, and Abby had succumbed to another case of heatstroke. They hadn't made love in months, but being bedridden for a few days had left her easily persuaded towards sex.

They were yanked from their moment of euphoria by the sound of the front door bursting open and rapid footsteps approaching the bedroom. Abby panicked a little, her limbs unresponsive and her mind hazy from pleasure as she pawed ineffectually for a weapon that was well out of reach. "Sis!" called Carmina's voice.

Abby relaxed somewhat knowing that it was just her sister. "Don't come in here!" she called back. Poor Johann looked utterly lost as to what he should do, presented with a choice between finishing for the first time in too long or removing himself from Abby to minimise his own embarrassment. He didn't get time to decide; Carmina burst through the door anyway, and squeaked in surprise at the sight of Johann's bare backside. Abby shrieked and pulled the blanket over them both. "I said-"

"There's been another murder!" Carmina interrupted, covering her eyes and turning away from the sight of the beast with two backs, just in case one or the other was apparently not enough to prevent her from seeing it.

Abby felt any lingering arousal dissipate in an instant as the situation went from awkward to serious. "I'll be out in a moment," she responded.

"Can't we finish?" pleaded Johann, lowering his voice.

"I'm still here, you know!" Carmina reminded him, evidently better at hearing than Johann was at talking quietly.

"No, we cannot! Someone's been murdered, Johann, that's a little more important," Abby scolded, pushing him off and out of her.

"I'll just take care of myself and catch up later, then," he muttered bitterly, keeping himself wrapped in blankets as Abby hopped about the room, dressing in a sartorial panic.

"By every god, I can still hear you!" whined Carmina. Abby rolled her eyes and pulled on the bare minimum clothing before marching her little sister from the room. It was still too hot to be running about in armour.

Carmina was quick to address her mistake as she led Abby to places unknown. "I'm sorry for walking in like that, I thought you said-"

"It's fine," Abby dismissed it quickly, her temper frayed. "Who's the victim?"

"Vanessa," Carmina claimed. "They haven't found the killer yet, Markus asked me to get you."

Abby went silent a few moments, struggling to remain composed. She'd grown to respect Vanessa greatly in the small amount of time that they'd spent in each other's company, and she knew just how important the woman was to those she represented. "Where are we going?"

"The chapel in Lapden," Carmina informed her.

"Would you fetch the others for me? The same who helped last time, plus the council. And Jenna," Abby requested. Carmina turned without delay, heading back the way they'd come.

Labour had resumed as the very worst of summer's glaring warmth had passed, construction and other industries picking up again right after new crops had been sown. In most cases, the buildings that had burned down during the elemental attack had been forgotten, their replacements concentrated in the gulf between the two villages in an attempt to bring physical unity. Consequently, the gap had diminished a little. Abby took advantage of the secluded walk to prepare her mind.

She'd not had occasion to visit the chapel in Lapden before, and as she strode purposefully into the village she found herself regretting not doing so when it would have been a pleasant experience. It didn't take her long to get directions, and she soon arrived to find the remaining three members of the Lapden council waiting at the entrance. "Abby," greeted Yasmine, her eyes puffy from crying. "Thanks for coming, this is just awful."

Abby nodded glumly. "I've sent for all the people that helped me investigate the last murder," she informed them. "We'll do everything we can."

"Good. Vanessa was the best of us, we need to find whoever did this," insisted Montgomery.

"What do we know so far?" Abby asked. "Any obvious suspects I should know about?"

She was met with a series of shrugs from the Lapden council. "We were hoping you could tell us. This is more your area of expertise, as we understood it, you should probably take a look," suggested Markus.

Abby inclined her head respectfully and headed inside the chapel. Arthur was sat on a pew within, staring at his wife's bloodied body in shock and grief.

"Miss Koning," greeted Friedrich, standing watch over the bereaved.

"Call me Abby," she insisted, grimacing as she got a closer look at the corpse. Vanessa's face was contorted in horror and agony, the body laying in a puddle of blood. "Who found her?"

"Amelia Ackerman. She says she came straight to me. I questioned her already, but she didn't know anything about it," Friedrich claimed.

Abby nodded and moved over to sit beside Arthur. "I'm so sorry about this," she said, putting a single arm around his shoulders.

He looked up, giving Abby a proper view of the horror written on his face. She ruled him straight off the suspects list; she'd seen the face of loss enough times now to be sure that this was the real thing. "Find who did this," he managed, his voice shaky.

"Believe me, Arthur, I'm going to do everything I can," she assured him. She knew better than to promise results, after last time. "I need to look at the body - perhaps it's best you leave now. We'll turn it over to you when we've examined it fully?"

Arthur shook his head adamantly. "Abby, I am seventy-one years old. Blood and wounds do not shock me as they once might have. I'll stay, and have these last moments with my wife before we bury her," he insisted, his expression hardening.

"If you're sure," Abby allowed, getting to her feet and easing herself around the pool of blood. She didn't require Johann so much for this inspection; it was clear that Vanessa had been stabbed several times through and around the heart. She couldn't see any other injuries on her front, and so she rolled the body over. It was limp, as of yet unaffected by rigor mortis. "Have we got an approximate time of death yet?" she asked Friedrich.

"Amelia found her a little under an hour ago. That's all I've got," he informed her. Abby nodded and lifted the back of Vanessa's shirt. There it was - just like before, only larger. She wiped away the blood with her hand for certainty's sake, but there could be no mistaking it. The symbol of Corsein oozed red before her.

She heard Tahgri's voice outside and turned to see her team amassing at the door with the others. Abby left the body and joined them, glancing about. "Where are Johann and Jaina?" she asked.

"Two guesses what Johann's doing," Carmina commented, rolling her eyes. "I couldn't find Jaina, but I asked some people to send her this way if they saw her."

Abby sighed and shook her head in disbelief. "Typical. Well, I just looked at the body - it's got the same mark on it as Owen's had, so I suppose we're dealing with a serial killer. You may as well take a look."

Carmina and Aurelius nodded and moved into the chapel to inspect the crime scene for themselves. "When was the first murder? That was in your chapel, wasn't it?" asked Yasmine.

Abby nodded. "That must've been almost a year ago now. It was last autumn."

"So, no obvious connection between the dates of the murders then?" Yasmine considered.

Abby thought carefully, recalling the rather unforgettable memory of Tahgri waking her on the morning of the first murder. It had been three hundred and twenty-six days since then, and one extra day since the murder actually occurred. "Hey, Abby! Did you see the water?" Carmina called from inside the chapel, interrupting her train of thought.

"Just a second!" Abby called back, finishing her calculations. "It was the twenty-ninth of September on the first murder, and it's the twenty-second of August now. I don't know about you but I don't see any connection there," she informed Yasmine before excusing herself to see what Carmina had spotted. Samson and Daniel followed her into the chapel.

Carmina pointed to a patch of floor at the left edge of the building. It was only a small amount, most of it had already soaked into the wood or evaporated, but there was still a little water sitting on the floorboards. "Well spotted," Abby commended her, eyeing it curiously. There had obviously been a substantial amount of water spilled at some point, but no bucket to be seen.

"What do you make of it?" asked Daniel.

Abby shrugged, her brain flinging wild and improbable explanations around. "I'm not sure yet. Keep looking, I might've missed something else. Aurelius, Friedrich, can I borrow you both?" Abby asked. They followed her back outside. "We need to talk to any potential witnesses. Can you ask around the village and get anyone who's been in the chapel today to come and talk to me at the court?"

"Me too?" questioned Tahgri.

Abby shook her head. "No. Yasmine, Jenna, Katherine, Michael, and Markus - if you could go with them and fetch people for me that would be great. Daniel, Samson, stay here with Car and make sure nobody messes up the crime scene, please. Tahgri, I'd like to talk to you alone."

"What about me?" asked Montgomery.

"Stay here with the others. Arthur might need the company," she suggested before leading Tahgri to the court.

"What's on your mind?" he asked once they were alone.

"Please tell me you've got an alibi this time?"

"I do. I was with Jenna," Tahgri claimed, much to Abby's relief.

"Good. Then I need you to go back to New Cray and watch Patrick, if you can. Be subtle about it," she instructed.

"You think it was him?" asked Tahgri.

"I think he's our biggest suspect right now. He's the only one I've known to take any issue with Vanessa - we'd be daft not to keep an eye on him," Abby explained.

"I'll do my best, but I'm not known for my subtlety," he reminded her. It didn't worry Abby - Patrick wasn't known for being observant, or anything other than pig-headed for that matter.

She left Tahgri to his task and walked over to the court, taking a seat in the main room. It wasn't long before the first person strolled in to see her. "Hey there," she greeted the man, gesturing him over.

"Abby, right?" he asked. He was noticeably nervous. No doubt he was aware that she wanted him for questioning in relation to Vanessa's murder, and had been told little else.

"That's right. I won't waste your time, mister - I'd like you to tell me every single detail about your visit to the chapel today," she requested.

"Call me Emmett," he introduced himself. "Mind if I sit down?"

Abby gestured to the bench beside her, and Emmett seemed to relax as he realised that he wasn't immediately being accused of anything. He seemed a rather unremarkable man; average height, average build, brown hair, and a tan from working outdoors. "I went to the chapel this morning after I ate. I didn't see anything, I'm afraid."

"Was there any particular reason you went to the chapel?" she asked.

"To... pray," he said, looking embarrassed.

"Was there anything in particular that you were praying for?" she continued.

"My wife. She suffers awfully from the heat. The crops, too; now that it's cooled down a little bit I was praying for some luck, I suppose," he explained, seeming sceptical about her line of questioning.

"How would you describe your faith?" she asked him.

"We've had trying times. I'd be lying if I said it was as strong as it used to be," he admitted.

Abby nodded, satisfied that he wasn't their man. Another stranger came through the court doors ahead of them, younger this time. She addressed both of them with her next question. "And you didn't notice anything or anyone out of the ordinary, either on the way to, or back from the chapel?"

"Afraid not," Emmet claimed.

"Anyone with blood on their clothes, perhaps. Or even someone you didn't recognise?" she pressed the matter.

Emmet shook his head glumly. "Me neither," said the newcomer.

"Thank you, Emmett. If you think of anything you might've missed, please let me know as soon as you can," Abby dismissed him.

"I'll be sure to," he agreed, getting up to leave.

"And good luck with the wife!" Abby called after him.

"I was told I was wanted here?" the second man greeted her, stepping closer warily.

"That's right. I'm Abby," she smiled at him. "You went to the chapel today?"

"Sebastian," he returned. "And yes, I did."

"Could you tell me when that was, and why?" she requested, straight to business.

"I went to pray, of course. Must've been some time around midday," he explained.

"Are you a man of great faith?" she asked.

"I wouldn't call it *great*. Not all sins are crimes, though," he insisted somewhat condescendingly.

She resisted the urge to bicker with him and glanced over at the door as her third visitor came through - a middle-aged woman. "No, they're not. Did you see Vanessa on your way back?" Abby asked.

Sebastian shook his head. "No. I did see *her*, though," he claimed, glancing over his shoulder at the newcomer.

"Hi. I was told you had some questions for me?" the woman asked awkwardly. "I'm Amelia."

"Amelia Ackman?"

"Ackerman," corrected Amelia, approaching with a nervous smile.

Abby wished everyone wouldn't be so nervous when dealing with her. It would only make it harder to pick out the guilty. "Just a moment, Amelia," she insisted. "Sebastian, you said you saw Amelia on your way out of the chapel?"

"Not exactly. It was on my way back home. I think I was pretty much home already, in fact," he clarified.

Abby nodded. "How long would you say it took you to walk from the chapel to Amelia?"

"Well, I stopped to draw some water. Five minutes, maybe. Definitely not ten," he mused

Abby smiled. "Thanks. You can go now," she offered.

"Good luck with the questions," he returned before leaving. Whether he was being sincere or not, Abby couldn't tell.

"So, Amelia - you said you found Vanessa's body in the chapel. When abouts was that?"

"Around midday, miss."

"Do you recall seeing Sebastian on your way there?"

Amelia nodded. "Sure. It was near his place, just like he said."

"And do you know how long it took you after that to get to the chapel?"

"Couldn't have been much more than five minutes. I stopped to chat with a friend of mine on the way there."

"Who was the friend?" Abby demanded.

"Grace Anthony," she claimed, clearly reluctant to draw others into the investigation.

"And when you got to the chapel, what did you do?" Abby continued, making a mental note to cross-reference the story with Grace.

"I opened the doors and saw the body. I took maybe one step inside, realised what I was looking at, then I went straight to Friedrich," she explained.

"Alright. Did you see anyone you didn't recognise on the way there? Anyone that stood out in any way, maybe with blood on their clothes?" Abby asked.

Amelia bit her lip, looking lost in thought for a few moments. "No. Nothing like that," she insisted.

"Alright. Thank you, Amelia. You've been a big help," concluded Abby.

"Good luck," Amelia said before leaving, accidentally bumping into Johann on the way out. Jaina was accompanying him, her hair slightly damp from what little the sun hadn't caught.

"Where were you two?" Abby demanded.

"You know exactly where I was," Johann muttered unapologetically.

"Bathing, sorry. You caught me rather off-guard," admitted Jaina.

Abby just sighed, deciding not to make a big deal out of it. "Come on, you should see the body," she suggested, getting to her feet and gesturing to the door they'd just come through.

"We already did. Serial killer, huh?" commented Johann.

"What do you make of it?" questioned Abby. "The time of death seems to have been almost exactly midday."

"The wounds are consistent with the weapon from last time, but they clearly put a lot more force behind it. There should've been more blood spray, which I'm guessing means the murderer stabbed Vanessa from the front and got a nice spattering of red," explained Johann.

"In the middle of the day? I struggle to believe they got covered in blood without being seen," commented Jaina.

Abby nodded and adjusted her hair. "In this sunlight, with that much blood on them? Somebody would've told us by now, unless they were covering for the murderer," she contemplated.

"What, you're suggesting a conspiracy?" asked Johann.

Abby shook her head. "Simpler than that - they weren't covered in blood. From what I can tell, the killer had a fairly small window. There were ten minutes, fifteen at most between Vanessa entering the chapel and the body being found. They go in, shut the doors behind them, stab Vanessa, and carve the symbol into her back. We found water on the floor, so I'm thinking they washed themselves up before they left."

Johann shook his head. "They couldn't have washed the blood off of their clothes with water alone."

"Maybe they brought a change of clothes? It would be the simplest explanation," commented Jaina.

"Alright, let's work with that. Perhaps they stab Vanessa, strip, wash themselves down, and change into new clothes?" suggested Abby.

"Or maybe they stripped *before* killing Vanessa, so that they didn't have to change clothes?" Johann theorised.

"Both possible, though I'm not sure how likely it is that they'd have been able to get naked in front of Vanessa without her screaming for help," commented Jaina.

Abby nodded. "And I doubt they got naked outside the chapel, either. Too obvious. Either way, we're looking for somebody who was carrying a bucket of water."

"Unfortunately, that probably doesn't narrow it down a whole lot in this heat," Jaina noted.

Abby sighed, frustrated on that particular point. Nobody would look twice at a bucket. "It's the best lead we've got," she admitted.

"Ummm," hummed a voice from behind Jaina and Johann. They parted to reveal a young girl, no more than nine years old. She looked rather withdrawn, perhaps shy around strangers.

"Hey there," greeted Abby, smiling encouragingly at her. "Are you looking for us?"

"Are you Abby?" the girl questioned.

"I am Abby. Did you go to the chapel today?" she enquired.

"Tried to, but the door was locked," the girl claimed.

Alarm bells went off in Abby's head. "When was this?" she probed.

The girl thought for a few moments. "It was before the guard was shouting."

"Do you mean Friedrich? Is Friedrich the guard?"Abby probed.

The girl shrugged. "The man who's always with Arthur."

Abby was sure that could only be Friedrich. "Where was that?" she asked. "Where was the guard shouting?"

"In the chapel," said the girl.

"Perhaps Friedrich would've been shouting for help when he saw the body?" Jaina interjected.

"Is that right? Was the guard in the chapel shouting when he found Vanessa?" Abby pressed for more information.

The girl nodded faintly. "He wanted help."

"Thank you. What's your name, young lady?" Abby asked.

"Melissa, ma'am," the girl introduced herself.

"Alright Melissa, how long before that shouting did you find the door was locked? Five minutes maybe?" Abby probed.

"I guess," Melissa recalled, nodding.

Abby leaned in to pay close attention to every word the girl said. "Did you hear anything from inside?"

"No," she claimed, shaking her head resolutely.

"Could you tell me *exactly* what happened? You arrived at the chapel and..." Abby began for her, hoping it'd help coax out more description.

"I tried to pull the door open but it was locked. I knocked, but nobody answered, so I waited outside," Melissa explained.

"When you pulled on the door, did it give at all, or not budge?" Abby enquired.

The girl thought for a moment. "It moved a bit, but it went right back again."

"And you didn't hear anything from inside when you knocked, or when you were waiting outside?" Abby reiterated.

"No," the girl repeated.

"What happened next? Who went in and out of the chapel after that?" Abby asked.

"The woman who opened the door, she went in," said Melissa. "Then she left, and came back with the guard and Arthur. They all went in."

"Alright, stop me if I'm getting anything wrong here," Abby began, putting together Melissa's story. "You went to the chapel at midday or so but the door was locked, so you waited outside. Nothing happened with the chapel until the woman opened the door. She left quickly, and the *same* woman came back with Arthur and his guard. Then they went inside, and the guard started shouting?"

Melissa nodded. "Yes ma'am."

"And nobody went in or out of the chapel while you were waiting, right?" Abby tried.

"Nobody," agreed Melissa, shaking her head.

"They must've left through one of the windows and used the alleyway to get clear of the chapel," Jaina remarked.

"Thanks, Melissa, you've been very helpful. You can go now," Abby allowed. Melissa performed a sort of shallow curtsy before leaving. It was such a sweet contrast to the rest of the investigation that Abby's heart felt like it was swelling at the sight.

"No locks around these parts, last I checked," commented Johann.

"Yup. They barred the door - I didn't check for that," Abby admitted. She knew that the others would've missed it as well, with the doors wide open. She gestured for them to follow her back to the chapel.

Montgomery stepped out to greet them as they arrived. "Any luck?" he asked.

"Some. Just a moment," Abby requested. She led the others inside and closed the doors behind them. The nicks on the inside handles were clear to see - small, but definitely there. "I need a sword," she demanded, glancing around for one. Not even Samson or Daniel were currently armed with any blades larger than a hunting knife.

"I'll go find you one," offered Johann, opening the doors to leave.

"Montgomery, would you go to the court and redirect anyone looking for me to here?" Abby requested.

"Certainly," agreed Montgomery, giving Arthur a consolatory pat on the shoulder before following Johann out of the chapel.

"What are you thinking?" enquired Jaina.

"I'm thinking we've got more to go on this time, but we're going to have to ask absolutely everyone. We'll have to sift through and cross-examine stories again," Abby informed her.

Jaina groaned. "I think it's time we made full use of that ink, then."

"Why don't you get on that?" Abby suggested. The lawyer nodded reluctantly and took off after the other two.

"May I take the body now?" asked Arthur, still sat beside the corpse.

"I can have somebody help you move her, if you like. Before you go, though, could I ask you some final questions?" Abby requested.

"If it helps you catch who did this," Arthur agreed solemnly.

"Did Vanessa have any enemies that you know of?" she began.

"Only Patrick," he claimed, just as Abby had feared he would. Daniel and Samson exchanged concerned looks.

"We'll talk to him when we move on to interviews in New Cray. If he had anything to do with it, we'll know soon," Abby assured him. "Were you with anyone around midday today?"

"I was talking with Friedrich at the well for a short while. Then a woman came and informed us of... this," he gestured to his wife's body.

"Amelia Ackerman. Yeah, alright, that all fits. Can you confirm the location of anyone else prior to that? Anyone you saw around ten minutes before can be immediately ruled off as a suspect," she explained.

Arthur began to rattle off several unfamiliar names. Abby tried to remember them all until she could write them down, though she knew that she would have to check them again later. "Thanks, Arthur. Let me know if there's anything I can do for you. Help with the burial, perhaps," she offered.

"There's only one thing you can do for me, Abby. I want justice, that's all," he said sternly.

"I'll keep at it, then," she assured him. Arthur went to lift his wife from the pool of blood, and Carmina rushed over to help him. Vanessa stained them red as they carried her outside.

"Can we talk?" Daniel asked, pouncing on the opportunity as soon as Arthur was out of earshot.

"As long as it's not about your dad," Abby agreed. Their silence told her that it was. "He's a suspect, guys, there's no point dressing it up. There are plenty of others, try not to worry about it too much."

"You'll be fair, right?" asked Samson.

"Of course I'll be fair!" Abby sighed. "Give me some credit, please?"

"Sorry," muttered Samson. The brothers seated themselves on a pew, clearly struggling not to pester her on the matter.

Inspecting every last corner of the chapel revealed no more clues, and so Abby waited. Johann returned soon enough, offering her a borrowed sword - Friedrich's, if she wasn't mistaken. She closed the doors and slid the blade through the handles; it flexed as she pushed against it, but held strong, quickly springing back and shutting the doors. Just as Melissa had described.

"That'll about do it," commented Johann. "What next?"

"I reckon it's time for the big bit. We get absolutely everyone from Lapden into the court and interview all of them. Jaina's sorting out ink and paper, we can write things down this time," Abby instructed. She retrieved the sword, and they took to the streets once more.

***

Once again, Abby found her team tasked with interviewing an entire village. It took long enough to get everyone there, but once they began, things progressed relatively quickly. They managed to get everyone's statements written down before dark, and knowing that they'd have to do the same with the entire population of New Cray, they decided to call it a night. They promised to keep the Lapden council informed regarding the investigation, and took their work with them.

Abby joined her family for dinner that night, sharing in an ostrich that Eric had caught. They were all hungry from a full day's work, but her mind was still preoccupied with the investigation, and she barely even registered the conversation as her brain churned through theories on who could have done it and why. Disappointingly, nobody had been able to recall any individual that met the profile, and some people were resorting to supernatural explanations for the killer's improbable subtlety. Abby preferred a simpler explanation, however; whoever the murderer was, they simply didn't stick out of the crowd.

It wasn't until her father called her name that she was drawn from her thoughts. "Abby?" he probed, waving a hand in front of her face.

"Huh? Sorry, did I miss something?" she asked, focusing on him.

"I asked how the investigation is looking this time," he repeated, the obvious question.

"Better than last time. I'm hoping we make a breakthrough tomorrow when we talk to people here. I think it was more likely someone from New Cray than Lapden," she informed him.

"What makes you think that?" asked Elizabeth.

"Mainly the locations," Abby told her. "During the first investigation we didn't rule out the possibility that the murderer was from Lapden, but it would've been easier for someone who lived here to get away with it. The same could be said in reverse for this murder, but if the killer was from Lapden why would they kill here to draw attention away from themselves, then cause trouble in Lapden when everyone's already looking elsewhere? Perhaps I'm reading too much into it, but that's my thinking, anyway."

"Well, they were both in chapels. Was the chapel in Lapden built at the time of the first murder?" enquired Alexander.

Abby opened her mouth to answer, then realised she didn't know. "That's a good question," she muttered.

"It was. Some people got spooked and started going there to pray after Owen was murdered. I remember that," Elizabeth recalled.

"Damn, I thought I was on to something there," Alexander sighed. "By the way, do we all have to be interviewed again tomorrow?"

"Yep," Abby smiled apologetically.

"Even me?" questioned Eric.

"Even you," Abby confirmed. "Cross-examining stories could help us pick out a liar. It also narrows down the suspects list to people who have no reliable witnesses as to their location at the time of the murder."

"Fair enough," Eric grunted. "By the way, I meant to ask - did one of you borrow my spare musket?" he enquired, leaving Abby to relapse into her musings on the mystery. She was stuck in her own thoughts again before she even heard the answer.

Eventually, they all bid each other goodnight, and Abby strolled off towards the chapel, feeling the need for prayer and further reflection. The tranquility of the walk there was shattered by Jenna. "Are you alright?" the bandit asked, intercepting her halfway to her destination.

"I'm fine. What do you want?" Abby demanded.

Jenna seemed slightly put off by the curt reply, but answered anyway. "I guess I wanted to thank you for letting me be part of this. For not treating me like a criminal."

"You are a criminal," Abby reminded her.

"Yeah, but you treat me differently. Like I'm worth listening to," she continued.

Abby forced herself to drop the stern attitude. It was something of a defence she'd adopted to prevent herself from accidentally giving away that Jenna's blood oath was nothing but an elaborate ruse. "I treat you like you're worth listening to because you are, Jenna. You're a criminal, sure enough, but you're also a person. You made mistakes because you were desperate. I can't hold that against you forever," she allowed.

"I'm glad you can't," said Jenna. "I thought the blood oath would make it right, but you're still the only one who'll even look at me."

Abby frowned and strode into the chapel, Jenna still in tow. "It might take them a long time to warm to you, but they're wrong not to trust you. Still, I suppose you'll have to make do with me until people start talking to you."

"Right. Anyway, I was thinking - you want to catch this guy, right? Why not use the blood oath?"

"We're not assuming the gender of the killer at the moment," Abby corrected, kneeling to pray. "And nobody's going to agree to a blood oath, that's why not. It's easy to abuse, not to mention it would use a lot of resources which we can't spare at the moment. It took us long enough just to scrape together the things for yours."

"But maybe just, I don't know, a minor one? So they can't lie to you or something," suggested Jenna.

"Still, I doubt anyone would agree to that. Everyone has secrets and not all of them are illegal. I wouldn't expect them to trust me not to abuse it, and the materials would still be a lot even if they were reduced."

Jenna nodded glumly. "Fair enough."

Abby closed her eyes to pray but was interrupted by Jenna again. "So what secrets do *you* have?" she asked with a girlish sort of playfulness.

"Alright, fine. *Most* people have secrets. Now be quiet a few moments while I pray," Abby ordered. She didn't mind talking to Jenna, but this line of questioning didn't bode well for anyone.

The bandit remained as silent as the grave whilst Abby muttered her prayer. "Lords above us, I am sure that these murders cannot be your will. I know I can't blame our misfortunes on you, but I feel that I must know now. Corsein, if this villain acts outside of your faith and your power, send me a sign that I might know my duty."

16
Oracle of Fates

Abby stood there, dazed and confused. She was somewhere outside the chapel now. It didn't take her long to figure out where, mostly due to the smell; she was stood in a latrine - the western one, to be precise.

Letting out a faint grunt of disgust, she tried to clamber out, but her limbs had a different plan. She didn't feel in control of herself - it was almost as though she was an observer within her own body. She looked down at her feet, and even in the dark it was quite clear that she stood upon a freshly filled hole. Despite never having instructed her body to do so, she knelt, digging with her fingers.

"Abby! Abby!" came Jenna's voice. She blinked, wondering why the bandit was on top of her all of a sudden. She was in the chapel again, laying on her back. Forcing Jenna away from her, she sat up and looked around, in control of her body again.

"Are you alright? You passed out," the bandit informed her.

Abby scrambled unsteadily to her feet, a sense of purpose filling her as she realised what had happened. "Fetch me a spade. Meet me by the western latrine," she ordered. Jenna hesitated at the strange command. "Immediately," Abby added, and the bandit sprinted out the door right away, unwilling to suffer the painful fate that supposedly awaited her should she break the oath.

Abby strode to the latrine, her heart pounding with excitement. It seemed an odd sensation to be coupled with such a place, but this was special; the Maralor had given her a sign, whether symbolic or literal. She carefully lowered herself into the ditch, digging her feet into either side to avoid stepping in excrement as she searched for the exact spot that had been revealed to her. It didn't take her long to find it, though it had been covered rather deliberately with human waste. Wrinkling her nose, she climbed up on the side and waited for Jenna to return.

The bandit arrived quickly, Tahgri immediately behind her. "What on Panora is going on? Are you alright?" he asked. No doubt Jenna had fetched him out of some concern that Abby had lost her mind.

"I'm fine," she assured them, hopping across the ditch to retrieve the spade from Jenna.

"So what's going on?" Tahgri repeated as he watched.

"I prayed and had a vision!" Abby informed him, carefully shovelling aside the topmost layer of soil.

"A vision that claimed you should dig up the latrine?" he questioned, understandably sceptical.

Abby nodded. "Yes! Look!" she enthused, reaching down into the dirt. It hadn't been buried deep, the first of it appearing after only a few inches. She pulled it free and continued digging, excavating more of the bloodied fabric with every stroke until she reached what seemed to be the bottom of the pile. Triumphantly, she handed the spade back to Jenna and held the ruined linens out for the pair of them to see.

"Is that what I think it is?" asked Tahgri, squinting in the darkness.

"It must be! Let's get some light on it," Abby insisted, gesturing for the pair to follow. They did so, almost as excited as she was to see what came of it.

She led them to Johann's, calling for him as she entered. Judging by the lack of response, he wasn't in. Muttering under her breath, Abby set the bloody rags down on one of his medical benches and set about the fiddly business of lighting an oil lamp in the dark. "Was there any movement from Patrick?" she asked Tahgri.

"Nothing suspicious, at least. He went to the well once, and he didn't seem out of sorts," Tahgri claimed. Abby nodded, unsurprised. Although Patrick had believable motives, she thought him too incompetent to have fooled her investigations for this long. Having Tahgri watch him had been a smart precaution, but little more than that.

After several attempts at ignition, she managed to light the lamp and illuminate the cloth. Ignoring the faint odour of urine, she examined the garment, the others watching curiously as she brushed the dirt off. It had been torn into crude strips, presumably to obfuscate the evidence. "Any clues?" asked Tahgri.

"Give me a moment," she insisted, beginning to arrange the pieces like some sort of sartorial puzzle. It wasn't easy, but the shapes of the bloodstains and the edges of the garment gave away its correct form, and eventually the whole thing came together. "I need you to go and get the tailor and his wife for me," she ordered. "Best not to tell anyone else about this for the time being."

"We'll be right back," Jenna assured her, and discarded the spade in a corner before bustling off with Tahgri. Abby waited with as much patience as she could muster.

Johann came in first. She was relieved to see him, since he was one of the few people that she could trust entirely. There were many others whom she wouldn't have thought to blame, but Johann was unique in that he'd been right next to her on the occasion of both murders.

"Hey," he greeted tiredly, pausing as he saw the new evidence beside her. "What's that?"

"We're pretty sure that this is the shirt the murderer wore when they killed Vanessa," she explained.

"May I see it?" asked Johann, perking up instantly with excitement. Abby nodded and gestured him over, too focused on the investigation to bother asking where he'd been. He set right to examining it under the light of the oil lamp. "These bloodstains seem consistent with Vanessa's wounds - I'd say this is the genuine article. Where did you get this?" he asked after a thorough inspection.

"It was buried at the latrine. Someone obviously tried to hide it."

Johann raised a brow. "Why were you digging at the latrine?"

"I prayed. The Maralor showed me where to look," she smiled.

"Huh. That's… intriguing," Johann said uncertainly. Abby supposed she couldn't blame him for doubting it, but she was glad that he didn't dwell on the matter. "So… what next?"

"Jenna and Tahgri should be back soon. They're fetching Samiel and Ephenra," she explained. "I'm hoping they can tell me whose this was."

Johann grinned broadly and kissed her right on the lips. "I knew you'd get him eventually," he said confidently.

She returned the kiss. "*Them*, not *him*. And I haven't got them quite yet," she reminded him. Johann didn't seem discouraged.

The tailor and his wife burst through the door, Tahgri and Jenna in close pursuit. "Over here," Abby called out. "I need you to look at this and tell me who it belongs to."

"We can try," agreed Ephenra. She stepped forwards, brushing her messy hair back behind pointy ears and inspecting the bloodied rags.

Abby left her to it and smiled at Samiel. "Thanks for coming so quickly. I would've left it until morning, but this could well save lives."

"I'm glad we could help. Perhaps next time you could leave your pet criminal behind?" suggested the tailor, glancing snobbishly at Jenna.

The bandit clenched her jaw, but she'd long since been ordered not to voice venom in retaliation to people's intolerance of her. "Go back to Tahgri's. I'll see you tomorrow," Abby commanded her, showing a little mercy. Evidently relieved, Jenna scurried from the house to momentarily escape her persecution.

"This isn't one of ours," claimed Ephenra. "We didn't make this, and there's no clear indication of who it belonged to."

Samiel stepped forwards next, eyeing the shirt alongside his wife. "It is a man's shirt, though, of about average size. He'd obviously worn it for some time before it was finally destroyed," he added.

"A woman could have worn it, though, surely?" asked Tahgri.

Johann butted in with the expression of someone who'd just had a great epiphany. "Yes and no. They would have had to be *extremely* flat chested. There was nothing acting as a 'shelf', so to speak; if there had been, at least one of these bloodstains would have shown obvious malformation when the shirt was spread flat like this, but they're rather consistent."

Abby nodded excitedly. "So it's either a man or an extremely flat-chested woman, of average size or smaller. That certainly narrows down the suspects."

"So it seems," agreed Ephenra. "Can we take this with us? Perhaps we'll be able to figure out more after a night's rest," she suggested.

Both Samiel and Ephenra were too large to meet the profile - in one dimension or another. There was also no clear motive for them to have killed Vanessa. "Sure," Abby agreed. "Do you think you could stitch it back together? It doesn't have to be a proper job or anything, just as long as it'll hold up when I carry it around."

"Certainly," agreed Samiel, gathering up the scraps of the shirt. "Goodnight, all of you. We'll have it done for tomorrow."

Ephenra smiled politely and followed her husband out. "We'll be discreet," she assured them without being asked.

"Thanks guys," Abby dismissed them, turning back to the others. "I suggest we all get some sleep. We've got a big day tomorrow."

"Not so fast. I want to hear more about this vision," Tahgri insisted.

Johann nodded in firm agreement, a cheeky grin crossing his features. "I second this motion," he announced, perching himself on the medical bench they'd used as a table.

Abby chuckled. "Alright, fine. It only lasted a few seconds - I was in the chapel with Jenna, I prayed for a sign, and the next thing I know I'm standing at the latrines. I crouched down and started digging with my hands, then I woke up and I was back in the chapel," she shrugged. "I went straight to the spot in the vision and found the shirt buried there."

"Don't make this out to be a small matter, Abby. The gods themselves have aided you," Tahgri noted.

"I know, but I don't want people thinking I'm going to be spouting divine commandments or that I'm some sort of prophet, or anything like that. I'd appreciate it if this stayed between those of us conducting the investigation," she explained. She was thankful that only a few people knew so far; some sort of hysteria or misconception was the last thing she needed presently. She wanted people to think of her as their leader, not a zealot - and certainly not a madwoman or a heretic.

"So, what *exactly* did you pray for?" Tahgri pried, peering at Abby and looking very thoughtful indeed.

"A sign from Corsein. Something to show me if the murderer works outside of his will," she explained.

"Do you remember your exact words?" the paladin queried.

Abby bit her lip and tried to recall as accurately as she could. "I asked Corsein to give me a sign if the murderer operates outside of his faith and his plan," she informed him. "I can't remember it word for word, but that was the gist of it."

Tahgri nodded and gently rested a hand on Abby's shoulder. "Then we can be certain at last. This is not an act of misguided faith, but one of hatred for Corsein."

"It is," agreed Abby. "Now go and get some rest. I'll see you bright and early," she insisted. They exchanged their goodbyes before heading to bed, Johann and Abby theorising about the chief suspects. Patrick was still at the top of the list, but the only evidence to back it was him having made an enemy of Vanessa. Regardless of her thoughts on the matter, Abby would have to do the professional thing and interview him just like all the others. Her busy mind kept her awake for hours that night.

***

Eight hundred and twenty-eight days since we arrived in New Cray. Abby stretched, yawned, and set about her morning routine. She hurried through the usual tasks so that she could get back to the investigation as soon as possible, and before long she had her entire crew together again, gathered in Johann's front room.

"Alright. First things first, I'd like to say that we've actually got some decent evidence this time. If we approach this logically we can narrow the suspect list down very quickly," she addressed the assembly. "Here's what we know about the killer so far - some of this is new information, so please bear with me; they're either a man or an extremely flat-chested woman, they're of average size or smaller, and they have access to a sword. It's also been confirmed that the killer is acting - at least partly - out of hatred for Corsein," she summarised.

"How could you possibly know all of that?" asked Samson, frowning.

Abby had expected the question, and though she was a little reluctant to explain that right now, it was only fair that they all understood the evidence. She'd be sceptical too, were the roles reversed. "Last night I prayed to Corsein, and I received a vision whi-"

"That's not proper evidence! That's superstition!" Samson cut in, his own dislike of the Maralor doing him no favours.

"Let me finish," Abby demanded. "I found the killer's shirt, that's a fact - and whether you want to believe it or not, it was the vision that led me to it." The room went silent, mouths wide in surprise.

"Alright," Samson eventually agreed. "Who are our suspects?"

"Patrick's at the top of the list," she admitted. "I probably should've asked yesterday, but can you give me an alibi?"

The brothers went silent for another moment. "It wasn't him!" Daniel insisted, sounding worried.

"Please tell me that isn't a no?" Abby begged, glad that she at least had Tahgri's spying to fall back on.

Samson shook his head bitterly. "We can't - I was bathing around midday. We were all apart."

Daniel frowned at his brother. "I took over the farm from Samson a little before then. Dad was indoors," he claimed.

Abby nodded solemnly. "We're going to have to confirm those, or I won't be able to keep you two on the case," she informed them.

"Why not?!" complained Daniel. "We already know it wasn't either of us; we were asleep when the first murder happened, remember?"

"But this isn't the first murder. We're not ruling off two different killers," she told them. She felt bad for even suggesting that it could be one of them, but until proven otherwise, they were on the list of suspects along with their father.

"Fine. Well, Jaina might've seen me bathing," suggested Samson, looking hopefully to the lawyer.

"I'm sorry, but... to be frank, I didn't get close enough to be certain that it was you I saw. It could've been any number of people," Jaina returned, much to Samson's chagrin.

"I fetched water for the farm plenty of times around then. If someone remembers me going that way you have to rule me out," Daniel insisted.

"Could anyone have seen your dad? Even if it was just for a moment around midday," Abby tried.

Both of the boys shook their heads firmly. "He was inside, what do you think?" Daniel whined. "It wasn't him!"

"Don't panic, alright," she tried to calm them. "This isn't good, but if nobody saw him then that's a good defence that he couldn't have gone to Lapden, too. What are the chances of him walking all that way with a sword and a bucket, without anyone remembering him, right? I'll try to confirm your stories first thing, and if anyone witnessed them, you can stay on the investigation."

The brothers nodded glumly. "Fine, but keep us informed regardless, will you? It could be helpful," requested Daniel.

Abby turned to Carmina next. "Where were you when this happened, anyway?"

"We were having lunch," she claimed, gesturing to Aurelius.

"We didn't finish until well after the murder," he added.

Abby frowned. "You didn't share any with me?"

"There wasn't much to share," Carmina admitted guiltily.

Abby rolled her eyes. "Alright. Tahgri was with Jenna, so she can vouch for him. Let's confirm your stories, boys. After that we can start interviewing anyone who could possibly match the description; male, average size or smaller. Flat-chested women, too, and be professional about that part for goodness' sake."

The younger men shared a series of smirks. "Out of interest, where were you?" asked Daniel. "And yes, I know you don't exactly fit the profile."

"I was with Johann, same as last time," she informed them.

Typically, Carmina wasn't satisfied to leave it at that. "Underneath Johann, to be precise," she contributed. Abby sighed. *Adolescents.*

They set to work, starting by trying to confirm Samson and Daniel's alibis. Unfortunately, Jaina had been the closest thing to a witness for Samson, and the only person who claimed to have seen Daniel fetching water wasn't certain of the timing. Despite their protests, she had to keep the brothers out of the investigation.

Slightly dispirited by having to let the pair go, the rest of them began interviewing everyone who matched the profile, their workload greatly reduced by being able to instantly rule off so many people. As before, some of them had solid alibis and others didn't. Infuriatingly, Patrick fell into the latter category - not a soul had seen him until well after the murder. Whilst this kept him at the top of the suspects list, it certainly wasn't enough evidence by itself to declare him the culprit.

Next came the cross-examinations, and anyone who should've been able to confirm an alibi was interviewed - for the second time, in many cases. The vast majority were easily confirmed, with just a few who joined the Marshal family on the shortlist due to the uncertainty of their witnesses. By late afternoon, they finished with a list of about twenty suspects.

"What now?" quizzed Aurelius.

"Now I go and get the shirt. I need to talk with the tailors in Lapden, see if any of them made it. If that doesn't work I might be able to use it to spook a reaction out of someone on this list," Abby explained.

"By 'I', do you mean yourself, or all of us?" Aurelius continued to pry, sounding very much like he didn't care which it was.

"Tahgri and I. It's really only a one-person job, but you're welcome to come along if you feel like being bored," Abby chuckled.

"Nah, not after last time. I think I'll just get back to the field - see you later, alright?" Aurelius excused himself.

"Me too. Mum and dad could use the help," Carmina smiled. "Good luck."

"Alright. Thanks for your help guys, have a nice day," Abby called after them.

"So after Lapden we're just going to go back to the people on that list and try to scare a reaction out of them?" asked Tahgri, leading the way to the tailors.

"Pretty much. If we don't find out who the shirt belongs to soon, I'm thinking we go back to Patrick. I hate to say it, but he's looking pretty guilty on this one, whether he actually is or not."

"His sons, as well," Tahgri added.

Abby made sure to thank Samiel and Ephenra for their efforts as they collected the shirt. She and Tahgri checked in with the tailors in Lapden, and they soon concluded that the garment predated both villages. It was unfortunate, but there were still other avenues of investigation left, and so they returned to New Cray.

Jenna strode up to them as they neared the Marshal household. "Can I join you?" she asked.

Abby looked her over, recognising that she was in a poor mood - most likely due to the verbal abuse she so often received. "I need you to wait outside while we talk to Patrick. You can join us for the next ones," she offered.

The bandit followed them over and took herself aside so that she didn't get in the way. It was Daniel that answered the door, glancing at the shirt awkwardly. "I guess I can't blame you for doing your job," he muttered.

Abby smiled sweetly at him. "I'd appreciate it if you didn't. We'll be out of your hair shortly, we just need to talk to Patrick again. Alone." Though he was obviously reluctant, Daniel ushered them inside and left them to it.

Patrick was exactly as they'd left him after their initial interview; sat grouchily at a table. "What do you want now?" he demanded.

Abby was careful to observe his face as she seated herself opposite him. "Look familiar?" she asked, setting the shirt down between them.

Patrick squinted at the clothing. "If I'm not incredibly mistaken, it looks somewhat like a shirt," he said bitterly. He eyed it with a faint air of disgust, as though it were a filthy animal in his house.

"Lose the attitude," growled Tahgri, carefully balancing his bulk on a spare seat. "Despite your incompetence, Abby's done everything in her power to protect you from unfair treatment during this investigation. The least you can do is answer an honest question."

Abby stared commandingly at Patrick. After taking a few moments to get his temper under control, he responded more seriously. "It looks just like any other shirt to me, and it's not one of mine."

"That wasn't so hard, was it? Thanks, Pat. Let me know if you think of anyone whose it could be," she ordered, snatching the shirt and getting to her feet.

"My boys are on the suspect list, aren't they?" Patrick asked.

"I'm afraid they are. They fit the profile as well as you do, but try not to worry about it. There are plenty of people on that list and nobody's getting in any trouble until there's real proof," Abby reassured him.

"Be sure they don't," Patrick huffed, dismissing them with a wave of his hand.

Tahgri shut the door behind them as they left. "Was I too strong on that one?" he asked.

Abby shook her head. "No, that was perfect. I just wish people didn't take it so personally that we're investigating them. We've investigated literally everyone, after all."

"I suppose they feel somewhat accused. They'd be angrier if there was no investigation at all, though," he assured her.

Jenna rejoined them, matching their pace as Abby led the way to the next suspect on the list. "So, think you'll get lucky this time?" she asked, her mood brightening now that she was back in more tolerant company.

"It's hard to say, but it's looking that way. We've got a good profile now; it's hard to overstate how important that could be," said Abby.

"Well then, let's go and wave dirty clothing at people 'til we get our suspect," Jenna grinned.

Abby smiled and passed her the list - more to free up her own hands than anything, since Jenna couldn't read or write. "Our target's to get through these today. If you play nice you can stick with us all the way," Abby assured her.

"Thanks," returned Jenna. "I guess Patrick's innocent, then?"

"I think so. He barely reacted to the shirt - looked more offended that it was dirtying his table than anything else," Abby pointed out. "But I made the mistake of telling his boys about the shirt before talking to him. That was stupid of me."

"Don't beat yourself up over it. I would've done the same," claimed Tahgri. Abby imagined he was just trying to comfort her, but she was too focused on the investigation to doubt herself anyway.

Slowly but surely, they worked through the list, starting with New Cray and eventually moving back over to Lapden. Abby was looking for a reaction of panic or surprise when she presented the shirt, but mostly what she elicited was confusion or distaste. It was as they reached the penultimate entry on the list that Michael thundered up to them, dust from the dry earth kicking up around his boots as he skidded to a halt. "Abby, there's trouble. They're trying to arrest Patrick," he informed her, somehow managing not to sound particularly concerned despite the clear urgency with which he'd come to deliver the message.

"Who's 'they'?" demanded Abby, instantly furious.

"The Lapden council. Thought you might want to know," the smith clarified.

"Jenna, get the other council members to Patrick's!" Abby ordered, taking off in a sprint without a moment's delay. Tahgri and Michael tried to keep up as she made her way back towards the Marshal household, but neither of them had anywhere near her stamina.

Abby's legs were aching by the time she approached Patrick's house, the heat of the afternoon sapping her of energy. She was met with the concerning scene of Samson and Friedrich posturing for a fight, weapons out and weighing each other up. The entire Lapden council was there, as was Arthur. "Put down the swords!" Abby croaked as she slowed and staggered towards them.

They all faced her - except for Friedrich and Samson, who kept their eyes locked firmly on each other in the heat of the confrontation. "We're arresting Patrick. This has gone on long enough," said Montgomery.

"On what basis?" Abby demanded, breathing heavily and letting the bloodied shirt hang limply by her side.

"On the basis of the evidence! We were all there when Vanessa spoke to him in the court - you saw the look on his face. He meets all the criteria!" Montgomery continued. "You didn't think we wouldn't act on this when he's clearly the prime suspect, did you? Now, we demand this man step aside and let us arrest Patrick, before it comes to blows!"

Abby pushed through the crowd, glaring at Samson and Friedrich. "For crying out loud, put the swords down!" she ordered. They looked uncertainly at her, both wanting to trust her but unable to do so entirely. She decided to wait for Tahgri to get there before trying to disarm them; they would hold off on stabbing each other, that was enough for now.

"You didn't actually think you could just march over here and arrest people at random, did you?" she lectured Montgomery. "What happened between Patrick and Vanessa was almost a year ago now! He may be the prime suspect, but he's still just that - a suspect. Arresting someone just because it's possible they did it is unethical."

"Not to mention incredibly illegal. I should know," interjected Jaina, pushing past the crowd to stand beside Abby. The lawyer had never been such a welcome sight as right then and there.

"You can't seriously intend to let him get away with this!" Katherine snapped from amongst the Lapden council. "He's been an arse from the very start, and he clearly never wanted to assist the investigation. He's as guilty as can be."

209

"I have interviewed every person in Lapden and New Cray. Nobody has placed Patrick anywhere outside of his house near the time of the murder, and he doesn't exactly blend in these days - he's the palest man in either village! There's no way I'm going to believe he walked from his house to the chapel, and back again, without being recognised. Nobody's getting arrested for anything until there's real evidence against them," Abby insisted, hoping that the others would soon arrive to help defuse the situation.

Arthur stepped forwards next, cold anger on his face. "You promised me you'd see justice for Vanessa. Don't hold out on us," he demanded.

"Yes, I did! I promised I'd do my best to find justice! Not to arrest people without evidence, and just hope that they're the killer," she snapped.

"Well if you won't do anything, someone has to," insisted Markus. "I propose a vote; those for the arrest of Patrick, raise your hands."

Unsurprisingly, the entire Lapden council was in favour, joined by Katherine. "Johann and Michael will be here to vote soon," Abby told them, cautiously eyeing the swords that were being brandished.

"There's no need to wait," said Yasmine. "It wouldn't be the first time we've voted on issues without everyone present. You didn't have a problem with it before."

"No, but we're waiting for everyone this time," Abby insisted.

"Why should we?" Yasmine bickered.

"Because I'm telling, not asking," Abby warned her. She prayed to the Maralor that Michael would have her back on this one despite his bitter feelings towards Patrick.

The absent members of the council turned up before any more threats needed to be exchanged, Jenna and Tahgri following close behind them. "Sorry about the delay," grunted the paladin.

"Your swords. Now," Abby demanded, turning back to the source of the commotion. With Tahgri looming over him, Friedrich relinquished his weapon, and Abby took Samson's to keep things on a level.

What's going on?" demanded Johann, edging cautiously around the crowd.

"We're voting to arrest Patrick for murder," explained Montgomery.

"Then we should discuss with Abby, I suppose," said Johann. There were murmured complaints from the opposition, but the others ignored them and gathered around Abby to talk. "Do you think he's guilty?" asked the doctor.

"Not even a little. To kill Vanessa he'd have had to walk all the way from New Cray to Lapden whilst carrying a sword and a bucket of water, then back again. Can you imagine Patrick getting away with all of that without anyone even realising he'd left his house?" Abby questioned.

"No, he's not exactly subtle," agreed Johann before calling out to the assembly. "I vote not to arrest him!"

"You won't make many friends doing this," commented Michael, obviously unsure of himself.

"I'm not trying to make friends, Michael, I'm trying to do the right thing. Arresting an unpopular man for a crime he didn't commit isn't right," Abby insisted. She still found it rather unbelievable that she was actually defending Patrick, after everything he'd done.

Michael nodded bitterly and turned to face the crowd. It took him a few more moments to decide. "I vote to leave him be."

The gathering erupted into a series of angry objections. "Then we're going to have to come to some sort of agreement until we can settle this properly," insisted Montgomery, noting the even split between the eight elected.

"We don't have to do anything. The positions are binary; either the vote is for or against arresting Patrick. Until it's one or the other, we do nothing. That is *your* system, after all. The one I was elected to be a part of," argued Abby.

"Patrick murdered Vanessa. If it wasn't for that, she could vote too. I say we get one extra vote because of that," Montgomery tried.

"For goodness' sake, this is childish! The vote was a draw, and I'm not just going to sit here whilst you try to change the rules so that you can have your way," Abby retorted.

"I think it's time for you all to go home. Next time vote on the matter first, or don't come looking for trouble," Tahgri insisted with as much calm intimidation as he could muster.

"I can see now that inviting you to Lapden was a mistake," hissed Yasmine, joining Katherine in giving them a venomous parting look. Abby scowled, but didn't bother to waste breath on barbed words. The proponents of Patrick's arrest began to disperse.

Friedrich tried to retrieve his sword, but found his wrist caught in Tahgri's grip. "I think I'll hold onto this for now, in case you try to arrest anyone else," the paladin warned him.

Friedrich looked to Abby, silently appealing to her mercy. "You'll get it back tomorrow, but if we have to do this again, I'm keeping it," she threatened.

There was an awkward moment as the man considered his options, no doubt concluding that all he could do was obey. "Sorry about that," he mumbled before turning and following Arthur back to Lapden.

Abby let out a heavy breath of relief as the last of the opposition left. "Thanks for backing me up on this, all of you. I know it's not an easy choice, but it's the right one," she tried to assure those who remained.

"It is. There's no way a case like that would've held up in a real court. They're just angry," Jaina insisted. Johann and Michael nodded, though it was clear that the decision had been more difficult for the smith. Abby was proud of him for not choosing the easy path.

"What next?" asked Tahgri.

Before Abby could answer the question, Samson stepped over and hugged her tightly. No words were necessary, she wrapped her arms around him in return, speaking to the others over his shoulder. "What's next is that we get some dinner and sleep. We'll try to sort all of this out after a good rest," she insisted, withdrawing from the hug and offering Samson his sword back. "Don't do anything stupid with it," she warned him.

"I won't," he promised before disappearing into the safety of his home. She doubted he would resort to violence if he didn't have to, it wasn't his style.

"I'll loiter with Jenna a while and make sure they don't try to sneak back around for revenge," said Tahgri, leaning against Patrick's wall.

"Good idea, thanks guys. I'll bring you something to eat later," she promised before heading back home with Johann. Their own rebelling stomachs would also need tending to.

"So, what do we do if it does come to blows?" the doctor questioned. "I don't doubt that we've got the advantage physically, but that might not be the appropriate response if everyone sides with them."

Abby sighed. "I honestly don't know," she admitted. "For now we'll just have to hope that we can find the real killer before everyone tries to string up Patrick. It's all we can really do."

The evening passed by without any further trouble from Lapden, thankfully. Abby found herself awake later than usual that night, sat pondering on the bed with Johann's arms wrapped around her. The investigation was going less than perfectly, but that wasn't what was on her mind; she couldn't stop thinking about Johann's question - to what lengths would she have to go to protect democracy? How hard would she have to fight to do the right thing? Perhaps most scarily of all, she had to question if she'd subvert the entire system of rule if the majority sided against her. There was a word for people that did that. *Tyrant.*

17
A Gathering Storm

It had been more than a month since the confrontation with the Lapden council. Although they'd managed to interview the last two suspects and chase up every available lead, Abby and her friends were now all but officially unwelcome in Lapden, with very little to show for it. People had grown so concerned about the murderer that crude bolts were now a fixture of most doors. To make matters worse, Katherine had begun to sow seeds of discontent in New Cray, suggesting that another election would be a good idea after Abby's refusal to accept Patrick's supposedly obvious guilt. The man had been unpopular even before this, but now he'd replaced Jenna as the village's verbal punching bag.

Katherine was using everything she could to try and discredit Abby's authority, even the fact that she'd briefly resorted to cannibalism. The people of New Cray still had some respect for her, however; it wasn't a very effective reputation smear, given that almost everyone still alive in the village - including Katherine herself - had eaten the flesh. Abby took every opportunity she got to discredit the malicious attacks.

There were a couple of silver linings to the metaphorical clouds; the weather had cooled at last, and the elementals hadn't been seen for five weeks now. With the exception of one unlucky individual who had been caught out when sneaking to a well, the tactic of hiding had proven entirely effective. The drop in temperatures had also allowed for work to continue full time; Jenna was taking advantage of having the negative attention drawn elsewhere, and she'd been using her basic knowledge of irrigation to minimise the chances of the drought repeating itself, digging holes and ditches that Abby was only just beginning to understand the workings of.

She was helping Jenna work on the irrigation when she first heard the tempest. It rang across the distant sky, a thing of might that echoed on the horizon. It was day eight-hundred and fifty-eight, and the end of summer was about to be marked with the heaviest rainfall any of them had seen in years. Hours passed as she toiled away, the gloom of the oncoming storm ever increasing, blotting out most of the sun, and the gradually nearing thunder occasionally drowning out the sounds of her labour. It was during one such thunderous roar that she heard something that sounded more like a gunshot than the weather.

Eric almost crashed into Abby as she clambered out of the ditch to check everything was alright. Everything was not alright; the hunter was in full sprint away from a rapidly gaining monstrosity; a hideous thing with glistening, moistened scales covering the length of its serpentine body. She didn't believe it to be a creature of natural origin, its single pair of front arms making it unlike anything she'd ever seen in the wilds. Regardless of what it was or where it had come from, Abby only just managed to prepare the spade as a weapon before it reached her.

In a hefty movement, she bashed the creature over the head, causing it to reel and stop chasing Eric. It rounded on her as she prepared the tool a second time, and as quickly as one might expect from a serpentine being, it lunged. She caught it under the jaw with the tip of the spade, pushing back against it with all of her might. It proved to be somewhat stronger than her, however, and knocked her down with ease.

It came in for another strike, but this time she used her legs. Trying to take advantage of its physiology, she lodged her feet firmly against its shoulders and strained in an effort to keep its snapping jaws at bay. Abby lifted the spade again and rammed it deep and hard into the creature's maw until she felt flesh sever. Not content with that much, she yanked it back out and repeated the motion - there was a nasty crack of bone as she broke its jaw and dislodged many of its teeth. Eric helped her finish the thing off, stamping down on its already fractured skull and driving the spade further into its head.

She grasped Eric's hand as he offered it to her, and struggled back to her feet. Jenna came running to join them, glancing fearfully at the fallen creature. "What the fuck is that?" she questioned.

"Elemental," the hunter claimed, gesturing for them both to follow.

Moving so that the crops of the nearest fields were no longer in the way, Abby saw them; shrouded by rainclouds, an army of the creatures seemed to shimmer beneath the looming storm. "Fudge," she exclaimed, struggling to rationalise her thoughts past the fear. "I need you two to fetch all the fighters and help me get everyone into the houses by the eastern well. If we're lucky, we can just sit there and wait for them to pass by like we did with the fiery ones," she ordered. The pair took off towards the houses without delay. If they were lucky they'd have fifteen minutes to get everyone organised before they were set upon. It wasn't enough time to deal with Lapden as well - they could only hope that they'd noticed and were also doing the smart thing.

Just as before, Abby moved from house to house, directing everyone to the eastern well. It wasn't long before she reached Tahgri's, though it seemed that Eric had got there first, as the paladin was already pulling his armour on. "Help me get ready," he insisted.

Abby moved behind him to help. "I can't stay long. We've got to get everyone to the houses by the eastern well. If they pass us by we'll be safe there," she strategised.

"And if they don't pass by?" he questioned.

"Then slice them into fish steaks. At least we'll be assembled."

"Good thinking. I'll meet you there once I'm ready," agreed Tahgri.

Once she was confident that he could handle the rest of the armour quickly enough by himself, Abby took off again. She saw the others hastening her job; Daniel, Samson, Carmina, and Aurelius all knocking on doors and hurrying civilians along. They reached the east end of the village as the first of the elementals stampeded into New Cray.

Abby muttered a quick prayer to Rendick and yelled for Tahgri. Sure enough, the paladin soon came striding through the streets, braining the foremost aggressor with a single well-placed blow. The forerunners were different to the one she'd killed earlier; their forms were almost bear-like in size and shape, though they more resembled vicious sea creatures than anything she'd seen on land. Two more of them rounded on Tahgri, and though they struck him, his armour held strong as he butchered them with his trusty claymore. With the immediate threat dealt with, he jogged over to Abby and raised his visor. "Orders?" he questioned.

This time she didn't hesitate to lead in the slightest. "Join the others, and distribute the fighters as evenly as you can between the buildings. Try to keep quiet until they pass by," she ordered, pointing him in the right direction. She grabbed the dagger from his belt and handed him the spade she'd been carrying in return. "Good luck. I need to get my gear, I'll join you as soon as I can," she dismissed him, and readied her own knife - a more civilian blade - in her off-hand. They felt odd in her grasp; she knew from experience that dual-wielding weapons, especially longer ones, wasn't particularly practical. Even with shorter blades she wouldn't have recommended it for the majority of combatants, but she was practically a veteran by now.

She snuck off to the right, back towards Johann's. The doctor had long since evacuated to join the others, but Abby hadn't paused to fetch her armour when she'd gone by that way. She didn't even reach the door before she was approached by another of the creatures, this one identical to the first she'd faced. It reared up on its serpentine body, every inch of it dripping with rainwater as it lunged forwards. She felt its arms scrape against her shoulder as she ducked to avoid its fangs. Without giving it time to recover and attempt a second blow, she dug in with the blades, striking where she hoped its lungs were and rapidly eviscerating every inch of its underside. Its screeching resonated in the air, a sound that Abby thought no creature should be capable of producing.

She slit the elemental's throat to finish the job and sprinted through

Johann's door, rushing into their bedroom to pull on her armour. The sound of the rain against the woodwork was quickly joined by the furious hammering of something heavier, and a few moments later she heard the front door burst open. Pulling on her helmet, she ran through to the next room to see what hideous monstrosity was upon her this time. It uncoiled from around one of the medical benches and lunged at her, receiving a knife through each eye for its efforts. The only sound it made was the gentle slapping of its body against the woodwork as it slumped to the ground.

She returned to the bedroom and grabbed the last of her gear. Testing the combination of hammer and knife left her dissatisfied, and so she tucked the spare weapon into her belt and decided to stick to the two blades for now. A large part of her wished that she still had her shield.

Abby tried to make her exit, only to find one of the bulkier creatures trapped in the doorframe. It struggled to get its broad shoulders through, eyeing her hungrily and scrambling in an attempt to make ground. Aware of the constraints of time, she opted not to fight it for now and opened the shutters, flinging herself out the window to escape instead. She heard the sounds of woodwork splintering and smashing distantly behind her as she dashed towards the east end of the village, but she didn't look back. The rain beat down upon her all the way.

The sight she arrived to was one she'd feared; the creatures - rather than pass straight through - seemed to have amassed around the occupied buildings. Perhaps they'd seen the people entering, or perhaps it was something else that drew the elementals to the villagers trapped inside, but the aqueous creatures clearly knew where their targets were hidden. She snuck up behind the swarm, readying her knives and moving as quietly as she could, hoping the rain would keep them from hearing her. The elementals closest to the occupied houses were battering furiously at the woodwork, and it would only be matter of seconds before it began to give way to their brutish strength. She had to do something quickly if she wanted to minimise the casualties.

The first of her would-be victims sniffed the air as she approached. It hesitated a moment, as did Abby, then it rounded on her with a hiss. She sighed and dashed forwards, ramming both knives through the creature's skull as its claws scraped uselessly off of her breastplate. "TO ARMS!" she bellowed, dashing to the nearest empty house. Parts of the swarm broke away from the crowd and began to chase her.

She hoped that those capable of fighting had heard her, as she was immediately forced to defend herself again when the creatures chased her inside. The door served as a filter for the attackers, making their numbers nearly worthless.

Once again, one of the larger creatures became trapped in the narrow doorway. Abby brought one knife down in a feint, and the other up, severing its throat neatly when it tried to bite her. The creature thrashed and slumped, making the doorway even less passable. Still, some of the more slender, snake-like creatures tried their luck. The next attacker's constricted movement helped her, and she lunged forwards to deliver a series of vicious slashes to its head and underside as it pushed through the gap. She didn't quite pull it off flawlessly this time, a single fang causing a shallow gash in her right shoulder. Still, it was worth it to have almost completely sealed the main entrance.

She could hear the creatures outside, slithering around and bashing at the woodwork to try and get in. Abby had no idea whose house she'd taken shelter inside, but she'd have to apologise for any damage caused when she got the opportunity to do so. *If* she got the opportunity to do so.

Something splintered loudly behind her, and she darted through the house to see what was going on. One of the creatures had damaged the latch on a set of shutters, denting them inwards. She waited beside them, knives at the ready, and soon enough it struck again, ripping the wood apart and slamming the shutters wide open. It seemed startled to see her already there, and she wasted no time in driving Tahgri's knife through both of its jaws, holding on tightly as it thrashed and split its own face in two against the blade.

The elemental fell down and staggered off below the window. Abby could see more of them out there, scrambling over one another in order to be next into the breach. Still, others hammered against the woodwork to try and create more entrances. She wished she could see how well the others were getting on with their own defence, but with the horde of monsters stealing her focus it was impossible.

The serpentine creatures continued to storm the house from every available entrance. She held them off for a minute or two more as they destroyed the other shutters, but she was only buying time until she was entirely surrounded. Deciding it best to make her exit while she still could, she eventually clambered out of the window and hauled herself onto the roof, her injured shoulder protesting the effort.

The heavier of the creatures seemed to be having trouble following her up onto the roof, and so she took a moment to survey the scene - it seemed that the others were now fighting at the doorways and windows, repelling the elementals as they battered at the woodwork. Some of the monsters began to close in on her again, their rippling tails propelling them up towards the roof, true to their serpentine form. Taking a calming breath, Abby dashed to the edge and jumped across to the next building. She knew they would pursue her easily enough, and so she continued to use her momentum to jump until she reached the roof of one of the besieged houses.

She readied her knives and leapt from the rooftop onto a creature below. It thrashed as gravity drove her weapons through the top of its skull, the brain taking a few moments to catch on to the fact that it was already dead. She clambered through the nearest window, assisted by the defender - Samson. "We thought they'd got you!" he grunted, barely sparing a moment to bring her to her feet before readying his sword to cut down the invaders again.

"They almost did!" Abby gasped, wiping blood from her shoulder. Without further delay, she moved through the crowd of scared civilians and saw to defending some of the numerous breaches.

The house was crowded, poorly suited for all but the crudest forms of fighting. For that reason, Abby was actually thankful that she'd only had access to shorter weapons. The defence went on, the enemy's numbers dwindling in the choke-points and the sounds of the melee interspersed with thunder and gunshots. It wasn't until the walls themselves started to give way that the attackers became truly problematic, coming in from all angles. "Form a square!" Abby yelled as the elementals endangered the exposed civilians.

The response was crude but somewhat helpful. Those with weapons both proper and makeshift formed the outer lines of the shape, protecting the huddled civilians in the very centre of the house. With such a crowd of people behind them, the defenders couldn't simply be bowled over. Their enemies kept coming until their own bodies had piled high enough to stop them.

People screamed as lightning struck the building, showering them all with fragments of wood. Abby felt something batter against her helmet and dropped to the floor, keeping as low as possible as the building collapsed around her.

The inner walls cracked near the base, leaving them all in a sort of darkened crawlspace. Trusting the dim light to guide her, Abby managed to pull herself free of the wreckage, immediately finding herself face to face with another of the larger creatures. Before she could attack, its mouth wrapped around her head and squeezed. The helmet proved stronger than its teeth, but she could still feel the metal warping under pressure, and so she was swift to bring her knives to work, stabbing blindly at the creature as the stench of fish filled her nose. She drove each strike as deep as she could until it released its jaws from her and collapsed, the numerous wounds proving too much for it.

She wasn't given time to recover fully before the snake-like body of another elemental began to wrap around her. She gasped as it started to constrict painfully about her legs, but even as her arms were pushed close to her torso she managed to dig the blades deep into its scaled sides. The very motion that compressed her body tore the creature apart, allowing her to push one fist through its entire being. The knives carved the way, fluids oozing down her arm as she forced her shoulder through it, ripping her way out through a wall of flesh. The muscles loosened as it died, and Abby struggled her way free of its restraining tail.

The elementals seemed to be thinning out at last, though they were still far from done. In some cases it was hard to tell which were alive and which were dead, the shimmering of rainwater on motionless scales easily mistakable for movement in the gloom. Glancing down at her breastplate, she noted that the previous creature had deformed the iron with its strength. It would be more work for the smithy, assuming anyone survived to run it.

She could see Tahgri ahead of her. He stood amidst the wreckage of a different house, cutting through the creatures with weary blows. He normally looked far more graceful in the motions, and Abby could tell that the length of the engagement had taken its toll on him. She worked her way towards him, her legs protesting after the abuse they'd received.

As luck would have it, the collapsed roofs had probably done the civilians more good than harm, forming a barrier between the elementals and their prey long enough for the fighters to regroup and cut down the majority of the aggressors. "We can't stop. We need to help Lapden!" Abby panted as the last of the creatures fell.

There was some hesitance, but Carmina and Samson formed up with her. "We're right behind you," they agreed. Aurelius and Daniel were soon beside them as well, their expressions grim but their wounds minor.

"I'm done in, Abby," admitted Tahgri. "And you're bleeding," he added after a moment. He sagged and sat down, lifting his visor.

"They're nothing," she assured him, glancing at the various scrapes she'd endured. She'd had much worse injuries, and unless the elementals were venomous she would be just fine. "If you can't fight, I'm going to need your sword. Get all the civilians out of this wreckage, gather them at the barn and defend them as best you can from any stragglers," she ordered. Tahgri offered her his claymore freely, and she exchanged it for her hammer and the return of his own knife. The sword felt reassuring in her grasp, a gleaming weapon that promised to cleave straight through any unarmoured opponent. "Everyone who can fight, follow me!" she barked.

The walk to Lapden felt shorter than it used to be. There was a gap of barely two hundred metres between the villages now, but Abby didn't rush her band of fighters across it. As urgent as the situation was, they'd been exhausted from combat before the walk, and moving faster would only have left them all too weak for the fight when they arrived. They got there in their own time.

The group took to the streets, moving as one. There were only bodies to be found at first, and it seemed likely that Lapden had sustained worse losses than New Cray once again, most likely due to a lack of military leadership. They followed the trail of corpses through the village, and when they finally encountered living elementals, Tahgri's sword proved incredibly effective against them. They slaughtered every creature they encountered.

The bodies littering the floor grew thicker as they neared the court, both those of the civilians and the elementals. Abby tried not to let her thoughts linger on what the population of Lapden would be after this. Suffice to say that any remaining council members would probably prove to be a great over-representation.

She finally took off in a sprint as she saw movement inside the court. Friedrich's armour was hanging limply from a mangled mess of half-eaten limbs on the stairs up. His was one amongst many corpses, and all of them had died recently by the looks of it. Hoping she wasn't too late, Abby plunged through the front doors and into the reception.

The elementals were everywhere, slithering about and battering at the two doors to the main room. They must've been barred from the inside, as they didn't immediately give. The fighters charged, bludgeoning and hacking the creatures apart. The front room was soon clear of threats, but there were still screams and the unmistakable sounds of combat coming from behind the ravaged double-doors.

Without delay, Abby set to finishing what the elementals had started, and with the help of Aurelius and Samson they managed to get one door down. The windows at the rear of the building were wide open, shutters smashed apart where the elementals had sought access to the crowd of civilians inside. It was a slaughter on both sides, all sorts of weapons - of proper forging or improvised origin - seeing use as the court was flooded with monsters. Before long the floors were slick with fluids and covered with bodies, making combat difficult for elementals and citizens alike. Still, they slogged on until it was truly over.

Abby hefted the claymore one last time. Numerous as the aqueous monstrosities had been, she eventually found herself fighting the last one. A single mighty blow severed it from shoulder to gut, the stench of fish spilling out of it instead of organs. "Thank the Maralor, I think that's the last of them," she panted.

"Fuck the Maralor. We did this ourselves," commented Samson.

Abby frowned, but didn't contest his beliefs. She turned to Aurelius, relieved to see that he and Carmina were still alive, if a little bloodied. "Get me a count of the dead," she ordered. "The rest of us need to get back to New Cray."

He nodded and set out to see how effective the watery horde had been compared to their fiery cousins. Abby turned to lead the way back, but was confronted by Montgomery, clambering shakily over the corpses to get to her. "We need to talk!" he insisted.

Abby pushed past him, not bothering to pause as she answered. "I think I've heard enough of what you've got to say already. I'm going back home to make sure we're ready for the next attack."

"But what about us? All of our fighters are dead now. We won't survive another attack!" he called after her, following gingerly.

Abby turned to face him this time, seeing a near-perfect opportunity to take back control of the churlish popularity contest that government here had become. "Fighters aren't your problem, Montgomery. What you don't have are leaders. Frankly, after what you and Katherine have been up to, you're lucky to have me around to help at all," she snarled at him. The battle still had her blood running hot, to say the least.

Montgomery faltered, struggling for a response. "So you're just going to leave us to die?!" he questioned.

Abby smirked and shook her head. "No, that's the sort of thing you'd do. If you want to survive, help Aurelius get a count of the dead, then gather absolutely everyone outside the chapel in New Cray."

Montgomery's face briefly flickered with anger, but he swallowed his pride and nodded, turning to arrange the scattered flock that was Lapden. Abby simply led her fighters back to New Cray, the rain lashing them every step of the way.

***

The rain had finally stopped. Abby stepped out from the shelter of the chapel and took to the steps with Tahgri, watching as the crowd gathered in front of her. There were fewer people than she'd expected - it was sad to see that the combined population of New Cray and Lapden was now approximately the same as New Cray's alone had been a year ago.

She'd been quick to check on all of her friends and family, of course - her father had received a nasty gash on his arm, which was actually the product of his own embarrassing knife-work in the heat of battle, but that was the worst injury that any of her friends or family had received. Aurelius hadn't yet given her the death count but she could see him in the crowd, and so she began. "Could all the council members step up, please," she called out. Montgomery and Markus stepped forth, along with most of New Cray's representatives. "What about Katherine and

Yasmine?" she asked the others.

"Yasmine's dead," Markus informed her with a stony face. "I think Amanda was injured, Katherine said that she needed to be with her."

It was miserable news, even if they had been complicit in trying to turn New Cray against Abby. She opened her mouth to continue, but was interrupted by a ripple of murmurs spreading through the crowd. Daniel emerged from the dense gathering, the body of his father across his arms and angry tears on his face. "You did this!" screamed Samson, striding past his brother and pointing his sword at Montgomery and Markus. "Your lies killed my father!"

Abby was - oddly - more shaken by this than any of the other deaths she'd noted so far. Perhaps it was because she'd assumed that Patrick's sons had got him to safety in the early stages of the attack, or perhaps because of the accusation Samson had made. She wanted nothing more than to comfort the boys, but for the sake of New Cray she remained focused. "Tahgri," she muttered softly. "Could you take them aside? Tell them I'll be with them in just a moment," she requested.

Tahgri approached the pair, and Carmina soon joined them. Whatever words they exchanged, they seemed to convince the boys to come with them without causing any more of a scene. Tahgri led the others off to the side, helping them carry the body to his house.

Abby took one last look at them before turning to address the crowd. "I'm disappointed in the sort of behaviour we've seen lately, especially from people purporting to want democracy. I hope you all think about the effect that this division has caused, but first we've got to address the bigger problem. The elemental problem," she began. Nobody reacted much, a solemn look of acceptance on many faces, and guilt on others. "What we have right now is a tactical issue, and it's clear that some methods which have worked previously against other elementals haven't worked at all against this new threat. I have every reason to believe that they'll return sooner or later, and so I've devised a plan to deal with them. It's going to require a lot of effort and cooperation, but I believe that once constructed it will prove entirely effective against fire, water, maybe even earth. If you want to put aside petty squabbles and work together, I suggest you stick around. Anyone who doesn't - feel free to go, but know that we'll remember who turned their backs on us."

Nobody moved to leave, all of them much preferring the option that didn't involve inevitable death. "Excuse me a few minutes while I deal with Patrick's sons. Don't go anywhere just yet," Abby insisted, and strode off after the others.

The sobbing was audible as she approached Tahgri's house. She entered to the sight of Carmina embracing Samson, and decided to offer

Daniel the same comfort. "I'm so sorry about this," she condoled. He had clearly taken it the hardest of the two, and wept against her shoulder for a full minute before managing to compose himself even a little. Tahgri stood by the body, unable to do anything but watch awkwardly.

"You need to see this," Samson said angrily, detaching himself from Carmina and handing Abby a folded piece of paper with her name on one side. She frowned and took it, though she noticed that hers wasn't the only one - Samson had another with 'Boys' written on it in place of a specific name, but she dismissed that as being none of her business and unfolded hers, peering at the contents.

Abby,

I know we've had our disagreements, especially in the last year or so. I'm sorry about that, but I guess you don't care too much about what I think now that you're on the council and I'm not. You stood up for me when nobody else would because you knew I wasn't guilty, so that gives me some hope that you'll live up to my father's expectations.

I suppose this is my way of setting things right before I go. By the time you read this I'll be dead, so there's no reason to lie about it - I never killed anyone, and I don't know who did. I wish you luck in finding the real murderer.

Abby frowned and glanced at Patrick's body upon realising that this was a suicide note. She'd noticed that his corpse was strangely free of blood, and the marks around his neck explained why; he must've hanged himself either during or immediately after the attack. She looked back to the letter.

I should've stayed on to fix this, but things have gone from bad to worse here, and I don't see it getting any more bearable. We're better than we were given credit for, me and my boys. We didn't deserve to have our family torn apart like it has been.

All I ask is that you take care of Samson and Daniel. I know you wouldn't do it for me, so do it because it's the right thing to do.

Patrick

She folded the letter away, feeling as though her heart had been used as a juggling ball. "What are you gonna do about this?" demanded Samson. "They bullied him to this point, that's got to be a crime!"

Abby took a deep breath and thought carefully on how to handle it. Something had to be done, and the people in this room - elected or otherwise - had the power to do it. She looked between them sternly as she spoke. "I'm going to strip Katherine, Montgomery, and Markus of power. I promise you I'll consider some real punishments in time, but right now we can't afford to lose more people than we already have. I need all of you to back me up on this or it won't work."

Daniel stood abruptly. "Whatever you do to them, I'm in. I want to see those bastards' faces when they realise they're fucked," he agreed, drying his eyes.

"You're going to strip them of their power? What difference does that make?" questioned Samson, clearly dissatisfied with her plan. "They're murderers, we should execute one of them as an example!"

"Absolutely not," Abby sighed. "I don't want to execute anyone. That's a dark path to start down."

"They started down their own dark path!" Samson snapped. "You have to do *something* about it, imprison them at least. We can't have cowards and murderers living with us."

"We can't imprison anyone, Sam. We don't have a prison. We don't even have stocks. Besides, we need them with us; numbers are the only safety we have right now," she tried to remind him.

"I'll execute one of them myself, then! Katherine maybe, she was the worst. You don't even have to get involved - and it's not like she can fight worth a damn. Nobody except Amanda will miss her, and she won't be around for much longer, either," Samson ranted. Carmina took his hand, trying to calm him a little.

"Sam, I don't have enough time or enough people to stop you from killing Katherine. Even if I tried, you could kill her in her sleep, that's the truth," Abby admitted. "But what do you think will happen when people start to worry that they're next in line? They'll get scared, they'll leave, and we'll be left on our own to fight the elementals. I know it's not fair on either of you, but we can't afford to punish them any worse than this. Not right now."

"She's right," contributed Carmina, embracing Samson again.

Daniel stepped over and put a hand on his brother's shoulder. "She is. Play it smart. The slow knife, alright?"

Samson brushed Daniel's hand off of him, but solemnly nodded his acceptance. "Fine. I'll go along with you, but only because there's no better choice. They should be punished. And I mean *really* punished."

Abby nodded, and glanced at Tahgri to see if he'd come to the same conclusion. "If you think it'll work, I'm with you every step of the way," agreed the paladin, though the situation clearly weighed heavily on him.

"Come on then. This won't take too long," Abby insisted, gesturing for them to follow. They left Patrick's corpse behind for the time being and returned to the crowd, the others standing beside her on the chapel steps.

"I have here a letter addressed to me from Patrick. I'm inclined to believe that men with the intention of killing themselves tell few lies, so when he wrote that he isn't the murderer and doesn't know who is, I believed him," she called out, waving the paper. "As a consequence of the bullying and unfair behaviour that led to his suicide, I'm going to respond with a little of my own; Katherine, Montgomery, and Markus are, of this moment, no longer on the council. Jaina, Johann, Michael, and myself are now in charge. This isn't negotiable, unless of course you think you'd survive another attack after everyone who can fight properly leaves New Cray with me."

The crowd exploded into a raucous discussion, the other council members staring at Abby in disbelief. "You can't do that!" Montgomery insisted. "Who made you the leader?"

"Who made you the executioner?" Abby snapped back. "You drove Patrick to suicide by spreading malicious rumours without evidence. Frankly, you deserve to be in stocks, so be glad I'm not doing that."

The remains of the Lapden council stepped forwards, Montgomery raising his voice to the crowd. "Will you stand for this? We were elected! What gives Abby the right to decide who's in power?"

The crowd was clearly divided on the matter. Abby stepped up beside the other two, calling out again. "Do you think these people will be able to protect you when the elementals come again? I suspect you'll find that their brand of democracy is a dull blade."

"Democracy has worked for us so far, and would continue to work for us if we stuck to it!" Markus insisted. "She's playing on your fears so that she can take charge. Is that what you all want? A dictator?"

"Democracy worked for us, until we realised that we had elected children where we should've elected leaders!" Abby rebuked. "These people have no mind for the real problems, all they do is talk. Elementals won't listen to reason, and they won't respect our democracy. Why don't you tell these people, Montgomery? Tell them all about *your* plan to deal with the elementals."

Montgomery floundered uncharacteristically in the face of a question that couldn't be answered with rhetoric. Someone in the crowd booed, and that was all it took - the hesitation and uncertainty made him look weak and stupid - perhaps even more so than he actually was.

"You have no plan! You want power but you don't know what to do with it. Give us some real solutions, or stand down so that better leaders can do it for you," Abby demanded. Defeated, the deposed councilmen shuffled awkwardly into the crowd.

Abby raised her hands to draw attention, not that she needed any more than she already had. "Now listen closely; anyone who's capable of acting as a mason or any other form of builder, please stand out here on the left," she requested, gesturing. "And anyone who can assist Michael in smithing a bell, please stand on the right."

A small group of craftsmen formed to Abby's left, though only the smith from Lapden stepped to the right. "We're going to need a big bell. The kind that can be heard at least a couple of miles away," she informed them. "You two may as well set right to it, because this needs to be done as quickly as possible."

Michael stepped down from behind her and greeted the other smith before leading him off to get started. Hopefully it wouldn't take too long to gather enough metal for what they needed.

"We're going to be building a tower that goes underground as well as above. It'll be right between the villages, and it's going to be made partly of stone. I'll talk with the town planners soon, but I suggest you all get gathering materials. As for the rest of you, we need to dig a pit at least eight feet deep. I'll be along soon to show you where to start," Abby continued. She turned to look at everyone who had remained on the steps beside her. "That means us, too. We should get started now. Daylight's burning."

There were murmurs of agreement as people set off to work. Abby walked with Carmina, making her way over to supervise the labourers. "So, you and Samson..?"

"Sort of, but this really isn't the time," Carmina smiled apologetically at her. "Later, alright?"

"Fair enough," Abby agreed, trudging onwards.

Aurelius joined them, matching their pace. He remained stoically quiet for a while, but before Abby could ask if there was something beyond the obvious souring his mood, he finally spoke. "Ninety-five dead," he confirmed.

Abby swallowed the bitter news and nodded. "We'll have to find time to bury them at some point. How bad are the wounded?"

"Pretty bad. Johann's tending them still, might as well round it up to a hundred," he admitted, then veered off to get away from them.

"Aurelius! What's wrong?" Abby called, following him.

He turned around, glowering. "What do you think is wrong? What the fuck was that back there?" he demanded.

"That was us taking back control. All those politics were killing us," Abby responded, smiling sadly at her brother.

"You mean those politics that *you* introduced in the first place?" he returned, jabbing a finger into her breastplate.

"It was good at first! It encouraged people to talk and help each other out," Abby reminded him, batting away his hand. "But this division would've been the end of us. I didn't vote for that."

"Sweetie... I know you meant well by it," commented Alexander, approaching along with his wife. "But that was a bit extreme. You can't just bluff about uprooting our family like that. We need to talk about these things. It was meant to be a democracy, right?"

"We're worried about you," admitted Elizabeth. "You made a lot of enemies when you sided with Patrick, and those things you said? Markus was right - you're using people's fear to control them."

Carmina shook her head. "It had to be done! Look at what they did, you can't expect us to just stand by and let something like that happen again," she differed. "The only reason people let it go on for this long was because nobody liked Patrick."

Abby nodded. "We didn't have any real choice - they were making the wrong decisions. This might be our last chance to do the right thing."

Aurelius groaned. "Listen to yourself. The 'wrong decisions'? Who decides what the wrong decisions are? You can't just have democracy until they disagree with you - this was a power-grab, plain and simple. I wonder if you would've tried to kick them all out if they'd voted to execute Jenna, too."

"Oh come on!" Abby moaned. "Is it such a bad thing to want to spare some lives? You were wrong about Jenna, get over it."

She only saw the fist coming because he hesitated. She lowered her head a little, letting his knuckles batter against her forehead. "Aurelius!" her parents exclaimed in shock.

He went for another blow, but Abby deflected everything he threw at her with ease, grabbing his limbs and locking them in place with her own, embracing him in such a way that he couldn't get free. "Stop!" she insisted, squeezing him tightly. She could feel him giving in to her. Surrendering. "This is exactly what I'm talking about. I know you're scared and angry, but these petty arguments will kill us. I'm sorry for talking on your behalves, and I'm sorry for undermining democracy, but the choice was never more than an illusion. We need to unite against the elementals. Everything else is just a distraction that'll kill us all."

"She's right," Tahgri commented from behind her. Abby didn't know how long he had been standing within earshot, but she was glad he was here. "The elementals are only going to grow in number. Out here we have bandits, droughts, and a serial killer to contend with already - any more divisions we make amongst ourselves will be the end of us. It may be wrong to do away with democracy, but sometimes positions of power force us to make the kind of decisions which pit sin against sin. Life isn't as black and white as you'd all like it to be."

Abby stepped back from Aurelius, struggling not to cry as Tahgri's words made her realise what she'd become. "I'm sorry," she apologised again. "I know it was wrong, but I'd do it again if I had to. I'd rather you hated me, if the alternative is you dying."

Carmina stepped closer hesitantly. "How much longer do you think we could've survived if we hadn't done that?" she asked her brother.

"None of us could've lasted much longer," Tahgri answered for him. "Abby's always done the right thing, it's just that the right thing keeps getting worse. Save your blows for the elementals."

Aurelius gave Abby a distrusting look and stormed off. She hoped he came to see reason soon, because knowing that someone in her family could view her with anything other than love was breaking her heart.

"What are we building, anyway? Surely not just a tower?" asked the paladin.

Abby restrained her emotions and composed herself as she considered the best way to explain what she had in mind; the bastion that would bring permanent safety to New Cray. "A fortress."

"A fortress made of stone? I don't seem to remember those doing much to stop the elementals back home," Tahgri commented.

Abby shook her head and glanced up at him. "I suppose not, but the fortresses in Luthania weren't designed with elementals in mind. You've got to trust me. It'll work."

Tahgri nodded grimly. "I trust you."

"No turning back now," Carmina insisted, looking to her parents. "Let's get to work."

Alexander hesitated, stepping up to Abby and reaching out to touch her forehead where Aurelius had struck her. "Are you alright?" he asked.

"I'll live," Abby grunted. Her father gave her an awkward little smile and followed the rest of the family to start digging.

Alone with Tahgri now, Abby sighed. "They don't understand, do they? If only they could."

"They won't. You're a leader now, Abby. I've never once disagreed with your decisions, but this won't be the last time others do. No good deed goes unpunished."

228

18
Red Rain

Eight days had passed since work on the fortress had begun. They were still excavating, the masons and other craftsmen waiting patiently to be able to begin construction. The weather had grown milder, with only gentle rains and relatively mellow heats following the storm. Still, it was only a matter of time before extreme weather beset them once again, and more elementals along with it.

Abby sat opposite Jaina and Tahgri, discussing the defences and how quickly they could feasibly build them without putting a stop to other essential industries. It had been discovered - no doubt through sheer recklessness - that the aqueous elementals were as edible as common fish, and they'd preserved well enough to feed the workforce for a short while. They would have no troubles with food this season, so at least they didn't have to worry about agriculture.

She frowned and glanced over at the closed shutters as she heard it, a distant sound that would've been lost amongst the pouring rain if not for its pitch. "Did you hear that?" she asked.

Tahgri had evidently been oblivious to it, but Jaina nodded. "That sounded like a scream to me," she stated anxiously.

"Tahgri, grab your sword," Abby ordered, her fears confirmed.

Jaina briefly braved the rain, opening a shutter and peering outside as the paladin equipped himself. "It's not elementals, as far as I can see," she informed them. Without delay, Abby led the group out the front door. The woodwork was still a splintered wreck from the last attack; repairs had seemed unimportant compared to work on the fortress.

Others nearby must have heard the scream as well, as they stepped outside to look around curiously despite the weather. "Where'd it come from?" Abby asked as she passed their neighbour.

"Not a clue," he responded, ducking back inside to keep dry. Abby frowned and walked on

The source of the commotion soon became clear - Johann was stood near the chapel, crouched over the body of Mrs. Sutton and trying to stem the bleeding from her neck. "Johann! What happened?" Abby demanded, jogging over to him.

He glanced across at her and shook his head rapidly. "It wasn't me! I just got here. I heard screaming and I was... gods, she's not even dead yet, just unconscious - but I don't think I can save her from this. I didn't

229

see who killed them," he claimed, running one bloody hand through his hair. It was unnerving to see Johann lose his composure. He was always the one who viewed the injured and dying with indifference, but the violence of this situation was evidently too close for comfort.

"Them?" Abby asked, unsettled by his use of a plural. Johann simply pointed at the chapel.

She headed inside. Even with the other victim laying on their front, it barely took a moment for Abby to identify the body. "Katherine," she muttered.

"Orders?" requested Tahgri, following her inside. Jaina hung back, cursing and muttering heatedly with Johann.

"Hang on," Abby insisted, stepping over and checking the symbol on Katherine's back. It wasn't quite as usual; the outer circle was only about three-quarters finished. She moved over to check the other body for the same mark, but found it entirely absent. Lowering her voice, she gave Tahgri the desired orders. "See if you can find Francine's husband, he ought to be told about this. Samson and Daniel, as well - they wanted Katherine dead. Send them all over here." She'd have added Amanda to that list, but the woman had succumbed to her injuries three days ago despite Johann's best efforts.

Tahgri loped off, and Abby looked to Johann and the small group of people approaching the scene. It was a grey afternoon, the bleak weather matching the looks of the people. "How much blood would the killer have on them?" she asked the doctor.

"Enough. The arterial spray should've gone all over them," Johann claimed, getting to his feet and trying to compose himself.

"Everyone get inside the chapel," Abby ordered. "Anyone who's still here couldn't have done this without being covered in blood, so please go where we can rule you out." Eager to be seen as innocent, the crowd stampeded inside the chapel and took seats, being sure to keep clear of Katherine's corpse.

"Johann, Jaina - I need you to gather the usual crew while I talk to this lot," Abby instructed.

"Are you sure you want Aurelius?" the lawyer asked. It was no secret that Abby had hardly spoken to her brother since they'd fought, and she'd barely done any better with her parents, either.

"Yeah. Tell him it's important, obviously," Abby returned. She'd just have to hope that he'd put aside their differences, for now.

Jaina nodded. "Alright. We'll be right back," she promised, taking Johann by the arm and striding off with him.

Abby stepped back inside the chapel, sparing a brief grimace at the sight of Mrs. Sutton's blood washing away in the rain. Nobody recovered from a throat injury like that. She would never wake up. "Alright! We're sitting in a fresh crime scene right now. Did anyone hear or see anything other than that scream?" she asked the assembly. Nobody spoke.

Samson appeared in the doorway, not a fleck of blood on him to tie him to the crime. "Was it the same killer?" he asked, coldly regarding Katherine's limp form as he strode over.

Abby glanced at the corpse again. Katherine's throat had been slit, her blood messily painting the walls. "Both of them were, presumably. Mrs. Sutton has no symbol cut into her, but Katherine does," she explained.

"Any theories yet?" Samson enquired. He hadn't really had enough time to recover from his father's suicide; his words were disinterested and world-weary.

Abby stepped back over to Katherine's body, showing Samson the symbol of Corsein. Most of the crowd peered as well, sating their own morbid curiosities. "He didn't finish it," she pointed out. "I'm thinking he killed her, but got interrupted by Mrs. Sutton whilst he was carving the symbol. He charged Mrs. Sutton down and stabbed her in the neck, but not before she managed to scream. He's probably still out there, running or hiding."

One of the men on the pews cleared his throat loudly, getting to his feet. "Did you hear that there were two screams?" he enquired.

Abby frowned and looked the man over, trying and failing to recall his name. "Two? I only heard one, when was the second?"

He nodded confidently. "One was really loud. I heard that, then a few moments later there was another, quieter that time."

"Did they both sound like the same person?" Abby probed.

The man shrugged. "Both women, I think," he clarified. There were a few agreeable nods and glances between those gathered.

"Alright. What do we do now?" Samson asked, looking around at the assembled crowd.

"We look for the killer, of course. Were you working on the fortress with the others?" Abby asked.

"No, I was inside. I think Daniel was at the fortress, though."

Abby pursed her lips, reconsidering Samson's possible involvement. He'd wanted Katherine dead, certainly - still, she doubted he could've got away without a single drop of blood on his clothes. "Alright. Go and get Daniel, and start gathering people who were working with him," she ordered. "If they can all account for each other at the time of the scream, we can start ruling people out that way. Process of elimination." Samson nodded and pushed past her, unenthusiastically strolling off to fetch the workforce.

Abby stepped back outside as Mr. Sutton sprinted over. She noted the dirt of use and lack of blood on his clothes as he knelt by the body, and ruled him off as a suspect as well. He clutched his wife tightly and she spewed up a little blood, accompanied by a faint gurgling sound. "She's still alive?" he dared to hope.

"Her lungs are full of blood. I'm afraid you just forced it up when you moved her," Abby informed him. She hated to be so blunt, but there was nothing else she could say without giving him false hope.

He began to cry, angry and shocked tears slipping down his cheeks. "Who did it?" he demanded, struggling to form coherent words through his emotions. "Who killed my wife?!"

"We don't know yet," Abby confessed. "Some of us are out looking right now. If we're lucky, we can still catch them with blood on their hands - literally. Were you with anyone from about ten minutes ago until now?" she asked.

It took a moment for him to compose himself enough to give a proper answer. "I was digging with the others," he managed, gesturing off to the north. Given the state of his clothes, she didn't doubt it.

"Alright. We're already gathering people who were digging there. If you could point out anyone you were with at the time, we can rule them off as suspects," Abby explained. Mr. Sutton nodded bitterly and clung to his wife, her blood seeping into his clothes and the rain disguising his tears.

Tahgri rejoined them, stopping in front of Abby. "Jaina and Johann are still trying to find the others," he informed her, embedding the tip of his sword in the ground.

"Alright, thanks. Could you fetch me the shortlist from last time?" Abby requested. "It should still be at Johann's."

Tahgri headed for the doctor's, Carmina passing him by on her way to the crime scene. She ground to a halt beside Abby and stared worriedly at the corpse. "Where were you about ten minutes ago?" Abby enquired.

Her sister clearly had to force herself to focus. "Uh, I was working the farm," she claimed.

Abby nodded and glanced about, unused to having so little assistance on these matters. "Any idea where Aurelius has got to?"

"No idea. Haven't seen him all morning," Carmina claimed. "He's probably still sulking."

The crowds began to swarm in. They gathered in a circle, watching in horror as Mr. Sutton held his dead wife. "Go and start looking around for anyone with blood on their clothes," Abby commanded her sister. "And make sure you stay armed!"

Carmina made her way back out through the thickening crowds as Abby called out. "Alright, listen up. Some of you were working on the fortress today. I want everyone who was to form a line." They followed her commands, murmuring quietly amongst themselves. "Mr. Sutton will identify anyone he's absolutely certain was working with him at the time of the murder."

The rain slowed to a drizzle as the bereaved left his wife and began to pick out those he remembered. Abby ushered the men and women that were selected into the chapel, dismissing protests from those who cried foul when their alibi wasn't corroborated. They were about halfway finished when Aurelius finally joined them. "What's the plan?" he asked, eyeing Mrs. Sutton's corpse. "Jaina told me it's the same killer?"

"Seems like it, yeah. Plan's the same as always; ask lots of questions. Where were you about fifteen minutes ago?" Abby enquired.

"I was having lunch. Alone," he claimed. He seemed calmer than he had been a week ago, hiding his anger at her behind a thin veneer of professionalism. "I went to the latrine after, that's why it took me so long to find out about this."

They were interrupted by one of the men lined up in front of Mr. Sutton. "No he wasn't, he was digging with us earlier. Walked off a little before the scream, so if he had lunch it wasn't fifteen minutes ago," he claimed. A few of the others in the line nodded and muttered, seemingly convinced that this was the case.

"Were you at the fortress at all today?" Abby interrogated Aurelius.

He shook his head, scowling. "No! I went hunting this morning, then I had lunch. I came here as soon as Jaina found me," he insisted.

Abby was about to try and figure out who was lying and why, when a voice called out from the other side of the crowd. "Let us through!" it insisted, and the people slowly parted. Samson escorted a young girl through. Abby just about recognised her as the Wilkinsons' daughter, Michelle; she was soaked and breathless - and pointing a finger right at Aurelius. "It was Aurelius! I saw him!" she insisted.

Samson drew his sword, and Aurelius took a panicked step back from the accusing finger. "Stop!" snapped Abby, stepping in front of Samson and trying to calm the bristling crowd. Her heart panicked against her will as she struggled to remain professional.

"She's talking shit!" snapped Aurelius, which did nothing to help calm the situation.

"Everybody ease up. Aurelius, just don't move," Abby warned him. Looking very scared indeed, he stood immobile, putting his hands up in surrender. "Michelle, tell me what you saw."

The girl gestured at Aurelius again. "I was on my way to the chapel, and I heard this scream, so I went to look. I saw him stab Francine!" she insisted. "Then he started chasing me with his knife!"

"Liar!" hissed Aurelius. Mr. Sutton stormed towards him, and before Abby could prevent it, it went straight to blows. Mr. Sutton was bigger, probably stronger, and definitely angrier, but Aurelius had had proper training. The older man was soon bent double from a series of knee-strikes, clutching his gut.

"Everyone calm down!" Abby snapped, dragging Aurelius away from Mr. Sutton and confiscating all of his weapons. He looked lost, perhaps understanding that his reaction had only made things worse for himself. "Take care of Mr. Sutton, please," she ordered the crowd.

"I think it's time for you to step down from this investigation, Abby," Samson objected, watching a few concerned citizens help Mr. Sutton.

She shook her head resolutely, but handed him Aurelius' weapons. "Absolutely not," she differed. "I'm going to handle him like I would any other suspect. Come with me, all of you. We're going to talk about this sensibly and check the story with other witnesses just like we did for everyone else."

Michelle was clearly nervous about going near Aurelius, hesitating at the edge of the crowd when Abby gestured her over. "He won't hurt you," Samson assured her. "I'll protect you." The girl took his hand, still looking somewhat hesitant as she was escorted over.

"We'll talk at the doctor's," Abby instructed them, being sure to keep Aurelius as far away from the girl as she could.

"What about the rest of us?" asked someone from the crowd. Others murmured around them, no doubt wondering the same thing.

"If Mr. Sutton can't rule you out as a suspect, go and take shelter in the barn. I'll let you all know what comes of this soon," she instructed. The reluctance was clear on some of their faces, but Abby was too busy worrying to care about their opinions.

"You can't possibly believe this! I couldn't have done it, I'm not even on the short list for the first two!" Aurelius whined as he was marched towards the doctor's house. Abby remained gloomily silent, weighing up the possibilities in her mind. None of it seemed to add up.

Johann almost bumped into her at the door. "Oh! There you are," he greeted, backing up rapidly to let them all enter. "I was just going to find you - Tahgri asked me to direct you to the cemetery, apparently Daniel found some bloodstained clothes there. He didn't want to move them before one of you had a look."

Abby shook her head glumly and gestured to the seats. "I'll deal with it shortly. Sit with us, please," she instructed. Perhaps recognising the seriousness in her voice, the doctor obeyed without question.

Aurelius moved shakily around the table and took a seat opposite them all. "Where have you been in the last hour? Tell me everything,"

Abby demanded.

"I told you! I got back from hunting, I had lunch, and I went to the latrine. She's lying through her teeth!" he insisted, pointing at Michelle.

Abby slammed his hand down onto the table before he could scare the girl any more. "Control yourself," she ordered, wrestling to restrain her emotions. "It wasn't just Michelle. All those people said they saw you working on the fortress, and then she specifically pointed at you and said she saw *you* stab someone! You must understand how bad this looks." Whether she believed it or not, Abby knew that many would view his naming by the witness as hard proof of Aurelius' involvement. Johann stared, slack-jawed at the revelation.

"Have you got any proof that you really were at the latrine?" Samson pressed, putting an arm around Michelle's shoulders to calm her down again.

"What are you expecting, huh? I could go and scoop up my shit, would that be proof enough?" Aurelius growled, frustration and fear evident on his face as he glared at his accusers. "How reliable are these witnesses, anyway? It was pissing it down outside - they could've easily mistaken someone else for me."

"Average size with brown hair isn't exactly a unique appearance," the doctor contributed helpfully. Abby found herself momentarily frozen as his words made her draw the connection.

"You're fucking right it's not!" Aurelius concurred. In a blur of motion, Abby shot to her feet, grabbing her chair and slamming it into Samson's head. He went down with a look of astonishment upon his face, his consciousness fading before he even hit the floor.

Michelle screamed and backed away rapidly to the other side of the room. "What the fuck?!" questioned Johann, hopping to his feet and staring at Abby in horror.

"Arrest him," Abby ordered, pointing weakly at Samson. Her mind panicked and struggled to formulate a plan. "It's Daniel. Aurelius looks just like him!"

"What? Are you sure?" asked Aurelius, looking rather alarmed.

Abby moved over and grabbed Michelle by the arm. "Johann, did Daniel go with Tahgri to the cemetery?" she asked.

Johann clapped his hands to his forehead as he realised what was happening. "Oh shit. Yes he did," he informed her.

"Tie Samson up, then send help!" she barked, haste causing her to almost trip over her discarded seat as she led Michelle out the door. "Michelle, get somewhere safe. Tell everyone you can find to come to the cemetery!"

She didn't pause to hear the response. She was already sprinting.

235

19
Tombstone

The residual rainwater splashed under her boots as she sprinted towards the cemetery. She couldn't afford to wait for help; every second she wasted was another second that Tahgri could be stabbed in the back, and every single step made her stomach churn with disbelief at what had happened. The depth of Daniel's betrayal was almost too much to bear. She could barely fathom how it could be him, but it simply had to be.

Abby's gut lurched as she heard the gunshot, and she vomited from nerves, barely even slowing down as she spewed fish and bile across the ground to her side. She could hear Daniel yelling as she approached.

The cemetery was rather out of the way, which was no doubt why he had lured Tahgri there. It was the perfect place to get away with murder, barely visible or audible from most of the village. When she came into view of the pair, Tahgri was already on the floor, struggling back to his feet. Daniel gave up on reloading the stolen musket and drew his sword instead. "Drop it!" Abby cried out, hurtling towards him.

Alarmed, he went on the offensive against Tahgri. He timed it well, barreling into the paladin as hard as he could. Such a thing should've been foolish due to Tahgri's superior size, weight, and armour, but he was weakened by injury. The pair crashed to the ground, and Daniel was soon on his feet again, triumphantly gripping Tahgri's claymore. "Well, it seems you brought a knife to a swordfight," he commented, tossing away his own inferior weapon. As much as Abby hated to admit it, she wasn't sure she could fight Daniel like this. Her armour was still sat in the smithy, and her knife wasn't suited to parrying blades. She hadn't paused to grab any larger weapons in her rush to get there.

Tahgri tried to tug Daniel's feet out from under him, but the murderer brought the sword down heavily on the offending arm. The paladin groaned and slumped, his armour only just saving the limb. "Put the sword down, Daniel," Abby insisted. "It doesn't have to end like this."

"Liar," he smirked. "This is the only way it can end. If I get rid of you two, who's going to stop me?" he questioned, his features cold and serious. Taking advantage of the distraction, Tahgri reached across himself and drew his knife, slamming it into Daniel's leg. The young man screamed in pain and limped away from the fallen paladin.

Abby darted forwards. "Knife!" she demanded, and Tahgri threw the bloodied weapon limply towards her; she caught it mid-run, adjusting it in her hand even as she charged at Daniel. The murderer staggered back and raised the sword to finish his victim, but Abby moved too fast, trapping the blade with Tahgri's cruciform knife.

Before she could sink her other weapon into Daniel's gut, he shunted her backwards, swinging the sword wildly. Abby retreated, letting his injured leg bleed and weaken. If Tahgri hadn't also been injured she would've let Daniel waste energy until victory was easy.

She waited for him to get close enough to attempt another strike, then dipped back out of range, only to lunge forwards again the moment the blade had wasted itself on thin air. She tried to gut him with the knives, but merely scratched the surface of his stomach before he brought the sword around and pommelled her in the head with it. She staggered and grasped his wrist to prevent him doing it again, ramming her elbows into any part of his form that she could reach. They struggled for control of the sword, but her own raw strength proved inferior once again. He barged her back, and somewhere in the process of it all he managed to knock Tahgri's knife from her grasp.

Abby backpedalled, recovering and taking in her surroundings again. She knew that Daniel was aware of his advantages and his disadvantages, she knew everything he'd been taught and then some. He went for the obvious, limping forwards for a predictable strike; a thrust with as much force as he could put behind it. She sidestepped, allowing him to follow up with an overhead strike. One last dodge, and the sword crashed down on the cemetery's most prominent monument - William's tombstone. Abby kept just out of reach, smirking at Daniel.

"Wipe that look off your face! You haven't won yet," he snarled, oblivious to the lioness stalking up behind him. Just a couple more steps. It roared and pounced on the murderer, the sword flailing uselessly as heavy paws battered his head into the earth. He didn't stand a chance.

Abby waited just a moment to make sure it was safe to approach. "Thank you," she whispered, grabbing the sword and leaving Daniel to Ersei's quadrupedal weapon of retribution. Tahgri was still alive; gazing up at the sky with tired eyes and wheezing breathlessly, but still alive. "Stay with me! I told Johann to get help, they'll be here soon," Abby assured him, fighting back tears as she stepped over and took note of his wounds. The shot had scattered all over his chest, going clean through the armour. The fact that he was still alive at this point gave her some hope that it wasn't fatal.

The paladin propped himself up against a wooden grave ornament and coughed up blood. "It must've hit the lung," he commented, wiping his chin. "Listen to me; do you swear to uphold the will of the Maralor in all you do, and to fight for truth and justice?" he asked, his voice weak.

"I do," she agreed, desperately hoping that the ceremony would keep him focused a little longer whilst Johann got there.

"And do you swear to dedicate your life to the greater good, and to do your duty to the gods, king, and country?" he whispered.

"I do," she agreed again, clutching his armoured form carefully.

He wheezed, struggling to sit up straighter. "Just hang on!" Abby begged, tears flooding down her cheeks and adding to the moisture of the sodden earth. "Johann will be here any minute." She glanced around to see if they'd caught up with her yet; the lioness had snuck off already, and Eric had taken its place looming over Daniel, but there was still no sign of the doctor. Given that she'd ordered him and Aurelius to tie up Samson, she couldn't be sure how far behind he was.

Tahgri shook his head sluggishly. "Hand me my sword," he insisted. With a sob, Abby did as he instructed, helping him to grip it. He raised his voice as much as he could. "Arise, Dame Paladin," he managed, the sword gently tapping each of her shoulders. His work done, he let the weapon fall softly to the earth.

By the time Johann arrived, Tahgri was no more. Abby clung to his armoured chest and wailed, begging the Maralor to give him back, but it was not to be. Corsein had drawn his fate.

A gathering crowd watched in silent mourning as Abby wept, but it was some minutes before anyone dared to disturb the scene. "Do you want me to kill him?" Eric asked coldly, still crouched beside Daniel's battered form.

Abby glanced at the man that had killed Tahgri, laying there on his grandfather's grave. "He's still alive?" she managed through her tears.

"His injuries are mostly superficial," clarified Johann. "But if I don't deal with his leg he'll bleed out."

Abby reluctantly got to her feet and went to inspect Daniel for herself. He was bloodied and battered, but the Maralor clearly had a good reason for not killing him outright. Tahgri had once told her that their role was not as glamorous as the stories would have people believe, and he had been right. "Make sure he lives," she instructed, her first act as a paladin one of justice rather than revenge. "I need him to confess."

20
Heroes and Villains

"Sir Dunwolf was a man that each of us should strive to be a little alike," she began, struggling to accept that he was gone even as she gave the eulogy. "Eric once told me that what makes a hero, is fighting for the greater good - even when you don't know if you'll walk away from it. Tahgri was selfless, strong, and righteous; the epitome of our order. He touched our town in a way that drew out the best in us, and he fought 'til the end. He will always be our hero."

The crowd of Tahgri's friends and acquaintances muttered sombre agreement before Abby continued. "His last act in life was to ordain me in the hope that I'd continue to do good in his place. I intend to do just that, but we all know that you don't have to be a paladin to make Panora a better place. Love and respect each other. Help each other. If you won't do it just because it's right, do it in memory of Tahgri."

She hoped it hadn't been too brief. Her parents seemed suitably moved, though Carmina and Aurelius just looked depressed. They'd been almost as close to Tahgri as Abby had been, after all, and it hadn't even been a day since his death, yet. She joined the crowd as others said their last goodbyes, adding her own little prayer to all the others. They were going to spare the time to make a suitable monument for him; a tombstone to stand proudly next to William's. It seemed fitting to Abby - both men had done great things for New Cray in similar measure.

When the whole upsetting affair was over, she walked away from the funeral in isolation, allowing herself a few moments of lonely sorrow. A few moments was all she would get, though - Markus and Montgomery approached her as she entered the town properly. "My condolences," said the pair in unison, looking incredibly uncomfortable at the situation.

"We both want to apologise about that whole misunderstanding with Patrick. We went too far," Markus tried.

"Misunderstanding? You mean that thing where you two helped bully him into suicide?" Abby replied sharply. "Don't think you're completely free of all that just yet. If this town didn't already have enough problems I might've arrested you both already."

There was no real way in which they could answer that, and so they merely followed her in silence for a few moments. "So, what do we do about the boys?" Montgomery finally asked before she could get away. "The people want to know, sooner rather than later."

Abby frowned. "Don't presume to tell me what the people want. That's not your place anymore," she reminded them. "I'm going to talk to Daniel to determine Samson's guilt, then they'll both be handled in accordance with Jaina's interpretation of the law."

"Which will be death, yes? For Daniel, at least," Markus questioned. Abby simply nodded.

They didn't dare press her for more information, for which she was grateful. Tahgri was barely cold and she was already being bombarded by the needs of the town, which was more stress than she cared for. "We'll leave you to your business, Dame Koning. We're sorry again, about all of this," Montgomery concluded before leading Markus away. Despite everything, she had to admit that it sounded good. *Dame Koning.*

She went to the chapel first, deciding to pray before pushing herself into confronting Samson and Daniel. The bodies were gone, but the blood still stained the woodwork; Abby struggled not to see the people that had died in here when she knelt at the altar. She said her usual prayer, just to help her focus on what needed to be done, and what was expected of her as a paladin.

She stayed there a short while before heading to Johann's house. Eric had volunteered to guard Samson there, whereas Daniel was being kept at his own home by Michael. She took a moment to calm herself before walking into the building through the gaping hole that had once been their front door.

Samson lay bound to one of the medical benches, a furious bruise covering the side of his face where she'd struck him. He glared at her venomously. "Do you know why you're here?" she asked him.

"So you can frame me and keep your brother out of trouble, maybe?" he snapped back.

Abby shook her head, studying his expressions as she sat opposite him. Eric simply leant against the wall, watching. "Your brother is the murderer. I saw him attacking Tahgri with my own eyes, and then he tried to kill me," she explained.

Samson looked away from her, glaring at the ceiling as he digested the new information. "So I'm related to the wrong person then, is that it?" he asked, obviously still struggling to believe it.

"You can't honestly expect me to believe that you had no idea. You gave him a false alibi for the first murder, and you tried to stop the investigation yesterday when the opportunity arose," she pointed out.

Samson shook his head fervently. "I said he went to bed, which he did! And how do I know that you're telling the truth about Tahgri?" he countered.

From what Abby could tell, his reactions were genuine. She gestured to Eric, who explained tiredly. "It's true. I arrived after Tahgri got shot, only others there were Abby and Daniel, and unless you think Tahgri's last act was to ordain his own killer..." he trailed off, shrugging.

Once again, Samson went quiet. No doubt this was all very hard for him to comprehend. Either that, or he was doing a very good job of acting innocent. "I... didn't know about Tahgri. You're sure it was Daniel that killed the others?" he eventually asked, his voice weakening.

"He didn't deny it. I'm going to talk to him again, but first I want the truth. What's your explanation for all of it? How could he keep it secret from you?" she demanded.

"How could I possibly know?! Maybe he snuck out again after he went to bed. You'd have to ask him," he snapped.

"And the other two murders?" she continued.

"I wasn't with Daniel at the time of the other murders, you know that," Samson argued. "And I didn't claim to be, either."

Abby had expected those answers, and the first alibi had never exactly been an incredibly solid one. "What about the gun? And trying to stop the investigation?"

He nodded. "I didn't think it was fair for you to investigate your own brother as a suspect, that's all. You took us off the team when Vanessa was murdered because we couldn't prove our alibis - this seemed just as good a reason to take you off."

"Seems convenient that you tried to take over as soon as you had a scapegoat, but a fair point," she agreed. "And the gun?"

"What gun? I never saw a fucking gun, all the victims were stabbed!"

"He shot Tahgri," she reminded him. "Couldn't beat him in a fair fight... must've stolen the gun from Eric a while ago, we didn't think too much of it at the time. Anything else you want to say? If you miss something it might be the difference between you being found innocent or guilty."

Samson paled slightly and went quiet for a few moments. "I'm sorry about Tahgri, really, but I liked him too. He was my teacher. I've never told you anything but the truth, as far as I knew it, now let me go! You can't keep me here," he insisted.

"Watch me. You may not like to admit it, but I know best. If I let you go before confirming you're innocent, you're going to be lynched, Sam. You wouldn't last until dawn," Abby warned him.

It was clearly taking all of Samson's self control not to snap at her. "I want to speak to Carmina," he growled.

"Nobody's stopping her. If she wanted to speak to you, she'd have done it by now. Whatever was going on between you two, I think you can consider this a hiatus, at least," she informed him. That was the gentle version - she'd offered to let Carmina talk to Samson and had been informed that they were done. Even if he was found innocent, Carmina wasn't sure she could ever trust him again.

Samson spat on her boots and returned to glaring at the ceiling. Abby left, hoping he'd prove to be innocent, and that if he did he'd find it in himself to forgive her methods.

She paused as she reached the Marshal household, calming herself in preparation. She supposed it wasn't really their house anymore, there wasn't a plural. If Samson proved to be innocent it would be his house alone. Even if she'd wanted to, there was no way she could get away with letting Daniel live after all the murders he'd committed.

She walked through the door, receiving a polite nod of greeting from Michael. "Want me to leave?" he asked.

"No. Stay," she requested. Normally she might've valued the option of privacy, but right now she couldn't trust herself to be alone with the murderer. She'd never felt such a burning anger at someone in all her life.

Daniel was tied firmly to a chair on the other side of the main room. Johann had done a good job on the injuries - the claw marks across his face were just deep enough to scar, though the bruising around them made it look worse than it was. The lioness had been remarkably gentle about rendering Daniel unconscious, no doubt due to whatever divine mandate had brought it to the cemetery in the first place.

Abby sat opposite him and considered how to begin the interrogation. It had seemed like such a straightforward affair, just a moment ago, but she struggled to start now. Beneath the injuries, Daniel looked angry, but there was also a hint of regret. "How about we start with you confessing to your crimes?" she suggested. He remained entirely silent, the regret vanishing as his face twisted into hatred. "Don't you care about what you've done, even a little?" she asked. Still, he remained silent.

She edged a little closer to him. "You can play it like that if you want, Daniel, but if you don't answer my questions you're going to land your brother in serious trouble," she warned him.

That seemed to do the trick. Daniel's eyes widened slightly and he shook his head. "Leave Samson out of this! He never did anything."

"So you're saying, but at the moment I'm inclined to believe that you two worked together to get away with the crimes. I suppose you're going to have to placate me, aren't you," Abby continued.

Daniel sagged, his stubborn attitude deflating instantly. "I didn't think you were capable of being such a cold bitch," he muttered.

"Better that than a murderer," she retorted. "Don't try to turn this on me, you're the only one who's at fault here. Or perhaps Samson as well, should I say."

"Fine, I'll play your game. What do I have to do to prove that he's innocent?" Daniel asked.

"Tell me the truth. All of it," she demanded. "Let's start with the first murder. Don't leave a thing out, I want to hear every little detail."

"Owen," Daniel muttered. He hesitated a few moments then sighed. "Alright. Owen was an accident, really," he began.

Abby scoffed. "And I suppose your knife slipped and carved a symbol of Corsein miraculously, did it?"

"Not like that. I mean I never planned to kill him. Samson was pissed at the gods; he would've been mad if he knew I'd gone to the chapel, so I snuck out after dark to pray. I wanted to know why grandpa had to die. Why him, of all people," he explained.

Abby nodded. "William was a good man, but he was old. You can't blame Corsein for taking someone at his age," she insisted. She didn't know why she was bothering, it didn't matter what he thought about the gods anymore. "So why'd you kill him, then? Going from praying to murder, that's quite a leap."

"Owen stuck around while I was there, said he was sorry for our loss or something. The usual shit I guess. Then he said something that really got to me; 'Corsein had a plan for him' or something like that. I guess I wanted to put Owen's money where his mouth was; if he really believed that was Corsein's will, he had to believe his own death was, too."

Abby sighed and shook her head. She refrained from arguing with him this time, though, simply searching for the facts. "That really drove you to slit his throat? That still seems like a big jump."

Daniel shrugged, the chair creaking as his arms tugged at the ropes. "I was angry, what did you expect? It was almost too easy," he told her.

Abby grimaced, disgusted by how casually he could talk about it. "So you carved the symbol and went home?"

He nodded. "I did. Cleaned the blood off my hands and knife, then went right back to bed. Nobody even noticed I was gone, and you know what? It felt good to get one up on the gods."

"I suspected it was Samson for a time," Abby admitted. "He wasn't exactly subtle about his dislike of the Maralor after William died, but you were. Barely a peep out of you about them."

"Samson probably would've held back, too, if he'd known it was me. You probably thought my whole family was involved, so I did my best to seem less… bitter," Daniel explained.

"So your anger was just bubbling away inside you that whole time?" she enquired.

"Like you wouldn't believe."

Abby realised that she was going off-topic again, and forced herself to focus. "I guess not all the victims were random, though, were they?"

"No, only Owen was," Daniel confirmed. Abby gestured for him to elaborate. "Dad told me all about Vanessa. If it hadn't been for that pack of rodents running Lapden, things would've been different."

"Tell me about Vanessa," she demanded. "You brought water to the chapel, so I guess it was premeditated. How did you do it?"

"I planned that for months," he admitted. "After the first murder I had a pretty good idea of how you'd investigate it, so I planned around that. I watched Vanessa sometimes when the weather allowed for it, figured out that she went to the chapel on the same days every week. That was a nice coincidence, made my job a lot easier. It was still hot, so Samson and I were taking turns on the field. I figured if he thought I was farming he'd vouch for my alibi, and even though Lapden was pretty busy, I knew that nobody would remember me. I noticed that in the first investigation - people have shit memories. It practically takes a slap in the face to get anything to sink in."

Abby nodded glumly. He wasn't wrong, and if that hadn't been the case he almost definitely would've been caught that time, especially as he'd been incorrect about Samson vouching for his whereabouts. "So how did it go down? Don't spare me the details," she insisted. In part, she wanted to see if he slipped up and accidentally pointed to Samson's involvement, but she was also curious to know exactly how much of her theorising had been correct at the time.

"I brought a spare shirt and a bucket of water with me, hid my sword in my trousers and stayed around the chapel until I saw her go in. She noticed when I barred the door; I tried telling her that I just wanted to talk, but she saw the knife. I had to put my hand over her mouth to stop her screaming while I stabbed her. I carved the symbol, cleaned myself up, and changed shirt."

"What about your trousers and boots?" Abby questioned, certain that he must've got blood on them both. "Didn't you change them?"

"I wore leather. The blood scrubbed right out while it was still wet," he claimed. "I put the bloody shirt in the bucket so that nobody would see it, and the sword in my trousers again."

"Right. So how come you brought a change of shirt, anyway? Did you plan for it to get messy, or was it just a precaution?" she urged him on.

"I was getting to that," he frowned. "Someone tried the door just as I was about to leave, so I went through a window instead. As soon as I got back to Lapden I ripped up the shirt and buried it. I'd planned to wait a couple more days before planting it to frame you."

Abby scowled. She was glad that he'd failed, but the thought that he could turn on her like that was still infuriating. "Why me?" she asked. "I was never anything but kind to you."

"It was never personal," he said with a hint of guilt. It seemed so very odd that he could feel bad about betraying her but not about murdering people. "I figured if you were suspected, nobody would trust you to investigate other murders. Even if you were never proven guilty, people would still be suspicious of you. Nobody would ever think it was me." If it hadn't been for divine intervention it might have worked, too. That was the scariest part.

"The tailors were all sure that it wasn't a shirt they'd made," Abby recalled. "Where did you get it?"

"It was one of grandpa's older ones, tatty old thing. We kept them more out of sentimental value than anything, and I knew that nobody would notice it missing."

Abby nodded. "So, what about Katherine and Mrs. Sutton?"

"Katherine was the target, obviously," he claimed. "Samson would've killed her one day, I reckon, but I didn't know when. I kind of raced him to the mark. Figured since I already had blood on my hands I should be the one to do it. I didn't want him to be guilty as well."

"I guess you didn't plan it so well that time," she commented.

Daniel shrugged. "I always knew I was playing with fire. That just made it more exciting to be honest. Anyway, I didn't think Katherine would be much of a challenge."

"So what exactly happened? How did you even know she was there?"

"Katherine was predictable. She went to the chapel at least once a day after Amanda got injured. More, since she died. She was helping dig, not that she was much good at it. I just waited until she took a break and followed her. I did her just like Owen, but I hadn't thought anyone else would turn up there, since it was raining. I guess I really fucked up on that one," he admitted, chuckling grimly.

Abby nodded bitterly. "That would be one way of putting it. So, Mrs. Sutton walked in on you did she?"

"Yeah. I wasn't done carving the symbol yet. She didn't notice the body at first, so I tried to play it off. Figured if I killed her before she screamed I could still get away with it. Didn't quite work out."

"Seems odd to me that you kept killing in chapels and carving the symbol even after it stopped being about William," Abby commented.

Daniel smirked. "Seemed the thing to do, I guess. My way of getting mad at Corsein," he dismissed it, as though it were little more significant a habit than biting fingernails or cracking knuckles. "Anyway, as soon as I finished her off I got seen by some girl. Just my bloody luck."

"And then what?" Abby demanded, gesturing for him to finish.

"And then she ran away screaming, obviously. I chased her at first, but I figured I'd just be seen by someone else if I caught her anyway. I knew there was no coming back from that."

"You almost got away with it - the girl mistook you for Aurelius," Abby informed him. "If I hadn't known better he'd probably be in your place right now."

Daniel winced. "I'm sorry about that, really. I know we look a lot alike, but I never planned that. It was never personal."

"You made it personal when you murdered Tahgri," she spat, barely resisting the urge to batter him.

Daniel sighed and shook his head. "It wasn't, though. I thought I was fucked, then. The way I saw it, the only way I was getting away clean was by covering my tracks with chaos and killing anyone smart enough to figure it out," he explained.

"That's an awful plan! How could you possibly think it was a good idea?" she demanded, struggling to believe the sheer savagery of it.

"I never said it was a *good* plan," he said bitterly. "I panicked, couldn't think of a better option. I managed to get home and change my clothes, then I hid the gun in the cemetery and lured Tahgri out there."

"You should've slit your own throat then and there, and spared us your wickedness," Abby growled. "What about the musket, anyway? That was stolen ages ago. Did you always plan to kill someone with it?"

Daniel hesitated for too long. "Samson stole the musket, but he never knew!" he blurted out. "He never knew I killed anyone. He just wanted a gun for the elementals, I swear. Please… it was never Samson."

Abby clenched her jaw. Theft was also a crime, and Samson had lied to her about it, but no matter how much people might argue with her, that was all she believed him to be guilty of. She couldn't take her anger out on him. It just wasn't right. "I believe you," she admitted, much to the relief of Daniel.

"It's the truth," he emphasised. "I'll do anything you like - I'll confess in public, even take a blood oath like Jenna's if I have to. Just leave Samson out of it, please?"

Abby glared coldly at him. "Blood oath? You murdered five people, Daniel. You're going to die," she informed him remorselessly.

He nodded, seeming unsurprised at the response. Still, tears forced themselves to his eyes. "And Samson?" he enquired one last time.

"I'm not sure if I'll be able to protect him, now that people associate him with your crimes. I won't sentence him to death, but I can't promise that someone else won't take it into their own hands. You only have yourself to blame for that. Your dad, too. He would still be alive if you hadn't murdered Vanessa. You killed your family legacy."

"I'm already dead, spare me the lecture," he managed through the tears. "If you want to do something self-righteous, you keep my brother alive. It's the right thing to do."

"I can't promise that," she returned. She could've promised to try, of course, but it would've been a lie; perhaps the situation had made her more cynical, but as far as she was concerned, Samson was a lost cause. "Michael, would you help me get him outside?" she requested.

The smith was strong from years of hammering metal into shape, and between them it wasn't so hard to carry Daniel outside, still bound firmly to his chair. A crowd began to form as people speculated on what would happen, and by the time they arrived at the chapel they were encircled by citizens of New Cray, and loiterers from Lapden who had perhaps been waiting just for this.

"Jaina, what's the punishment for five murders?" Abby called out as they set down Daniel's chair at the top of the steps.

"Hanging," the lawyer called back, just as expected.

Abby nodded and looked to the still-growing crowd. "Daniel is guilty of five murders, and has confessed to his crimes. I don't think I need to elaborate on the details; everyone already knows them. The punishment is to be hanged by the neck until dead."

She crouched beside Daniel and untied him. She'd expected him to put up one last token fight as she stood him up on the chair, but all he did was cry as she tied his noose. Johann helped her without instruction, his height allowing him to tie the other end above the chapel doorway. "May the Maralor have mercy on your soul," Abby finished, and kicked the chair down the steps.

The crowd jeered, angry and aggrieved citizens calling Daniel out for what he was. *Coward. Murderer.* Some threw rocks at him, some spat. He struggled until he grew weak, then he fell from consciousness, and the only motion that remained was from lingering momentum; the slow pendulum of his body. A ghost of his final movements. Although Abby felt some of the great weight lift from her shoulders as she watched the light leave his eyes, she didn't enjoy killing Daniel. None of this would bring back Tahgri.

"Samson is innocent, and will be released tomorrow, provided that he cooperates," she announced. She didn't stay to hear what the crowd had to say about that. It was almost over now.

She returned to the doctor's, where Eric greeted her once again. "You alright?" he asked her, no doubt taking in her moody appearance.

The answer to his question was painfully obvious, and so she didn't bother to respond. "I need a moment alone with him," she ordered. Eric left her to it without further ado.

Samson's spirited defiance seemed to have crumbled in her absence. "Can I go yet?" he asked grumpily, watching her as she sat beside him.

"No, not yet. I know you stole the musket," she informed him. "I'm going to pretend that didn't happen, just don't expect any other favours from me. Daniel confessed to the murders, but people still won't trust you. You should keep a low profile."

Tears began to well in Samson's eyes as he digested the information. She would have felt sorry for him if he'd been absolutely innocent. "Can I see him?" he asked.

"You don't want to - we hanged him," Abby told him. "I'll let you out of here when I reckon you're not going to do anything stupid. They'll string you up next to him if you do."

Samson began to wail in mourning, and Abby left before any insults or accusations could leave his mouth. She headed straight to her family's home to rest, the woes of the day proving too much for her to continue. She was given pause when she arrived, however; Jenna was sitting at the table in the main room. "Hey," Abby greeted her.

"Hey," Jenna returned, fidgeting miserably. Despite the blood oath, Tahgri had grown on the woman. She may not have known him as well as Abby had, but she was evidently still saddened by his death. "I was wondering what this means for me?"

"Absolutely nothing. Carry on as you were," Abby instructed.

Jenna shook her head quickly. "I mean the oath. Without him, I guess it doesn't work anymore, does it?"

Abby shrugged, the amusing facade of the blood oath falling short of making her smile this time. "I guess not, but nothing needs to change. Take the day off then get back to work. That's what I'll be doing."

"Really? You trust me not to break the law or run off?" Jenna asked, clearly unsure of herself.

"If you intended to do that, you wouldn't have come here to have this conversation with me," Abby pointed out.

The bandit nodded thoughtfully. "I guess not. I don't want out, I like it here. Especially now that people stopped hassling me all the time."

"And we don't need to remind them about your past by giving you a new oath. Why change something that works, right?"

"Does that make us friends, now?"

"Seems so," Abby agreed. She gave Jenna a brief, half-hearted hug before going to get some rest in Carmina's bed. "I'll see you tomorrow."

Jenna let her be, and Abby settled down to try to sleep and escape her depression. It would still be there when she awoke of course, waiting for her - but tomorrow she would have the strength to deal with it.

21
One Thousand Days

Abby knelt in prayer, clutching the reforged blade close to her bosom. The smiths had recovered Tahgri's gear, resizing his sword and armour to fit her. The spare metal had made a fine pair of warhammers, but even though they were more in keeping with her style, it was the sword that gave Abby a sort of comfort in Tahgri's absence. No matter how much she missed the paladin, the weapon made her feel like part of him was still there to guide her.

Today marked her one-thousandth day in New Cray, and though she had no desire to celebrate it, there was still plenty of good news to take with the bad; Jenna had stuck to her word and stayed, becoming an honest citizen. Abby hadn't bothered to reveal the truth about her blood oath, and she wasn't sure she ever would. She'd never told Mr. Sutton that his wife had been cheating on him, either - it seemed somehow wrong to reinforce his grief with that knowledge.

The fortress was almost complete, now. The whole structure consisted of a short, stone bell tower connected by a staircase to a subterranean hall, the walls, floor, and ceiling of which were all made of wood. It would simply be expanded to fit the population of New Cray as it grew, and with this bastion, Abby was certain that it would grow.

She could hear them testing the bell; it wasn't so loud from within the bowels of the fortress, but she was sure that it would be very audible from outside, even in the middle of a storm. All they needed to do now was finish the portcullises and prepare some heavier weapons to repel the earthen elementals.

She finished her prayers and stood again, leaving the altar that sat proudly at the end of the hall. The last of the day's warmth caressed her skin as she walked back upstairs and out into the open, strolling over to a comfortable patch of grass. Aurelius joined her there as she observed the sunset. It bathed the masonry of the tower in a beautiful, orange glow. Tahgri would've been proud of it. He would've been proud of *her*.

"I guess you were right," Aurelius admitted. "This would never have worked out if it had been up to Montgomery and Markus. They probably would've argued against it just to avoid being in the same room as you."

"Yeah, probably. They'll warm to it when they realise it's the only thing saving them," she predicted.

"You know, I never apologised for hitting you."

"It wasn't much of a hit," she teased, smiling at him.

Aurelius chuckled "Laugh it up. Next time I'll go for the crotch."

"So we're alright then?" she asked.

Aurelius put his arm around her shoulders. "Yeah, we're good," he assured her. They'd reconciled a little since their disagreement; it was hard for him to hate her when she'd saved him from the unfortunate case of mistaken identity, after all. Still, that particular violent exchange had been an awkward stain on their familial bond until now.

The distant future was uncertain, and the elemental threat showed no sign of slowing down, but at least one thing was clear for now; they would remain.

34230255R00148

Printed in Great Britain
by Amazon